Tl

REV. W. HENRY JONES
AND
LEWIS L. KROPF.

PREFACE.

A vast and precious store of Folk-Lore is to be found amongst the Magyars as yet but little known to English readers, and so it is hoped that this work on the subject may prove of some value to the student of Comparative Folk-Lore. The difficulty of the language is one which makes it well nigh impossible for the unaided foreigner to do anything like justice to the stories. We laboured together often till dawn to make the translation as literal as possible, that the reader might have as true a rendering of the Magyar story-teller's method and manner as so different a tongue as English would permit.

Whilst engaged on the Finnish stories we received the greatest help from Finnish friends, especially Mr. A. Nieminen, Dr. Fagerlund, Dr. Krohn, Dr. Rancken, Professor Freudenthal, Mr. Halleen, and Mr. Walter von Bonsdorff. In the Lapp stories [Pg vi]Professor Friis of Christiania has ever been a true helper. Amongst numerous kindly helpers we tender thanks to Dr. Retzius, Stockholm; Professor Gittée, Charleroi; the Rev. Henry Jebb, of Firbeck Hall; Mr. Quigstad, of Troms; Mr. Nordlander; Mr. O. P. Petersson, Hernösand; Mr. Lindholm; Dr. R. Köhler; Baron Nordenskjöld; and the Rev. Walter H. James, rector of Fleet.

We regret that we cannot do more than acknowledge the courtesy of the late Dr. Greguss (Buda Pest), whose lamented death removed a scholar and friend to Englishmen.

If this collection adds a mite to the knowledge of man, our labours will not have been in vain.[1]

W. H. J.

L. L. K.

[1]Mr. Kropf desires it to be stated, that he is not responsible for the Introduction and Notes beyond supplying certain portions of the material for their compilation.

[Pg vii]

INTRODUCTION.

Before the arrival of the Magyars, Hungary was the "cock-pit of eastern Europe;" its history one incessant struggle between nation and nation, which either perished or was driven out by some more powerful neighbour. First we hear of the subjection of what was known as Pannonia, by the Romans; then, when that great power began to wane, a motley horde under the great Attila swept down and founded a kingdom. "Attila died in Pannonia in 453. Almost immediately afterwards the empire he had amassed rather than consolidated fell to pieces. His too-numerous sons began to quarrel about their inheritance; while Ardaric, the King of the Gepidae, placed himself at the head of a general revolt of the dependent nations. The inevitable struggle came to a crisis near the river Netad, in Pannonia, in a battle in which 30,000 of the Huns and their confederates, including Ellak,[1] Attila's eldest son, were slain. The nation thus broken rapidly dispersed. One horde settled under Roman protection in Little Scythia (the Dobrudsha); others in Dacia Ripensis (on the confines of Servia and Bulgaria), or on the southern borders of Pannonia."[2] A tradition asserts that the Magyars are descendants of those Huns, who, after their defeat, returned to their homes in Asia. On the other hand, one of their most learned men says, we cannot [Pg viii]"form an accurate idea as to the part the Hungarians took in the irruption of the Huns, with which event they are associated in national tradition." But yet he adds, "we fairly claim that the ancestors of the Hungarians took part in the great devastating campaigns which Attila carried on against Rome and the Christian West, as far as France." Legend carries us still further back, saying that the giant Nimrod had two sons named Hunyor and Magyar, from whom the Huns and Magyars descended.[3] Leaving legend, in history we find that the Magyars appeared in Europe about 884, first on the Ural, later on the banks of the middle Volga; and then, marching westward, passed over the Danube and the Bug, crossing the Carpathians between 888 and 900, under Álmos, the father of Árpád,[4] the founder of modern Hungary, who is said to have claimed the country as his inheritance from Attila. The Magyars, then, are part of the numerous hordes of Turco-Tartar origin which, impelled by some mighty impulse, left their home amid the [Pg ix]Altai mountains, and, conquering the divided forces on the rich plains of Hungary, settled down, and so founded the race whose tales form the body of this work.[5]

Another people, the Székely,[6] speak a dialect of Magyar, which, like other Magyar dialects, differs but slightly from the written language. This race claims to be descendants of those Hunnish tribes that remained in Europe after the defeats. They say, that when the Magyars arrived in modern Hungary they found a Magyar-speaking people (the Székely) inhabiting parts of Transylvania. This is confirmed to some extent by the statement of Constantinus Porphyrogenitus, who, writing about 950, asserted that, amongst others, some Magyar tribes lived on the banks of the rivers Maros and Körös (Transylvania). Kriza, too, quotes several Székely sayings referring to the Székely-Magyar relationship, *e.g.*:

"A Székely has borne the Magyar."

"If there were no Székelys in the world, there would not be any Magyars."

"There is the same difference between a Székely and a Magyar as there is between a man's son and his grandson."

"Let the Magyar be thankful, that the Székely is his acquaintance."

With regard to the alleged descent of the Székelys from the [Pg x]Huns, the evidence in proof of such a pedigree is very meagre. First, it has not as yet—with any degree of accuracy—been determined who the Huns were. Prof. Vambéry has, with infinite pains, collected and analysed some seventy words, mostly proper names—all that has come down to us of the old Hunnish language—and come to the conclusion that the Huns and Avars for the greater part belonged to the Turco-Tartar branch of the Ural-Altaic race; yet he is bound to acknowledge that he would gladly welcome a few historical facts to support him in his conclusions, which are built upon an almost entirely philological basis.[7] Indeed, it seems as though the term "Hun" was a sort of conventional designation, like "Scythian," or "Barbarian" with the ancient Greeks and Romans; or "Frenghi" with the modern Turks. Attila and the various races he pressed into his service were, of course, the Huns *par excellence.* After his death and the fatal battle near the river Netad his hordes appear to have well-nigh vanished from Europe; but their terrible deeds left an indelible impression upon the people who were unfortunate enough to have been brought into contact with the "scourge of God" and his fierce warriors. In the lapse of time all kinds of weird traditions gathered round their names, in the usual way, when great names pass into the possession of the Folk Historian;[8] and so they drifted through legends of saints into the region of myths. Thus we find the name Hüne (Heune, Hewne, Huyne) becomes synonymous with "giant," and to this day the Westphalian and Dutch peasant speaks of the great tumuli as "Hünen gräber"—graves of the giants, or Huns.[9] To add to the confusion, it would appear that [Pg xi]there were some German tribes who were known as Hunes. Mr. Karl Blind has pointed out in the *Gentleman's Magazine*,[10] that our own Venerable Bede speaks of Hunes as being among the tribes of Germany that came over to Britain together with the Saxons. Elsewhere[11] he explains "the tribal origin of Siegfried (of the Nibelungen lied) as a German Hüne;" a word which has nothing whatever to do with the Mongolian Huns. We know mediæval writers were not very particular about facts, and the *licentia poetica* was claimed not only by poets, but also by historiographers, as an indisputable privilege. Thus, João Barros, in his chronicle of Clarimundus,[12] calmly tells us that Count Henry of Portugal, the Navigator, was of Hungarian descent, and that he found the statement in a Magyar book.[13] This alleged pedigree was the cause of a fierce controversy amongst Hungarian savants, and was fully threshed out in the early part of the present century.[14]

Vigfusson[15] remarks that the northern poet, whom he designates the "Tapestry poet," uses Hunar (Huns), Hynske (Hunnish) as a vague word for "foreign." Probably the East Baltic folk would have been Huns to the earlier poets. With regard to the German and Scandinavian Huns, it is noteworthy what Olaus Magnus writes with regard to the "Huns" of his time. The learned prelate says that "in [Pg xii]provincia Middelpadensi versus Boreales partes Suetiæ superioris, ubi ferè major pars virorum Huni nomine appellantur tamquam populi clarius contra Hunos olim belligerantes ac triumphantes."[16] His statement is borne out by his colleague, Joannes Magnus,[17] who asserts that "non desunt qui dicant ipsos Hunnos à Septentrionale parte Scandiæ utra Helsingorum terras ex Medelphatia primum erupisse: in qua etiam hodie plurimi præstantissimæ fortitudinis homines inveniuntur, qui Hunni proprio nomine appellantur, quique magna et præclara opera in tyrannos, qui patriæ libertatem vexaverat, peregerunt."

In the face of all this, it is quite evident how difficult a task awaits those who attempt to identify the lineal descendants of the Huns: and those who uphold the Hunnish descent of the Székelys do not appear, as yet, to have advanced sufficient historical grounds to establish the connection of the modern Székelys with the Huns of Attila.[18]

[Pg xiii]

It is well known that the Hun descent of the Magyars and Székelys has equally been questioned. Savants of such authority as Budenz and Hunfalvy disclaim the Hun relationship, and endeavour to prove the Finn-Ugrian origin of the Magyars. Whereas Professor Vambéry, in his work on the "Origin of the Magyars," which received so favourable a reception at the hands of the whole learned world, defends, as we saw above, a Turco-Tartar descent.

It lies far beyond the limits of this work to give even a brief outline of the history of the Székelys: yet a few data may not be out of place to show that, although they are at the present time, and mayhap always have been, a Magyar-speaking people, yet they are in many respects distinct from the race known as the Magyars. Ibn Dasta, an Arab writer,[19] at the end of the ninth century, informs us that in his time some Bulgarians lived on the banks of the River Itil (Volga); and that they consisted of three tribes, viz.: the Berzuls, the Esseghels, and the Uz. He further says that "the first territory of the Magyars lies between the country of the Bisseni and the Esseghel Bulgarians."

Another Arab writer, Ibn Muhalhal, about the middle of the tenth century, mentions a people named "Jikil," who lived next to the "Bajnak." If the writers who would identify in this Ashkal, Esseghel, or Jikil people, the parents of the Székely race, be right in their conclusions, then the Siculi (as they are called in Latin deeds) are of Bulgarian descent.[20] But we know [Pg xiv]full well how dangerous it is to build up theories on a mere similarity of names amongst barbarous or semi-barbarous races. The first reliable information we have about them is that about the year 1116 A.D. Bisseni and Siculi formed the body-guard of the Magyar King Stephen II. in his war against the Czechs. They supplied the vanguard of the army of King Géjza against Henry of Austria about 1146. More than half a century later, *i.e.* A.D. 1211, Andreas II. presented some uninhabited territory in Transylvania to the Teutonic knights; and, in a deed dated 1213, William, Bishop of Transylvania, granted the tithes of his territory to the same order, but reserved to himself the right of collecting them from all Magyar or Székely immigrants who might settle on the lands in question.[21] King Béla IV. ordered the Székelys[22] to supply him with one hundred mounted warriors in war; and later on, to show them his gratitude for their faithful services, he created them military nobles:[23] "Quod non sub certo numero (in a body as hitherto) sed eo modo sicut servientes regales, per se et personaliter armata nobiscum exercituare teneantur."[24] The Székelys of Hungary Proper gradually disappear, but the Siculi of Transylvania figure throughout the pages of Hungarian history as a separate people, with institutions and privileges of their own, and acting as a sort of border-fencibles in the numerous wars with the enemies of the Magyars. They furnished a separate title to the Prince of Transylvania,[25] and, although recent reforms have swept away old barriers, yet one still hears people speaking of the three nations of [Pg xv]Transylvania, viz. the Magyars, the Székelys, and the Saxons.[26] Whether they ever spoke a language of their own we are unable to say; they speak several dialects, which have been carefully studied by Kriza,[27] himself a Székely by birth, and which possess peculiarities not to be found amongst the Magyars, or any other part of the realm of St. Stephen. A passage[28] in a work entitled "Hungaria et Attila," by Nicolaus Oláh, Archbishop of Esztergom (died 1568), might, perhaps, be quoted to prove that an independent Székely language had existed once, but there is an ambiguity about the statement of the learned prelate which makes it useless to the philologist. At any rate, we do not possess a single scrap of the old language, if it ever existed.

Having thus made ourselves acquainted with the Székelys, we may proceed to consider the other Magyar-speaking nationalities.

The Csángós[29] are Hungarian settlers in Moldavia; there are so many similarities in their tongue to the Székely dialects that Hunfalvy appears to be quite confident that they are a people of Székely origin.[30] Of late years an attempt has been made to resettle them in the less populous crown lands in Hungary; the result, as one might expect, is, that some are content, whilst others lust after the flesh-pots of Moldavia.

Next come the Kúns (Cumanians). The non-Magyar writers,[31] who have made the old language of this people their study, declare it, with almost unanimous consent, to be a Turkish dialect, whereas the Magyar writers, with very few exceptions, staunchly defend the Magyar origin of the Cumanians.[32]

[Pg xvi]

Foremost in the ranks of the latter party was the late Stephen Gyárfás, who denied that a *lingua Cumenesca* had ever existed, and that the various extant specimens are the remnants of the language of a people of Magyar descent, who had become Turks during the lapse of centuries.[33] His most powerful antagonist is Count Géjza Kuun, the learned editor of the *Codex Cumanicus*,[34] who espouses the cause of the Turkish party. Besides the valuable Glossary preserved in the Codex, several versions of the Lord's Prayer and other scraps of the Cumanian tongue are in existence, and have been examined by competent scholars, and pronounced to be of undoubted Turkish origin.[35]

Jazygo-Cumanians have been quoted in the note, and so we [Pg xvii]proceed to consider the next race—if one may use the word—viz.: the Jazyges, formerly a military tribe, who, together with the Cumanians, live in central Hungary, in the vicinity of the capital, and occupy a territory on the banks of the rivers Danube, Zagyva, Sárrét, Tisza, and Körös.

From time immemorial, until quite recent times, they enjoyed certain privileges and administered their own affairs in three districts—the Jászság, Kis-Kúnság, and Nagy-Kúnság, entirely separate from the surrounding population, thus forming a state within a state. They had however to surrender some of their old rights in 1848, and by the law of 1876 (cap. xxxiii.), which readjusted the political divisions of the kingdom, the limits of their territory disappeared altogether from the map of Hungary.[36] With regard, then, to the nationality of the Jász people, they are found at all periods of history in company with the Cumanians, and so, as their institutions are the same as their fellow armigerents, [Pg xviii]we may safely assume with Hunfalvy that they are a branch of the Cumans, if they be not offspring of the same mother-stock.

Next come the Palócz folk,[37] who live scattered among the other races in several of the northern counties of Hungary, and speak a dialect of their own. Hunfalvy asserts that they are the same people as the "Polovczi" mentioned by early Russian and Slavonic writers. And as Jerney, in his paper *The Palócz Nation and The Palócz Chronicle*, has proved beyond doubt that, whatever the Magyar Chronicles and Byzantine writers relate anent the Cumans can be traced, statement for statement, in Russian and Polish writers, with reference to the Polovczi, Hunfalvy draws the conclusion that the Palócz people are Cumans.[38]

Their name first occurs in Russian Annals A.D. 1061, and the Magyar savant to whose rich store of learning this work is so deeply indebted thinks that the migration of the Cumans into Hungary took place in two distinct streams, one, an earlier one, from the North, *viâ* the Slave countries across the Northern Carpathians, and another, later one from the south-east, through the passes and defiles of the south-eastern extension of the same range of mountains.

Before leaving this part of the subject, the reader must be reminded that all the foregoing races or nationalities at the present time speak one or other Magyar dialect,[39] and that the [Pg xix]old Cuman tongue is the only other language of which we know anything.[40]

Having, we hope, somewhat cleared the way as to people amongst whom the stories have been collected, we may now proceed to say a few words about the tales themselves. Of course, the stories will be found to bear a strong resemblance to other collections, as indeed they must do; the very fact of the striking way in which not only tales, but even little superstitions, reappear in all manner of strange places,[41] is of itself a fact which is of the deepest interest to those who study the history of man. We have attempted to give some few variants to the tales in this work, chiefly confining ourselves to Lapp and Finnish tales, which are but little known in England, and of which, as of the Magyar, there is a rich store. The more one considers comparative folk-lore, the more one is convinced that many of these tales were the common property of mankind before they migrated from their Asiatic [Pg xx]home.[42] Of course local circumstances often colour the stories, but do not change the theme. Amidst the stories from Hungary we find, as we might presume, the Székely stories telling of snow-clad mountains, whilst those from the banks of the Danube dwell on the beauties of the Hungarian plains. The fierce conflicts of the past, too, have left their marks on the stories, and so we find the Turkish Sultan[43] and the Dog-headed Tartar[44] as the tyrants of the tale; and even, in one case, so modern a fact as the French invasion[45] is used to frighten an old-world witch. We see later on the influence of Mohammedanism, and also the marks of Christianity,[46] in some tales which become as it were, a folk-lore palimpsest. Nor must we omit other ways by which the tales have been modified. Many of the mediæval romances were, of course, translated into Hungarian; and even to this day the penny bookstall is always present at fairs and popular gatherings where "yards of literature" are to be obtained for a nominal sum. The vendor cannot afford a booth or stall, so a [Pg xxi]mat or tarpaulin is spread on the ground, and weighted at the four corners with brickbats or paving stones, hence the Hungarian name "ponyva-irodalom" (tarpaulin literature). Here we find mediaeval romances, bits of national history, biographies and panegyrics of famous robbers, the wicked doings of the mistress of some castle and her punishment, the exploits of Magyar heroes, the chronicles of Noodledom, in prose, or versified by some such favourite poet of the people as Peter Tatár; and by this means certain tales have been imported, others modified. Then again, the wandering students were entertained by the country folk during their peregrinations, and no doubt in return amused the old folks with the latest news from the town, and the young ones with tales from the Greek and Roman Mythologies.[47] Another mode of dissemination and modification was the soldiers. When the Hapsburgs were at the height of their glory the emperor-king's soldiers were scattered far and wide over Europe; and, after long years of service in an infantry regiment and absence from home, the old private returned to his native village, and at eventide in the village inn related how he, as "Sergeant of Hussars," caught with his own hand the Emperor Napoleon, and only let him go at the earnest entreaties of his wife, and upon receiving a rich bribe in gold.[48] The old soldier was well received in every family, and enjoyed great authority as a man who had seen the world. The children sat upon his knee, or stood round about him open-mouthed, and listened to his marvellous yarns.[49]

In Hungary, as in other countries, until the labours of the Brothers Grimm directed attention to the importance of the Folk-tales, nothing was done in the way of collecting them; and, [Pg xxii]even after Grimm's work appeared, no move was made in Hungary until Henszlman read his paper in 1847 before the Kisfaludy Society on the "Popular Tales of Hungary," in which paper he examined some 14 tales which afterwards appeared in Erdélyi's Collection, vols. 1 and 2. Ladislaus Arany in May 1867 read another paper before the same society and according to his calculation some 240 tales had been collected up to that date: the collections quoted by him were as follows:—

John Erdélyi,[50] *Folk-Songs and Popular Tales*, 3 vols.	co ntaining	4	ales
George Gaál,[51] *Hungarian Folk-Tales*, 3 vols.	"	3	
John Erdélyi, *Hungarian Popular Tales*, 1 vol.	"	3	
Ladislaus Merényi, *Original Popular Tales*, 2 vols.			
Ladislaus Merényi, *Popular Tales from the Valley of the Sajó*, 2 vols.	"		
Ladislaus Merényi, *Popular Tales from the Banks of the Danube*, 2 vols.		5	
Ladislaus Arany, *Original Popular Tales*, 1 vol.	"	5	
John Kriza,[52] *Wild Roses*, 1 vol.[53]	"	0	
Julius Pap, *Palócz Folk-Poetry*, 1 vol.	"		
[Pg xxiii]Count John Majláth,[54] *Hungarian Fairy Tales, Sagas and Popular Tales*, translated from the German by G. Kazinczy, 1 vol.	"		
Maurus Jókai, *Witty Tales of the Hungarian Folk*, 1 vol.	"		
	To tal,	40	

Of these, Erdélyi's first collection and Kriza's *Wild Roses* are the most important, and the translation of them form the bulk of this volume. Since 1867 the work of collecting the Popular Tales has been going on steadily, and the *Hungarian Language Guardian* (Magyar Nyelvör) is a paper specially devoted to the purpose: publishing popular sayings, proverbs, children's games, nursery rhymes, &c. Very little of the Folk-lore treasure is known outside of Hungary. There is Count Majláth's collection, which appeared originally in German, and also a German edition of Gaál, and one by Stier, which contains some of Erdélyi's stories. In English the only translations we are aware of are the tale of "The talking grapes, the smiling apple, and the tinkling apricot," from Erdélyi's collection, which was translated by Mr. E. D. Butler, and appeared in a London suburban paper; and another tale, "The Round Stone," in the February number of the *St. Nicholas Magazine*, 1882; so that this collection opens up new ground. The great difficulty in considering these tales—in common with the Finn, Esthonian, and Lapp—is the language; and the aim of the present translation is but to be as literal as possible in its rendering of the stories; there being no attempt [Pg xxiv]whatever made to polish or beautify the tales, but simply an endeavour to reproduce as near as may be the stories as told by the people; in many cases, especially with regard to the Székely stories, this has been a work of very great difficulty, on account of the dialect, and must plead for the many shortcomings in the translations.

A brief consideration of some points in Magyar Folk-lore may be found of interest in a study of the stories. And I am indebted for the following information on giants, fairies, and witches to a valuable paper, entitled *Mythological Elements in Székely Folk-lore and Folk-life*, read by Kozma before the Hungarian Academy in 1882.

I. GIANTS.[55]

Many of the characteristics of the Magyar giants are the same as those to be found in the Greek and German mythologies, but we do not find anything extraordinary in their appearance, such as one eye—as Cyclops[56], or sundry heads as the northern giants, nor redundant fingers and toes as the Jews; they are simply big men. There is no trace of any struggle between the gods and the giants in Magyar mythology.

They are said to be sons of witches,[57] and as tall as towers,[58] and step from mountain-top to mountain-top as they walk.

The length of their stride and the pace at which they walk is illustrated in a tradition, according to which the giants who inhabited a fortress called Kadicsavár, near the River Nyikó, [Pg xxv]were in the act of shaving when the bells rang first from the church-tower of Gyula-Fejérvár, at the second ringing they dressed, on the third ringing they sat in church.[59]

Near Szotyor in Háromszék[60] there is a rock, which is called the "Giant's Stone," on the top of this there is a cavity resembling in shape the heel of a man; the diameter of this hole is five feet, and popular tradition says it is the imprint of a giant's heel.

When the giant is angry he strikes a blow with his fist on the rock, and traces of his fist are shown now-a-days on a rock near Ikavar; his footstep is shown in the neighbourhood of Kézdi-Borosnyó, on a rocky ledge near a spring, where he used to come down to drink.

With one foot he stands on the mountain where Csiki-Bálványos-vár castle stands; with the other on a mountain opposite, and bending down, he picks up the water of the River Olt, running in the valley below, in a gigantic bucket, with one swoop.

He mounts a horse of such size that it stands with its hind legs on a mountain in Bodok in Háromszék, while its fore-legs rest on another mountain in Bickfalú, and its head reaches far into Wallachia, where it grazes in a green clover-field.

On short outings he walks; on long journeys he goes on horseback; his steed is a tátos,[61] with whom he holds many conversations. On returning home from a long ride he throws his mace, weighing forty hundredweights, from a distance of forty miles (= about 180 English miles), which drops into the [Pg xxvi]courtyard of the castle, and penetrating into the ground taps a subterranean spring.[62]

While the giant of the Germans lives during the flint-period, and uses gigantic stones and masses of rock as weapons, the Hungarian giant uses swords and maces of iron and copper, and also goes in for wrestling. He is not a cannibal. He is fond of a good supper and warm food, and is not a teetotaller. He always takes plenty of provisions on the journey.

Kozma has come across a tale, "Iron-made Peter," in which there figure six giants, each of whom is proficient in one thing or another. They bear names which characterise their special accomplishments. In English they would be as follows: Sharp-eye, Fast-runner, Far-thrower, Glutton, Drinker, Shiverer. The first is sitting on a mountain-peak reaching up to heaven's vault, and keeps on bowing in every direction, muttering "Which way shall I look? Is there nothing else to be seen? I have already seen everything in the world." The second is wandering about a vast plain, the boundaries of which cannot even be seen, and is moaning, evidently in great trouble. "Where shall I run? In which direction? No sooner do I start than I am at the end of this place." The third is seen sitting among huge pieces of rock, and crying, "Where shall I throw now? Which way? The whole world is covered by the stones I have thrown." The fourth is watching a bullock roasting, and continues yelling, "Oh, how ravenously hungry I am! What can I eat?" The fifth is rolling about on the sea-shore, roaring, "Oh, how thirsty I am! What will become of me? What can I drink? If I drain the ocean there will not be left anything for to-morrow!" The sixth is shivering on the top of a huge stack of wood all in a blaze, and exclaiming, "Oh, how cold I am! I am freezing."

[Pg xxvii]

The hero of the tale finds suitable employment for each of the giants. "Fast-runner" goes on an errand into the seven-times-seventh country, and returns in five minutes, although he goes to sleep on the road from the sleeping draught administered to him by a witch. "Sharp-eye" discovers him asleep; and "Far-thrower" knocks away the pillow from underneath his head, thus enabling him to return by the appointed time. "Glutton" consumes 366 fat oxen within six hours. "Drinker" empties during the same interval the contents of 366 casks, each holding 100 buckets of wine. "Shiverer" creeps into a furnace, which has been brought to, and kept in, a glowing heat for the last twenty-four years by twenty-four gipsies,[63] and by so doing lowers the temperature so that his mates, who have gone with him, are shivering with cold although they are wrapped up in thick rugs.[64]

The giants in northern regions live in six-storied diamond castles, or in golden fortresses which swivel round on a leg; more generally, however, they inhabit fortresses built by their own hands on the top of lofty mountains or steep rocks. In Székelyland the ruins of thirty-six such castles are existing, all of which are ascribed by the people to the giants. Some of their names show this; they are called the "Giant's Rock," the "Giant's Castle," the "Giant's Hill." In one case (Egyeskö in Csikszèk) they show the giants' table and bench in the rock. Sometimes, however, the castles are inhabited by fairies.

Tall mountain chains are sometimes said to be roads built by giants. Their names are "Attila's Track," "Devil's Ridge," &c. These roads were constructed by devils and magic cocks who were in the service of the giants. Hence also the name "Cocks' Ridge." In one case, however, near Száraz Ajta, the [Pg xxviii]ridges were made by giants themselves,[65] who used silver-shared ploughs drawn by golden-haired bullocks for this purpose.

The giants left their homes when "the country was given away to mankind," or when "modern mankind commenced to exist." When the husbandmen appeared and began to till the lands in the valleys and lowlands the giants did not associate with men, but kept to their castles and only visited the impenetrable woods.

There is a tale which occurs in several localities about a giant's daughter who finds a husbandman, picks up him and his team and puts them into her apron and carries them off as toys, showing them to her father. The father exclaiming angrily, "Take him back, as he and his fellow-creatures are destined to be the lords of the globe," or "Their anger might cause our ruin," or "They will be our successors." We thus see that, while in the German tale the giant of Nideckburg in Alsacia bids his daughter to take back the ploughman and his team for fear that by preventing his tilling the land the bread-supply might fail, in the Hungarian tales the giant openly acknowledges the superior power of the human race.[66]

The giants, unlike their brethren in foreign lands, are gregarious and live under a royal dynasty. They hold assemblies, at which their king presides. Several royal residences exist in Székeland. Near Besenyö there is one that is called "Csentetetö." Tradition has even preserved the giant-king's name, which was Bábolna. This king used to convoke the other [Pg xxix]giants to the assembly with huge golden bells. On feeling his approaching death he ordered the bells to be buried in a deep well in the castle, but on feast days they are still to be distinctly heard ringing, which sets the whole rock vibrating.

The name of another king of giants is to be found in Kriza's "Prince Mirkó" (Kutyafejü = Dogheaded.)

Sometimes the giants were good-natured and full of kindness towards the weak.[67]

They marry, their wives are fairies, so are their daughters. They make very affectionate fathers. They had no male issue, as their race was doomed to extermination. They fall in love, and are fond of courting. Near Bikkfalva, in Háromszék, the people still point out the "Lovers' Bench" on a rock, where the amorous giant of Csigavár used to meet his sweetheart, the "fairy of Veczeltetö."

The giants lived to a great age. Old "Doghead" remembers a dream he dreamt 600 years ago. His friend Knight Mezei finds him after a separation of 600 years, and they live happy for a great many years after.[68]

They have magic powers. They know when a stranger is hidden in their home. Doghead knows who has thrown back his mace from a distance of 180 English miles. They are acquainted with the conjuring formulæ and charms of the fairies, and know how to overcome them. They have a thorough knowledge of geography, and can give advice to those who enter their service, &c. They have great physical strength, and can build huge castles and roads, subdue whole countries, amass treasures[69] which they have guarded even after their death. Magic beings, animals, and implements await their commands.

[Pg xxx]

In the castle of Hereczvára, near Oltszem, the giants were negroes, and their servants were black dwarfs. Among the magic animals who guarded the giant's treasures we may mention the bullock with golden hair, the tátos, &c. Of weapons, charms, &c., Doghead's copper mace, Prince Mirkó's magic sword, the wine kept in a cask in the seventh cellar, each drop of which equals the strength of five thousand men.

The king of the giants of Görgény is bullet-proof; but if a man who is the seventh son of his mother (and all the elder brothers of whom are alive) casts a bullet, at the first appearance of the new moon, by a fire of wheat straw, this bullet will kill the monarch. Such a man was found, and the bullet was made, and it killed the king. The other giant, now being without a leader, evacuated the fortress and withdrew to Hungary Proper. Thus we see a giant can only be killed with a magic weapon.

In one of Kozma's tales the hero is in possession of a rusty padlock, from which two giants appear whenever he commands. They produce by charms, a golden cloak, and a golden fortress on the swivel principle, which they hand over to their master in a nutshell. They then clothe the poor lad in a copper suit and seat him on a copper steed so that he may appear decently dressed before the king; they change his miserable hovel into a fine palace at eleven o'clock, and at noon the whole royal family, who are his guests, sit down to a sumptuous dinner; they carry their master and his royal bride across a sea of flames, &c. There are several other tales which attribute the power of flying to giants.

Some of the giants have grown old and died a natural death. The greater part of them, however, were killed by enterprising knights. They have buried their treasures in deep wells, in huge mountains, or in extensive cellars under the fortresses. In the well of the Várhegy in Száraz-Ajta there lies[Pg xxxi] hidden the silver plough and the golden bullock; in the cellar the silver plough with the fluid gold. In the cellars of Hereczvára in black casks the accumulated treasure of the negro-giants is guarded by the black dwarfs, who spend their time in eating, drinking, and dancing. In the cellar of Kézdi-Szent-Lélek castle the treasure is guarded by a copper greyhound.

In the well and cellar of the Várbércz, near Kis-Borosnyó, the gigantic golden bells and other treasures of the king of giants are guarded by two black goats. Near Angyalos, in the Bábolna dyke, King Bábolna's golden sun and golden lamb are guarded by two black greyhounds and a snow-white stallion in full harness. In the well of Csigavàr there is a gold bucket on a golden chain, and in the bowels of the Tepej mountain, near Alsó-Rákos, the rams with golden fleece, &c.

Some of the cellar doors open every third, others every seventh year. People have been inside, but were careless and lost the treasure on the way back to the surface, others were more careful, and succeeded in bringing some of it out; but the moment the wind touched it it changed into dry leaves or bits of charcoal. Some unwise people have been foolhardy enough to try the expedition a second time, but the huge iron doors closed behind them. But whereas the natives have hitherto been unsuccessful in recovering the hidden treasure, foreigners come and carry it off wholesale on the backs of horses, which are shod with shoes turned the wrong way.[70]

[Pg xxxii]

II. FAIRIES.[71]

Fairy, in Hungarian, "tündér," from the same root as "tün" (verb) and "tünés" (noun) = comparitio, apparitio, and "tündökōl" = to shine. Cf. the Mongolian "Tinghir."

The queen of the fairies is sometimes called a goddess. Thus, south of the sulphur cave, Büdös, near Altorja, behind a mountain called the Priests' Mountain, is situated the very ancient village of Ikafalva, through which runs a brook named Furus. According to the tradition, the ancestors of the people of the village were led to this place more than 1,000 years ago, in the time of the conquest of the country, by a hero who encouraged his warriors in the name of "the goddess Furuzsina." The hero fell in the struggle, and on the spot where his blood had flowed a spring appeared, close to which the warriors built the present village, and named the brook after their goddess. The water of this brook is collected, even at the present day, into ponds; and drinking from this "blood and water" has made the villagers so strong that they have quite a name for physical strength in the neighbourhood. If a lad of Ikafalva performs some feat of pluck or strength they say: "It is no wonder, he has grown up on Furus water!"

Although the fairies, as a rule, are kind, good-natured persons, and take the hero's part in the tales, the Székely folk-lore furnishes a case to the contrary, *i.e.* that of two fairies, "Firtos" and "Tartod," the former being the queen of the good, the latter the queen of the bad, fairies.[72]

[Pg xxxiii]

Kozma has found another variation of the first-named tale in "Fairy Helena." Helena's father blows across a broad river, whereupon a golden bridge appears. The young fairy takes a "kourbash," and wipes a rusty table-fork with it, which at once changes into a steed with golden hair, on which her lover, the prince, flees to Italy. When they discover that they are followed, Helena spits on the floor,[73] on the door-handle, and on the hinge of the door, whereupon the planks, the handle, and the hinge commence to speak to the king's messengers from behind the closed door, and the fugitives gain time to make their escape. Her father is sent after them in the shape of a gigantic spotted eagle, who with the tip of one wing touches heaven and with the other earth. On the road the same things happen as in "Fairy Elizabeth," with this difference, that Helena's mother changes into a buffalo who drinks all the water in the pond on which the lovers swim about as ducks, whereupon they change into worms; and, as the mother cannot find them in the mud, she pronounces the curse of oblivion upon them.

Their means of charming were: The pond of beautifying milk, dresses, tears, the saliva, fascinating look, word of command, rejuvenating herb, rejuvenating water, wound-healing herb, water of life and death, iron bar, copper bridle, leather belt, gold and diamond rod, copper and gold whip, at the cracking of which dragons and devils appear; magic wand, curse of oblivion, sleeping draughts (wine), and the table that covers itself. The daughter of Doghead rides on a tátos. The magic animals in their service are: the cat and the cock, although the loud crowing of the latter has, by indicating the time, very often a fatal influence on fairies who are forgetful. One fairy queen, Dame Rapson, has the devil himself in her service.

[Pg xxxiv]

Their conjuring formulae are: "You are mine, I am thine." "Be there, where you have come from!" "Fog before me, smoke behind me." "Hop, hop! let me be, where I wish to be." "Hop, hop! they shall not know where I have come from, nor where I am going to! Let me be, where my thoughts are!" They can teach their magic formulae to their heroes.

As to *their occupations.* Of serious ones, our tales only mention embroidery. Their more favourite pastimes seem to be: bathing, banquets, singing, frivolous dances, and love adventures. After their nocturnal dances, flowers spring up where their feet have touched the ground. If anybody approaches them while they are dancing, they, in their unbounded merriment, drag him also into the dance.

On one occasion they enticed a shepherd into Borza-vára Cave, and kept him there for three days, amusing him with singing, dancing, playing music, and cajoling; finally they invited him to a game of cards and dismissed him with a big hatful of gold. From the castle-hill of Makkfalva the merry song of the fairies can be heard now every night as they dance round the castle-walls to the strains of music. They are reserved in their love; but, having made their choice, they are faithful, and their passion has no bounds. The daughter of Doghead is an instance of this; she reveals to her hero her father's charms, in order to ensure his victory in his struggle for life and death. The young and pretty mistress of Kisvártetö Castle, near Zsögöd, in the county of Csík, stood on a rock-ledge, waiting for the return of her husband from the war, till she faded away in her grief. The impression of her foot can still be seen in the rock. The fairy daughter of the giant who inhabited the castle near Bereczk fell in love with a hero who played the flute, disguised as a shepherd, at the foot of the rock; but her haughty father smashed the shepherd with a huge piece of rock, which is still[Pg xxxv] to be seen in the bed of the brook. His daughter thereupon escaped from the father's castle, and built a castle (Leányvár = Maiden's Castle) near Ojtoz for herself, where she spent the rest of her days mourning for her lover, until grief killed her. Another such a pretty tale is associated with Firtos Castle. The fairy who lived here was in love with a knight; and, notwithstanding that her father forbade the intercourse, they secretly met in the garden every night. One beautiful moonlight night she was standing on the brink of the rock, when, as she extended her arm to assist her lover up the steep slope, the knight's horse slipped, and they were precipitated arm in arm into the depth below, and thus perished, united for ever in death. The horse caught on a projecting piece of rock, and petrified. "Firtos's horse" is still to be seen. Dame Rapson's daughter, Irma, a fairy, also fell a victim to prohibited love, and fell from a lofty peak where her mother's castle stood, with her lover, Zelemir, into the depth below, where Dame Rapson found them, and died of a broken heart. They all three were buried under the rock below, which tradition names "Zelemir's Tower."

At the south angle of the Firtos there is a group of rocks which is called "Fairy Helena's Carriage," in which the fairies who lived in the castle used to drive out on moonlight nights. But one night they were so much engrossed in their enjoyments that they returned home late; and lo! the cock crew, and the carriage turned into stone.

The fairies live in castles on lofty mountain peaks. They build their castles themselves, or inherit them from giants. Sometimes they are at a great distance, as *e.g.*Fairy Elizabeth's Castle in the town of Johara, in the "Land of Black Sorrow."

Kozma enumerates the names of about 23 castles which belonged to fairies and which still exist. The castle of Kadacs formerly belonged to giants, upon whose extinction the fairies moved into it. Dame Rapson's castle near Paraja was built of[Pg xxxvi] materials which were carried up on the almost perpendicular side of the rock, to a height which makes one's head swim, by a magic cat and cock. The road leading to the castle was constructed by the Devil for a "mountain of gold," and a "valley of silver." Dame Rapson owed the Devil his wages for several years, although he kept on reminding her of it, till at last the cunning fairy presented him with a gold coin between the tips of her upheld fingers, and a silver coin in her palm, explaining to him that the gold coin is the mountain and the silver coin the valley.[74] The Devil, seeing that he was outwitted, got into a fearful rage and destroyed the road, the traces of which are still shown as far as the Görgény (snow-clad) mountains, and is still called "Dame Rapson's Road." The tale about building the road for a mountain of gold and valley of silver is also mentioned in connection with the Várhegy, near Köszvényes-Remete, but in this case it is Fairy Helen's daughter who cheats the devil. There is such a dam also at the foot of the Sóhegy, near Paraja, extending as far as Mikhàza, and this bank too is called "Dame Rapson's Road," and also "Devil's Dyke." A dam, similar to the "Cock's Ridge," near Rika, extends in the neighbourhood of Gagy and Körispatak in the direction of Firtos, and is called "Pretty Women's Road," or "Fairies' Road." Another high dam with a deep moat at its southern side, and also called the "Fairies' Road," is to be seen between Enlaka and Firtos. Under the Szépmezö (Beautiful Meadow) in Háromszék, the golden bridge of the fairies lies buried. On the outskirts of Tordátfalva there is a peak called "Ebédlö-Mál" (ebédlö = dining-place) on which the fairies coming from Firtos to Kadacsvára used to assemble to dinner.

In some localities *caves* are pointed out as the haunts of fairies [Pg xxxvii]such as the caves in the side of the rock named Budvár. We have already mentioned the cave Borza-vára near the castle of Dame Rapson; another haunt of fairies is the cave near Almás, and the cold wind known as the "Nemere" is said to blow when the fairy in Almás cave feels cold. On one occasion the plague was raging in this neighbourhood; the people ascribed it to the cold blast emanating from the cave, so they hung shirts before the mouth of the cave, and the plague ceased. (Mentioned by L. Kőváry.)

The fairies have beautiful flower-gardens in the castle grounds, and in the centre of the garden there is generally a golden summer-house which swivels round on a pivot. On moonlight nights they returned to water their flower-beds long after they had disappeared from the neighbourhood. The peonies (Whitsun-roses) that bloom among the ruins of Dame Rapson's Castle are even nowadays known among the people as Dame Rapson's roses.

The fairies live an organised social life. Several of their queens are known, as *e.g.* Dame Rapson and Fairy Helen. The latter was the most popular among them. The queens had court-dames, who were also fairies, and who lived near their queen's castle, as *e.g.* the court-dames of Dame Rapson lived in Borza-vára Cave. They also live a family life—their husbands being giants or heroes, their children fairy-girls. Those of them, however, who waste their love on ordinary mortals all die an ignoble death.

Although they have disappeared from earth, they continue to live, even in our days, in caves under their castles, in which caves their treasures lie hidden. The iron gates of Zeta Castle, which has subsided into the ground and disappeared from the surface, open once in every seven years. On one occasion a man went in there, and met two beautiful fairies whom he addressed thus: "How long will you still linger here, my[Pg xxxviii] little sisters?" and they replied: "As long as the cows will give warm milk."[75] (See Baron B. Orbán, *Description of Székelyland*, 3 vols.)

Their subterranean habitations are not less splendid and glittering than were their castles of yore on the mountain peaks. The one at Firtos is a palace resting on solid gold columns. The palace of Tartod, and the gorgeous one of Dame Rapson are lighted by three diamond balls, as big as human heads, which hang from golden chains. The treasure which is heaped up in the latter place consists of immense gold bars, golden lions with carbuncle eyes, a golden hen with her brood, and golden casks filled with gold coin. The treasures of Fairy Helen are kept in a cellar under Kovászna Castle, the gates of the cellar being guarded by a magic cock. This bird only goes to sleep once in seven years, and anybody who could guess the right moment would be able to scrape no end of diamond crystals from the walls and bring them out with him. The fairies who guard the treasures of the Pogányvár (Pagan Castle) in Marosszék even nowadays come on moonlight nights to bathe in the lake below.

Other fairies known by their names are: Tarkö (after whom a mountain near Csik-Gyergyó takes its name) with her twin daughters Olt and Maros (the names of the two principal rivers of Transylvania, the sources of which are on the Tarkö); their mother touched them with her magic wand, and they were transformed into water-fairies, they then went in search of their father, who at the time when the elements were put in order [Pg xxxix]was transformed into the Black Sea.[76] Another fairy is Mika, the warrioress fairy, who with her father Kadicsa led the remnants of Attila's Huns to their present place of sojourn.[77]

As mentioned before, there were good and bad fairies. The most complete tale about good and bad fairies is the one about Firsos and Tartód, fully mentioned by Ipolyi.[78] The castle of Dame Vénétur (near Bereczk), the bad fairy who defied God, was swallowed up by the earth, and she herself turned into a stone frog.[79]Dame Jenö (Eugen), who lived in Énlak Castle, drove out one day, and on her way home her coachman happened to remark that: "If the Lord will help us, we shall be home soon!" to which she haughtily replied: "Whether he will help us, or whether he won't, we shall get home all the same." At that moment she and her carriage were turned into stone and the people still call a rock "Dame Jenö's Carriage." (There is also another place called "Dame Jenö's Garden.") The fairy who lived in Sóvár Castle near Csik-Somlyó, was spinning on the Sabbath, and while doing so used the Lord's name in vain, and was, with her spinning-wheel turned into stone. Her stone distaff is shown to this day. A pond near Székely-Keresztur named "Katustava" (*i.e.* Kate's Pond) contains a sunken house which once upon a time belonged to a woman who was punished for doing her washing on a feast-day. Even now the children stand round the pond and sing out: "Boil up, boil up, Catherine! boil up, boil up, Catherine! We do our soaping on Saturday and rinse our clothes on Sunday!" In days gone by, the water used to boil up with great force and the little folks were [Pg xl]dispersed, and had to run away in consequence of the rush of water. They returned, however, and threw stones into the pond, and the water boiled up again vehemently. Aged people say that in their childhood the pond was ten to twelve yards in diameter, and the water boiled up to a height of two or three feet. Its present diameter is not more than a couple of feet, and the boiling up has also considerably decreased in proportion. The pond will perhaps disappear altogether, but its name will last, as the whole close of fields is named after it. (Kate's Pond Close).

A clear Christian influence can be traced in the four last tales. Mohamedanism[80] has also left behind its traces in the tales in which fairies figure who kidnap girls.

Such a fairy was Dame Hirip, who lived on the Városdal, near Gyergyó-Szens-Miklós. She used to stand on the castle tower with a wreath in her hand, waiting for her two sons, who were engaged at the bottom of the mountain, cutting down the sweethearts of the girls they had kidnapped; until, at last, two heroes clad in mourning killed them; whereupon their mother faded away with the wreath she held in her hand. On mount Bükkös, which skirts the valley of the Úz, lived another kidnapping fairy, who kidnapped a girl every year from the shores of the Black Sea. On one occasion she happened to kidnap the sweetheart of the King of the Ocean-Fairies, the loveliest maid in the sea; the King pursued her and impeded her flight, and tired her out by raising a hurricane and shower of rain. He overtook and caught her at a place called "Stone Garden;" and, seizing her, killed her by flinging her on to a rock. A mineral healing spring sprung up where her blood flowed on the ground.[81]

[Pg xli]

III. WITCHES.

The degenerate descendants of bad fairies are witches;[82] in Hungarian, "boszorkány;" in Turkish-Tartar, "Boshûr Khân;" which signifies one who worries, annoys, or teases. They appear sometimes as green frogs, sometimes as black cats; and they find a demoniacal delight in "plaguing" people. Sometimes they appear as horses and kick their enemies cruelly;[83] if such a horse be caught and shod, the horse-shoes will be found on the hands and feet of the witch next day.[84]

In nearly every village, one or two such old women are to be found who are suspected, but nobody dares to do them any harm.[85]

It is a very simple thing to see the witches. After the autumn sowing is over the harrow is to be left on the field over winter. In the morning of St. George's Day one has to go out in the field, make the harrow stand upright, stand behind it, and observe through it the herd of cattle as they pass by. You will then notice the head witch between the horns of the bull, and the minor witches between the horns of the other beasts.[86] But if you do not know the necessary protecting formula, then you are done for.

If you do not like to risk this, there is another way. Dye the first egg of a black hen, and take it with you to church in your pocket on Easter Sunday, and observe the people as they walk [Pg xlii]into church. Some of them will have great difficulty in passing through the door on account of the length of their horns. When leaving the church, you must go out before them and put down the egg; or stand at the meeting of two cross-roads; or else they will carry you off. Witches, or other evil spirits, have no power at cross-roads. The popular tales describe the witches as mothers of giants, or dragons.[87] The witch is capable of changing forms by turning somersaults.[88] They appear then as a puddle, brook, golden pear-tree, fiery oven, &c. They grow so old that their lower lips hang down as far as their knees; their eyelids also become elongated, so that if they wish to see anything the eyelid has to be lifted up with a huge iron rod, weighing 300 hundred-weights.

They exercise their magic powers: (1) in a defensive way;[89] (2) in an aggressive way, by bewitching, the cause of which is some real or fictitious offence, or evil intention. Thus by magic you can make the woman appear who has taken away the cow's milk, and you can make her give back the milk. The *modus procedendi*is as follows: take a rag saturated with milk, or a horse-shoe or chain which has been made hot in a clear fire, place it on the threshold and beat it with the head of a hatchet; or make a plough-share red hot, and plunge it several times into cold water. In order to keep away intruders it is a rule that the first woman who enters the house while the incantation proceeds is severely beaten, because she is the culprit. Sometimes the ridiculous thing happens that the man has to thrash his own wife, if she happens to be the first comer.

By magic one can make a young man marry under all circumstances a girl previously selected. Of such a young man they say, "They have dug up a big weed[90]for him;" or, "They [Pg xliii]are boiling his 'kapcza'[91] for him." The latter seems to indicate some charm. The sorceress summons toads, holds an unintelligible conversation with them, and hands some mysterious charm which has to be placed under the threshold of the selected young man's house. The person, however, who orders the incantation will die the same year.

Some kinds of severe illness or accidents can be produced by planting in secret certain magic plants on the selected person's ground; the illness will last, and the consequences of the accident be felt, until the plants are removed. If the owner plants these plants himself they will serve as a preventative.

Thieves can be found out or bewitched, and they dread the thing so much that very often they return in secret the stolen articles.

There are various formulæ to cause marriage or produce sickness. One of them may be mentioned here.[92] The person who orders the incantation steals from the selected victim some article of dress, and takes it to the sorceress, who adds three beans, three bulbs of garlic, a few pieces of dry coal, and a dead frog to it, and places these several articles in an earthenware pot under the victim's gate or threshold, accompanied by these words: "Lord of the infernal regions and of the devils, and possessor of the hidden treasures; give to ... (name of the victim) some incurable illness—(or inflame ... with irresistible love towards ...)—and I will join your party!"

[Pg xliv]

In a Hungarian paper, published in 1833, we read

Some woman in Transylvania grew tired of her husband, and consulted a sorceress about the means of getting rid of him. The sorceress (a Wallachian old woman) visited the woman's house, and they both retired to the garret, where the sorceress laid out an image in clay, which was intended to represent the unfortunate husband, and surrounded it with burning wax tapers, and both women engaged in prayer for the quick departure from this life of the husband. The latter, however, appeared on the scene and put an end to the proceedings.

Amidst the vast pile of superstitions still current amidst the peasantry, we may note the following, from a very valuable work by Varga János, entitled *A babondák könyve, Arad*, 1877; a volume which won the prize offered at the time by the Hungarian physicians and others, for the best work written on the existing superstitions of the Magyar people. Its chief aim is to instruct the people, and is written in *very* popular language.

To this day old women (Roman Catholics) do not swallow the consecrated wafer at communion; but save it and carefully wrap it in a handkerchief, and keep it in a drawer at home, as it will prevent the house from being burnt down. An epidemic raged all over Hungary, and the people in one of the villages attributed the outbreak of cholera to an old woman who had died shortly before, and who was said to have been a witch in her lifetime. The corpse was dug up, and replaced in the grave face *downwards*, in order to stay the plague. When the rinderpest broke out in another village they had recourse to the same remedy. The corpse of the witch was unearthed, and reburied face downwards. As this had no effect, the shift of the corpse was turned inside out and put on again. As the pest still continued, the heart of the witch was taken out and divided into four pieces, and one quarter burnt at each of the four[Pg xlv] corners of the village, and the herd driven through the smoke. One year, when there was a drought in the country, in a northern village, amongst the Slováks, a young girl was let down into a well, in order to bring on the rain.

Ghosts.[23] There is a proverb saying that: "The good souls do not wish to come back, and the bad ones are not allowed to return;" but still people believe in ghosts.

Sprites. (Evil spirits, garabonczas.) The father of the garabonczas is the devil; the mother, a witch. The garabonczas mostly appears as a poor wandering student begging for milk in the village. If he be well treated no harm will happen to the village, but if he be sent away from the door, he will bring on hail and will destroy the crops belonging to the place. He generally rides officially on dragons or tátos.

Exchanged children, or táltos.[24] If a child be born with some defect (say without an arm, &c.) or with some supernumerary member (say six fingers or six toes) or with a big head, people say it is an exchanged child; it is a child of some witch who exchanged her offspring for the baby, while the baby's mother was in bed. Babies born with teeth are especially considered to be children of witches. Such unfortunate creatures are very badly treated by the people, and even by their own parents. The name "táltos" sticks to them, even when grown up. A knife stuck into a slice of garlic and placed under the pillow of the woman in childbed is an effective remedy against babies being exchanged by witches.

Goblins[25] (Lidércz) are the servants of evil spirits or the evil [Pg xlvi]spirits themselves. One favourite form they like to appear in is the "wandering fire," or will-o'-the-wisp. A hen that crows (a hermaphrodite bird) is also a goblin; and a combination of cock and hen is hatched from the first egg laid by the young hen, or from very small undersized eggs as are sometimes laid by fowls. A little decrepit, undeveloped chicken is also always looked at with suspicion. The good housewife breaks the first egg laid by a young hen, or a very small egg, to prevent the goblin's being hatched. The crowing hen is executed, the neck being laid on the threshold and cut off with a hatchet; if the head jumps into the yard, then no matter, but if it hops inside the house, then it means that the house will be burnt down. (In Germany some hundred and seventy years ago a crowing hen was brought before the judges, sentenced to death, its neck cut off by the public executioner in the market-place, and the body burnt at the stake.)

Roadside wanderers or inhabitants of graves.[26] Sickly, yellow, haggard-looking people are said to live in graves or crypts at night. The Magyar people are very good-natured, and their hospitality is well known. But such a grave-inhabitant can reckon upon having no mercy. If they stop and rest anywhere somebody is sure to die in the neighbourhood. If anybody look at them it will bring on jaundice; if anybody touch them the healthy person will dry up; children die if touched or kissed by such a creature.

There is a rich mine of Folk-Medicine, as yet but little worked by western students: a few examples will be found in "Székely Folk-Medicine," *Folk-lore Journal*, April 1884, and we append a few more, which may be of interest, from an old MS.[97]

Jaundice is brought on by looking through the window of a [Pg xlvii]house where there is a corpse laid out, and seeing it. It is cured by taking nine "creepers" from the head of a person with the same Christian names as the patient; put the nine insects into an apple; bake the whole, and give it to the patient for internal application. Then take the foeces[98] of a person of the same Christian name; place them in a hard-boiled egg, having first removed the yolk; sew the egg in a small bag, and place it *secretly* under the altar, and allow three masses to be said over it; then hang it round the patient's neck, who has to wear it for nine days. The cure is to be repeated nine times. There is a marginal note in the book to the effect that our "doctor" had altogether six cases under treatment, but not one of the patients got beyond the first stage of the cure.[99]

Pleurisy. Take a trough in which the dough has been kneaded and taken out; pour water into it cross-ways (diagonally from corner to corner) then pour water in cross form over the peel; scrape out the trough and knead with one finger the scrapings into a flat cake and place it on the aching side. Varga also gives a form of prayer which has to be recited when the dough is placed on the side. The same prayer is prescribed for toothache and sore throat.

Scurvy. (In Magyar "süly.") The scorbutic place is to be rubbed with a piece of rancid bacon, and the following ditty sung:—

"Sü-sü, lentils-süPeas-sü,—pumpkin-sü,Onion-sü,—77 sorts of sü,

I order thee, in the name of the Blessed Virgin Mary to disappear!"

[Pg xlviii]

Cataract in the eye. This is cured with a long prayer, commencing I † N † R † I, and, if it has no effect, another (shorter) prayer is mumbled, and the performer breathes upon the eye.

Gangrene is also cured by prayers; a little garlic and broken glass is placed upon the wound.

Another way is to bury three hairs of the patient in the gutter under the eaves, and then to say the Lord's Prayer. When the medicine-man arrives at the words "as in earth," he drops a slice of garlick, this is afterwards buried in some secluded spot. If anybody steps on this place he will be affected by the same disease.

Hydrophobia is cured by a mixture of the following nine ingredients:—

1. A kind of small, vermilion, flat beetle;
2. Some dittany gathered before St. John's Day;
3. Splinters of tree struck by lightning before St. George's Day;
4. Some cantharides;
5. Young buds of ash gathered in early spring;
6. Rue gathered before St. George's Day;
7. "St. Ivan's beetle" (? glow-worm);
8. "Christmas crumb"[100] and eggshell from between two Christmases;
9. On Midsummer Day, at early dawn, the medicine-man walks out barefoot, and the weeds, grasses, flowers, &c. that stick to his sole or toes form ingredient No. 9.

The mixture is to be taken internally.

Epilepsy is treated with an oil prepared by the quack out of horseradish; also some brimstone and other things.

External wounds and sore nails are cured by placing a live toad on the place.

[Pg xlix]

The rash called *St. Anthony's Fire*. A man whose Christian name is Anthony has to produce sparks with steel and flint.[101]

Scab is treated with an ointment made of beef-fat and brimstone; the ointment to be used for three days, and to be followed up by a hot-air bath. As these useful establishments only exist in large towns, the unfortunate sufferer is put inside a hot oven.

Quinsy.—With the child's finger stroke the throat of a lizard,[102] caught before St. George's Day.

Cramp.—Place a left-hand window-frame across the child suffering from cramp, or burn feathers under its nose.

Hand of Glory.[103]—The little finger of the human foetus has all the virtues of (and is used for the same purpose as) the hand of glory. All the famous brigands are believed to have one of these articles in their possession.

When a person is *in extremis* they place him or her, bed and all, in a line with and under the main joist of the ceiling. If the dead person's eyes are left open somebody will soon follow him or her.

Superstitious Days.

Friday. Work commenced or finished on Friday is sure to fail.

Who laughs on Friday will cry on Sunday.

To sneeze on Friday the first thing in the morning when the stomach is empty means some great catastrophe.

To start on a journey on Friday is unlucky.

[Pg l]

He or she who is taken ill on Friday will never again leave their bed.

A guest on Friday means one week's distress.

Dough kneaded on Friday will not rise.

Linen washed on Friday will give the wearer some skin disease.

If the fires are lighted in the rooms for the first time on Friday the house will be burnt down.

If a baby gets its first tooth on a Friday the front teeth will come all right but no more.

If a baby commence to talk on a Friday it will, when grown up, stammer or remain mute altogether.

If the new year commence with a Friday all the crops will fail.

If a hen commence to sit on her eggs on a Friday the eggs become addled.[104]

St. Matthias. "It is better trust the ice after St. Matthias' Day than in you, my dear little maid." *Erdélyi*, vol. 3. Folk-Song No. 200.

St. George's Day is a very lucky day.

A butterfly caught before St. George's Day brings great luck.

Snakes caught before St. George's Day make a powerful medicine.

The skin of a marmot caught before St. George's Day will make a purse which will never be empty.

[Pg li]

The person who sees a swallow or stork before St. George's Day will live as many years as the bird flaps its wings.

Procure the wing of a bat caught before St. George's Day and wrap up money in it; then you will never be without cash.

On the night following St. George's Day one can listen to the conversation of the witches and overhear their secrets about good and bad herbs.

All the medicines gathered before St. George's Day are very powerful.

Christmas Eve.—Roman Catholics fast on this day—eating no meat, using instead fish and vermicelli with crushed poppy seed and honey. Those who stand on "Lucy's chair" during midnight mass can tell who is a witch and who is not. St. Lucy's Day is December 13th, and on that day some begin to make a small chair, or stool, working at it, on each following day, so as to get it ready by Christmas Eve. The maker then takes it to midnight mass, and sits upon it in order to discover who are witches in the parish. All those who turn their backs to the altar whilst he (or she) sits on the stool, are witches. "Lucy's chair" is also said of anything that is being made very slowly. On this day, too, the farmer's wife and servants wrap their heads up in cloaks, and, armed with big brushes (a sort of brush tied athwart the end of a pole), go round and catch the hens and touch their hinder parts, believing that it will cause them to lay more eggs. The twelve days following St. Lucy's are called Lucy's Kalendar, and are very carefully observed. If the first, second, third, &c., be raining, windy, foggy, &c., so will the first, second, third, &c., months of the next year be.

Christmas Day.—Every hour of this day is significant and pregnant with good or evil. It seems as if on this day every good angel descended from heaven to scatter blessings, and every[Pg lii] demon ascended from the infernal regions to shower curses on the heads of men.[105]

Even the remnants of food have their magic power. The well-known "Christmas crumb" forming an important ingredient in many folk-medicines.

Whoever picks up an apple or nut from the ground will be covered with sores; and if anyone steps upon a reel of cotton (or gets entangled in it) upon this day, he will, without fail, have an attack of the "evil of Lazarus."

A sort of basket made of twisted or plaited straw, such as is used for taking dough to the bakers, is filled with hay and put under the table to receive the "little Jesus," who is said to get into it. Maize put under this basket is said to fatten fowls to a wondrous extent, and cattle thrive marvellously on the hay. Whosoever eats nuts without honey will lose his teeth.

Whosoever does not eat a slice of garlic with honey on this holy day will get a sore throat.[106]

There are several Finnish superstitions with regard to this season, *e.g.*:

In West Bothnia one must not spin on St. John's Day (which is called a half-holyday), or the sheep will be attacked with disease during the year. Cf. the well known saying that a spinning wheel is unlucky on board a ship.

Fire must not be taken out of a house on Christmas Eve,[107] or else the so-called "black ears" will grow among the barley. See *Suomen Muinaismuisto-yhdistyksen, Aikakauskirja*, v. p. 109.

[Pg liii]

If the corn is found to be very much entangled when cut, it is said that the farmer slept crooked in bed on Christmas Eve. In some villages, on "Knuts Day," Jan. 13th, a young girl is dressed up as a bride, and called "twenty-days' bride" (twenty days after Christmas), and driven through the village. The day ends with a dance, and a collection for the "bride," who is generally one of the poor. Straw, too, was laid on the room floors in remembrance of the Saviour's bed. A light burnt all night on the settle.[108] These customs still exist in some places.

A yule-cross used to be erected at the house-door on Christmas Eve.

To return to the Magyars. The bread at Christmas time is baked in curious forms, just as it is in Finland, where, *e.g.*, in Åbo, it is made in the form of a fish, &c., and called "Kuse" and "Kasa," in other parts in the form of animals, &c. (cf. the "Yuldoos" in Northumberland).

New Year's Eve and *New Year's Day*.[109] Molten lead is cast into water to see the future husband's trade. Watch which way the cock crows on the dawn of the new year, for in that direction your future partner will surely come. Turn your pillow at midnight (December 31st), and you will see whom you are to marry, in your dreams. Any one born at midnight will become a great person. Whosoever is whipped on New Year's Day will be whipped every day in the new year! Indeed, anything done on this day will be repeated during the year. It is unlucky to sow on this day, as it prevents the hens laying. If you put on new linen you will cause your skin to be covered with sores. New Year's morn is spent in wishing each other a happy new year; just as, in many parts of England (*e.g.* Hull) the juvenile [Pg liv]population call and expect to receive their reward in the shape of coin of the realm.

In Vienna they say: "to have Schweinsglück," or "Sauglück," *i.e.*, "a pig's luck," or a "sow's luck;" and so one sees in some houses a cook appear, bearing a sucking pig on a tray, and wishing all a happy New Year, expecting a New Year's box in return.

According to Paul Kelecsényi, the following custom is observed at Kolony, in the county of Nyitra. Girls make a bonfire, and leap through the flame. From their mode of leaping the spectators gather when the girl will be married. The performance is accompanied by a song, of which a few verses will suffice as a specimen:

"We lay a fire,We lay it square,At one corner sit five old men,At the other sit good looking matrons,At the third sit handsome young bachelors,At the fourth sit pretty young maidens.Then the fire is lighted.John A's (the name of an unmarried man) is about to catch fire.Let us extinguish it! (Susie.)Oh! don't let us forsake the poor people!Jane B's (generally John A's sweetheart) store house is about to catch fire.Let us....Oh! don't...."

Then follow verses, like the following, and all more or less unintelligible:

"How high the branch of the tree has grown,[The tree] has sent out branches.It is bending and bending across the oceanInto the courtyard of John A.Of [to?] pretty Helena with the silken yellow tresses."

See Erdélyi's *Folk-Songs and Stories*, vol. iii. pp. 148-150. "Szent Iván Éneke."

[Pg lv]

On St. John the Baptist's Day[110] the glow-worm is gathered, and also at dawn the medicinal herbs for certain cures (see supra). On this day it is also customary to jump over "St. John's fire;" any person doing this will not die during the year.

On the Day of St. Paul's Conversion all the bears turn round in their sleep in their winter dens.

On the Night of St. Andrew's every girl will dream about her future husband; if she manage to procure a shirt of a young man and place it over-night under her pillow, she will so bewitch him that he will follow her like her shadow.

On Saturday before Easter all snakes, frogs, toads, &c., can be driven away in the morning when the cattle's bell is heard.

On Palm Sunday, swallow without chewing three buds blessed by the priest and brought from church, and this will prevent a sore throat.

St. Martin. On this day, in conformity with an old custom, the Jewish community of Pozsony (Pressburg) yearly present a fat goose to the King of Hungary. This deputation is always received personally.

St. Michael. The bier in Magyar is called "St. Michael's horse."

St. Stephen.—See *Notes and Queries*, "Magyar and Finn Songs on St. Stephen's Day," 6 S. viii. 487, and x. 485, with which we may compare the following:—

VAUSENOTTES: La cérémonie de crier les *valantins*: les garçons se nommoient *vausenots* et les filles *vausenottes*: ces mots viennent de *vouser* ou *vauser*, qui eux-mêmes viennent de *vocare*, nommer, et de *nuptiae* noces: comme si l'on disoit appeler aux noces: aux mariages: cette cérémonie s'est pratiquée longtemps dans le pays Messin. *Voyez Valantin.*

VALANTIN: Futur époux, celui qu' on désignoit à une fille le jour des *brandons*, ou premier dimanche de carême, qui, dès [Pg lvi]qu'elle étoit promise, se nommoit*valantine*: Et si son *valantin* ne lui faisoit point un present ou ne la regaloit avant le dimanche de la mi-carême, elle le brûloit sous l'effigie d'un paquet de paille ou de sarment, et alors les promesses de mariage étoient rompues et annuliés.

BRANDON: Tisson allumé, feu, flambeau: de-là ou a appelé *dimanche des brandons*, le premier dimanche de carême, parce qu'on allumoit des feux ce jour-là, il était encore nommé le jour de *behourdi*, *behourt*, *bordes*, *bourdich*, termes qui signifioient une joûte une course de lances. Il se nomme encore dans quelques provinces, le jour de *grand feux*, des *valantins*, le jour des *bulles* ou des *bures*, le dimanche des *bordes*; au figuré, l'ardeur de l'amour et son flambeau, *brando*. On appelle à Lyons, *brandons*, des rameaux verds auxquels on attache des gâteaux, des oublies et des bugnes, le premier dimanche de carême.

BULE, *bulle*; Feu de rejouissance.

BORDE. One of the meanings of the diminutive of "borde," viz.: "bordelle" "on a appliqué ensuite aux lieux de débauche."[111]

Heltay Gáspár, the typographer of Kolozsvár, wrote his book in 1552 against this custom as practised in Hungary.

The following Finnish superstitions at certain times may here be noted for comparative purposes:—

Lent. Witches are said to have cut off the sheep's wool at this time, and given it to the evil one; who in return gave them good luck with their sheep and butter.

Shrove Tuesday. Women are not to spin on this day; because, if they do, the sheep will suffer from diseases.

If the sun shines on this day there will be a fine summer. Much sledging must be done if long flax is desired; and seven meals must be eaten without drinking, if thirst is to be avoided during the summer heats.

[Pg lvii]

Good Friday. It was not customary formerly to make a fire on this day.

Easter. On Easter Eve cut off the wool from between the sheep's ears; so the young folks burn straw and tar-barrels to frighten the Easter witches (in the parishes of Wörå and Munsala). If anyone wishes to see the witches, as they ride in mid-air on their broomsticks, he must sit on the roof of a three-times-removed house. (Houses in Finland are built of wood, and often sold and removed to another site.)

May 1st. As the weather is this day, so will the rest of the year be.

Eve of St. John Baptist. On this night the young girls go out into rye-fields with bits of colored worsted, and tie them round the stalks that are chosen. The stalks are then cut off just above the worsted. Next morning the stalk that has grown the most during the night foretells the future of the maiden. The red one foretells purity; green, love; yellow, rejection; black, grief; blue, old maid; white, death; speckled, an illegitimate child. The stalk is then taken up and placed under the pillow, and whatever the sleeper then dreams will undoubtedly happen.

A Finnish lady friend relates that she and one of her friends on this night gathered nine different sorts of flowers, and, having made wreaths of them, put them under their pillows—as it was said that next morning there would be a lock of hair the colour of the future husband's found in each wreath. In order to make sure, each of the young ladies, unknown to the other, cut a lock off her own head and placed it in her friend's wreath, but, unfortunately, one of the ladies also put a lock of her own hair in her own wreath, and thus next day found she was doomed to have two mates! In some parts, when the farmers return from church, they see who can get home first, as that one will get his harvest in first the following year.

[Pg lviii]In some places straw is burnt on this night, but it is more common to burn wood (which fires are called Kokko). In some parts these fires are burnt on Maunday Thursday night. In Honkojoki, after the Kokko is burned two persons go and stand each on a wood stack, and begin throwing the logs into a heap, each trying his best to throw more than his rival. This done, the logs are counted, and, if found to be an odd number, it is regarded as an omen of misfortune. The girls are dressed in white on this night. In the southern parts of the country stones used to be rolled down the hill sides on this night. The houses are decorated on the outside with young birches and inside with leafy boughs, &c. For dressing with flowers and leaves at this time see *Hofberg*, "Digerdöden."

St. Bartholomew.—According to some, seed ought to be sown this day.

St. Matthew's Day.—People disguise themselves so as not to be recognised. A sledge, too, is drawn by a ram, with a straw man as driver.

St. Thomas's Eve.—A Swedish superstition regards this as the goblins' special night, and one story (*Hofberg*, "Tomten") relates how no one would go into a smithy that night on this account, and if anyone looked through the door he would see the goblins forging silver bars, or "turning their own legs under the hammer."

In the Highlands, even in modern times, there were May-Day bonfires, at which the spirits were implored to make the year productive. A feast was set out upon the grass, and lots were drawn for the semblance of a human sacrifice; and whoever drew the "black piece" of a cake dressed on the fire was made to leap three times through the flame.[112]

In many parts of France the sheriffs or the mayor of a town [Pg lix]burned baskets filled with wolves, foxes, and cats, in the bonfires at the Feast of St. John; and it is said that the Basques burn vipers in wicker panniers at Midsummer, and that Breton villagers will sacrifice a snake when they burn the sacred boat to the goddess who assumed the title of St. Anne.[113]

Varga also gives the following information on numbers:

13 is very unlucky.[114] If thirteen sit down to table, one will die.

9 also plays an important part. See folk-medicine. Hydrophobia breaks out in nine days, weeks, months, or years. Nine different ingredients often make up the mixture—nine different shoots of nine different trees. If a cow be bewitched, a cure with nine ants' nests is used. Most medicines are taken nine times; the patient has to bathe nine times, &c. &c.

7 is very superstitious. The seventh child plays an important part in everything; only a seventh child can lift hidden treasures. A seventh child seven years old has great magic power. In digging for treasures seven people club together, each member removes seven spades-full of earth in one night. Seven times seven, or seventy-seven is also a magic number. The devil's grandmother is 777 years old.

3 very often occurs in fairy-tales. It is an important number with witches. It is said there are 33,333 witches in Hungary.

[Pg lx]

Superstitions about Animals.

It would be more easy to enumerate those animals about which there are not superstitions, but we will give a few instances from Varga.

The Death-Bird (a kind of small owl).—If the death-bird settles on the roof, and calls out three times "kuvik," somebody will die in that house.

The Owl.—The well-known servant of witches. It procures them the required number of snakes, lizards, &c.

The Cuckoo.—It will tell you how many years you have to live. It sucks the milk out of the udder of the cow. There is also another bird credited with this.

The Crowing-hen.—See *supra*. p. xlvi.

The Swallow and stork are favourite birds. To catch a swallow is very unlucky. To disturb its nest will set the roof on fire. If you kill it, your arm will shrivel up. Of this bird the people say that it dies; of all others, they perish. (A human being "dies" = "meghal" in Hung. = "stirbt" in German; an animal "perishes" = "megdöglik," = "crepirt.") If you see the first swallow, stroke your face and sing, "I see a swallow; I wash off the freckles"—and the freckles will disappear. The stork is, also, a sacred bird. It must not be caught or killed; to disturb its nest will set the house on fire. He who sees for the first time in the year a stork standing, will be very lazy during the year; if flying, then fresh and very healthy.

Lark, Plover,[115] *Quail,* and *Pigeon.*—When Christ was hiding himself he went among some underwood, his pursuers were about to follow him there, when the lark rose and sang: "Nincs, nincs, nincs, nincs, nincs, sehol itten." (He is not—he is nowhere [Pg lxi]here). The pursuers were about to leave, when out of malice the quail flew up and called "Itt szalad, itt szalad" (Here he runs, here he runs); the pursuers thereupon returned, and Christ took refuge in a shrubbery; then the plover flew up and cried "bú vik, bú vik" (he is hiding), and the pigeon added "a bokorban, a bokorban" (in the bush). Christ blessed the lark, hence it rises high up in the sky and sings merrily, whereas the three other birds were accursed to never fly on a tree, but to hide themselves among grass, in the mud, in old ruins.

See Arany László "Magyar Népmeséinkröl" (On our Magyar Popular Tales), a paper read before the Kisfaludy Society on May 29, 1867. Cf. *Hofberg*, Horsgötten.

Newt.—If you swallow a newt with the water drawn from a well, it will grow quite a monster in your stomach, and eat its way through. The monster will have a head as a calf; immense immoveable eyes; a skin like a human being; its voice like a baby's, and its head covered with fur, like that of a wild cat.

Snake.—There is a snake in every house; if it creep out of its hole, some great misfortune will happen. It is therefore unlucky to disturb it. The skin of a snake caught before St. George's Day, drawn over a stick, makes a powerful weapon; it will break iron in two.

Snakes and Frogs.[116]—If a snake or frog get into a man's stomach, it can be allured out by placing some steaming milk near the mouth of the patient. If they die inside, the patient has to take internally some powderized stork's stomach. [Cf. "Liber Quartus Practicae Haly," cap. 49, "De eius medela qui leporem marinum aut ranam biberit," p. 207, verso (Leyden, [Pg lxii]1523)]. The so-called frog-rain; the frogs drop from the clouds, or that they are drawn up by the clouds from lakes, &c.

Lizard, see "Quinsy" and "St. George's Day," pp. xlix. and li.

Cat.—The black cat is a favourite disguise of the witch. When the cat is cleaning herself, you must observe at whom she looks first, when finished; the person so looked at will go to a ball, or some other amusement. If the cat uses one paw only, a guest will arrive; he will come from the direction in which the cat stroked her paw the last time. If a cat be uneasy, &c., it will rain.

Donkey.—There are three indents on the bulrush as if made with teeth. The tradition is, that the donkey on which Christ sat commenced to nibble the reed, but before it had time to bite it off, Christ rode away. The traces of the teeth are still plainly visible. The cross on the donkey's back is said to be the stains left by Christ's blood, as it ran down on both sides.—Arany László *loc. cit.*

Raven.—There is a well-known Magyar folk-song commencing the thus:—

"The raven washes his brood on Good Friday."

Clocks.—The ticking of the clock-beetle forbodes death in the house.

Dog.—The witch will sometimes appear as a black dog. If a dog whine in his sleep, it is a sign of conflagration; if it bark in its sleep, robbers are due. If a dog howl,[117] it smells a dead body, and somebody will die in the house.

The Sow with a litter of nine, *the Horse* without a head, *the Bull* with horns pointing downwards, are favourite forms assumed by witches.

The Tortoise.—When Christ was walking on earth, He appeared as a beggar, and begged for alms at a Jew's house. The [Pg lxiii]mistress of the house was very mean; and in order not to be obliged to give anything, she hid under a trough used for kneading bread, and told her little girl to say that she was not to be found. When the girl said that her mother was not at home, Christ replied: "May she never be able to get home!" The girl waited in vain for her mother to come forth; and when she opened the closet door, an ugly thing crawled out, with a trough-like shield grown to its back. This is the origin of the tortoise.

Superstitions about Plants.

Varga supplies the following notes on this subject:

Deadly Nightshade works miracles in folk-medicine. One of its uses is to cure maggots in beasts. It is not used internally nor applied externally. The medicine-man approaches the plant wherever it grows, makes a hole into the ground close to the root, then bends the plant gently down, sticks the top of it into the hole and buries it, taking care not to break the plant. Then he repeats the following formula:—"Do you hear, deadly nightshade? I herewith bury you, and will not again liberate you until the maggots that have got into the left rump of John So-and-So's cow clear out from there."

Vervain or "lock-opening herb."—Open the skin on the palm of your hand, place a small leaf of vervain under the skin and let the wound heal over; then at the touch of such hand all locks and bars will open. All the more famous brigands of old are said to have had such power.

Clover.—Clover with four leaves is very lucky.

Wolf's-milk.—The milky juice oozing from the broken stem of this plant will beautify the skin.[118]

[Pg lxiv]*The Wolf's-bane leaf*, the ökörfark kóró (lit. the dried oxtail)[119], and *the Rue* are very important herbs in folk-medicine.

Some other plants are said to have had this power, that if at dusk you switch with them three times in the air you hit the witch, and you can hear her moaning.

The Lily is the flower of the dead. If any body be executed innocent, three yellow lilies will grow on his grave.

Superstitions about Stones.

The Diamond is blown, like glass, by thousands and thousands of snakes in caves, who bury them in the sand.

The Carbuncle glows in the dark.

The Garnet. While the person who wears these stones is healthy the garnet is of a beautiful red colour; when the wearer ails the stones turn pale.

The Opal is an unlucky stone.

Sundries.[120]

Astronomy. The milky way came about in this way. The driver of a cart of straw was very drunk; the straw was badly loaded and fell off in all directions as the drunken driver drove his horses irregularly over the way.

*Comets forebode a great war or the pest.

Many people get out at the left side of the bed, pull on the left side first of their trousers, the left sleeve of their coat, and undress left first because it is good for toothache.

*If your palm itches, you receive money; rub it to your hair, and you get as much money as you touched hairs.

[Pg lxv]*Right eye itching, you will cry; left eye, you will be merry; whose eyes jump about will get beaten.

*Singing in right ear, bad news; left, good news.

If a family gets into a new house, somebody will die; a dead body's eyes left open, he is looking for somebody to follow him. If you pity an animal when it is being slaughtered it dies very slowly.

*If a knife, fork, or scissors drop and stick upright in the ground, a guest will arrive. If by accident one more plate is laid on the table than necessary, a very hungry guest will come.

Where there is a baby in the house, you must sit down or you will take away its sleep. If you stare at the baby, you spoil it with your eye. To counteract this, put your hat on the child's head or spit on the baby. If the mischief is already done, drop a piece of live coal into a glass of water, and make the child drink of it, and bathe his eyes with the water. At the same time wish the "spoiling" back to the person from whom it came.

If a spider lowers itself on somebody at night, it is lucky; in the daytime, unlucky.

*If the fire is noisy (a series of small explosions) there will be high words or some scrimmage in the house. If you dream of fire, you will be robbed. If in your dream you see yourself as bride or bridegroom, you will die. If you dream that you are dead, you get married. If, at meals, you sit between two brothers or sisters, you will get married.

If a woman in the family-way looks into the window, where there is a corpse, the baby will be dumb. If the woman sends away a beggar, she will bear twins.

In stormy weather stick a hatchet in the threshold, and the hail-clouds will roll by. *Make the sign of a cross with the poker against the sky and the rainbow will appear.

When it rains and the sun shines too, the devil beats his wife. [Pg lxvi]If it thunders without lightning, the devil has got hold of a poor sinner. If you abuse the rain, the angels cry and the devil tears his hair.

If the cow is bewitched and will not allow herself to be milked, place the pail over her head; or go to the cemetery, procure a decayed old wooden cross, and beat the animal with it.

If the cow kicks, cover her head with an old apron and stick holes through the apron with the pitchfork. *The witch will feel the stabbing from the prongs. If the witch has taken away the milk of the cow, procure nine ants'-nests,[121] bury this with nine pieces of bread on the road over which the cattle goes, so that the cow may step over it. Then after three days knead the bread and soil together and make the cow eat it, and her milk will be restored.

Or pour some of the milk into a fiery oven, and the fire will burn the witch who spoilt the cow.

It is not good to look at a cow while calving, because her milk will not come. The first week's milk is to be given to the poor, or it will be difficult to milk the cow afterwards.

Do not call a child "a frog," or it will with difficulty learn to talk. Do not step over it, or you stop its growing. Do not say thanks for a medicine, or it will lose its power. Do not wish the fisher or hunter "good luck," or he will have a poor day. To meet a priest is unlucky; to meet a Jew lucky.

If a child suffers from epileptic fits, take the shirt it has worn during one of the fits and wrap it around one of the (wooden) crosses in the cemetery, this will cure the child; but the person who removes it will catch the disease. When a child loses its first tooth, the mother ought to eat the tooth in a piece of bread, and then she will never suffer from toothache. When a child sees a swallow for the first time in Spring, it must spit several [Pg lxvii]times into the palms of its hands and pretend to wash its face; this will prevent freckles.

The following is said to cure abscesses: Boil together peas, beans, lentils, and millet in a new pot, and when the mess is ready bathe the affected place therein; then take pot and contents at dawn to the cross-roads, and dash it to the ground. The abscesses will disappear, the first person who steps over the mess will get them.

When sweeping the house the dust must not be swept towards the door but from it, and the sweepings burnt; then luck will never desert the house.

A loaf that has been cut should never be placed so that the cut part faces the door, because that would cause lack of bread.

When the bread is taken from the oven, if a few red-hot cinders be thrown into the oven it is as good as throwing them down your enemy's throat!

*Whenever water is drawn from a well, great care must be taken that a little is returned, to propitiate the angry sprite of the well.

Manners at Table.

"Whereas other learned and wise nations keep their heads covered while they are at meals, the Magyars uncover themselves at table. Perhaps they follow this custom because they remember the words of St. Paul (1 Cor. ii.), who says that every man praying, having his head covered, dishonoureth his head; the Magyars, however, not only often commence their meals with a prayer, but mention the Deity as often as they drink, and wish to those, in whose honour they lift their glasses, good luck and bliss, and pray to God for these, which custom is not always followed by other nations. Therefore they think it is better not to cover the head than to be obliged to uncover [Pg lxviii]themselves so many times."[122]—*From "A Kopaszsagnac diczireti" (the praise of baldness). Kolozsvár, 1589; author unknown.*

Drinking Custom.—The Finnish word "ukko," at the present day, means "the host," "the master of the house;" formerly "yli-jumala" meant "the chief-God," "the God of the weather and fertility." Wherefore Väinämõinen prays to him when sowing the first seed (Kalevala, I. runes 317-330).

The heathen Finns, after spring sowing,[123] sacrificed with "Ukko's cup" (Ukon malja). Jacob Grimm compares Ukko's cup to Thor's drinking vessel.[124]

In 1886, or thereabouts, the Magyar Academy of Science came into possession of some XVIth and XVIIth century deeds written in Magyar, and relating to the sale of certain vineyards in the Hegyalja, where the famous vines of Tokaj[125] grow. From these deeds it appears, that in each case the bargaining for [Pg lxix]the vineyard was followed by a drinking-bout, at which one of the men would lift up his glass; and if nobody objected to the sale the bargain became confirmed and binding upon all parties concerned. The ceremony of lifting up the cup that should serve as a sign that the bargain was struck was called "Ukkon poharat fölmutatui," = show up Ukko's glass, and the name of the person who performed the ceremony is mentioned in the deed in every case. Thus, in one of these documents, dated "Tállya, December 28, 1623," we read as follows: "In witness thereof, we the above named magistrates and sworn men, in conformity with the living old custom of our ancestors, have drunk áldomás[126] &c. Ukko's glass was held up[127] by John Kantuk de Liszka."

Thus, while the Finnish Agricola in 1551 condemns the custom of "drinking Ukko's cup" of the ancient Finns as a superstition, in Hungary, in the Hegyalja, it was, according to deeds bearing dates from 1596 to 1660, a ceremony "in accordance with the old law and living custom."[128]

See Paul Hunfalvy's "Magyarország Ethnographiája," Budapest, 1876, pp. 242 & seq.

[1]"Aladár," in Hungarian tradition.

[2]*Enc. Britt.* "Huns."

[3]See "Rege a csoda-szarvasról, by Arany János, an English translation of which has been published by Mr. Butler in his *Legends, Folk Songs, &c.*, from the Hungarian." Cf. *Hungary*, by Professor Vambéry, cap. iii.

[4]According to Hungarian history, Árpád found numerous small nationalities inheriting Attila's realm, with each of whom he had to settle separately. The number of nationalities has been further increased by fresh arrivals from Asia, and immigrants from Western Europe during the past ten centuries: thus we hear of the continuous irruption of Besseni (Petchenegs) during the reign of Stephen the Saint (first King of Hungary, A.D. 1000); of Cumani in the time of Salamon (A.D. 1060) and his successors; and of Tartars under Batu Khan (A.D. 1285) in the time of Béla IV. During this last invasion large tracts of land became depopulated, the inhabitants having either perished or fled; so that the king was obliged to invite immigrants from Western Europe, and this was the origin of the Saxon settlements in Transylvania. This will to some extent show the difficulties which beset the writer who attempts to give a sketch of the races inhabiting modern Hungary. A further difficulty, in tracing the origin of such races, is due to the variety of spelling adopted by different writers in describing the same race, and the unscrupulous use of the names Huns, Scythae, &c. when writing about tribes inhabiting regions beyond the borders of the then known civilised world. *Vide infra*, p. x.

[5]We have attempted to give but a brief sketch of the Magyars, feeling that when there is so lucid a work as "Hungary," by so well-known an authority as Professor Vambéry, within the reach of all, and dealing with this subject in a way that it would be folly for us to attempt, we may content ourselves with referring all readers to that work, and to *Der Ursprung der Magyaren* by the same author.

[6]The Székely (in German "Székler," in Latin "Siculus") inhabit the eastern parts of Transylvania, the territory occupied by them forming an oblong strip between the Saxon settlement of Besztercze and Brassó (Kronstadt), with two branches to the west known as

Marosszék and Udvarhelyszék. Another district (szék) inhabited by them, Aranyos-szék, lies in the western part of Transylvania between the districts of Torda and Alsó-Fejér.

[7]*The Nationality of the Huns and Avars*, a paper read before the Hungarian Academy of Sciences, Oct. 4, 1881. Cf. also "The Origin of the Magyars," by the same author.

[8]See p. 380, *infra*.

[9]Kozma says, that in the two above-mentioned countries the word "Huns" was used, up to the thirteenth century, among the people as equivalent to giants, who figured in fairy tales. Simrock and Grimm are inclined to see real persons in them, and say they were the Huns, and in later history the Magyars.

[10]1883, vol. i. pp. 466, 467.

[11]*Cornhill Magazine*, May, 1882.

[12]The first edition appeared in 1520. Cf. *Diccionario Bibliographico Portuguez* (Lisboa, 1859) *sub voce* "Barros."

[13]He asserts that his chronicle is a translation of "ex lingua Ungara." So far as one knows, the *original* remains undiscovered and unknown!

[14]Cf. Geo. Fejér, *Henricus Portagulliae Comes origine Burgundus non Hungarus*, Budæ 1830, and other dissertations by M. Holéczy, &c. in the British Museum. Press Mark 10632/1.

[15]*Corpus Poeticum Boreale*, by Vigfusson and Powell. Oxford, 1883, p. lxi, vol. i.

[16]*Historia de Gentium Septentrionalium variis conditionibus &c.* (Basileæ, 1567). Lib. ii. cap. xviii.

[17]*De Hunnis et Herulis* Libri Sex. Joannes Magnus died in 1544. His chronicle appeared interspersed with Olaus Magnus' work. Cf. Lib. viii. cap. xiii.

[18]Cf. Paul Hunfalvy's polemic work, *A Székelyek*. Budapest, 1880. The same learned writer in his well-known *Ethnography of Hungary*, disputes the separate origin of the Székelys, and maintains that they are not a distinct people from the Magyars, but that they are Magyars who have migrated from Hungary Proper into their modern Transylvanian homes. This assertion gave rise to severe criticism on the part of the defenders of the old tradition like Dr. John Nagy, Farkas Deák, and others; and the above mentioned pamphlet was a reply, wherein the author further defends his assertion, on the testimony of comparative philology and history. One powerful argument in favour of the separate origin is, that for centuries the Székely population has kept distinct not only from the Saxons, but also from the Magyars in Transylvania; they had privileges which were denied to the Magyars. Their administration until recently was quite distinct. Their name first occurs in a deed signed by William, Bishop of Transylvania, dated 1213, in which the Bishop renounces his right of collecting tithes from settlers in the Bárczaság "a waste and uninhabited" track of land, if those settlers be neither Magyars nor Székelys.

[19]Abu-Ali Achmed ben Omar ibn Dastás. *Information regarding the Kozars, Burtás, Bulgarians, Magyars, Slavs and Russ.* Edited by D. A. Chvolson, St. Petersburg, 1869 (in Russian); quoted by Hunfalvy in his *Ethnography of Hungary*.

[20]Abn Dolif Misaris ben Mohalhal *De Intinere Asiatico*—Studio Kurd de Schloezer. Berolini, 1845. Cf. Defrémery *Fragments de Geographes, &c.* in *Journ. Asiat.* ser. iv. tom. xiii. 466. Both quoted by Colonel Yule in *Cathay and the Way Thither*. London, 1866. Vol. i. pp. cxi. and clxxxvii.

[21]On the river Vág (in the North of Hungary Proper).

[22]Hunfalvy *The Székelys*, pp. 40-42.

[23]*Ib.* p. 41.

[24]Cf. *Republica Hungarica*, ex off. Elzeviriana, 1634, p. 12. "Nemo apud illos (Ciculos) ignobilis esse censetur, etiam si manu aratrum tractet, aut caprino gregi praesit."

[25]Georgius Rákóczy. Dei Gratia Princeps Transylvaniæ ... et Siculorum Comes, &c.

[26]Prior to 1876, the Székelys administered their own affairs, and were divided into five "széks" (*sedes*).

[27]His essay, entitled "A few words on the Székely Dialects," was published at the end of his work, *Vadrózsâk*, vol. i.

[28]Quoted *infra*, p. xix.

[29]*Vide infra*, p. 380.

[30]*Opus citatum*, p. 34.

[31]Such as Klaproth.

[32]Cf. Hunfalvy *Ethnography*, p. 408.

[33]Cf. *The History of the Cumanians*, and also *The Nationality and Language of the Jazygo-Cumanians*, by Stephen Gyárfás. Budapest, 1882.

[34]Budapest, 1880. The original MS. is in the Bibliotheca Marciana in Venice. It was discovered by Cornides in 1770. Klaproth first made it known in his "Mémoirs relatifs à l'Asie," III. and Roesler published a specimen of its grammar in his "Romänische Studien," pp. 352-356.

[35]Count Géjza Kuun has, we are glad to say, not yet spoken his last word; for that indefatigable scholar is busily engaged on a large work on his favorite subject, which, judging by the extracts he read (June 1st, 1885) before the Hungarian Academy of Sciences, promises to rank with the best writings of modern philologists.

It may be of interest here to quote one of the Cumanian children's rhymes:

Heli, heli, jáde üzürményüzbe her!Zeboralle, sarmamamile,Alo bizon sasarma,Düzüsztürmö dücsürmöHej ala hilalaZeboralle dücsürmö.(Wolan, wolan, ich löse das Gelübde,Der Lenz ist da!Mit Gebeten, ZauberzeichenMache ich den ZauberUnschädlich. Ich preise dich!Es ist nur ein Gott.Mit Gebeten preise ich dich).

Vide Ungarische Revue, viii.-ix., Heft. 1885, p. 644.

[36]How dangerous a practice it is to build up history upon no other ground than the mere similarity in the sound of the names of nationalities is shewn in the history of the modern Jazyges. This name has led many a chronicler astray. Their Magyar proper name is "Jász," which, according to Hunfalvy (*Ethnography of Hungary*, p. 376) is derived from the word "ijász," i.e. "an archer," or "bowman," a name describing their original occupation. In some old deeds of the xivth and xvth centuries, they are called "Jassones" and "Pharetrarii," and things kept straight until Ranzanus the Papal Nuncio at the Court of Matthias Corvinus appeared on the scene, and, struck by the sound of the name "Jassones" and finding that they lived on the very territory which, according to Ptolemy, was occupied by the Jazyges: Metanastae in his time, at once jumped to the conclusion that they were lineal descendants of the wild horsemen mentioned by the classic author. We know how hard anything false dies, and so we find this statement copied by subsequent writers, and even disfiguring the pages of so excellent a work as Smith's *Dictionary of Greek and Roman Geography*, sub. art. "Jazyges." A still wilder mistake was made by a scribe of King Sigismund, who re-christened the Jász folk "Philistæi," which afterwards appears in many deeds. It would appear to be reasoned out thus; a "Jász," or "bowman," must naturally handle a bow and arrow; but an arrow is called "pfeil" in German, which comes from the old German "phil," hence Jász-Philistæi, Q. E. D! Cf. Hunfalvy's *Ethnography loco citato*.

[37] *Vide infra*, p. 412, &c.

[38]*Ethnography of Hungary*, p. 362.

[39]The true born Magyar repudiates with scorn the idea that there is any such thing as a dialect, boasting that rich and poor speak the same tongue. Cf. *Galeoti Martii, de Matthiæ egregie, sapienter, fortiter et jocose dictis ac factis libellus*, ed. Cassoviæ, 1611. "Unde fit ut carmen lingua Hungarica compositum rusticis et civibus, mediis et extremis, eodem tenore intelligatur." Galeoti was an Italian by birth, and Papal Nuncio at the Court of Matthias I. (Corvinus), King of Hungary.

[40]There is a passage in the writings of Nicolaus Oláh (*Hungaria et Attila*, cap. xix. § 3) which at first sight seems to ascribe a separate language to each of the peoples named in the text. According to him, "the whole of Hungary in our days (xvith century) contains various nations, viz., Magyars, Germans, Czechs, Slováks, Croats, Saxons, Székelys, Wallachs, Servians, Cumans, Jazyges, Ruthens, and finally Turks, and all these (nations) "differenti inter se utuntur lingua," except that some of the words may appear somewhat similar and identical in sound in consequence of (their) protracted use and (the continuous) contact (of the said nations with each other)." Against this, we may urge, that if the language of the Székelys, for example, differed no more from the Magyar than the German speech from that of the Saxons, they can scarcely be described as two different languages. Moreover, another writer says, that the "Hungari nobiles ejusdem regionis (Transylvaniæ) passim intermixti Saxonibus, cum Ciculis propemodum tam sermone, quam vestitu et armis conveniunt." See *Respublica Hungarica*, 1634. We have good reasons for believing that the passage has been copied by the Elzevirian compiler from the *Chronigraphica Transylvaniæ* of George Reijchersdorffer, 1550.

[41]Cf. Simpleton stories and lying stories, many of which as told in Hungary, Finland, and Flanders, and even amongst the Lapps, are identical with those we hear in Yorkshire, Lincolnshire, Northumberland, and Norfolk.

[42]Professor Vambéry says: there are many features in Hungarian Folk-Tales which can be found in the tales of China, and other Asiatic countries, ancient and modern. The characteristics of the chief personages in the tales show that the tales have been imported by the Magyars from their old Asiatic homes, although a Slavonic influence cannot be denied.

[43]P. 239 *infra*. See also remains of the Turkish occupation and their barbarous doings in the children's rhyme:

"Lady bird, lady bird, fly away, fly away,For the Turks are coming!They will throw you into a well full of salt water:They will take you out, and break you on the wheel."

Dark wine produced at Eger (Erlau) is called "Turk's blood."

[44]Pp. 70, 118.

[45]P. 5, *infra.*

[46]"Stephen the Murderer," "Fisher Joe," and the "Baa Lambs" in this collection. Cf. "Die Engel-lämmer" *Aus der im Auftrage der Kisfaludy-Gesellschaft von Lad Arany und Paul Gyulai besorgten.* Ungarische Revue viii. ix. Heft, 1885, p. 640, and note, which says: "Eines der wenigen ungarischen Volkmärchen, in welche die christliche Mythologie hineinspielt."

[47]Cf. Such stories as "Handsome Paul," p. 29 *infra et seq.*

[48]See all this beautifully sketched by Czuczor, in his poem *Joannes Háry.*

[49]That the Magyar soldier can tell stories may be seen in Gaál's tales, most of which Arany tells us have a most undesirable flavour of the barracks about them.

[50]John Erdélyi (born 1814, died 1868), Hungarian poet and author, elected Member of the Hungarian Academy of Science, 1839.

[51]These tales were collected from soldiers: and are full of unnecessary flourishes and coarse barrack-room jokes.

[52]John Kriza (born 1812, died 1875), born in a small village of Székely parents. Unitarian minister, professor, poet, and author, elected Member of the Academy, 1841.

[53]A second volume has, I believe, since appeared.

[54]Ladislaus Arany objects to this collection, on the ground that the collector has tried to improve on the original popular form, and endeavoured to produce something classic, and thus spoiled the stories.

[55]Giant in Magyar is: "Óriás" i. e. a tall man, tall father. Cf. pp. 99, 147, 318, 340. Cf, numerous stories of giants and what they are like in Friis.*Lappiske Eventyr* and Hofberg. *Svenska Sägner.*

[56]See pp. 146 and 388.

[57]See "Knight Rose," p. 57.

[58]See "Knight Rose," p. 55.

[59]Cf. "Handsome Paul," p. 26 *infra*, where another illustration of their size will be found; also the giant in Swedish tale who travelled from Dalecarlia to Stockholm, and the bread was still warm in his knapsack when he ended his journey.

[60]Cf. *Friis.* "Jetanis." *Hofberg.* "Bron öfver Kalmarsund" "Ulfgrytstenarna" "Ruggabron" and "Stenen i Grönan dal."

[61]Vide pp. 345 and 392 *infra.*

[62]Vide "Prince Mirkó," p. 72.

[63]In Hungary, the village blacksmith is a gipsy as a rule.

[64]Vide "Shepherd Paul," p. 244 and note p. 407.

[65]Cf. "A Lincolnshire tale," p. 363.

[66]Cf. Story as found in Finland, Lapland, and Sweden, of Kaleva's daughter, who, finding a man, put him and his horse and plough into her apron, and carrying them off to her mother, asked what sort of a dung beetle this was she had found scratching the earth, receiving a similar answer to the above-mentioned one. Cf. Hofberg. *Svenska Sägner,* Jätten Puke. Dybeck, *Runa* 1845, p. 15, and Thiel *Danmarks. Folksagn* ii. p. 228.

[67]Vide "Handsome Paul" and "Fairy Elizabeth."

[68]See "Prince Mirkó."

[69]Cf. *Rancken,* "Munsala," 22 i.: Wörå, 22: where a description of buried treasures will to be found. Also *Hofberg,* "Den forlärade skatten," "Guldvaggan," "Skatten i Säbybäcken," "Skattgräfvarna," vide *infra.* pp. xxx. xxxvii.

[70]Amongst the numerous stories of hidden treasures, I may note two I heard in my own parish lately. There is a chest of gold buried in Mumby Hill, and an old man went by "his'sen," and dug and dug, and would have got it, but so many little devils came round him, he had to give up.

The other tale is a long story of a man who went to an old house, and every thing he did "a little devil" did, and as the man could not be frightened a vast hidden treasure was revealed to him.—W. H. J.

[71]Rancken, *Några åkerbruksplägseder i Finland.* Munsala, 22, c. and d. Hofberg. *Svenska Sägner* "Skogsråęt och Sjörået," and "Ysätters-Kajsa."

[72]"Fairy Elizabeth," "Handsome Paul," "Knight Rose," and "Prince Mirkó" are full of the doings of fairies.

[73]Cf. Ralston, *Russian Folk-Tales,* "The Baba Yaga," p. 143. *Afanassieff,* i. No. 3 b.

[74]This is the nearest translation. In the original a hyphen between gold and mountain, silver and valley, alters the meaning.

[75]*i.e.* "For ever." A form of orientalism which frequently occurs in Magyar folk-poetry. For instance,

"My rose I will not marry youUntil there are no fish in the lake,And as there always will beCf. You see, my rose, I cannot marry you."

[76]The waters of the two rivers flow into the Theiss, this into the Danube, and the Danube into the Black Sea.

[77]Baron Orbán's *Székelyland.*

[78]Bishop Arnold Ipolyi, *Magyar Mythology.*

[79]Ladislaus Köváry, *Historical Antiquities.*

[80]In consequence of the Turkish rule over Hungary. Buda was 157 years in the hands of the Turks.

[81] *Vide* Baron Orbán, *Székelyland.*

[82]One must be careful not to confound, as many writers do, the witches of fairy tales, with the old women who are designated as witches by the common people.

[83]Cf. Many Lincolnshire and Yorkshire tales.

[84]Cf. *Rancken,* "Purmo" 27, and "Munsala," 25.

[85]It is interesting to note that, although prosecution for witchcraft was only abolished in England under George II. in 1736, in Hungary it was abolished under Coloman the Learned, who reigned 1095-1114, for a very cogent reason, "Witches are not to be prosecuted, as they do not exist!"

[86]The Hungarian cattle have long erect horns like those of the Roman campagna.

[87]Cf. p. 203 *infra.*

[88]As the wolf in the Finnish tale, "The Golden Bird."

[89]See *Folk Medicine.*

[90]Charm-weed.

[91]Square pieces of linen without seam or hem, wrapped round the bare foot, instead of socks.

[92]Only lately, a man in my own parish said that when "Maud was a young 'un, she was amazin' badly. The doctors could do nowt for her: she was all skin and bone. Doctors said it wor a decline; but a' didn't believe it, for she did sqweäl amazin'. It was all an owd woman who used to sell pins and needles." It appears, this old woman always gave, and insisted upon giving, Maud, some little thing; and at last they perceived the child was "witched"; so the next time the old woman appeared, another daughter ordered her off, and the child recovered; the same old woman is said to have "witched" another child in the parish in like manner. I may add "Maud" is now a fine strapping girl, and vows vengeance on the witch.—W. H. J.

[93]Cf. *Hofberg,* "Bissen," the manner of "laying ghosts," is noticed, *ib.* "Herrn till Rosendal."

[94]In some parts of Finland the same superstition is, or was, current (*e.g.* in Munsala). Unbaptized children are specially liable to be changed by the trolls, but this may be prevented by putting Holy Scripture in the cradle, or silver coins, scissors, or other sharp tools. Cf. *Hofberg,* Svenska Folksägner "Bortbytingen."

[95]Cf. *Hofberg* "Mylingen," "Tomten." See also *Några åkerbruksplägseder bland svenskarne i Finland* af Dr. J. Oscar I. Rancken.

[96]Cf. *Rancken.* "Munsala," 22 g.

[97]This belonged formerly to a well-known medicine man, who practised over three countries. There are hundreds and hundreds of cures in it.

[98]This class of ingredients occupied an important place in the pharmacopœia of the physicians of the middle ages. Cf. *Liber Secundus Practicae Haly* cap. 51, "De stercoribus et fimis," p. 178 (Lyons 1523).

[99]

"I physicks 'em, I bleeds 'em, I sweats 'em,And if they *will* die, I lets 'em."

[100]See "Christmas Day."

[101]Steel and flint are still in extensive use among smokers in rural districts.

[102]The Magyar name of quinsy is torokgyik, *i.e.* throat-lizard.

[103]Varga does not seem to know anything about

"The dead, shrivelled hand ...... of the gentleman dangling up there."

[104]So far is this day considered unlucky in Portugal that we heard of a Portuguese young lady who had ordered a harp from England: it unfortunately arrived at her house on Friday, and was sent away till Saturday, although she was "dying to try it!" Tuesday is also regarded as unlucky in Portugal.

On St. Peter's Day, in Portugal, the saint is said to have a holiday, and take the keys with him, and the fisher-folk assert that if anyone is drowned on that day the chances are he will be sent to the "wrong place."

Cf. "Ma foi sur l'avenir bien fou qui se fiera,Tel qui rit vendredi, dimanche pleurera."—

Racine au commencement de la comédie des Plaideurs.

[105]One is said to be most liable to be punished at this time on this account.

[106]Garlic is said to be a charm against evil. See *Notes and Queries*, 6 S. ix. 5.

[107]It is a common superstition in many parts of Yorkshire that fire must not go out of the house between New and Old Christmas Day. An old nurse told us she once went home during this time and her neighbours would not even give her a match that she might light her candle and so find her own.

[108]Cf. Yorkshire, Yule-candle.

[109]Lead is cast in Finland to see whether fortune or misfortune is in store; in these degenerate days "stearine," has been used by impatient souls. See also Burnaby, *Ride to Khiva*, cap. xxii.

[110]Elton's *Origins of English History*, 270, 271.

[111]See *Glossaire de la langue Romane*, par J. B. B. Roquefort. Paris, 1808.

[112]See Cormac's Glossary, under "Beltene," *Revue Celtique*, iv. 193; Grimm, *Deutsche Mythol.* 579.

[113]"C'était en beaucoup d'endroits en France l'usage de jeter dans le feu de la Saint-Jean des mannes ou des paniers en osier contenant des animaux, chats, chiens, renards, loups. Au siècle dernier même dans plusieurs villes c'était le maire ou les échevins qui faisaient mettre dans un panier une ou deux douzaines de chats pour brûler dans le feu de joie. Cette coutûme existait aussi à Paris, et elle n'y a été supprimée qu'au commencement du règne de Louis XIV."—Gaidoz, *Esquisse de la Religion des Gaulois*, 21.

[114]In the West-end of London there is a house where No. 13 is cancelled, and the house re-numbered 15A for the very same reason. The people are*comme il faut*, and consider themselves educated.

[115]Plover.—*Notes and Queries* 4th S. viii. 268. On the Lancashire Moors there is a tradition that the plovers contain the souls of those Jews who assisted at the Crucifixion.

[116]Hungarian saying: "To speak snakes and frogs after a man," to say everything that is bad about him.

[117]Or dig.

[118]I (writes a Magyar friend) have seen a youth use this stuff to produce a beard and moustache, and the whole of his skin was covered with ugly sores.

[119]German name, Himmelbrandt, Wollkraut, Königskerre; French, bouillon blanc, molène.

[120]The superstitions marked * have been in Lincolnshire and Yorkshire quite lately.

[121]The small heap of soil thrown up by ants.

[122]The modern custom is to lift the glass and say "Isten éltesse!" ("may God let you live.")

[123]The Finnish reformer, Michael Agricola, in his preface to the 1551 edition of the Finnish Psalms, prepared by him, mentions the idols and sacrifices of the old Finns. The passage relating to this matter is in verses, and especially of the *Carialians* he says the following: "*Egres* creates them peas, beans, and carrots, cabbage, flax, and hemp; *Köndös* guards their cleared grounds and ploughed fields as they superstitiously believe; and when they finished their spring-sowing, then they drank Ukko's Cup."

"Kuin kevä-kylvä kylvettiinSilloin Ukon malja juottiin."

[124]"Wie Thor's cleinne trank man Ukko zu ehren volle Schale." *Mythol Vorr* xxviii. In Sweden, as toasts, the only word they mention is "skål," cup; this is a meagre reminder of "Thor's Schåle."

[125]Not Tokay; that is German. We have a hazy recollection that one of the Popes—it may have been Sylvester II. (A.D. 1000) or Pio Nono—upon receiving a small cask of Tokaj wine, exclaimed "Talc vinum summum pontificem decet!" or words to this effect.

[126]"Áldomás," from "áldani" (Latin offerre and benedicere) hence—"sacrificium" and "benedictio." Cf. "Ultemaš"—"preces" in Cheremiss. In the district of Hradist in Moravia, "oldomaš pit"—"áldoma's drink." In modern Magyar the word "áldozni" is used for to sacrifice. Whether the Magyar and Finnish Ukko are the same, or whether it is a mere coincidence, we are not prepared to say. Hunfalvy makes much of it.

[127]Ukkon-pohar-felmutato volt.

[128]In modern times the bargain is first settled and the "liquor" comes afterwards, *tout comme chez nous* in England.

[Pg lxx]

PRINCE CSIHAN (NETTLES).

There was once—I don't know where, at the other side of seven times seven countries, or even beyond them, on the tumble-down side of a tumble-down stove—a poplar-tree, and this poplar-tree had sixty-five branches, and on every branch sat sixty-six crows; and may those who don't listen to my story have their eyes picked out by those crows!

There was a miller who was so proud that had he stept on an egg he would not have broken it. There was a time when the mill was in full work, but once as he was tired of his mill-work he said, "May God take me out of this mill!" Now, this miller had an auger, a saw, and an adze, and he set off over seven times seven countries, and never found a mill. So his wish was fulfilled. On he went, roaming about, till at last he found on the bank of the Gagy, below Martonos, a tumble-down mill, which was covered with nettles. Here he began to build, and he worked, and by the time the mill was finished all his stockings were worn into holes and his garments all tattered and torn. He then stood expecting people to come and have their flour ground; but no one ever came.

One day the twelve huntsmen of the king were chasing a fox; and it came to where the miller was, and said to him: [Pg 2]"Hide me, miller, and you shall be rewarded for your kindness." "Where shall I hide you?" said the miller, "seeing that I possess nothing but the clothes I stand in?" "There is an old torn sack lying beside that trough," replied the fox; "throw it over me, and, when the dogs come, drive them away with your broom." When the huntsmen came they asked the miller if he had seen a fox pass that way. "How could I have seen it; for, behold, I have nothing but the clothes I stand in?" With that the huntsmen left, and in a little while the fox came out and said, "Miller, I thank you for your kindness; for you have preserved me, and saved my life. I am anxious to do you a good turn if I can. Tell me, do you want to get married?" "My dear little fox," said the miller, "if I could get a wife, who would come here of her own free will, I don't say that I would not—indeed, there is no other way of my getting one; for I can't go among the spinning-girls in these clothes." The fox took leave of the miller, and, in less than a quarter of an hour, he returned with a piece of copper in his mouth. "Here you are, miller," said he; "put this away, *you will want* it ere long." The miller put it away, and the fox departed; but, before long, he came back with a lump of gold in his mouth. "Put this away, also," said he to the miller, "as you will need it before long." "And now," said the fox, "wouldn't you like to get married?" "Well, my dear little fox," said the miller, "I am quite willing to do so at any moment, as that is my special desire." The fox vanished again, but soon returned with a lump of diamond in his mouth. "Well, miller," said the fox, "I will not *ask* you any more to get married; I will get you a wife myself. And now give me that piece of copper I gave you." Then, taking it in his mouth, the fox started off over seven times seven countries, and travelled till he came to King Yellow Hammer's. "Good day, most gracious King Yellow Hammer," said the fox; "my life and death are in your majesty's hands. I have heard that you have an unmarried daughter. I am a messenger [Pg 3]from Prince Csihan, who has sent me to ask for your daughter as his wife." "I will give her with pleasure, my dear little fox," replied King Yellow Hammer; "I will not refuse her; on the contrary, I give her with great pleasure; but I would do so more willingly if I saw to whom she is to be married—even as it is, I will not refuse her."

The fox accepted the king's proposal, and they fixed a day upon which they would fetch the lady. "Very well," said the fox; and, taking leave of the king, set off with the ring to the miller.

"Now then, miller," said the fox, "you are no longer a miller, but Prince Csihan, and on a certain day and hour you must be ready to start; but, first of all, give me that lump of gold I gave you that I may take it to His Majesty King Yellow Hammer, so that he may not think you are a nobody."

The fox then started off to the king. "Good day, most gracious king, my father. Prince Csihan has sent this lump of gold to my father the king that he may spend it in preparing for the wedding, and that he might change it, as Prince Csihan has no smaller change, his gold all being in lumps like this."

"Well," reasoned King Yellow Hammer, "I am not sending my daughter to a bad sort of place, for although I am a king I have no such lumps of gold lying about in my palace."

The fox then returned home to Prince Csihan. "Now then, Prince Csihan," said he, "I have arrived safely, you see; prepare yourself to start to-morrow."

Next morning he appeared before Prince Csihan. "Are you ready?" asked he. "Oh! yes, I am ready; I can start at any moment, as I got ready long ago."

With this they started over seven times seven lands. As they passed a hedge the fox said, "Prince Csihan, do you see that splendid castle?" "How could I help seeing it, my dear little fox." "Well," replied the fox, "in that castle dwells your wife." On they went, when suddenly the fox said, "Take off the clothes you have on, let us put them into this hollow tree, and [Pg 4]then burn them, so that we may get rid of them." "You are right, we won't have them, nor any like them."

Then said the fox, "Prince Csihan, go into the river and take a bath." Having done so the prince said, "Now I've done." "All right," said the fox; "go and sit in the forest until I go into the king's presence." The fox set off and arrived at King Yellow Hammer's castle. "Alas! my gracious king, my life and my death are in thy hands. I started with Prince Csihan with three loaded wagons and a carriage and six horses, and I've just managed to get the prince naked out of the water." The king raised his hands in despair, exclaiming, "Where hast thou left my dear son-in-law, little fox?" "Most gracious king, I left him in such-and-such a place in the forest." The king at once ordered four horses to be put to a carriage, and then looked up the robes he wore in his younger days and ordered them to be put in the carriage; the coachman and footman to take their places, the fox sitting on the box.

When they arrived at the forest the fox got down, and the footman, carrying the clothes upon his arm, took them to Prince Csihan. Then said the fox to the servant, "Don't you dress the prince, he will do it more becomingly himself." He then made Prince Csihan arise, and said, "Come here, Prince Csihan, don't stare at yourself too much when you get dressed in these clothes, else the king might think you were not used to such robes." Prince Csihan got dressed, and drove off to the king. When they arrived, King Yellow Hammer took his son-in-law in his arms and said, "Thanks be to God, my dear future son-in-law, for that He has preserved thee from the great waters; and now let us send for the clergyman and let the marriage take place."

The grand ceremony over, they remained at the court of the king. One day, a month or so after they were married, the princess said to Prince Csihan, "My dear treasure, don't you think it would be as well to go and see your realm?" Prince Csihan left the room in great sorrow, and went towards the [Pg 5]stables in great trouble to get ready for the journey he could no longer postpone. Here he met the fox lolling about. As the prince came his tears rolled down upon the straw. "Hollo! Prince Csihan, what's the matter?" cried the fox. "Quite enough," was the reply; "my dear wife insists upon going to see my home." "All right," said the fox; "prepare yourself, Prince Csihan, and we will go."

The prince went off to his castle and said, "Dear wife, get ready; we will start at once." The king ordered out a carriage and six, and three waggons loaded with treasure and money, so that they might have all they needed. So they started off. Then said the fox, "Now, Prince Csihan, wherever I go you must follow." So they went over seven times seven countries. As they travelled they met a herd of oxen. "Now, herdsmen," said the fox, "if you won't say that this herd belongs to the Vasfogu Bába, but to Prince Csihan, you shall have a handsome present." With this the fox left them, and ran straight to the Vasfogu Bába. "Good day, my mother," said he. "Welcome, my son," replied she; "it's a good thing for you that you called me your mother, else I would have crushed your bones smaller than poppy-seed." "Alas! my mother," said the fox, "don't let us waste our time talking such nonsense, the French are coming!" "Oh! my dear son, hide me away somewhere!" cried the old woman. "I know of a bottomless lake," thought the fox; and he took her and left her on the bank, saying, "Now, my dear old mother, wash your feet here until I return." The fox then left the Vasfogu Bába, and went to Prince Csihan, whom he found standing in the same place where he left him. He began to swear and rave at him fearfully. "Why didn't you drive on after me? come along at once." They arrived at the Vasfogu's great castle, and took possession of a suite of apartments. Here they found everything the heart could wish for, and at night all went to bed in peace.

Suddenly the fox remembered that the Vasfogu Bába had no [Pg 6]proper abode yet, and set off to her. "I hear, my dear son," said she, "that the horses with their bells have arrived; take me away to another place." The fox crept up behind her, gave her a push, and she fell into the bottomless lake, and was drowned, leaving all her vast property to Prince Csihan. "You were born under a lucky star, my prince," said the fox, when he returned; "for see I have placed you in possession of all this great wealth." In his joy the prince gave a great feast to celebrate his coming into his property, so that the people from Bánczida to Zsukhajna were feasted royally, but he gave them no drink. "Now," said the fox to himself, "after all this feasting I will sham illness, and see what treatment I shall receive at his hands in return for all my kindness to him." So Mr. Fox became dreadfully ill, he moaned and groaned so fearfully that the neighbours made complaint to the prince. "Seize him," said the prince, "and pitch him out on the dunghill." So the poor fox was thrown out on the dunghill. One day Prince Csihan was passing that way. "You a prince!" muttered the fox; "you are nothing else but a miller; would you like to be a house-holder such as you were at the nettle-mill?" The prince was terrified by this speech of the fox, so terrified that he nearly fainted. "Oh! dear little fox, do not do that," cried the prince, "and I promise you on my royal word that I will give you the same food as I have, and that so long as I live you shall be my dearest friend and you shall be honoured as my greatest benefactor."

He then ordered the fox to be taken to the castle, and to sit at the royal table, nor did he ever forget him again.

So they lived happily ever after, and do yet, if they are not dead. May they be your guests to-morrow!

[Pg 7]

STEPHEN THE MURDERER.

There was once, I don't know where, over seven times seven countries, or even beyond that, a very, very rich farmer, and opposite to him lived another farmer just as rich. One had a son and the other a daughter. These two farmers often talked over family matters together at their gates, and at last arranged that their children should marry each other, so that in case the old people died the young people would be able to take possession of the farms. But the young girl could not bear the young man, although he was very fond of her. Then her parents threatened to disinherit her if she did not marry as she was bid, as they were very wishful for the marriage to take place.

On the wedding morning, when they arrived at church, and were standing before the altar, the bride took the wedding ring and dashed it on the floor before the clergyman, saying, "Here, Satan, take this ring; and, if ever I bear a child to this man, take it too!" In a moment the devil appeared, snatched up the ring, and vanished. The priest, seeing and hearing all that was done, declined to proceed with the ceremony, whereupon the fathers remonstrated with him, and declared that if he did not proceed he would lose his living. The wedding thereupon was duly celebrated.

As time went by the farmers both died; and the young folks, who couldn't bear each other before, at last grew very fond of each other, and a handsome boy was born. When he was old enough he went to school, where he got on so well that before long his master could teach him no more. He then went to college, where he did the same as at school, so that his parents [Pg 8]began to think of him taking holy orders. About this time his father died; and he noticed that every night when he came home from the college that his mother was weeping: so he asked her why she wept. "Never mind me, my son," said she; "I am grieving over your father." "But you never cared much for him," said he; "cheer up, for I shall soon be a priest." "That's the very thing I'm weeping over," said his mother; "for just when you will be doing well the devils will come for you, because when I was married to your father I dashed the wedding-ring on the ground, saying, 'Here, Satan, take this ring; and if ever I bear a child to this man take it too.' One fine day, then, you will be carried off by the devil in the same way as the ring." "Is this indeed true, mother?" said the student. "It is indeed, my son." With that he went off to the priest, and said, "Godfather, are these things which my mother tells me concerning her wedding true?" "My dear godson," replied the priest, "they are true; for I saw and heard all myself." "Dear godfather, give me then at once holy candles, holy water, and incense." "Why do you want them, my son?" asked the priest. "Because," replied the student, "I mean to go to hell at once, after that lost ring and the deed of agreement." "Don't rush into their hands," said the priest; "they will come for you soon enough." But the more the priest talked the more determined was the student to set off at once for the infernal regions.

So off he went, and travelled over seven times seven countries. One evening he arrived at a large forest, and, as darkness set in, he lost his way and roamed about hither and thither looking for some place to rest; at last he found a small cottage where an old woman lived. "Good evening, mother," said he. "Good luck has brought you here, my son," said she. "What are you doing out here so late?" "I have lost my way," replied the student, "and have come here to ask for a night's lodging." "I can give you lodging, my son, but I have a murderous [Pg 9]heathen son, who has destroyed three hundred and sixty-six lives, and even now is out robbing. He might return at any moment, and he would kill you; so you had better go somewhere else and continue your way in peace, and mind you take care not to meet him."

"Whether he kill me or not," said the student, "I shall not stir an inch." As the old woman could not persuade him to go he stayed. After midnight the son returned, and shouted out loudly under the window, "Have you got my supper ready?" He then crept in on his knees, for he was so tall that he could not enter otherwise. As they sat at table he suddenly saw the student. "Mother, what sort of a guest is that?" said he. "He's a poor tramp, my son, and very tired." "Has he had anything to eat?" "No; I offered him food, but he was too tired to eat." "Go and wake him, and say, 'Come and eat'; because whether he eat or whether he let the food alone he will repent it."

"Hollo!" said the student, "what is the matter?"

"Don't ask any questions," replied the old woman; "but come and eat." The student obeyed, and they sat down to supper. "Don't eat much," said the old woman's son, "because you will repent it if you do eat and you will repent it if you don't." While they were eating the old woman's son said, "Where are you going, mate—what is your destination?" "Straight to hell, among the devils," quoth the student.

"It was my intention to kill you with a blow; but now that I know where you are going I will not touch you. Find out for me what sort of a bed they have prepared for me in that place."

"What is your name?"

"My name," said he, "is Stephen the Murderer."

In the morning, when they awoke, Stephen gave the student a good breakfast, and showed him which way to go. On he [Pg 10]travelled till at length he approached the gates of hell. He then lighted his incense, sprinkled the holy water, and lighted the holy candles. In a very short time the devils began to smell the incense, and ran out, crying, "What sort of an animal are you? Don't come here! Don't approach this place; or we will leave it at once!"

"Wherever you go," said the student, "I tell you I will follow you; for, on such and such a date, you carried off from the church floor my mother's wedding-ring; and if you don't return it and cancel the agreement, and promise me that I will have no more trouble from you, I will follow you wherever you go." "Don't come here," cried they; "stop where you are, and we will get them for you at once."

They then blew a whistle and the devils came hastily out from all directions, so many you could not count them, but they could not find the ring anywhere. They sounded the whistle again, and twice as many came as before, but still the ring was not to be found. They then whistled a third time, and twice as many more came. One fellow came limping up, very late. "Why don't you hurry," cried the others; "don't you see that a great calamity has happened? The ring can't be found. Turn out everybody's pockets, and on who ever it is found throw him into the bed of Stephen the Murderer." "Wait a moment," cried the lame one, "before you throw me into Stephen the Murderer's bed. I would rather produce three hundred wedding-rings than be thrown into that place:" whereupon he at once produced the ring, which they threw over the wall to the student, together with the agreement, crying out that it was cancelled.

One evening the student arrived back at Stephen the Murderer's. The latter was out robbing. After midnight, as usual, he returned, and when he saw the student he woke him, saying, "Get up, let's have something to eat! And have you been to hell?"

[Pg 11]"I have." "What have you heard of my bed?" "We should never have got the ring," said the student, "if the devils had not been threatened with your bed." "Well," said Stephen, "that must be a bad bed if the devils are afraid of it."

They got up the next morning, and the student started for home. Suddenly it struck Stephen the Murderer that as the student had made himself happy he ought to do as much for him. So he started after the student, who, when he saw him coming, was very much afraid lest he should be killed. In a stride or two Stephen overtook the student. "Stop, my friend; as you have bettered your lot, better mine, so that I may not go to that awful bed in hell."

"Well then," said the student, "did you kill your first man with a club or a knife?" "I never killed anybody with a knife," said Stephen, "they have all been killed with a club." "Have you got the club you killed the first man with? Go back and fetch it."

Stephen took one or two strides and was at home. He then took the club from the shelf and brought it to the student; it was so worm-eaten that you could not put a needle-point on it between the holes. "What sort of wood is this made of?" asked the student. "Wild apple-tree," replied Stephen. "Take it and come with me," said the student, "to the top of the rock." On the top of the rock there was a small hill; into this he bade him plant the club. "Now, uncle Stephen, go down under the rock, and there you will find a small spring trickling down the face of the stone. Go on your knees to this spring and pray, and, creeping on your knees, carry water in your mouth to this club, and continue to do so till it buds; it will then bear apples, and when it does you will be free from that bed."

Stephen the Murderer began to carry the water to the club, and the student left him, and went home. He was at once made a priest on account of his courage in going to hell; and [Pg 12]after he had been a priest for twenty-five years they made him pope, and this he was for many years.

In those days it was the rule—according to an old custom—for the pope to make a tour of his country, and it so happened that this pope came to his journey's end, on the very rock upon which the club had been planted. He stopped there with his suite, in order to rest. Suddenly one of the servants saw a low tree on the top of the rock, covered with beautiful red apples. "Your holiness," said he to the pope, "I have seen most beautiful red apples, and if you will permit me I will go and gather some." "Go," said the pope, "and if they are so very beautiful bring some to me." The servant approached the tree; as he drew near he heard a voice that frightened him terribly saying, "No one is allowed to pluck this fruit except him who planted the tree." Off rushed the servant to the pope, who asked him if he had brought any apples.

"Your holiness, I did not even get any for myself," gasped the servant, "because some one shouted to me so loudly that I nearly dropped; I saw no one, but only heard a voice that said, 'No one is allowed to pluck this fruit but the man who planted the tree.'"

The pope began to think, and all at once he remembered that he had planted the tree when he was a lad. He ordered the horses to be taken out of his carriage, and, with his servant and his coachman, he set off to the red apple-tree. When they arrived, the pope cried out, "Stephen the Murderer, where are you?" A dried-up skull rolled out, and said, "Here I am, your holiness; all the limbs of my body dropped off whilst I was carrying water, and are scattered all around; every nerve and muscle lies strewn here; but, if the pope commands, they will all come together." The pope did so, and the scattered members came together into a heap.

The servant and the coachman were then ordered to open a [Pg 13]large, deep hole, and to put the bones into it, and then cover all up, which they did. The pope then said mass, and gave the absolution, and at that moment Stephen the Murderer was delivered from the dreadful bed in hell. The pope then went back to his own country, where he still lives, if he has not died since.

THE LAMB WITH THE GOLDEN FLEECE.

There was once a poor man who had a son, and as the son grew up his father sent him out to look for work. The son travelled about looking for a place, and at last met with a man who arranged to take him as a shepherd. Next day his master gave him a flute, and sent him out with the sheep to see whether he was fit for his work. The lad never lay down all day, very unlike many lazy fellows. He drove his sheep from place to place and played his flute all day long. There was among the sheep a lamb with golden fleece, which, whenever he played his flute, began to dance. The lad became very fond of this lamb, and made up his mind not to ask any wages of his master, but only this little lamb. In the evening he returned home; his master waited at the gate; and, when he saw the sheep all there and all well-fed, he was very pleased, and began to bargain with the lad, who said he wished for nothing but the lamb with the golden fleece. The farmer was very fond of the lamb himself, and it was with great unwillingness he promised it; but he gave in afterwards when he saw what a good servant the lad made. The year passed away; the lad received the lamb for his wages, and set off home with it. As they journeyed night set in just as he reached a village, so he went to a farmhouse to ask for a night's lodging. [Pg 14]There was a daughter in the house who when she saw the lamb with the golden fleece determined to steal it. About midnight she arose, and lo! the moment she touched the lamb she stuck hard-and-fast to its fleece, so that when the lad got up he found her stuck to the lamb. He could not separate them, and as he could not leave his lamb he took them both. As he passed the third door from the house where he had spent the night he took out his flute and began to play. Then the lamb began to dance, and on the wool the girl. Round the corner a woman was putting bread into the oven; looking up she saw the lamb dancing, and on its wool the girl. Seizing the peel in order to frighten the girl, she rushed out and shouted, "Get away home with you, don't make such a fool of yourself." As the girl continued dancing the woman called out, "What, won't you obey?" and gave her a blow on her back with the peel, which at once stuck to the girl, and the woman to the peel, and the lamb carried them all off. As they went they came to the church. Here the lad began to play again, the lamb began to dance, and on the lamb's fleece the girl, and on the girl's back the peel, and at the end of the peel the woman. Just then the priest was coming out from matins, and seeing what was going on began to scold them, and bid them go home and not to be so foolish. As words were of no avail, he hit the woman a sound whack on her back with his cane, when to his surprise the cane stuck to the woman, and he to the end of his cane. With this nice company the lad went on; and towards dark reached the royal borough and took lodgings at the end of the town for the night with an old woman. "What news is there?" said he. The old woman told him they were in very great sorrow, for the king's daughter was very ill, and that no physician could heal her, but that if she could but be made to laugh she would be better at once; that no one had as yet been able to make her smile; and moreover the king had issued that very day a proclamation stating that whoever made her laugh should have her for his wife, and share the [Pg 15]royal power. The lad with the lamb could scarcely wait till daylight, so anxious was he to try his fortune. In the morning he presented himself to the king and stated his business and was very graciously received. The daughter stood in the hall at the front of the house; the lad then began to play the flute, the lamb to dance, on the lamb's fleece the girl, on the girl's back the peel, at the end of the peel the woman, on the woman's back the cane, and at the end of the cane the priest. When the princess saw this sight she burst out laughing, which made the lamb so glad that it shook everything off its back, and the lamb, the girl, the woman, and the priest each danced by themselves for joy.

The king married his daughter to the shepherd; the priest was made court-chaplain; the woman court bakeress; and the girl lady-in-waiting to the princess.

The wedding lasted from one Monday to the other Tuesday, and the whole land was in great joy, and if the strings of the fiddle hadn't broken they would have been dancing yet!

FISHER JOE.

There was once a poor man, who had nothing in the world but his wife and an unhappy son Joe. His continual and his only care was how to keep them: so he determined to go fishing, and thus to keep them from day to day upon whatever the Lord brought to his net. Suddenly both the old folks died and left the unhappy son by himself; he went behind the oven and did not come out till both father and mother were buried; he sat three days behind the oven, and then remembered that his father had kept them by fishing; so he got up, took his net, and went fishing below the [Pg 16]weir: there he fished till the skin began to peel off the palms of his hands, and never caught so much as one fish. At last he said, "I will cast my net once more, and then I will never do so again." So he cast his net for the last time and drew to shore a golden fish. While he was going home he thought he would give it to the lord of the manor, so that perhaps he might grant a day's wages for it. When he got home he took down a plate from the rack, took the fish from his bag, and laid it upon the plate; but the fish slipped off the plate and changed into a lovely girl, who said, "I am thine, and you are mine, love." The moment after she asked, "Joe, did your father leave you anything?" "We had something," replied her husband; "but my father was poor and he sold everything; but," continued he, "do you see that high mountain yonder? it is not sold yet, for it is too steep and no one would have it." Then said his wife, "Let's go for a walk and look over the mountain." So they went all over it, length and breadth, from furrow to furrow. When they came to a furrow in the middle his wife said, "Let us sit down on a ridge, my love, and rest a little." They sat down, and Joe laid his head on his wife's lap and fell asleep. She then slipped off her cloak, made it into a pillow, drew herself away, and laid Joe upon the pillow without waking him. She rose, went away, uncoiled a large whip and cracked it. The crack was heard over seven times seven countries. In a moment as many dragons as existed came forth. "What are your Majesty's commands?" said they. "My commands are these," replied she: "you see this place—build a palace here, finer than any that exists in the world; and whatever is needed in it must be there: stables for eight bullocks and the bullocks in them, with two men to tend them; stalls for eight horses and the horses in them, and two grooms to tend them; six stacks in the yard, and twelve threshers in the barn." She was greatly delighted when she saw her order completed, and thanked God that He had given her what He had promised. "I shall now go," said she, "and wake my husband." When [Pg 17]she came to him he was still asleep. "Get up, my love," said she, "look after the threshers, the grooms, the oxen, and see that all do their work, and that all the work be done, and give your orders to the labourers; and now, my love, let us go into the house and see that all is right. You give your orders to the men-servants, and I will give mine to the maids. We have now enough to live on;" and Joe thanked God for His blessings. He then told his wife that he would invite the lord of the manor to dine with him on Whit Sunday. "Don't leave me," replied his wife; "for if he catch sight of me you will lose me. I will see that the table is laid and all is ready; but a maid shall wait on you. I will retire into an inner room lest he should see me."

Joe ordered the carriage and six, seated himself in it, the coachman sat on the box, and away they went to the lord's house; they arrived at the gate, Joe got out, went through the gate, and saw three stonemasons at work in the yard; he greeted them and they returned the greeting. "Just look," remarked one of them, "what Joe has become and how miserable he used to be!" He entered the castle, and went into the lord's room. "Good day, my lord." "God bless you, Joe, what news?" "I have come to ask your lordship to dine with me on Whit Sunday, and we shall be very pleased to see you." "I will come, Joe;" they then said good-bye and parted. After Joe had gone the lord came into the courtyard, and the three masons asked him "What did Joe want?" "He has invited me to dine with him," was the reply, "and I am going." "Of course; you must go," said one of them, "that you may see what sort of a house he keeps."

The lord set out in his carriage and four, with the coachman in front, and arrived at the palace. Joe ran out to meet him, they saluted each other, and entered arm in arm. They dined, and all went well till the lord asked, "Well, Joe, and where is your wife?" "She is busy," said Joe. "But I should like to see her," explained the baron. "She is rather shy when in [Pg 18]men's society," said Joe. They enjoyed themselves, lighted their pipes and went for a walk over the palace. Then said the baron to his servant, "Order the carriage at once;" it arrived, and Joe and he said "Farewell." As the baron went through the gate he looked back and saw Joe's wife standing at one of the windows, and at once fell so deeply in love with her that he became dangerously ill; when he arrived at home the footmen were obliged to carry him from his carriage and lay him in his bed.

At daybreak the three masons arrived and began to work. They waited for their master. As he did not appear, "I will go and see what's the matter with him," said one of them, "for he always came out at 8 a.m." So the mason went in and saluted the baron, but got no reply. "You are ill, my lord," said he. "I am," said the baron, "for Joe has such a pretty wife, and if I can't get her I shall die." The mason went out and the three consulted together as to what was best to be done. One of them proposed a task for Joe, *i.e.* that a large stone column which stood before one of the windows should be pulled down, the plot planted with vines, the grapes to ripen over night, and the next morning a goblet of wine should be made from their juice and be placed on the master's table; if this was not done Joe was to lose his wife. So one of them went in to the baron and told him of their plan, remarking that Joe could not do that, and so he would lose his wife. A groom was sent on horseback for Joe, who came at once, and asked what his lordship desired. The baron then told him the task he had to propose and the penalty. Poor Joe was so downcast that he left without even saying "good-bye," threw himself into his carriage, and went home. "Well, my love," asked his wife, "what does he want?" "Want," replied her husband, "he ordered me to pull down the stone column in front of his window. Since my father was not a working-man, how could I do any work? Nor is that all. I am to plant the place with vines, the [Pg 19]grapes have to ripen, and I am to make a goblet of wine, to be placed on his table at daybreak; and if I fail I am to lose you."

"Your smallest trouble ought to be greater than that," said his wife. "Eat and drink, go to bed and have a good rest, and all will be well." When night came she went out into the farmyard, uncoiled her whip, gave a crack, which was heard over seven times seven countries, and immediately all the dragons appeared. "What are your Majesty's commands?" She then told them what her husband required, and in the morning Joe had the goblet of wine, which he took on horseback lest he should be late; he opened the baron's window, and, as nobody was there, he placed the goblet on the table, closed the window, and returned home.

At daybreak the baron turned in his bed. The bright light reflected by the goblet met his eyes, and had such an effect on him that he fell back in his bed, and got worse and worse.

The three masons arrived and wondered why their master did not appear. Said the tallest to the middle one, "I taught him something yesterday; now you must teach him something else." "Well," said the middle one, "my idea is this, that Joe shall build a silver bridge in front of the gate during the night, plant both ends with all kinds of trees, and that the trees be filled with all kinds of birds singing and twittering in the morning. I'll warrant he won't do that, and so he will lose his wife." When the baron came out they communicated their plan; he at once sent for Joe and told him what he required. Joe went away without even saying good-bye, he was so sad. When he got home he told his wife what the baron wanted this time. "Don't trouble yourself, my love," said his wife, "eat and drink and get a good rest, all shall be well." At night she cracked her whip and ordered the dragons to do all that was required, and so at daybreak all was done. The birds made such a noise that the whole of the village was awakened by them. One nightingale loudly and clearly to the baron sang, "Whatever [Pg 20]God has given to some one else that you must not covet; be satisfied with what has been given to you." The baron awoke and turned over, and, hearing the loud singing of the birds, rose and looked out of the window. The glare of the silver bridge opposite the gate blinded him, and he fell back in bed and got worse and worse. When the three masons arrived they could not enter, for the splendour of the silver bridge dazzled them, and they were obliged to enter by another gate.

As they were working, the shortest said to the middle one, "Go and see why his lordship does not come out; perhaps he is worse." He went in and found the baron worse than ever. Then said the shortest, "I thought of something, my lord, which he will never be able to do, and so you will get his wife." "What is that, mason?" demanded the baron. "It is this, my lord," said the mason, "that he shall ask God to dinner on Palm Sunday, and that he can't do, and so he will lose his wife." "If you can get Joe's wife for me you shall have all this property," said the baron. "It's ours, then," said they, "for he can't do that." Joe was sent for, and came at once to know what was required of him. "My orders are these," replied the baron, "that you invite God to dinner on Palm Sunday to my house; if you do not your wife is lost." Poor Joe went out without saying good-bye, jumped into his carriage, and returned home dreadfully miserable. When his wife asked him what was the matter he told her of the baron's commands. "Go on," said his wife; "bring me that foal, the yearling, the most wretched one of all, put upon it an old saddle and silver harness on its head, and then get on its back." He did so, said good-bye, and the wretched yearling darted off at once straight to heaven. By the time it arrived there it had become quite a beautiful horse. When Joe reached the gates of Paradise he tied his horse to a stake, knocked at the door, which opened, and he went in and greeted the Almighty. St. Peter received him, and asked him why he had come. "I've come," said he, "to [Pg 21]invite God to dinner at my lord's on Palm Sunday." "Tell him from me," said the deity, "that I will come, and tell him that he is to sow a plot with barley, and that it will ripen, and that I will eat bread made of it at dinner. That a cow is to be taken to the bull to-day, and that I will eat the flesh of the calf for my dinner."

With this Joe took leave, and the foal flew downward. As they went Joe was like to fall head-foremost off, and called upon the deity. St. Peter told him not to fear, it was all right; he would fall on his feet. When Joe arrived at home the barley was waving in the breeze and the cow was in calf. "Well, wife," said he, "I will go to the baron's and give him the message." So he went, knocked at the door, and entered the room. "Don't come a step further," cried the baron. "I don't intend to," said Joe: "I've come to tell you I have executed your commands, and mind you don't blame me for what will happen. The deity has sent you this message: you are to sow a plot with barley, and of it make bread for His dinner. A cow is to go to the bull, and of the calf's flesh He will eat." The baron became thoughtful. "Don't worry yourself, my lord," said Joe, "you have worried me enough, it is your turn now;" and so he said "good-bye," and went off home: when he got there the barley-bread was baking and the veal was roasting.

At this moment the deity and St. Peter arrived from heaven and were on their way to the baron's, who the moment he saw them called out to his servant, "Lock the gate, and do not let them in." Then said the deity, "Let us go back to the poor man's home, and have dinner there." When they reached the foot of the mountain St. Peter was told to look back and say what he saw, and lo! the whole of the baron's property was a sheet of water. "Now," said the deity to St. Peter, "let us go on, for the mountain is high, and difficult to ascend." When they arrived at Joe's he rushed out with outspread arms, fell to the ground, and kissed the sole of the deity's foot. He entered and [Pg 22]sat down to dinner, so did Joe and his wife and also St. Peter. Then said God to Joe, "Set a table in this world for the poor and miserable, and you shall have one laid for you in the world to come; and now good-bye: you shall live in joy, and in each other's love."

They are living still if they have not died since. May they be your guests to-morrow!

LUCK AND BLISS.

Luck and Bliss went out one day, and came to a town where they found a poor man selling brooms, but nobody seemed to buy anything from him. Bliss thereupon said, "Let us stop, and I will buy them all from the poor fellow, so that he may make a good bargain." So they stopped, and Bliss bought them all, and gave him six times the market value of them, in order that the poor man might have a good start.

On another occasion they came to the same town and found the man still selling brooms. Bliss bought them all, and gave him ten times their market value. They came a third time to the town, and the man was still selling brooms, whereupon Luck said, "Let me try now, for, see, you have bought them all twice, and in vain, for the man is a poor broom-seller still;" [Pg 23]so Luck bought them, but she did not give a penny more than the market price. They came to the town a fourth time and saw the man who had sold brooms leading wheat into town in a wagon with iron hoops on the wheels and drawn by four fine bullocks. When they saw this Luck said to Bliss, "Do you see that man who used to sell brooms? You bought them all twice for a very high price. I bought them but once, and that for the market value, and the consequence of my having done so is that he no longer sells brooms, as he used to do, but wheat, and it appears he must have got on well with his farm too."

THE LAZY CAT.

A lad married a lazy rich girl, and he made a vow that he would never beat her. The missis never did any work but went about from house to house gossiping and making all kinds of mischief, but still her husband never beat her. One morning as he was going out to his work he said to the cat, "You cat, I command you to do everything that is needed in the house. While I am away put everything in order, cook the dinner, and do some spinning; if you don't, I'll give you such a thrashing as you won't forget." The cat listened to his speech half asleep, blinking on the hearth. The woman thought to herself, "My husband has gone mad." So she said, "Why do you order the cat to do all these things, which she knows nothing about?" "Whether she does or whether she doesn't it's all the same to me, wife. I have no one else whom I can ask to do anything; and if she does not do all that I have ordered her to do you will see that I will give her such a thrashing as she will never forget." With this he went out to work, and the wife began to talk to the cat and said, "You had better get your work done, or he will beat you;" but the cat did not work, and the wife went from house to house gossiping. When she came home the cat was asleep on the hearth, and the fire had gone out; so she said, "Make the fire up, cat, and get your work done, or you will get a sound thrashing;" but the cat did no work. In the evening the master came home and found that nothing was done and that [Pg 24]his orders were not carried out; so he took hold of the cat by its tail and fastened it to his wife's back, and began to beat till his wife cried out, "Don't beat that cat any more! Don't beat that cat any more! it is not her fault, she cannot help it, she does not understand these things." "Will you promise then that you will do it all in her stead?" inquired her husband. "I will do it all and even more than you order," replied his wife, "if you will only leave off beating that cat."

The woman then ran off home to complain to her mother of all these things, and said, "I have promised that I will do all the work instead of the cat, in order to prevent my husband beating her to death on my back." And then her father spoke up and said, "If you have promised to do it you must do it; if not, the cat will get a thrashing to-morrow." And he sent her back to her husband.

Next time the master again ordered the cat what she had to do, and she did nothing again. So she got another beating on the wife's back, who ran home again to complain; but her father drove her back, and she ran so fast that her foot did not touch the ground as she went.

On the third morning again the master commenced to give his commands to the cat, who, however, was too frightened to listen, and did no work that day; but this time the mistress did her work for her. She forgot no one thing she had promised—she lighted the fire, fetched water, cooked the food, swept the house, and put everything in order; for she was frightened lest her husband should beat the poor cat again; for the wretched animal in its agony stuck its claws into her back, and, besides, the end of the two-tailed whip reached further than the cat's back, so that with every stroke she received one as well as the cat. When her husband came home everything was in order, and he kept muttering, "Don't be afraid, cat, I won't thrash you this time;" and his wife laid the cloth joyfully, dished up the food, and they had a good meal in peace.

[Pg 25]After that the cat had no more beatings, and the mistress became such a good housewife that you could not wish for a better.

HANDSOME PAUL.

There was once, over seven times seven countries, a poor woman who had a son, and he decided to go into service. So he said to his mother, "Mother, fill my bag and let me go out to work, for that will do me more good than staying here and wasting my time." The lad's name was Paul. His mother filled his bag for him, and he started off. As it became dark he reached a wood, and in the distance he saw, as it were, a spark glimmering amongst the trees, so he made his way in that direction thinking that he might find some one there, and that he would be able to get a night's lodging. So he walked and walked for a long time, and the nearer he came the larger the light became. By midnight he reached the place where the fire was, and lo! there was a great ugly giant sleeping by the fire. "Good evening, my father," said Paul. "God has brought you, my son," replied the giant; "you may think yourself lucky that you called me father, for if you had not done so I would have swallowed you whole. And now what is your errand?"

"I started from home," said Paul, "to find work, and good fortune brought me this way. My father, permit me to sleep to-night by your fire, for I am alone and don't know my way." "With pleasure, my son," said the giant. So Paul sat down and had his supper, and then they both fell asleep. Next morning the giant asked him where he intended to go in search of work. "If I could," replied Paul, "I should like to enter the king's service, for I have heard he pays his servants justly." [Pg 26]"Alas! my son," said the giant, "the king lives far away from here. Your provisions would fail twice before you reached there, but we can manage the matter if you will sit on my shoulder and catch hold of the hair on the back of my head." Paul took his seat on the giant's shoulders. "Shut your eyes," said the giant, "because if you don't you will turn giddy." Paul shut his eyes, and the giant started off, stepping from mountain to mountain, till noon, when he stopped and said to Paul, "Open your eyes now and tell me what you can see."

Paul looked around as far as he could see, and said, "I see at an infinite distance something white, as big as a star. What is it, my father?" "That is the king's citadel," said the giant, and then they sat down and had dinner. The giant's bag was made of nine buffalo's skins, and in it were ten loaves (each loaf being made of four bushels of wheat), and ten large bottles full of good Hungarian wine. The giant consumed two bottles of wine and two loaves for his dinner, and gave Paul what he needed. After a short nap the giant took Paul upon his shoulders, bade him shut his eyes, and started off again, stepping from mountain to mountain. At three o'clock he said to Paul, "Open your eyes, and tell me what you can see." "I can see the white shining thing still," said Paul, "but now it looks like a building." "Well, then, shut your eyes again," said the giant, and he walked for another hour, and then again asked Paul to look. Paul now saw a splendid glittering fortress, such a one as he had never seen before, not even in his dreams. "In another quarter-of-an-hour we shall be there," said the giant. Paul shut his eyes again, and in fifteen minutes they were there; and the giant put him down in front of the gate of the king's palace, saying, "Well, now, I will leave you here, for I have a pressing engagement, and must get back, but whatsoever service they offer to you, take it, behave well, and the Lord keep you." Paul thanked him for his kindness and his good-will, and the giant left. As Paul was a fine handsome fellow he was engaged at once, for the first three [Pg 27]months to tend the turkeys, as there was no other vacancy, but even during this time he was employed on other work: and he behaved so well, that at the end of the time he was promoted to wait at the king's table. When he was dressed in his new suit he looked like a splendid flower. The king had three daughters; the youngest was more beautiful than the rose or the lily, and this young lady fell in love with Paul, which Paul very soon noticed; and day by day his courage grew, and he approached her more and more, till they got very fond of each other.

The queen with her serpent's eye soon discovered the state of affairs, and told the king of it.

"It's all right," said the king, "I'll soon settle the wretched fellow; only leave it to me, my wife."

Poor Paul, what awaits thee?

The king then sent for Paul and said, "Look here, you good-for-nothing, I can see you are a smart fellow! Now listen to me: I order you to cut down during the night the whole wood that is in front of my window, to cart it home, chop it up, and stack it in proper order in my courtyard; if you don't I shall have your head chopped off in the morning." Paul was so frightened when he heard this that he turned white and said, "Oh, my king! no man could do this." "What!" said the king, "you good-for-nothing, you dare to contradict me? go to prison at once!" Paul was at once taken away, and the king repeated his commands, saying that unless they were obeyed Paul should lose his head. Poor Paul was very sad, and wept like a baby; but the youngest princess stepped into his prison through a secret trap-door, and consoled him, giving him a copper whip, and telling him to go and stand outside the gate on the top of the hill, and crack it three times, when all the devils would appear. He was then to give his orders, which the devils would carry out.

Paul went off through the trap, and the princess remained in prison till Paul returned; he went out, stood on the hill, and [Pg 28]cracked his whip well thrice, and lo! the devils came running to him from all sides, crying, "What are your commands handsome Paul?" "I order you," replied Paul, "by to-morrow morning to have all that large forest cut down, chopped, and stacked in the king's courtyard;" with this he went back to prison and spent a little time with the princess before she went away. The devils entered the wood, and began to hew the trees down; there was a roaring, clattering, and cracking noise as the big trees were dragged by root and crown into the king's yard; they were chopped up and stacked; and the devils, having finished the task, ran back to hell. By one o'clock all was done.

In the morning the first thing the king did was to look through the window in the direction of the wood; he could not see anything but bare land, and when he looked into the courtyard he saw there all the wood chopped and stacked.

He then called Paul from prison and said, "Well, I can see that you know something, my lad, and I now order you to plough up to-night the place where the wood used to be, and sow it with millet. The millet must grow, ripen, be reaped, threshed, and ground into flour by the morning, and of it you must make me a large millet-cake, else you lose your head." Paul was then sent back to prison, more miserable than ever, for how could he do such an unheard-of thing as that? His sweetheart came in again through the trap-door and found him weeping bitterly. When she heard the cause of his grief she said, "Oh, don't worry yourself, dear; here is a golden whip, go and crack it three times on the hill-top, and all the devils will come that came last night; crack it again three times and all the female devils will arrive; crack it another three times and even the lame ones will appear, and those enceinte come creeping forth. Tell them what you want and they will do it."

Paul went out and stood on the hill-top, and cracked his whip three good cracks, and then three more, and three more, such [Pg 29]loud cracks that his ears rung, and again the devils came swarming in all directions like ants, old ones and young ones, males and females, lame and enceinte, such a crowd that he could not see them all without turning his head all round. They pressed him hard, saying, "What are your commands, handsome Paul? What are your commands, handsome Paul? If you order us to pluck all the stars from heaven and to place them in your hands it shall be done."

Paul gave his orders and went back to prison, and stayed with the princess till daybreak.

There was a sight on the hill-side, the devils were shouting and making such a din that you could not tell one word from another. "Now then! Come here! This way, Michael! That way, Jack! Pull it this way! Turn it that way! Go at it! See, the work is done!"

The whole place was soon ploughed up, the millet sown, and it began to sprout, it grew, ripened, was cut, carted in wagons, in barrows, on their backs, or as best they could. It was thrashed with iron flails, carried to the mill, crushed and bolted, a light was put to the timber in the yard, it took fire, and the wood crackled everywhere, and there was such a light that the king in the seventh country off could see to count his money by it. Then they brought from hell the biggest cauldron they could find, put it on the fire, put flour into it and boiling water; as the millet-cake was bubbling and boiling they took it out of the pot and put it into Mrs. Pluto's lap, placed a huge spoon into her hands, and she began to stir away, mix it up, and cut it up with her quick hands till it began to curl up at the side of the cauldron after the spoon. As it was quite done she mixed it well once more, and being out of breath handed the spoon to Pluto himself—who was superintending the whole work,—who took out his pocket-knife—which was red-hot—and began to scrape the cake off the spoon and to eat it with great gusto.

Mrs. Pluto then took the cake out with a huge wooden spoon, [Pg 30]heaped it up nicely, patted it all round, and put it on the fire once more; when it was quite baked she turned it out a large millet-cake in the midst of the yard, and then they all rushed back, as fast as they could run, to hell.

Next morning, when the king looked through the window, an immense millet-cake was to be seen there, so large that it nearly filled the whole yard; and he, however vexed he was, could not help bursting out into a loud laugh. He gave instant orders for the whole town to come and clear away the millet-cake, and not to leave so much as a mouthful. Never was such a feast seen before, and I don't think ever will be again: some carried it away in their hands, some in bags, some in large table-cloths, sacks, and even in wagons; everybody took some, and it went in all directions in every possible manner, so that in three hours the huge cake was all gone; even the part that had stuck to the ground was scraped up and carried away. Some made tarts of it at home, pounded poppy-seed, and spread it over them; others wanted pork to eat with it, others ate it with fresh milk, with dried prunes, with perry, with craps, with cream-milk, sour-milk, cow's-milk, goat's-milk; some with curds; others covered it over with cream-cheese, rolled it up and ate it thus; better houses mixed it with good buffalo-milk, and ate it with butter, lard, and cream-cheese, so that it was no longer millet-cake with cream-cheese, but cream-cheese with millet-cake! There were many who had never eaten anything like it before, and they got so full of it they could just breathe; even the king had a large piece served up for his breakfast on a porcelain plate; he then went to the larder for a large tub, which was full of the best cream-cheese of Csik like unto the finest butter; he took a large piece of this, spread it on his cake, set to and ate it to the very last. He then drank three tumblerfuls of the best old claret, and said, "Well, that really was a breakfast fit for the gods!" And thus it happened that all the millet-cake was used up, and then the king sent for Paul and said to him, [Pg 31]"Well, you brat of a devil, did you do all this, or who did it?" "I don't know." "Well, there are in my stables a bay stallion, a bay mare, two grey fillies and a bay filly, you must walk them about, in turn, to-morrow morning, till they are tired out; if you don't I'll have your head impaled." Paul wasn't a bit frightened this time, but began to whistle, and hum tunes to himself in the prison, being in capital spirits. "It will be very easy to walk these horses out," said he; "it's not the first time I've done that." The matter looked different however in the evening when his sweetheart came and he told her all about it. "My love," said she, "this is even worse than all the rest, because the devils did all your former tasks for you, but this you must do yourself. Moreover, you must know that the bay stallion will be my father, the bay mare my mother, the two grey foals my elder sisters, and the bay foal myself. However, we shall find some way of doing even this. When you enter the stable we all will begin to kick so terribly that you won't be able to get near us; but you must try to get hold of the iron pole that stands inside the door, and with it thrash them all till they are tame; then you must lead them out as well as you can; but don't beat me, for I shall not desert you." His love then gave him a copper bridle, which he hid in his bosom, and buttoned his coat over it. And his lady-love went back to her bedroom; for she knew there was plenty of hard work in store for her on the morrow; for the same reason she ordered Paul to try to sleep well.

In the morning the jailer came, and brought two warders with him, and led Paul to the stable to take the horses out for a walk. Even in the distance he could hear the snorting, kicking, pawing, and neighing in the stable, so that it filled the air. He tried in vain to get inside the stable-door, he had not courage enough to take even one step inside. Somehow or other, however, he got hold of the iron pole, and with it he beat, pounded, and whacked the bay stallion till it lay down in agony. He then took out his bridle, threw it over its head, led it out, jumped upon its back, and [Pg 32]rode it about till the foam streamed from it, and then led it in and tied it up. He did the same with the bay mare, only she was worse; and the grey foals were worse still, till by the end he was nearly worn out with beating them. At last he came to the bay foal, but he would not have touched her for all the treasure of the world; yet, in order to deceive the others, he banged the crib, box, manger, and posts right lustily, till at last the bay foal lay down. With this the mare, who was the queen, said to the bay stallion, "You see it was that bay foal who was the cause of all this. But wait a bit, confound her!" she cried after them as he led her out of the stable; "I also have as many wits as you, and I will teach you both a lesson. Never mind, my sweet daughter, you have treated us all most cruelly with that iron pole, but you shall pay for it shortly." When

Paul heard this he was so frightened he could hardly lead the foal. "Don't be afraid," said the foal, "let's get away from here, and the sooner the better, never to return, or woe betide us!" They cantered up to the house, where she sent him in to get money, and jewellery, and the various things they would need, and then galloped off as fast as she could with Paul on her back, over seven times seven countries, till noon; and just as the sun was at noon the foal said to Paul, "Look back; what can you see?" Paul looked back and saw in the distance an eagle flying towards them, from whose mouth shot forth a flame seven fathoms long. Then said the foal, "I will turn a somersault, and become a sprouting millet-field; you do the same, you will become the garde champêtre, and when the eagle, which is my father, comes, if he ask you if you have seen such and such travellers, tell him, yes, you saw them pass when this millet was sown." So the foal turned over and became a sprouting millet-field, and Paul became the garde champêtre. The eagle arrived, and said, "My lad, have you not seen a young fellow on a bay foal pass this way in a great hurry?" "Well, yes," replied Paul, "I saw them at the time this millet was sown, but I can't [Pg 33]tell you where they may be now." "I don't think they can have come this way," said the eagle, and flew back home and told his wife all about it. "Oh! you baulked fool!" cried she, "the millet-field was your daughter, and the lad Paul. So back you go at once, and bring them home."

Paul and his foal rode on half the afternoon, and then the foal said, "Look back, what can you see?" "I see the eagle again," said Paul, "but now the flame is twice seven fathoms long; he flies very quickly." "Let's turn over again," said the foal, "and I will become a lamb and you will be the shepherd, and if my father ask you if you have seen the travellers say yes, you saw them when the lamb was born." So they turned over, and one became a lamb and the other a shepherd; the eagle arrived and asked the shepherd if he had seen the travellers pass by, and was told that they were seen when the lamb was born. The king returned and told his wife all, who drove him back, crying, "The lamb was your daughter and the shepherd, Paul, you empty-headed fool." Paul and the foal went on a long way, when the foal said, "What can you see?" He saw the eagle again, but now it was enveloped in flames; they turned over and the foal became a chapel, and Paul a hermit inside; the eagle arrived and inquired after the travellers, and was told by the hermit that they had passed by when the chapel was building. The eagle went back a third time, and his wife was in an awful rage and told him to stay where he was, telling him that the chapel was his daughter and the hermit Paul. "But you are so dense," said she, "they can make you believe anything; I will go myself and see whether they will fool me."

The queen started off as a falcon. Paul and the foal went still travelling on, when the foal said, "Look back, what can you see?" "I see a falcon," said Paul, "With a flame seventy-seven yards long coming out of its mouth." "That's my mother," said the foal, "We must be careful this time, Paul, for we shall [Pg 34]not be able to hoodwink her with lies; let us turn over quickly, she will be here in a second. I will be a lake of milk and you a golden duck on it; take care she doesn't catch you, or we are done for." They turned over and changed; the falcon arrived and swooped down upon the duck like lightning, who had just time to dive and escape. The falcon tried again and again till it got quite tired; for each time the duck dived and so she missed him. In a great rage the falcon turned over and became the queen. She picked up stones and tried to strike the duck dead, but he was clever enough to dodge her, so she soon got tired of that and said, "I can see, you beast, that I cannot do anything with you; my other two daughters died before my eyes to-day from the beating you gave them with the iron pole, you murderer. Now I curse you with this curse, that you will forget each other, and never remember that you have ever known each other."

With this she turned over, became a falcon, and flew away home very sad, and the other two changed also, this time into Paul and the princess. "Nobody will persecute us now," said she, "let us travel on quietly. The death of my two sisters is no sad or bad news to me, for now when my father and mother are dead the land will be ours, my dear Paul;" so they wandered on, and talked over their affairs, till they came to a house; and as the day was closing they felt very tired and sat down to rest and fell asleep. After sunset they awoke and stared at each other, but couldn't make out who the other was, for they had forgotten all the past, and inquired in astonishment "Who are you?" and "Well, who are you?" But neither could tell who the other was; so they walked into the town as strangers and separated. Paul got a situation as valet to a nobleman, and the princess became a lady's maid in another part of the city. They lived there for twelve months, and never once remembered anything that had happened in the past. One night Paul dreamt that the bay stallion was in its last agony, and soon afterwards died; the lady's maid, at the same time, dreamt that the bay mare [Pg 35]was dying, and died; by this dream they both remembered all that had happened to each other; but even then they did not know that they were in the same town. On the day following this dream Paul was sent by the nobleman's son secretly with a love-letter to the nobleman's youngest daughter where the lady's maid lived. Paul took the letter, and handed it to the lady's maid so that she might place it in her mistress's hands; then he saw who the lady's maid was, that it was his old sweetheart, the beloved of his soul; now he remembered how often before he had given her letters from his young master for the young lady of the house, and how he had done a little love-making on his own account, but never till now had he recognised her. The princess recognised Paul at a glance and rushed into his arms and wept for joy. They told each other their dreams, and knew that her father and mother—the bay mare and bay stallion of yore—died last night. "Let us be off," said the princess, "or else the kingdom will be snatched from us." So they agreed, and fixed the day after the morrow for the start. Next morning the official crier proclaimed that the king and queen had died suddenly about midnight; it happened at the very moment they had had their dreams.

They started secretly by the same road, and arrived at home in a day.

The king and queen were still laid in state, and the princess, who was thought to be lost, shed tears over them.

She was soon afterwards crowned queen of the realm, and chose Paul for her consort, and got married; if they have not died since they are still alive, and in great happiness to this day.

[Pg 36]

THE TRAVELS OF TRUTH AND FALSEHOOD.

A long time ago—I don't exactly remember the day—Truth started, with her bag well filled, on a journey to see the world. On she went over hill and dale, and through village and town, till one day she met Falsehood. "Good day, countrywoman," said Truth; "where are you bound for? Where do you intend going?" "I'm going to travel all over the world," said Falsehood. "That's right," said Truth; "and as I'm bound in the same direction let's travel together." "All right," replied Falsehood; "but you know that fellow-travellers must live in harmony, so let's divide our provisions and finish yours first." Truth handed over her provisions, upon which the two lived till every morsel was consumed; then it was Falsehood's turn to provide. "Let me gouge out one of your eyes," said Falsehood to Truth, "and then I'll let you have some food." Poor Truth couldn't help herself; for she was very hungry and didn't know what to do. So she had one of her eyes gouged out, and she got some food. Next time she wanted food she had the other eye gouged out, and then both her arms cut off. After all this Falsehood told her to go away. Truth implored not to be left thus helpless in the wilds, and asked that she might be taken to the gate of the next town and left there to get her living by begging. Falsehood led her, not to where she wanted to go, but near a pair of gallows and left her there. Truth was very much surprised that she heard no one pass, and thought that all the folks in that town must be dead. As she was thus reasoning with herself and trembling with fear she fell asleep. When she awoke she heard some people talking above her head, and soon discovered that they were [Pg 37]devils. The eldest of them said to the rest, "Tell me what you have heard and what you have been doing." One said, "I have to-day killed a learned physician, who has discovered a medicine with which he cured all crippled, maimed, or blind." "Well, you're a smart fellow!" said the old devil; "what may the medicine be?" "It consists simply of this," replied the other, "that to-night is Friday night, and there will be a new moon: the cripples have to roll about and the blind to wash their eyes in the dew that has fallen during the night; the cripples will be healed of their infirmities and the blind will see." "That is very good," said the old devil. "And now what have you done, and what do you know?" he asked the others.

"I," said another, "have just finished a little job of mine; I have cut off the water-supply and will thus kill the whole of the population of the country-town not far from here." "What is your secret?" asked the old devil. "It is this," replied he; "I have placed a stone on the spring which is situated at the eastern corner of the town at a depth of three fathoms. By this means the spring will be blocked up, and not one drop of water will flow; as for me I can go everywhere without fear, because no one will ever find out my secret, and all will happen just as I planned it."

The poor crippled Truth listened attentively to all these things. Several other devils spoke; but poor Truth either did not understand them or did not listen to what they said, as it did not concern her.

Having finished all, the devils disappeared as the cock crew announcing the break of day.

Truth thought she would try the remedies she had heard, and at night rolled about on the dewy ground, when to her great relief her arms grew again. Wishing to be completely cured, she groped about and plucked every weed she could find, and rubbed the dew into the cavities of her eyes. As day broke she saw light once more. She then gave hearty thanks to the God [Pg 38]of Truth that he had not left her, his faithful follower, to perish. Being hungry she set off in search of food. So she hurried off to the nearest town, not only for food, but also because she remembered what she had heard the devils say about cutting off the water supply. She hurried on, so as not to be longer than she could help in giving them her aid in their distress. She soon got there, and found every one in mourning. Off she went straight to the king, and told him all she knew; he was delighted when he was told that the thirst of the people might be quenched. She also told the king how she had been maimed and blinded, and the king believed all she said. They commenced at once with great energy to dig up the stone that blocked the spring. The work was soon done; the stone reached, lifted out, and the spring flowed once more. The king was full of joy and so was the whole town, and there were great festivities and a general holiday was held. The king would not allow Truth to leave, but gave her all she needed, and treated her as his most confidential friend, placing her in a position of great wealth and happiness. In the meantime Falsehood's provisions came to an end, and she was obliged to beg for food. As only very few houses gave her anything she was almost starving when she met her old travelling companion again. She cried to Truth for a piece of bread. "Yes, you can have it," said Truth, "but you must have an eye gouged out;" and Falsehood was in such a fix that she had either to submit or starve. Then the other eye was taken out, and after that her arms were cut off, in exchange for dry crusts of bread. Nor could she help it, for no one else would give her anything.

Having lost her eyes and her arms she asked Truth to lead her under the same gallows as she had been led to. At night the devils came; and, as the eldest began questioning the others as to what they had been doing and what they knew, one of them proposed that search be made, just to see whether there were any listeners to their conversation, as some one must have [Pg 39]been eaves-dropping the other night, else it would never have been found out how the springs of the town were plugged up. To this they all agreed, and search was made; and soon they found Falsehood, whom they instantly tore to pieces, coiled up her bowels into knots, burnt her, and dispersed her ashes to the winds. But even her dust was so malignant that it was carried all over the world; and that is the reason that wherever men exist there Falsehood must be.

THE HUNTING PRINCES.

Once there was a king whose only thought and only pleasure was hunting; he brought up his sons to the same ideas, and so they were called the Hunting Princes. They had hunted all over the six snow-capped mountains in their father's realm; there was a seventh, however, called the Black Mountain, and, although they were continually asking their father to allow them to hunt there, he would not give them permission. In the course of time the king died, and his sons could scarcely wait till the end of the funeral ceremonies before they rushed off to hunt in the Black Mountain, leaving the government in the hands of an old duke. They wandered about several days on the mountain, but could not find so much as a single bird, so they decided to separate, and that each of them should go to one of the three great clefts in the mountain, thinking that perhaps luck would serve them better in this way. They also agreed that whoever shot an arrow uselessly should be slapped in the face. They started off, each on his way. Suddenly the youngest one saw a raven and something shining in its beak, that, he thought, was in all probability a rich jewel. He shot, and a piece of steel [Pg 40]fell from the raven's beak, while the bird flew away unhurt. The twang of the bow was heard all over the mountain, and the two elder brothers came forward to see what he had done; when they saw that he had shot uselessly they slapped his face and went back to their places. When they had gone the youngest suddenly saw a falcon sitting on the top of the rock. This he thought was of value, so he shot, but the arrow stuck in a piece of pointed rock which projected under the falcon's feet, and the bird flew away; as it flew a piece of rock fell to the ground which he discovered to be real flint. His elder brothers came, and slapped his face for again shooting in so foolish a manner. No sooner had they gone and the day was drawing to an end than he discovered a squirrel just as it was running into its hole in a tree; so he thought its flesh would be good to eat; he shot, but the squirrel escaped into a hollow of the tree, and the arrow struck what appeared to be a large fungus, knocking a piece off, which he found to be a fine piece of tinder. The elder brothers came and gave him a sound thrashing which he took very quietly, and after this they did not separate. As it was getting dark and they were wandering on together a fine roebuck darted across their path; all three shot, and it fell. On they went till they came to a beautiful meadow by the side of a spring, where they found a copper trough all ready for them. They sat down, skinned and washed the roebuck, got all ready for a good supper, but they had no fire. "You slapped my face three times because I was wasting my arrows," said the youngest; "if you will allow me to return those slaps I will make you a good fire." The elder brothers consented, but the younger waived his claim and said to them, "You see, when you don't need a thing you think it valueless; see now, the steel, flint, and tinder you despised will make us the fire you need." With that he made the fire. They spitted a large piece of venison and had an excellent huntsman's supper. After supper they held a consultation as to who was to be the guard, as they had decided not to sleep without a [Pg 41]guard. It was arranged that they should take the duty in turns, and that death was to be the punishment of any negligence of duty. The first night the elder brother watched and the two youngest slept. All passed well till midnight, when all at once in the direction of the town of the Black Sorrow, which lay behind the

Black Mountain, a dragon came with three heads, a flame three yards long protruding from its mouth. The dragon lived in the Black Lake, which lay beyond the town of the Black Sorrow, with two of his brothers, one with five heads and the other with seven, and they were sworn enemies to the town of the Black Sorrow. These dragons always used to come to this spring to drink at midnight, and for that reason no man or beast could walk there, because whatever the dragons found there they slew. As soon as the dragon caught sight of the princes he rushed at them to devour them, but he who was keeping guard stood up against him and slew him, and dragged his body into a copse near. The blood streamed forth in such torrents that it put the fire out, all save a single spark, which the guarding prince fanned up, and by the next morning there was a fire such as it did one good to see. They hunted all day, returning at night, when the middle prince was guard. At midnight the dragon with the five heads came; the prince slew him, and his blood as it rushed out put the fire entirely out save one tiny spark, which the prince managed to fan into a good fire by the morning.

On the third night the youngest prince had to wrestle with the dragon with seven heads. He vanquished it and killed it. This time there was so much blood that the fire was completely extinguished. When he was about to relight it he found that he had lost his flint. What was to be done? He began to look about him, and see if he could find any means of relighting the fire. He climbed up into a very high tree, and from it he saw in a country three days' journey off, on a hill, a fire of some sort glimmering: so off he went; and as he was going he met [Pg 42]Midnight, who tried to pass him unseen; but the prince saw him, and cried out, "Here! stop; wait for me on this spot till I return." But Midnight would not stop; so the prince caught him, and fastened him with a stout strap to a thick oak-tree, remarking, "Now, I know you will wait for me!" He went on some four or five hours longer, when he met Dawn: he asked him, too, to wait for him, and as he would not he tied him to a tree like Midnight, and went further and further. Time did not go on, for it was stopped. At last he arrived at the fire, and found there were twenty-four robbers round a huge wood fire roasting a bullock. But he was afraid to go near, so he stuck a piece of tinder on the end of his arrow, and shot it through the flames. Fortunately the tinder caught fire, but as he went to look for it the dry leaves crackled under his feet, and the robbers seized him. Some of the robbers belonged to his father's kingdom, and, as they had a grudge against the father, they decided to kill the prince. One said, "Let's roast him on a spit"; another proposed to dig a hole and bury him; but the chief of the robbers said, "Don't let us kill the lad, let's take him with us as he may be very useful to us. You all know that we are about to kidnap the daughter of the king of the town of the Black Sorrow, and we intend to sack his palace, but we have no means of getting at the iron cock at the top of the spire because when we go near it begins at once to crow, and the watchman sees us; let us take this lad with us, and let him shoot off the iron cock, for we all know what a capital marksman he is; and if he succeeds we will let him go." To this the robbers kindly consented, as they saw they would by this means gain more than if they killed him. So they started off, taking the prince with them, till they came close to the fortress guarding the town of the Black Sorrow. They then sent the prince in advance that he might shoot off the iron cock; this he did. Then said the chief of the robbers, "Let's help him up to the battlements, and then he will pull us [Pg 43]up, let us down on the other side, and keep guard for us while we are at work, and he shall have part of the spoil, and then we will let him go." But the dog-soul of the chief was false, for his plan was, that, having finished all, he would hand the prince over to the robbers. This the prince had discovered from some whisperings he had heard among them. He soon found a way out of the difficulty. As he was letting them down one by one, he cut off their heads, and sent them headless into the fortress, together with their chief. Finding himself all alone, and no one to fear, he went to the king's palace: in the first apartment he found the king asleep; in the second the queen; in the third the three princesses. At the head of each one there was a candle burning; that the prince moved in each case to their feet, and none of them noticed him, except the youngest princess, who awoke, and was greatly frightened at finding a man in her bedroom; but when the prince told her who he was, and what he had done, she got up, dressed, and took the young prince into a side-chamber and gave him plenty to eat and drink, treated him kindly, and accepted him as her lover, and gave him a ring and a handkerchief as a sign of their betrothal. The prince then took leave of his love, and went to where the robbers lay, cut off the tips of their noses and ears, and bound them up in the handkerchief, left the fortress, got the fire, released Midnight and Dawn, arrived at their resting-place, made a good fire by morning, so that all the blood was dried up.

At daybreak in the town of the Black Sorrow, Knight Red, as he was inspecting the sentries, came across the headless robbers. As soon as he saw them he cut bits off their mutilated noses and ears, and started for the town, walking up and down, and telling everybody with great pride what a hero he was, and how that last night he had killed the twenty-four robbers who for such a length of time had been the terror of the town of the Black Sorrow. His valour soon came to the ears of the king, who ordered the Red Knight to appear before him: here he boasted of his valour, and [Pg 44]produced his handkerchief and the pieces cut from the robbers. The king believed all that he said, and was so overjoyed at the good news that he gave him permission to choose which of the princesses he pleased for his wife, adding that he would also give him a share of the kingdom. The Red Knight, however, made a mistake, for he chose the youngest daughter, who knew all about the whole affair, and was already engaged to the youngest prince. The king told his daughter he was going to give her as a wife.

To this she said, "Very well, father, but to whomsoever you intend to give me he must be a worthy man, and he must give proofs that he has rendered great service to our town." To this the king replied, "Who could be able or who has been able to render greater services to the town than this man, who has killed the twenty-four robbers?" The girl answered, "You are right, father; whoever did that I will be his wife." "Well done, my daughter, you are quite right in carrying out my wish; prepare for your marriage, because I have found the man who saved our town from this great danger." The young girl began to get ready with great joy, for she knew nothing of the doings of the Red Knight, and only saw what was going to happen when all was ready, the altar-table laid, and the priest called, when lo! in walked the Red Knight as her bridegroom, a man whom she had always detested, so that she could not bear even to look at him. She rushed out and ran to her room, where she fell weeping on her pillow. Everyone was there, and all was ready, but she would not come; her father went in search of her, and she told him how she had met the youngest of the Hunting Princes the night before, and requested her father to send a royal messenger into the deserted meadow, where the dragons of the Black Lake went to drink at the copper trough, and to invite to the wedding the three princes who were staying there; and asked her father not to press her to marry the Red Knight till their arrival; on such conditions she would go among the guests. [Pg 45]Her father promised this, and sent the messenger in great haste to the copper trough, and the young girl went among the guests. The feast was going on in as sumptuous a manner as possible. The messenger came to the copper trough, and hid himself behind a bush at the skirts of an open place, and as he listened to the conversation of the princes he knew that he had come to the right place; he hastened to give them the invitation from the king of the town of the Black Sorrow to the wedding of his youngest daughter.

The princes soon got ready, especially the youngest one, who, when he heard that his fiancée was to be married, would have been there in the twinkling of an eye if he had been able. When the princes arrived in the courtyard the twelve pillows under the Red Knight began to move, as he sat on them at the head of the table. When the youngest prince stepped upon the first step of the stairs, one pillow slipped out from under the Red Knight, and as he mounted each step another pillow fled, till as they crossed the threshold even the chair upon which he sat fell, and down dropped the Red Knight upon the floor.

The youngest Hunting Prince told them the whole story, how his elder brothers had slain the dragons with three and five heads, and he the one with seven heads; he also told them especially all about the robbers, and how he met the king's daughter, how he had walked through all their bedrooms and changed the candles from their head to their feet; he also produced the ring and the handkerchief, and placed upon the table the nose and ear-tips he had cut off the robbers.

They tallied with those the Red Knight had shown, and it was apparent to everybody which had been cut off first.

Everyone believed the prince and saw that the Red Knight was false. For his trickery he was sentenced to be tied to a horse's tail and dragged through the streets of the whole town, then quartered and nailed to the four corners of the town.

[Pg 46]The three Hunting Princes married the three daughters of the king of the town of the Black Sorrow. The youngest prince married the youngest princess, to whom he was engaged before, and he became the heir-apparent in the town of Black Sorrow, and the other two divided their father's realm.

May they be your guests to-morrow!

THE LAZY SPINNING-GIRL WHO BECAME A QUEEN.

A common woman had a daughter who was a very good worker, but she did not like spinning; for this her mother very often scolded her, and one day got so vexed that she chased her down the road with the distaff. As they were running a prince passed by in his carriage. As the girl was very pretty the prince was very much struck with her, and asked her mother "What is the matter?" "How can I help it?" said the mother, "for, after she has spun everything that I had, she asked for more flax to spin." "Let her alone, my good woman," said the prince; "don't beat her. Give her to me, let me take her with me, I will give her plenty to spin. My mother has plenty of work that needs to be done, so she can enjoy herself spinning as much as she likes." The woman gave her daughter away with the greatest pleasure, thinking that what she was unwilling to do at home she might be ashamed to shirk in a strange place, and get used to it, and perhaps even become a good spinster after all. The prince took the girl with him and put her into a large shed full of flax, and said "If you spin all you find here during the month you shall be my wife." The [Pg 47]girl seeing the great place full of flax nearly had a fit, as there was enough to have employed all the girls in the village for the whole of the winter; nor did she begin to work, but sat down and fretted over it, and thus three weeks of the month passed by. In the meantime she always asked the person who took her her food, "What news there was?" Each one told her something or other. At the end of the third week one night, as she was terribly downcast, suddenly a little man half an ell long, with a beard one and a-half ells long, slipped in and said, "Why are you worrying yourself, you good, pretty spinning-girl?" "That's just what's the matter with me," replied the girl; "I am not a good spinster, and still they will believe that I am a good spinster, and that's the reason why I am locked up here." "Don't trouble about that," said the little man; "I can help you and will spin all the flax during the next week if you agree to my proposal and promise to come with me if you don't find out my name by the time that I finish my spinning." "That's all right," said the girl, "I will go with you," thinking that then the matter would be all right. The little dwarf set to work. It happened during the fourth week that one of the men-servants, who brought the girl's food, went out hunting with the prince. One day he was out rather late, and so was very late when he brought the food. The girl said, "What's the news?" The servant told her that that evening as he was coming home very late he saw, in the forest, in a dark ditch, a little man half an ell high, with a beard one and a-half ells long, who was jumping from bough to bough, and spinning a thread, and humming to himself:—"My name is Dancing Vargaluska. My wife will be good spinster Sue."

Sue, the pretty spinning-girl, knew very well what the little man was doing, but she merely said to the servant, "It was all imagination that made you think you saw it in the dark." She brightened up; for she knew that all the stuff would be spun, and that he would not be able to carry her off, as [Pg 48]she knew his name. In the evening the little man returned with one-third of the work done and said to her, "Well, do you know my name yet?"

"Perhaps, perhaps," said she; but she would not have told his real name for all the treasures in the world, fearing that he might cease working if she did. Nor did she tell him when he came the next night. On the third night the little man brought the last load; but this time he brought a wheelbarrow with him, with three wheels, to take the girl away with him. When he asked the girl his name she said, "If I'm not mistaken your name is Dancing Vargaluska."

On hearing this the little man rushed off as if somebody had pulled his nose.

The month being up, the prince sent to see if the girl had completed her work; and when the messenger brought back word that all was finished the king was greatly astonished how it could possibly have happened that so much work had been done in so short a time, and went himself, accompanied by a great suite of gentlemen and court-dames, and gazed with great admiration upon the vast amount of fine yarn they saw. Nor could they praise the girl enough, and all found her worthy to be queen of the land. Next day the wedding was celebrated, and the girl became queen. After the grand wedding-dinner the poor came, and the king distributed alms to them; amongst them were three deformed beggars, who struck the king very much: one was an old woman whose eyelids were so long that they covered her whole face; the second was an old woman whose lower lip was so long that the end of it reached to her knee; the third old woman's posterior was so flat that it was like a pancake.

These three were called into the reception-room and asked to explain why they were so deformed. The first said, "In my younger days I was such a good spinster that I had no rival in the whole neighbourhood. I spun till I got so addicted to it [Pg 49]that I even used to spin at night: the effect of all this was that my eyelids became so long that the doctors could not get them back to their places."

The second said, "I have spun so much during my life and for such a length of time that with continually biting off the end of the yarn my lips got so soft that one reached my knees."

The third said, "I have sat so much at my spinning that my posterior became flat as it is now."

Hereupon the king, knowing how passionately fond his wife was of spinning, got so frightened that he strictly prohibited her ever spinning again.

The news of the story went out over the whole world, into every royal court and every town; and the women were so frightened at what had happened to the beggars that they broke every distaff, spinning-wheel, and spindle, and threw them into the fire!

THE ENVIOUS SISTERS.

A king had three daughters whose names were Pride, Gentleness, and Kindness. The king was very fond of them all, but he loved the youngest one, Kindness, the most, as she knew best how to please him. Many clever young gentlemen came to visit Kindness, but no one ever came near the other two, and so they were very envious of her, and decided they would get rid of her somehow or other. One morning they asked their father's permission to go out into the fields, and from thence they went into the forest. Kindness was delighted at having liberty to roam about in such pretty places; the other two were pleased that they had at last got the bird into their hands. As the dew [Pg 50]dried up the two eldest sisters strolled about arm in arm, whilst the youngest chased butterflies and plucked the wild strawberries, with the intention of taking some home to her father; she spent her time in great glee, singing and listening to the songs of the birds, when suddenly she discovered that she had strolled into an immense wood. As she was considering what to do, her two sisters appeared by her side, and said spitefully, "Well, you good-for-nothing! you have never done anything but try to make our father love you most and to spoil our chances in every way, prepare yourself for your end, for you have eaten your last piece of bread." Kindness lifted up her hands, and besought them not to harm her, but they cut off her hands, and only spared her life under the condition that she would never go near her home again; they then took her beautiful precious mantle from her, and dressed her in old rags; they then led her to the highest part of the forest, and showed her an unknown land, bidding her go there and earn her living by begging. The blood streamed from Kindness's arms, and her heart ached in an indescribable way, but she never uttered the slightest reproach against her sisters, but started off in the direction pointed out to her. Suddenly she came to a beautiful open plain, where there was a pretty little orchard full of trees, and their fruit was always ripening all the year round. She gave thanks to God that he had guided her there, then, entering the garden, she crouched down in a by-place. As she had no hands to pluck the fruit with she lived upon what grew upon low boughs; thus she spent the whole summer unnoticed by any one.

But towards autumn, when every other fruit was gone save grapes, she lived on these, and then the gardener soon discovered that the bunches had been tampered with and that there must be some one about: he watched and caught her. Now it so happened that the garden belonged to a prince, who spent a great deal of his time there, as he was very fond of the place. The gardener did not like to tell him of what had happened, as he [Pg 51]pitied the poor handless girl and was afraid his master would punish her severely. He decided therefore to let her go. Accidentally, however, the prince came past and asked who she was. "Your highness," replied the gardener, "I know no more of her than you do. I caught her in the garden, and to prevent her doing any more damage I was going to turn her out." "Don't lead her away," said the prince; "and who are you, unfortunate girl?" "You have called me right, my lord," said Kindness, "for I am unfortunate, but I am not bad; I am a beggar, but I am of royal blood. I was taken from my father because he loved me most; crippled because I was a good child. That is my story." To this the prince replied, "However dirtily and ragged you are dressed, still it is clear to me that you are not of low birth: your pretty face and polished speech prove it. Follow me; and whatever you have lost you will find in my house." "Your highness, in this nasty, dirty dress—how can I come into your presence? Send clothes to me which I can put on, and then I will do whatever you order." "Very well," said the prince; "stay here, and I will send to you." He went and sent her a lady-in-waiting with perfumed water to wash with, a gorgeous dress, and a carriage. Kindness washed and dressed herself, got into the carriage, and went to the prince. Quite changed in her appearance, not at all like as she was before, however much she suffered she was as pretty as a Lucretia; and the prince fell so much in love with her that he decided on the spot that he would marry her; and so they got married, with great splendour, and spent their time together in great happiness.

When the two elder sisters came home from the forest their father inquired where Kindness was. "Has she not come home?" said they; "we thought that she would have been home before us. As she was running after butterflies she got separated from us. We looked for her everywhere and called for her; as we got no answer we set off home before the darkness set in."

[Pg 52]The king gave orders that Kindness was to be looked for everywhere; they searched for days but could not find her; then the king got so angry in his sorrow that he drove the two elder girls away because they had not taken proper care of their sister. They set out into the world in quite another direction, but by accident arrived in the country where Kindness was queen; here they lived a retired life in a small town unknown to all. Kindness at this time was enceinte; and as war broke out with a neighbouring nation her royal husband was obliged to go to the field of battle. The war lasted a long time, and in the meantime Kindness gave birth to twins, two handsome sons; on the forehead of one was the sign of the blessed sun, on the other the sign of the blessed moon; in great joy the queen's guardian sent a letter containing the good news to the king by a messenger to the camp. The messenger had to pass through the small town where the envious sisters dwelt; it was quite dark when he arrived, and as he did not see a light anywhere but in their window he went and asked for a night's lodging; while he stayed there he told them all about the object of his journey; you may imagine how well he was received, and with what pleasure they offered him lodging, these envious brutes! When the messenger fell asleep they immediately took possession of the letter, tore it open, read it, and burnt it, and put in its place another to the king, saying that the queen had given birth to two monsters which looked more like puppies than babes; in the morning they gave meat and drink to the messenger, and pressed him to call and see them on his way back, as they would be delighted to see him. He accepted their kind invitation, and promised that he would come to them, and to no one else, on his return. The messenger arrived at the camp and delivered his letter to the king, who was very downcast as he read it; but still he wrote back and said that his wife was not to be blamed; "if it has happened thus how can I help it? don't show her the slightest discourtesy," wrote he. As the messenger went back [Pg 53]he slept again in the house of the two old serpent-sisters; they stole the king's letter and wrote in its place: "I want neither children nor mother; see that by the time I come home those monsters be out of my way, so that not even so much as their name remain." When this letter was read every one was very sorry for the poor queen, and couldn't make out why the king was so angry, but there was nothing for it but for the king's orders to be carried out, and so the two pretty babes were put in a sheet and hung round Kindness's neck, and she was sent away. For days and days poor Kindness walked about suffering hunger and thirst, till at last she came to a pretty wood; passing through this she travelled through a valley covered with trees; passing through this at last she saw the great alpine fir-trees at the end of the vale; there she found a clear spring; in her parching thirst she stooped to drink, but in her hurry she lost her balance and fell into the water; as she tried to drag herself out with her two stumps, to her intense astonishment she found that by immersion her two hands had grown again as they were before; she wept for joy. Although she was hiding in an unknown place with no husband, no father, no friend, no help whatever, with two starving children in this great wilderness, still she wasn't sorrowful, because she was so delighted to have her hands again. She stood there, and could not make up her mind in which direction to go; as she stood looking all round she suddenly caught sight of an old man coming towards her. "Who are you?" said the old man. "Who am I?" she replied, sighing deeply; "I'm an unfortunate queen." She then told him all she had suffered, and how she had recovered her hands that very minute by washing in the spring. "My poor good daughter," said the old man, bitterly, "then we are both afflicted ones; it's quite enough that you are alive, and that I have found you. Listen to me: your husband was warring against me, he drove me from my country, and hiding from him I came this way; not very far from here with one of my faithful servants I have built a hut [Pg 54]and we will live together there." The old man, in order to prove the miraculous curing power of the spring, dipped his maimed finger into it, which was shot off in the last war; as he took it out, lo! it was all right once more.

When the war was over, Kindness's husband returned home and inquired after his wife. They told him all that had happened, and he was deeply grieved, and went in search of her with a great number of his people, and they found her at last with her two pretty babes, living with her old father. On inquiry it was also found out where the messenger with the letters had slept and how the letters were changed. Pride and Gentleness were summoned and sentenced to death; but Kindness forgave them all their misdeeds, and was so kind to them that she obtained their pardon, and also persuaded her father to forgive them.

There is no more of this speech to which you need listen, as I have told it to the very end and I have not missed a word out of it. Those of whom I have spoken may they be your guests, every one of them, to-morrow!

KNIGHT ROSE.

A king had three sons. When the enemy broke into the land and occupied it, the king himself fell in the war. The young princes were good huntsmen and fled from the danger, all three, taking three horses with them. They went on together for a long time, till they did not even know where they were; on they journeyed, till at last they came to the top of the very highest snow-covered mountain, where the road branched off: here they decided to separate and try their luck alone. They agreed that on the summit of the [Pg 55]mountain, at the top of a tall tree, they would fix a long pole, and on it a white handkerchief. They were to keep well in sight of this white flag, and whenever the handkerchief was seen full of blood the one who saw it was to start in search of his brothers, as one of them was in danger. The name of the youngest was Rose; he started off to the left, the other two went to the right. When Rose came to the seventh snow-capped mount and had got far into it he saw a beautiful castle and went in. As he was tired with travelling and wanted a night's rest, he settled down. When even came the gates of the castle opened with great noise, and seven immense giants rushed into the courtyard and from thence into the tower. Every one of them was as big as a tall tower. Rose, in his fright, crept under the bed; but the moment the giants entered one of them said, "Phuh! What an Adam-like smell there is here!" Looking about they caught Rose, cut him up into small pieces like the stalk of a cabbage and threw him out of the window.

In the morning the giants went out again on their business. From a bush there came forth a snake, which had the head of a pretty girl; she gathered up every morsel of Rose's body, arranged them in order, and said, "This belongs here, that belongs there." She then anointed him with grass that had healing power, and brought water of life and death from a spring that was not far off and sprinkled it over him. Rose suddenly jumped up on his feet and was seven times more beautiful and strong than before. At this moment the girl cast off the snake-skin as far as the arm-pits. As Rose was now so strong he became braver, and in the evening did not creep under the bed, but waited for the giants coming home, at the gate. They arrived and sent their servants in advance to cut up that wretched heir of Adam; but they could not manage him, it took the giants themselves to cut him up. Next morning the serpent with the girl's head came again and brought Rose to life as before, and she herself cast off her skin as far as her waist. Rose was now twice as strong as a [Pg 56]single giant. The same evening the seven giants killed him again, he himself having killed the servants and wounded several of the giants. Next morning the giants were obliged to go without their servants. Then the serpent came and restored Rose once more, who was now stronger than all the seven giants put together, and was so beautiful that though you could look at the sun you could not look at him. The girl now cast off the serpent's skin altogether and became a most beautiful creature. They told each other the story of their lives. The girl said that she was of royal blood, and that the giants had killed her father and seized his land, that the castle belonged to her father, and that the giants went out every day to plunder the people. She herself had become a snake by the aid of a good old quack nurse, and had made a vow that she would remain a serpent until she had been avenged on the giants, and she knew now that although she had cast off the snake's skin she had nothing to fear because Rose was a match for the seven giants. "Now, Rose," said she, "destroy them every one, and I will not be ungrateful." To which he replied, "Dearest one, you have restored me to life these three times—how could I help being grateful to you? My life and my all are yours!" They took an oath to be true to each other till death, and spent the day merrily till evening set in, when the giants came, and Rose addressed them thus: "Is it not true, you pack of scoundrels, that you have killed me three times? Now, I tell you that not one of you shall put his foot within these gates! Don't you believe me? Let's fight!" They charged upon him with great fury, but victory was, this time, on his side; he killed them one after the other and took the keys of the castle out of their pockets. He then searched over every nook in the building, and came to the conclusion that they were safe, as they had now possession of the castle.

The night passed quietly; next morning Rose looked from the courtyard to the top of the snow-covered mountain, in the [Pg 57]direction of the white flag, and saw that it was quite bloody. He was exceedingly sorry, and said to his love, "I must go in search of my two elder brothers, as some mischief has befallen them; wait till I return, because if I find them I shall certainly be back."

He then got ready, took his sword, bow and arrow, some healing-grass, and water of life and death with him, and went to the very place where they had separated. On the way he shot a hare, and when he came to the place of separation he went on the same road by which his elder brothers had gone; he found there a small hut and a tree beside it; he stopped in front of the tree, and saw that his brothers' two dogs were chained to it; he loosed them, lighted a fire, and began to roast the hare. As he roasted it he heard a voice as if some one were shouting from the tree in a shivering voice; "Oh, how cold I am!" it said. "If you're cold," replied Rose, "get down and warm yourself." "Yes," said the voice, "but I'm afraid of the dogs." "Don't be afraid as they won't hurt an honest person." "I believe you," said the voice in the tree, "but still I want you to throw this hair between them; let them smell it first, then they will know me by it." Rose took the hair and threw it into the fire. Down came an old witch from the tree and warmed herself. Then she spitted a toad and began to roast it. As she did so she said to Rose, "This is mine, that is yours," and threw it at him. As Rose couldn't stand this he jumped up, drew his sword, and smote the witch; but lo! the sword turned into a log of wood, and the witch flew at him to kill him, crying, "It's all up with you also. I've killed your brothers in revenge because you killed my seven giant sons."[1] But Rose set the dogs at her, and they dragged her about till they drew blood. The blood was spilt on the log of wood and it became a sword again. Rose caught hold of it and chopped the old witch's left arm off. Now the witch showed [Pg 58]him the place where she had buried his brothers. Rose smote her once more with his sword and the old witch went to Pluto's. Rose dug out the bodies, put the bits together, anointed them with the healing-grass, and sprinkled them with the water of life and death, and they came to life again.

When they opened their eyes and saw Rose, they both exclaimed, "Oh! how long I have been asleep." "Very long indeed," said Rose, "and if I hadn't come you'd have been asleep still." They told him that soon after they had separated they received the news that the enemy had withdrawn from their country, and they decided to return, and that the elder should undertake the government of the land, and the other go in search of Rose. On their way they happened to go into the hut, and the old witch treated them as she was going to treat Rose.

Rose also told them his tale, and spoke to them thus: "You, my eldest brother, go home, and sit on our father's throne. You my other brother come with me, and let us two govern the vast country over which the giants had tyrannised until now:" and thus they separated and each went on his own business.

Rose found his pretty love again, who was nearly dead with fretting for him, but who quite recovered on his happy return. They took into their hands the government of the vast country which they had delivered from the sway of the giants. Rose and his love got married with the most splendid wedding-feast, and the bride had to dance a great deal; and if they've not died since they're alive still to this very day.

May they curl themselves into an eggshell and be your guests to-morrow.

[1]According to Kozma this is the only instance in the Székely folk-lore which accounts for the origin of giants.

[Pg 59]

PRINCE MIRKÓ.

There was once, I don't know where, a king who had three sons. This king had great delight in his three sons, and decided to give them a sound education, and after that to give them a place in the government, so that he might leave them as fit and willing heirs to his throne; so he sent these sons to college to study, and they did well for a while; but all of a sudden they left college, came home, and would not return. The king was very much annoyed at their conduct, and prohibited them from ever entering his presence. He himself retired, and lived in an eastern room of the royal residence, where he spent his time sitting in a window that looked eastward, as if he expected some one to come in that direction. One of his eyes was continually weeping, while the other was continually laughing. One day, when the princes were grown up, they held a consultation, and decided to ascertain from their royal father the reason why he always sat in the east room, and why one eye was continually weeping while the other never ceased laughing. The eldest son tried his fortune first, and thus questioned the king: "Most gracious majesty, my father. I have come to ask you, my royal sire, the reason why one of your eyes is always weeping while the other never ceases laughing, and why you always sit in this east room." The king measured his son from top to toe, and never spoke a word, but seized his long straight sword which leant against the window and threw it at him: it struck the door, and entered into it up to the hilt. The prince jumped through the door and escaped the blow that was meant for him. As he went he met his two [Pg 60]brothers, who inquired how he had fared. "You'd better try yourself and you will soon know," replied he. So the second prince tried, but with no better result than his brother. At last the third brother, whose name was Mirkó, went in, and, like his brother, informed the king of the reason of his coming. The king uttered not a word, but seized the sword with even greater fury, and threw it with such vehemence that it entered up to the hilt in the wall of the room: yet Mirkó did not run away, but only dodged the sword, and then pulled it out of the wall and took it back to his royal father, placing it on the table in front of him. Seeing this the king began to speak and said to Prince Mirkó, "My son, I can see that you know more about honour than your two brothers. So I will answer your question. One of my eyes weeps continually because I fret about you that you are such good-for-nothings and not fit to rule; the other laughs continually because in my younger days I had a good comrade, Knight Mezey, with whom I fought in many battles, and he promised me that if he succeeded in vanquishing his enemy he would come and live with me, and we should spend our old age together. I sit at the east window because I expect him to come in that direction; but Knight Mezey, who lives in the Silk Meadow, has so many enemies rising against him every day as there are blades of grass, and he has to cut them down all by himself every day; and until the enemies be extirpated he cannot come and stay with me." With this, Prince Mirkó left his father's room, went back to his brothers, and told them what he had heard from the king. So they held council again, and decided to ask permission from their father to go and try their fortunes. First the eldest prince went and told the king that he was anxious to go and try his fortune, to which the king consented: so the eldest prince went into the royal stables and chose a fine charger, had it saddled, his bag filled, and started on his journey the next morning. He was away for a whole year, and then suddenly turned up one morning, carrying on his [Pg 61]shoulder a piece of bridge-flooring made of copper; throwing it down in front of the royal residence, he walked into the king's presence, told him where he had been, and what he had brought back with him. The king listened to the end of his tale and said, "Well, my son, when I was as young as you are I went that way, and it only took me two hours from the place where you brought this copper from. You are a very weak knight: you won't do; you can go." With this the eldest prince left his father's room. The second prince then came in and asked the king to permit him to try his fortune, and the king gave him permission. So he went to the royal stables, had a fine charger saddled, his bag filled, and set off. At the end of a year he returned home, bringing with him a piece of bridge-flooring made of silver; this he threw down in front of the royal residence, and went in unto the king, told him all about his journey and about his spoil. "Alas!" said the king, "when I was as young as you I went that way, and it did not take me more than three hours; you are a very weak knight, my son: you will not do."

With this he dismissed his second son also. At last Prince Mirkó went in and asked permission to go and try his fortune, and the king granted him permission, so he also went into the royal stables in order to choose a horse for the journey; but he did not find one to suit him, so he went to the royal stud-farm to choose one there. As he was examining the young horses, and could not settle which to have, there suddenly appeared an old witch, who asked him what he wanted. Prince Mirkó told her his intention, and that he wanted a horse to go on the journey. "Alas! my lord," said the old witch, "you can't get a horse here to suit you, but I will tell you how to obtain one: go to your father, and ask him to let you have the horn which in his younger days he used to call together his stud with golden hair, blow into it, and the golden stud will at once appear. But don't choose any of those with the golden hair; but at the very last [Pg 62]there will come a mare with crooked legs and shaggy coat; you will know her by the fact that when the stud passes through the gates of the royal fortress the mare will come last, and she will whisk her tail and strike the heel-post of the fortress-gate with such force that the whole fort will quiver with the shock. Choose her, and try your fortune." Prince Mirkó followed the witch's advice most carefully. Going to the king he said, "My royal father, I come to ask you to give me the horn with which in your younger days you used to call together your stud with the golden hair." "Who told you of this?" inquired the king. "Nobody," replied Prince Mirkó. "Well, my dear son, if no one has informed you of this, and if it be your own conception, you are a very clever fellow; but if any one has told you to do this they mean no good to you. I will tell you where the horn is, but by this time, I daresay, it is all rust-eaten. In the seventh cellar there is a recess in the wall; in this recess lies the horn, bricked up; try to find it, take it out, and use it if you think you can." Prince Mirkó sent for the bricklayer on the spot, and went with him to the cellar indicated, found the recess, took the horn, and carried it off with him. He then stood in the hall of the royal residence and blew it, facing east, west, south, and north. In a short time he heard the tingle of golden bells begin to sound, increasing till the whole town rang with the noise; and lo! through the gates of the royal residence beautiful golden-haired horses came trooping in. Then he saw, even at the distance, the mare with the crooked legs and shaggy coat, and as she came, the last, great Heavens! as she came through the gates she whisked the heel-post with her tail with such force that the whole building shook to its very foundation. The moment the stud had got into the royal courtyard he went to the crooked-legged shaggy-coated mare, caught her, had her taken to the royal stables, and made it known that he intended to try his fortune with her. The mare said "Quite right, my prince; but first you will [Pg 63]have to give me plenty of oats, because it would be difficult to go a long journey without food." "What sort of food do you wish? Because whatever my father possesses I will willingly give to you," said the prince. "Very well, my prince," said the mare; "but it is not usual to feed a horse just before you start on a journey, but some time beforehand." "Well, I can't do much at present," said the prince; "but whatever I've got you shall have with pleasure." "Well, then, bring me a bushel of barley at once, and have it emptied into my manger." Mirkó did this; and when she had eaten the barley she made him fetch a bushel of millet; and when she had eaten that she said, "And now bring me half a bushel of burning cinders, and empty them into my manger." When she had eaten these she turned to a beautiful golden-haired animal like to the morning-star. "Now, my prince," said she, "go to the king and ask him to give you the saddle he used when he rode me in his younger days." Prince Mirkó went to the old king and asked him for the saddle. "It cannot be used now," said he, "as it has been lying about so long in the coach-house, and it's all torn by this, but if you can find it you can have it." Prince Mirkó went to the coach-house and found the saddle, but it was very dirty, as the fowls and turkeys had for many years roosted on it, and torn it; still he took it to the mare in order to put it on her, but she said that it was not becoming a prince to sit upon such a thing, wherefore he was going to have it altered and repaired; but the mare told him to hold it in front of her, and she breathed on it, and in a moment it was changed into a beautiful gold saddle, such as had not an equal over seven countries; with this he saddled the tátos (mythical horse). "Now, my prince," said she, "you had better go to your father and ask him for the brace of pistols and the sword with which he used to set out when he rode me in former days." So the prince went and asked these from his father, but the old king replied "that they were all rusty by this time, and of no use," but, if he really wanted them, [Pg 64]he could have them, and pointed out the rack where they were. Prince Mirkó took them and carried them to the mare, who breathed upon them, and changed them into gold; he then girded on his sword, placed the pistols in the holsters, and got ready for a start. "Well, my dear master," said the mare, "where now is my bridle?" Whereupon, the prince fetched from the coach-house an old bridle, which she blew upon and it changed into gold; this the prince threw over her head, and led her out of the stable, and was about to mount her when the mare said, "Wait a minute, lead me outside the town first, and then mount me;" so he led her outside the town, and then mounted her. At this moment the mare said, "Well, my dear master, how shall I carry you? Shall I carry you with a speed like the quick hurricane, or like a flash of thought?" "I don't mind, my dear mare, how you carry me, only take care that you run so that I can bear it."

To this the mare replied, "Shut your eyes and hold fast." Prince Mirkó shut his eyes, and the mare darted off like a hurricane. After a short time she stamped upon the ground and said to the prince, "Open your eyes! What can you see?" "I can see a great river," said Prince Mirkó, "and over it a copper bridge." "Well, my dear master," said the mare, "that's the bridge from which your eldest brother carried off part of the flooring: can't you see the vacant place?" "Yes, I can see it," said the prince, "and where shall we go now?" "Shut your eyes and I will carry you;" with this, she started off like a flash of lightning, and in a few moments again stamped upon the ground and said, "Open your eyes! Now what do you see?" "I see," said Prince Mirkó, "a great river, and over it a silver bridge." "Well, my dear master, that's the bridge from which your second brother took the silver flooring; can't you see the place?" "Yes," said he, "I can, and now where shall we go?"

"Shut your eyes and I will carry you," said the mare, and off she darted like lightning, and in a moment she again stamped [Pg 65]upon the ground and stopped and said to Prince Mirkó, "Open your eyes! What can you see?" "I see," replied he, "a vast, broad, and deep river, and over it a golden bridge, and at each end, on this side and that, four immense and fierce lions. How are we to get over this?" "Don't take any notice of them," said the mare, "I will settle with them, you shut your eyes." Prince Mirkó shut his eyes, the mare darted off like a swift falcon, and flew over the bridge; in a short time she stopped, stamped, and said, "Open your eyes! Now what do you see?" "I see," said the prince, "an immense, high glass rock, with sides as steep as the side of a house." "Well, my dear master," said the mare, "We have to get over that too."

"But that is impossible," said the prince; but the mare cheered him, and said, "Don't worry yourself, dear master, as I still have the very shoes on my hoofs which your father put on them with diamond nails six hundred years ago. Shut your eyes and hold fast."

At this moment the mare darted off, and in a twinkling of the eye she reached the summit of the glass rock, where she stopped, stamped, and said to the prince, "Open your eyes! What can you see?" "I can see, below me," said Prince Mirkó, "on looking back, something black, the size of a fair-sized dish." "Well, my dear master, that is the orb of the earth; but what can you see in front of you?" "I can see," said Prince Mirkó, "a narrow round-backed glass path, and by the side of it, this side as well as on the other side, a deep bottomless abyss." "Well, my dear master," said the mare, "we have to get over that, but the passage is so difficult that if my foot slips the least bit either way we shall perish, but rely on me. Shut your eyes and grasp hold of me, and I will do it." With this the mare started and in another moment she again stamped on the ground and said, "Open your eyes! What can you see?" "I can see," said Prince Mirkó, "behind me, in the distance, some faint light and in front of me such a thick darkness that I cannot even see [Pg 66]my finger before me." "Well, my dear master, we have to get through this also. Shut your eyes, and grasp me." Again she started and again she stamped. "Open your eyes! What can you see now?" "I can see," said Prince Mirkó, "a beautiful light, a beautiful snow-clad mountain, in the midst of the mountain a meadow like silk, and in the midst of the meadow something black." "Well, my dear master, that meadow which looks like silk belongs to Knight Mezey, and the black something in the middle of it is his tent, woven of black silk; it does not matter now whether you shut your eyes or not, we will go there." With this Prince Mirkó spurred the mare, and at once reached the tent.

Prince Mirkó jumped from his mare and tied her to the tent by the side of Knight Mezey's horse, and he himself walked into the tent, and lo! inside, a knight was laid at full length on the silken grass, fast asleep, but a sword over him was slashing in all directions, so that not even a fly could settle on him. "Well," thought Prince Mirkó to himself, "this fellow must be a brave knight, but I could kill him while he sleeps; however, it would not be an honourable act to kill a sleeping knight, and I will wait till he wakes." With this he walked out of the tent, tied his mare faster to the tent-post, and he also lay down full length upon the silken grass, and said to his sword, "Sword, come out of thy scabbard," and his sword began to slash about over him, just like Knight Mezey's, so that not even a fly could settle on him.

All of a sudden Knight Mezey woke, and to his astonishment he saw another horse tied by the side of his, and said, "Great Heavens! what's the meaning of this? It's six hundred years since I saw a strange horse by the side of mine! Whom can it belong to?" He got up, went out of the tent, and saw Prince Mirkó asleep outside, and his sword slashing about over him. "Well," said he, "this must be a brave knight, and as he has not killed me while I was asleep, it would not be honourable to [Pg 67]kill him," with this he kicked the sleeping knight's foot and woke him. He jumped up, and Knight Mezey thus questioned him: "Who are you? What is your business?" Prince Mirkó told him whose son he was and why he had come. "Welcome, my dear brother," said Knight Mezey, "your father is a dear friend of mine, and I can see that you are as brave a knight as your father, and I shall want you, because the large silken meadow that you see is covered with enemies every day, and I have to daily cut them down, but now that you are here to help me I shall be in no hurry about them; let's go inside and have something to eat and drink, and let them gather into a crowd, two of us will soon finish them." They went into the tent and had something to eat and drink; but all at once his enemies came up in such numbers that they came almost as far as the tent, when Knight Mezey jumped to his feet and said, "Jump up, comrade, or else we are done for." They sprang to their horses, darted among the enemy, and both called out, "Sword, out of thy scabbard!" and in a moment the two swords began to slash about, and cut off the heads of the enemy, so that they had the greatest difficulty in advancing on account of the piles of dead bodies, till at last, at the rear of the enemy, twelve knights took to flight, and Knight Mezey and Prince Mirkó rode in pursuit of them, till they reached a glass rock, to which they followed the twelve knights, Prince Mirkó being the nearest to them. On the top of the rock there was a beautiful open space, towards which the knights rode and Prince Mirkó after them on his mare, when all at once they all disappeared, as if the earth had swallowed them; seeing this, Prince Mirkó rode to the spot where they disappeared, where he found a trap-door, and under the door a deep hole and a spiral staircase. The mare without hesitation jumped into the hole, which was the entrance to the infernal regions. Prince Mirkó, looking round in Hades, suddenly discerned a glittering diamond castle, which served the lower regions instead of the sun, and saw that the twelve knights [Pg 68]were riding towards it; so he darted after them, and, calling out "Sword, come out of thy scabbard," he slashed off the twelve knights' heads in a moment, and, riding to the castle, he heard such a hubbub and clattering that the whole place resounded with it: he jumped off his horse, and walked into the castle, when lo! there was an old diabolical-looking witch, who was weaving and making the clattering noise, and the whole building was now full of soldiers, whom the devilish witch produced by weaving. When she threw the shuttle to the right, each time two hussars on horseback jumped out from the shuttle, and when she threw it to the left, each time two foot soldiers jumped from it fully equipped. When he saw this, he ordered his sword out of its scabbard, and cut down all the soldiers present. But the old witch wove others again, so Prince Mirkó thought to himself, if this goes on, I shall never get out of this place, so he ordered his sword to cut up into little pieces the old witch, and then he carried out the whole bleeding mass into the courtyard, where he found a heap of wood: he placed the mass on it, put a light to it, and burnt it. But when it was fully alight a small piece of a rib of the witch flew out of the fire and began to spin around in the dust, and lo! another witch grew out of it. Prince Mirkó thereupon was about to order his sword to cut her up too, when the old witch addressed him thus: "Spare my life, Mirkó, and I will help you in return for your kindness; if you destroy me you can't get out of this place; here! I will give you four diamond horse-shoe nails, put them away and you will find them useful." Prince Mirkó took the nails and put them away, thinking to himself, "If I spare the old witch she will start weaving again, and Knight Mezey will never get rid of his enemies," so he again ordered his sword to cut up the witch, and threw her into the fire and burnt her to cinders. She never came to life again. He then got on his mare and rode all over the lower regions, but could not find a living soul anywhere, whereupon he spurred his mare, galloped to the foot of the spiral staircase, and in another moment [Pg 69]he reached the upper world. When he arrived at the brink of the glass rock he was about to alight from his mare: and stopped her for this purpose, but the mare questioned him thus, "What are you going to do, Prince Mirkó?" "I was going to get down, because the road is very steep and it's impossible to go down on horseback." "Well then, dear master, if you do that you can't get below, because you couldn't walk on the steep road, but if you stop on my back, take hold of my mane, and shut your eyes, I will take you down." Whereupon the mare started down the side of the rock, and, like a good mountaineer, climbed down from the top to the bottom, and having arrived at the foot of the steep rock, spoke to Prince Mirkó thus: "You can open your eyes now." Mirkó having opened his eyes, saw that they had arrived in the silken meadow.

They started in the direction of Knight Mezey's tent, but Knight Mezey thought that Mirkó had already perished, when suddenly he saw that Mirkó was alive, so he came in great joy to meet him, and leading him into his tent, as he had no heir, he offered him the silk meadow and his whole realm, but Mirkó replied thus: "My dear brother, now that I have destroyed all your enemies, you need not fear that the enemy will occupy your country, therefore I should like you to come with me to my royal father, who has been expecting you for a very long time." With this they got on their horses, and started off in the direction of the old king's realm, and arrived safely at the very spot on the glass rock where Mirkó had jumped down. Knight Mezey stopped here, and said to Prince Mirkó: "My dear brother, I cannot go further than this, because the diamond nails of my horse's shoes have been worn out long ago, and the horse's feet no longer grip the ground." But Mirkó remembered that the old witch had given him some diamond nails, and said: "Don't worry yourself, brother. I have got some nails with me, and I will shoe thy horse." And taking out the diamond [Pg 70]nails, he shod Knight Mezey's horse with them. They mounted once more, and like two good mountaineers descended the glass rock, and as swift as thought were on the way home.

The old king was also then sitting in the eastern window, awaiting Knight Mezey, when suddenly he saw two horsemen approaching, and, looking at them with his telescope, recognised them as his dear old comrade Knight Mezey, together with his son, Prince Mirkó, coming towards him; so he ran down at once, and out of the hall. He ordered the bailiff to slaughter twelve heifers, and by the time that Knight Mezey and Mirkó arrived, a grand dinner was ready waiting for them; and on their arrival he received them with great joy, embraced them and kissed them, and laughed with both his eyes. Then they sat down to dinner, and ate and drank in great joy. During dinner Knight Mezey related Mirkó's brave deeds, and, amongst other things, said to the old king: "Well, comrade, your son Mirkó is even a greater hero than we were. He is a brave fellow, and you ought to be well pleased with him." The old king said: "Well, when I come to think of it, I begin to be satisfied with him, especially because he has brought you with him; but still I don't believe that he would have courage to fight Doghead also." Prince Mirkó was listening to their talk but did not speak. After dinner, however, he called Knight Mezey aside, and asked him who Doghead was, and where he lived. Knight Mezey informed him that he lived in the north, and that he was such a hero that there was no other to equal him under the sun. Prince Mirkó at once gave orders for the journey, filled his bag, and next day started on his mare to Doghead's place; according to his custom, he sat upon the mare, grasped her firmly, and shut his eyes. The mare darted off, and flew like a swift cyclone, then suddenly stopped, stamped on the ground, and said, "Prince Mirkó, open your eyes. What do you see?" "I see," said the Prince, "a diamond castle, six stories high, that glitters so that one can't look at it, although one could look [Pg 71]at the sun." "Well, Doghead lives there," said the mare, "and that is his royal castle." Prince Mirkó rode close under the window and shouted loudly: "Doghead! are you at home? Come out, because I have to reckon with you." Doghead himself was not at home, but his daughter was there—such a beautiful royal princess, whose like one could not find in the whole world. As she sat in the window doing some needlework, and heard the high shrill voice, she looked through the window in a great rage, and gave him such a look with her beautiful flashing black eyes, that Prince Mirkó and his mare at once turned into a stone statue. However, she began to think that perhaps the young gentleman might be some prince who had come to see her; so she repented that she had transformed him into a stone statue so quickly; and ran down to him, took out a golden rod, and began to walk round the stone statue, and tapped its sides with her gold rod, and lo! the stone crust began to crack, and fell off, and all at once Prince Mirkó and his mare stood alive in front of her. Then the princess asked; "Who are you? and what is your business?" And Mirkó told her that he was a prince, and had come to see the Princess of Doghead. The princess slightly scolded him for shouting for her father so roughly through the window, but at the same time fell in love with Prince Mirkó on the spot, and asked him to come into her diamond castle, which was six stories high, and received him well. However, while feasting, Prince Mirkó during the conversation confessed what his true errand was, viz., to fight Doghead; but the princess advised him to desist from this, because there was no man in the whole world who could match her father. But when she found that Mirkó could not be dissuaded, she took pity on him, and, fearing that lest he should be vanquished, let him into the secret how to conquer her father. "Go down," she said, "into the seventh cellar of the castle; there you will find a cask which is not sealed. In that cask is kept my father's strength. I hand you here a silver bottle, which you [Pg 72]have to fill from the cask; but do not cork the bottle, but always take care that it shall hang uncorked from your neck; and when your strength begins to fail, dip your little finger into it, and each time your strength will be increased by that of five thousand men; also drink of it, because each drop of wine will give you the strength of five thousand men." Prince Mirkó listened attentively to her counsel, hung the silver bottle round his neck, and went down into the cellar, where he found the wine in question, and from it he first drank a good deal, and then filled his flask, and, thinking that he had enough in his bottle, he let the rest run out to the last drop, so that Doghead could use it no more. There were in the cellar six bushels of wheat flour, with this he soaked it up, so that no moisture was left, whereupon he went upstairs to the princess, and reported that he was ready and also thanked her for her directions, and promised that for all her kindness he would marry her, and vowed eternal faith to her. The beautiful princess consented to all, and only made one condition, viz., that in case Prince Mirkó conquered her father he would not kill him.

Prince Mirkó then inquired of the beautiful princess when she expected her father home, and in what direction, to which the princess replied that at present he was away in his western provinces, visiting their capitals, but that he would be home soon, because he was due, and that it was easy to predict his coming, because when he was two hundred miles from home, he would throw home a mace weighing forty hundredweight, thus announcing his arrival, and wherever the mace dropped a spring would suddenly burst from the ground. Prince Mirkó thereupon went with the royal princess into the portico of the royal castle, to await there Doghead's arrival, when suddenly, good Heavens! the air became dark, and a mace, forty hundredweight, came down with a thud into the courtyard of the royal fortress, and, striking the ground, water burst forth immediately in the shape of a rainbow. Prince Mirkó at once ran into the courtyard [Pg 73]in order to try how much his strength had increased. He picked up the mace swung it over his head, and threw it back so that it dropped just in front of Doghead. Doghead's horse stumbled over the mace; whereupon Doghead got angry. "Gee up! I wish the wolves and dogs would devour you," shouted Doghead to the horse. "I have ridden you for the last six hundred years, and up to this time you have never stumbled once. What's the reason that you begin to stumble now?" "Alas! my dear master," said his horse, "there must be something serious the matter at home, because some one has thrown back your mace that you threw home, and I stumbled over it." "There's nothing the matter," said Doghead; "I dreamt six hundred years ago that I would have to fight Prince Mirkó, and it is he who is at my castle; but what is he to me? I have more strength in my little finger than he in his whole body." With this he darted off at a great speed and appeared at the castle. Prince Mirkó was awaiting Doghead in the courtyard of the fortress. The latter, seeing Prince Mirkó, galloped straight to him and said, "Well, Mirkó. I know that you are waiting for me. Here I am. How do you wish me to fight you? With swords? or shall we wrestle?" "I don't care how; just as you please," said Mirkó. "Then let us try swords first," said Doghead, and, getting off his horse, they stood up, and both ordered out their swords. "Swords, come out of the scabbards." The two swords flew out of the scabbards and began to fence over the heads of the combatants. The whole place rung with their clashing, and in their vehemence they sent forth sparks in such quantity that the whole ground was covered with fire, so that no one could stand the heat. Whereupon Doghead said to Mirkó, "Don't let us spoil our swords, but let us put them back into their scabbards, and let us wrestle." So they sheathed their swords and began to wrestle. When suddenly Doghead grasped Mirkó round the waist, lifted him up, and dashed him to the ground with such force that Mirkó sank to his belt. Mirkó was frightened, and quickly dipped his little finger into [Pg 74]the bottle. Whereupon he regained his strength, and, jumping out of the ground, made a desperate dash at Doghead, and threw him to the ground with such force, that he lay full length on the ground like a green frog; then he seized him by his hair and dragged him behind the royal residence, where a golden bridge stood over a bottomless lake. He dragged him on to the bridge, and, holding his head over the water, ordered his sword out of the scabbard and cut off his head, so that it dropped into the bottomless lake, and then he pushed the headless trunk after it.

Doghead's daughter saw all this, and grew very angry with Prince Mirkó, and as he approached her she turned her face away, and would not even speak to him; but Prince Mirkó explained to her that he could not do otherwise, for if he had spared Doghead's life he would have destroyed his; and that he was willing to redeem his promise, and keep his faith to the princess and take her for his wife. Whereupon the royal princess became reconciled, and they decided to get ready to go to Prince Mirkó's realm. They ordered the horses—Doghead's charger was got ready for the beautiful princess—and, mounting them, were about to start, when all at once deep sorrow seized Prince Mirkó, and the beautiful royal princess thus questioned him: "Why are you so downcast, Mirkó?" "Well, because," said Mirkó, "I'm anxious to go back to my country, but I am also extremely sorry to leave behind this sumptuous diamond castle, six stories high, which belonged to your father, for there is nothing like it in my country." "Well, my love," said the princess, "don't trouble about that. I will transform the castle into a golden apple at once, and sit in the middle of it, and all you will have to do is to put the apple into your pocket, and then you can take me with you and the castle too, and when you arrive at home you can re-transform me wherever you like." Thereupon the pretty princess jumped down from her horse, handed the reins to Mirkó, took out a diamond rod, and commenced to walk round the diamond castle, gently beating the sides of it with the [Pg 75]diamond rod, and the castle began to shrink and shrunk as small as a sentry box, and then the princess jumped inside of it, and the whole shrivelled up into a golden apple, the diamond rod lying by the side of it. Prince Mirkó picked up the golden apple and the diamond rod, and put them into his pocket, and then got on horseback, and, taking Doghead's horse by the bridle, he rode quietly home. Having arrived at home, Mirkó had the horses put in the stables, and then walked into the royal palace, where he found the old king and Knight Mezey quite content and enjoying themselves. He reported to them that he had conquered even Doghead, and that he had killed him; but the old king and Knight Mezey doubted his words. Therefore Prince Mirkó took them both by their arms, and said to them, "Come along with me, and you can satisfy yourselves, with your own eyes, that I have conquered Doghead, because I have brought away with me, not only his diamond castle, six stories high, but also his beautiful daughter, inside it, as a trophy of my victory." The old king and Knight Mezey were astonished at his words, and, still doubting, followed Mirkó, who took them into the flower garden of the king, in the middle of which Prince Mirkó selected a nice roomy place for the diamond castle, and placed the golden apple there, and commenced walking round, and, patting its sides with the diamond rod, the golden apple began to swell. It took a quadrangular shape, growing and growing, higher and higher, till it became a magnificent six-storied diamond castle; and then he took the old king and Knight Mezey by their arms, and led them up the diamond staircase into the rooms of the castle, where the princess, who was world-wide known for her beauty, met them, and received them most cordially. She bade them sit down, and sent lackeys to call the other sons of the old king and also the higher dignitaries of the court. In the dining-hall there was a big table, which could be opened out. She gave orders, and the table was laid of itself, and on it appeared all sorts of [Pg 76]costly dishes and drinks, and the assembled guests feasted in joy. The old king was highly satisfied with his son's doings, and handed over to Mirkó the royal power and the whole realm: he himself and Knight Mezey retired into quiet secluded life, and lived long in great happiness. The young royal couple who got married had beautiful children, and they are alive still, to this very day, if they have not died since. May they be your guests to-morrow!

THE STUDENT WHO WAS FORCIBLY MADE KING.

A student started on a journey, and as he went over a field he found some peas which were cracked. He thought that they might be of use to him as he was a poor lad, and his father had advised him to pick up anything he saw, if it was worth no more than a flea; so he gathered up the peas and put them in his pocket. As he travelled he was overtaken by night just when he arrived at the royal borough; so he reported himself to the king, and asked for some money for travelling expenses, and a night's lodging. Now the student was a comely lad, spoke grammatically, and had good manners. The queen noticed this, and as she had a daughter ready for marriage, she came to the conclusion that he was a prince in disguise, who had come in search of a wife. She told this to the king, and he thought it very probable. Both agreed that they would try to find out whether he really was a prince, and asked him to stay with them for two days. The first night they did not give him a very splendid bed, because they thought that if he were satisfied, he was but a student, if not, then he must be a prince. They [Pg 77]made his bed in the adjoining house, and the king placed one of his confidential servants outside of the window, that he might spy out all that the student did. They showed the bed to the student, and he began to undress when they left. As he undressed all the peas dropped out of his pocket, and rolled under the bed; he at once began to look for them and pick them up, one by one, and did not finish till dawn. The spy outside could not make out what he was doing, but he saw that he did not go to sleep till dawn, and then only for a short time, having spent the night arranging his bed; so he reported to the king that his guest had not slept, but had fidgeted about, appearing not to be used to such a bed. The student got up, and during breakfast the king asked him how he had slept, to which he replied, "A little restlessly, but it was through my own fault." From this they concluded that he already repented of not having shown them his true position, and thus having not got a proper bed. They believed, therefore, that he was a prince, and treated him accordingly. Next night they made his bed in the same place, but in right royal style. As the student had not slept the night before, the moment he put his head down he began to sleep like a pumpkin, and never even moved till dawn. He had no trouble with his peas this time, for he had tied them up in the corner of his handkerchief as he picked them up from under the bed. The spy reported to the king next morning that the traveller slept soundly all night. They now firmly believed that the student simply dressed up as such, but in reality was a prince. They tried to persuade him that he was a prince, and addressed him as such. The king's daughter ran after the student to get into his favour, and it didn't take much to make him fall in love with her, and so the two got married. They had lived a whole year together, when they were sent off to travel in order that the student-king might show his wife his realm. The student was very frightened that he might not get out of his trouble so well, and grew more and more alarmed, [Pg 78]till at last he accepted his fate. "Let come whatever is to come," thought he, "I will go with them, and then, if nothing else can be done, I can escape, and go back to college," for he had carried his student's gown with him everywhere. They started off and travelled till they came to a large forest. The student slipped aside into a deep ditch, where he undressed, in order to put on his student's clothes and to escape. Now there was a dragon with seven heads lazily lying there, who accosted him thus: "Who are you? What are you looking for here? What do you want?" The student told him his whole history, and also that he was just going to run away. "There is no need to run away," said the dragon, "that would be a pity, continue your journey; when you get out of this wood you will see a copper fortress, which swivels on a goose's leg. Go into it, and live there in peace with your wife, with your dog and cat, till the fortress begins to move and turn round. When this happens, be off, because if I come home and catch you there, there will be an end of you." The student went back to his travelling companions and continued his way until, emerging from the wood, he saw the fortress. They all went in and settled down as in their own, and all went on very well for two years, and he already began to believe that he really was a king, when suddenly the fortress began to move, and swivel round very quickly. The student was downcast, and went up on the battlement of the fortress, wandering about in great sorrow; he there found an old woman, who asked him, "What's the matter with your Majesty?" "H'm! the matter is, old woman," replied the student, "that I am not a king, and still I am compelled to be one," and then he told her his whole history up to that time. "There's nothing in that, my son," said the old woman, "be thankful that you have not tried to keep your secret from me. I am the queen of magic, and the most formidable enemy of the dragon with seven heads; therefore this is my advice: get a loaf made at once, and let this loaf be placed in the oven seven times [Pg 79]with other loaves, this particular loaf each time to be put in the oven the first and to be taken out last. Have this loaf placed outside the fortress gate to-morrow, without fail. When the dragon with the seven heads is coming, it will be such a charm against him that he will never trouble you again, and the fortress will be left to you with all that belongs to it." The student had the loaf prepared as he was told, and when the clock struck one after midnight the bread was already placed outside the fortress gate. As the sun rose, the dragon with seven heads went straight towards the fortress gate, where the loaf addressed him thus, "Stop, I'm guard here, and without my permission you may not enter; if you wish to come in, you must first suffer what I have suffered."

"Well," said the dragon, "I've made up my mind to enter, so let me know what ordeals you have gone through."

The loaf told him, that when it was a seed it was buried in a field that had previously been dug up: then rotted, sprouted, and grew; it had suffered from cold, heat, rain, and snow, until it ripened; it was then cut down, tied into sheaves, threshed out, ground, kneaded into dough, and then seven times running they put it in a fiery oven, each time before its mates: "If you can stand all this," concluded the loaf, "then I'll let you in, but on no other condition." The dragon, knowing that he could not stand all this, got so angry that he burst in his rage and perished. The student from that day became lord of the fortress, and after the death of his wife's parents became king of two lands; and if he has not died yet, he reigns still.

If I knew that I should fare as well as that student I would become a student this very blessed day!

[Pg 80]

THE CHILDREN OF TWO RICH MEN.

There lived, at the two corners of a country, far away from each other, two rich men; one of them had a son, the other a daughter; these two men asked each other to be godfather to their children, and, during the christening they agreed that the babes should wed. The children grew up, but did no work, and so were spoilt. As soon as they were old enough their parents compelled them to marry. Shortly afterwards their parents died and they were left alone; they knew nothing of the world and did not understand farming, so the serfs and farm-labourers had it all their own way. Soon their fields were all overgrown with weeds and their corn-bins empty; in a word they became poor. One day the master bethought himself that he ought to go to market, as he had seen his father do; so he set off, and drove with him a pair of beautiful young oxen that were still left. On his way he met a wedding-party, and greeted them thus, "May the Lord preserve you from such a sorrowful change, and may He give consolation to those who are in trouble," Words he had once heard his father use upon the occasion of a funeral. The wedding-party got very vexed, and, as they were rather flushed with wine, gave him a good drubbing, and told him that the next time he saw such a ceremony he was to put his hat on the end of his stick, lift it high in the air, and shout for joy. He went on further till he came to the outskirts of a forest, where he met some butcher-like looking people who were driving fat pigs, whereupon he seized his hat, put it on the end of his stick, and began to shout: which so frightened the pigs that they rushed off on all sides into the wood; the butchers got hold of him and gave him a sound beating, and [Pg 81]told him that the next time he saw such a party he was to say, "May the Lord bless you with *two* for every *one* you have." He went on again and saw a man clearing out the weeds from his field, and greeted him, "My brother, may the Lord bless you with *two* for every *one* you have." The man, who was very angry about the weeds, caught him and gave him a sound beating, and told him that the next time he saw such things he had better help to pull out one or two. In another place he met two men fighting, so he went up and began to pull first at one and then at the other, whereupon they left off fighting with each other and pitched into him. Somehow or other he at last arrived at the market, and, looking round, he saw an unpainted cart for sale, whereupon he remembered that his father used to go into the wood in a cart, and so he asked the man who had it for sale whether he would change it for his two oxen—not knowing that having once parted with the oxen he would not get them back again. The man was at first angry, because he thought he was making fun of the cart, but he soon saw that the man with the oxen was not quite right in his head, and so he struck the bargain with the young farmer, who, when he got the cart, went dragging it to and fro in the market. He met a blacksmith and changed the cart for a hatchet; soon the hatchet was changed for a whetstone; then he started off home as if he had settled matters in the most satisfactory manner. Near his village he saw a lake, and on it a flock of wild ducks. He immediately threw his whetstone at them, which sank to the bottom, whilst every one of the ducks flew away.

He undressed and got into the lake, in order to recover his whetstone, but in the meantime his clothes were stolen from the bank, and, having no clothes, he had to walk home as naked as when he was born. His wife was not at home when he arrived. He took a slice of bread from the drawer, and went into the cellar to draw himself some wine; having put the bread on the door-sill of the cellar, he went back to get his wine, as he did so he saw a dog come up and run away with his bread; he at [Pg 82]once threw the spigot after the thief, so the spigot was lost, the bread was lost, and every drop of wine was lost, for it all ran out. Now there was a sack of flour in the cellar, and in order that his wife might not notice the wine he spread the flour over it. A goose was sitting on eggs in the cellar, and as he worked she hissed at him. Thinking that the bird was saying, that it was going to betray him to his wife, he asked it two or three times, "Will you split?" Going up to the goose, it hissed still more, so he caught hold of it by the neck, and dashed it upon the ground with such force that it died on the spot. He was now more frightened than ever, and in order to amend his error he plucked off the feathers, rolled himself about in the floury mess, then amongst the feathers, and then sat on the nest as if he were sitting. His wife came home, and, as she found the cellar door wide open, she went down stairs, and found her husband sitting in the nest and hissing like a goose; but his wife soon recognised him, and, picking up a log of wood, she attacked him, saying, "Good Heavens, what an animal, let me kill it at once!" Up he jumped from the nest, and cried out in a horrible fright, "Don't touch me, my dear wife, it's I!" His wife then questioned him about his transactions, and he gave a full account of all that had happened; so his wife drove him away and said, "Don't come before my eyes again till you have made good your faults." She then gave him a slice of bread and a small flask of spirit, which he put in his pocket and went on his way, his wife wishing him "a happy journey, if the road is not muddy." On his way he met Our Lord Christ and said to him, "I'm not going to divide my bread with you, because you have not made a rich man of me." Then he met Death, with him he divided his bread and his spirits, therefore Death did not carry him off, and he asked Death to be his child's godfather.

Then said Death, "Now you will see a wonder"; with this he slipped into the spirit flask, and was immediately corked up [Pg 83]by the young man. Death implored to be set free, but the young farmer said, "Promise me then that you will make me a rich man, and then I will let you out." Death promised him this, and they agreed that the man was to be a doctor, and whenever Death stood at the patient's feet, he or she was not to die, and could be cured by any sort of medicine whatever: but if Death stood at the patient's head he was to die: with this they parted.

Our man reached a town where the king's daughter was very ill. The doctors had tried all they could, but were not able to cure her, so he said that he was going to cure her, if she could be cured, if not, he would tell them; so thereupon he went into the patient and saw Death standing at her feet. He burnt a stack of hay, and made a bath for her of the ashes, and she recovered so soon as she had bathed in it. The king made him so many presents that he became a very rich man: he removed to the town, brought his wife there, and lived in great style as a doctor. Once however he fell sick, and his koma [his child's godfather] came and stood at his head, and the patient begged hard for him to go and stand at his feet, but his koma replied, "Not if I know it," and then the doctor also departed to the other world.

THE HUSSAR AND THE SERVANT GIRL.[1]

The wife of a priest in olden times, it may have been in the antediluvian world, put all the plates, dishes, and milk-jugs into a basket and sent the servant to wash them in the brook. While the girl was washing she saw a cray-fish crawl out of the water, and, as she had never seen one in her life before, she stood staring at it, and was a little [Pg 84]frightened. It so happened that a hussar rode past on horseback, and the girl asked him, "Would you mind telling me, my gallant horseman, what sort of a God's wonder that yonder is?" "Well, my sister," said the soldier, "that is a cray-fish." The servant then took courage, and went near the cray-fish to look at it, and said, "But it crawls!" "But it's a cray-fish," said the soldier again. "But it crawls," said the servant abruptly. "But it's a cray-fish," said the soldier a third time. "Well, my gallant horseman, how can you stand there and tell me that, when I can see that it crawls?" said the servant. "But, my sister, how can you stand there and tell me, when I can see that it's a cray-fish?" said the soldier. "Well, I'm neither blind nor a fool, and I can see quite well that it's a-crawling," said the servant. "But neither am I blind nor a fool, and I can see that it is a cray-fish," said the soldier.

The servant got so angry that she dashed her crockery to the ground and broke it into fragments, crying, in a great rage, "May I perish here if it is not a-crawling!" The hussar jumped off his saddle, drew his sword, and cut off his horse's head, saying, "May the executioner cut off my neck like this if it isn't a cray-fish!" The soldier went his way on foot, and the servant went home without her ware, and the priest's wife asked, "Well, where are all the pots?" The servant told her what had happened between the soldier and her about a cray-fish and a-crawling. "Is that the reason why you have done all the damage?" said the priest's wife. "Oh, mistress, how could I give in when I saw quite well that it was a-crawling; and still that nasty soldier kept on saying it was a cray-fish?" The wife of the priest was heating the oven, as she was going to bake, and she got into such a rage that she seized her new fur jacket, for which she had given a hundred florins, and pitched it into the oven, saying, "May the flames of the fire burn me like this if you were not both great fools!" "What is all this smell of burning?" asked the priest, coming in. Learning what had happened [Pg 85]about a cray-fish and a-crawling, he took his gown and cut it up on the threshold with a hatchet, saying, "May the executioner cut me into bits like this if the three of you are not fools!" Then came the schoolmaster (his calf had got loose and run into the clergyman's yard, and he had come after it to drive it home): and, hearing what had happened, and why, he caught hold of a stick, and struck his calf such a blow on the head that it fell down dead on the spot, exclaiming, "If God will, may the fiery thunderbolt thus strike me dead if you all four are not fools!"

Then came the churchwarden, and asked what had happened there, and when he was told he got into such a rage that he picked up the church-box and dashed it on the ground in the middle of the yard, so that the box was broken to pieces, and the precious altar-covers and linen were rolling about on the dirty ground, saying, "May I perish like this, at this very hour, if the whole five of you are not fools!"

In the meantime the sacristan came in, and, seeing the linen on the floor, he threw up his hands and said, "Well, I never! whatever's the matter?" Then they told him what had happened, and why, whereupon he picked up all the covers and linen and tore them into shreds, saying, "May the devil tear me to atoms like this if you six are not a parcel of raving lunatics!"

News of the event soon got abroad, and the whole congregation gathered together and set the priest's house on fire, crying, "May the flames of the fire burn us all like this, every one of us, if all the seven were not fools!"

[1]The zest of this tale turns upon a similarity in the sound of the words in Magyar for "cray-fish," and "crawling."

[Pg 86]

MY FATHER'S WEDDING.

Once I discovered all of a sudden, it was before I was born, that my father was going to get married, and take my mother unto him. My father said to me, "Go to the mill and have some corn ground for bread for the wedding!" Whereupon I betook myself hurriedly like a smart fellow, I looked for a cloth, and took up into the loft three bags, and filled nine sacks with the best wheat of Dálnok, the best to be found; I put all nine sacks at once over my shoulder, and took them to the cart. I led out oxen and tried to yoke them, but neither of them could find it's old place; I put the off-side one on the near side, and the near-side one on the off side, and they were all right. I tried the yoke-pins, but they would not fit, I therefore put in lieu of one the handle of a shovel, and in place of the other a pole, and then all was right. I went to the mill with the team, and when I arrived there I stopped the oxen and stuck the whip into the ground in front of them to prevent them running away; I myself went into the mill to call the miller to assist me in carrying in the wheat. I couldn't find a soul in the mill. I looked around, under the bed, behind the oven, and saw that the green jug was not on it's peg; from this I knew that the mill was away gathering strawberries, so I thought, if this were so, I should have to wait patiently till it returned, but then I remembered that it was not its custom to hurry back, and by the time it got back my hair might be grey, and then it would be difficult for oxen to wait from year to year as I had not brought aught for them to feed on. So I rushed after it at a dog's trot, out on to the mount, and found it sniffing about the shrubs, so I cut a jolly good stick and began to bang it on both sides as hard as my strength allowed me, till I happened to hit it rather hard [Pg 87]with the stick, and, having struck it, I could hear it far away as it began to move down in the valley, and it ground away and made such a clatter; it was just grinding my wheat! In order to get down from the mount into the valley more quickly, I lay down on the ground and rolled down the slope, and after me all the stumps, who envied my pastime. Nothing happened to them, and the only accident I had was that I knocked my nose a little into some soft cow-dung, but I didn't carry it away altogether, and a good deal of it is left there still. The poor white horse fared much worse than that, as it was grazing at the foot of the mount, it got so frightened by us that it ran out of this world with a fetter fastened to it's feet, and has not returned to this very day. I rubbed my nose on the sward as a hen does, and went to see what had become of the oxen in the meantime: lo! the stock of my whip had taken root and become such a tall tree that it was as high as the big tower at Brassó[1] and the starlings had built their nests in it, and had so many young ones that you couldn't hear the clattering of the mill for their chirping.

Well, I was very much delighted, thinking that now I could catch a lot of young starlings; I knew how to climb well. I climbed the tree, and tried to put my hand into a hole but couldn't, so I tried my head, and that went in comfortably. I stuffed my breast full of starlings. When I tried to get out of the hole I could not; so I rushed home and fetched an adze, and cut myself out. I couldn't get down, as the tree was so thick and my head so giddy, so I called the miller to help me, but he, thinking that my complaint was hunger, sent me some miller-cake by his son, but I told him in a great rage that that was not what I wanted: so off he ran at once, and brought me a bushel of bran, handing it up on the end of a pale. I twisted the bran into a rope, so strong that it would bear a millstone, and I tried whether it would reach the ground, but it did not reach, so I doubled it up, then it not only reached, but trailed on the ground. I [Pg 88]began to glide down it, but a beetle aloft sawed it in two where it was tied to the bough, and down I dropped rope and all; but while I was falling to the ground, in the meantime, the young starlings in my breast got their feathers, took to their wings, and flew away with me. When we were flying over the river Olt, some women who were washing rags on the bank began to shout, "What the fiery thunderbolt is the boy doing that he flies so well? If he drops he will drop straight in the river and drown." I saw they were all staring at me, but from the chirping of the young starlings I couldn't clearly hear what they shouted: so I thought they were shouting that I should untie the waist-band of my shirt. I untied the waist-band of my shirt below the garter that tied my socks: with this the young starlings got out of my bosom all at once and all the wings I had flew away. Down I dropped into the middle of the river: with my splash the waters overflowed the banks and washed as far as the foot of the mountain: but when the waters flowed back into the bed of the river, (with the exception of a few drops that were lapped up by a thirsty shepherd-dog of Gidófalú) so many fish were left on the bank that they covered the whole place, from Málnás to Doboly and from Árkos to Angyalos and even the whole plain of Szépmezö. Well, there was a lot of fish! Twelve buffalo-carts were carting them away without interruption for a whole week, and the quantity didn't get less, you couldn't see that any had been taken away: but a stark naked gipsy brat came that way from Köröspatak, and he picked them up, put them into his shirt lap, and carried them all away.

I then remembered that they had not sent me here to play but to grind corn, so I started in the direction of where I had left the oxen to see what they were doing, and whether they were there still. I travelled for a long time till I got quite tired. I saw in a meadow a horse, and I thought I could easily get on it, and go where I wished to go, but it would not wait for me. I caught hold of its tail, turned it round, and so we stood face to face, and I said to it quite bumptiously: "Ho! stop, old nag. Don't be [Pg 89]so frisky." It understood the kind words and stopped dead, like a peg. I put the saddle on the grey and sat on the bay and started off on the chestnut; over a ditch and over a stile, so that the horse's feet did not touch the ground. In one place I passed a vineyard, and inside the hedge there was a lot of pretty ripe fruit. I stopped the grey, got down from the bay, and tied the chestnut to the paling. I tried to climb over the hedge, but couldn't, so I caught hold of my hair, and swung myself over. I began to shake the plum-tree, and walnuts dropped. I picked up the filberts and put them in my bosom. It was very hot, I was very thirsty, so that I nearly died of thirst. I saw that not very far away there were some reapers, and I asked, "Where can I get water here?" They shewed me a spring not far off. I went there, and found that it was frozen over. I tried in vain to break the ice with my heel, and then with a stone, but did not succeed, as the ice was a span thick; so I took the skull from my head and broke the ice with it easily. I scooped up water with it, and had a hearty drink. I went to the hedge and swung myself over by the hair into the road; then I untied the grey, got on the bay, and galloped off on the chestnut, over stile and ditch, so that my hair flew on the wind. In one place I passed two men. As I overtook them, they called out after me: "Where's your head, my boy?" I immediately felt my back, and lo! my head was not there; so I galloped back at a quick dog-trot to the spring. What did I see? My skull felt lonely without me, and had so much sense that as I forgot it there, it had made a neck, hands, waist, and feet, for itself out of the mud, and I caught it sliding on the ice. Well! I wasn't a bad hand at sliding myself, so I slid after it as fast as I could. But it knew better than I did, and so I couldn't possibly catch it. My good God! What could I do? I was very much frightened that I was really going to be left without a head but I remembered something, and thought to myself: "Never mind, skull, don't strain yourself, you can't outdo me." So I hurriedly made a greyhound out of mud, and set it after my skull. He [Pg 90]caught it in a jiffy, and brought it to me. I took it and put it on: I went to the hedge, and seizing myself by the hair, swung myself over the hedge: untied the grey, got on the bay, and galloped away on the chestnut, over a stile, and over a ditch, like a bird, till I came to the mill, where I found that my father had not had patience to wait for me, and so had set off in search of me; and, as he couldn't find me, began to bewail me, vociferating: "Oh! my soul! Oh! my son! Where have you gone? Oh! Oh! Why did I send you without anybody to take care of you? Oh! my soul! Oh! my son! Now all is over with you. You must have perished somewhere." As my father was always scolding me, and calling me bad names in my lifetime, I could never have believed that he were able to pity me so much. When I saw what was the matter with him, I called from a distance: "Console yourself, father, I am here, 'a bad hatchet never gets lost.'" It brought my poor old father's spirits back. We put the sacks full of flour on the cart and went home, and celebrated my father's wedding sumptuously. The bride was my mother, and I was the first who danced the bride's dance with her, and then the others had a turn, and when the wedding was over, all the guests went away and we were left at home by ourselves, and are alive at this date, if we are not dead. I was born one year after this, and I am the legitimate son of my father, and have grown up nicely, and have become a very clever lad.

[1]Cronstadt in Transylvania.

THE BAA-LAMBS.

There was once, somewhere or in some other place, I don't know where, over seven times seven countries, or even beyond them, a poor widow, and she had three unmarried sons who were so poor that one had always to go out to service. First the eldest went, and, as he [Pg 91]was going and going over seven times seven countries, and even beyond them, he met an old man, who accosted him, saying, "My younger brother, where are you going?" The lad answered, "My father, I am going to look for work." "And I am in need of a servant," the old man replied; so he engaged the lad on the spot to tend his baa-lambs. In the morning, as the lad went out with them, the old man told him not to drive them and not to guide them, but simply to go after them, as they would graze quietly if left to themselves. The lad started with the baa-lambs; first they came to a splendid meadow, he went in and trotted after them as his master had told him; then they came to a swift stream and the baa-lambs went over it, but the lad had not the courage to go into the water, but walked up and down the bank till evening, when the baa-lambs returned of their own accord, recrossed the water, and, as night had set in, he drove them home. "Well, my dear son," said his master, "tell me where you have been with the baa-lambs." "My dear father, I only followed after them. First of all they went into a large plain; after that we came to a great, swift stream; they got over the large sheet of water, but I remained on this side, as I did not dare to go into the deep water." As the poor lad finished his tale the master said, "Well, my dear son, I shall send you away, as I can see very well that you are not fit for service," and he sent him off without any pay. The lad went home, very much cast down. When he got home his two brothers asked him, "Well, dear brother, how did you get on in service?" "Hum, how did I get on, and what did I do? You'd better go yourselves and you will soon know." "Very well," they replied, and the second son went to look for service, met the same old man, and fared the same as his brother, and was sent home without anything. As he arrived home his younger brother met him and asked, "Well, dear brother, what sort of service did you get?" "Hum," replied he, "What sort of a place did I get? You had better go and then you also will know." "Very well," [Pg 92]replied the youngest, and he too went to try his luck. As he went along he met the same old man, and was engaged by him to tend his baa-lambs for a year; the old man told him, too, to walk after them, and not to leave them under any circumstances. Next morning the old man prepared the lad's bag, and let the baa-lambs out of the fold; they started off, and the lad followed them, step by step, till they came to a pretty, green plain: they walked over it, quietly grazing along as they went, till they came to the swift stream; the baa-lambs crossed it, and the lad followed them; but the moment he entered the water the swift current swept off his clothes and shrivelled his flesh, so that, when he got to the other side, he was only skin and bones; so soon as he reached the other bank the baa-lambs turned back and began to blow on him, and his body was at once fairer than it ever was before. The baa-lambs started off again till they came to a large meadow where the grass was so high that it was ready for the scythe, and still the cattle grazing on it were so ill-fed that a breath of wind would have blown them away; the baa-lambs went on to another meadow which was quite barren, and the cattle there had nothing to eat, yet they were as fat as butter; thence the baa-lambs went into a huge forest, and there, on every tree, was such a lamentation and crying and weeping as one could not conceive of; the lad looked to see what the meaning of the loud crying could be, and lo, on every bough there was a young sparrow, quite naked! and all were weeping and crying. From here the baa-lambs went sauntering on till they came to a vast garden; in this garden there were two dogs fighting, so that the foam ran from their mouths; still they could not harm each other. The baa-lambs went on further till they came to a great lake, and there the lad saw a woman in the lake, scooping with a spoon something from the water incessantly, and still she was not able to scoop the thing up. From there the baa-lambs went further, and, as they went, he saw a brook of beautiful, running water, clear like crystal, and, as he was very thirsty, he had half a mind to drink of it, but, thinking [Pg 93]that the spring-head was very much better, he went there, and saw that the water was bubbling out of the mouth of a rotting dead dog, which so frightened him that he did not taste a drop. From there the baa-lambs went into another garden, which was so wonderfully pretty that human eye had never seen the like before. Flowers of every kind were blooming, but the baa-lambs left them untouched, only eating the green grass, and, as they ate, he sat down under the shade of a beautiful flowering tree in order to partake of some food, when suddenly he saw that a beautiful white pigeon was fluttering about in front of him; he took his small blunderbuss, which he had with him, and shot at the pigeon, knocking off a feather, but the pigeon flew away; he picked up the feather and put it in his bag. From thence the baa-lambs started off home, the lad following them. When they arrived, the old man asked: "Well, my son, and how did the baa-lambs go?" "They went very well," answered the lad, "I had no trouble with them. I had merely to walk after them." As he said this, the old man asked him: "Well, my son, tell me where you have been with the baa-lambs." Then he told him that the baa-lambs first went into a pretty green plain, then they went through a swift stream; and he told him all—where he had been with them and so on. When he had finished his tale, the old man said: "My dear son, you see that wonderful pretty green plain where you went first with the baa-lambs represents your youth up to this day. The water through which you went is the water of life which washes away sin: that it washed away all your clothes and dried up your flesh means that it washes away all your previous sins: that on the other shore, upon the baa-lambs breathing on you, your body became purer, means that the holy faith, by the water of life, has penetrated all over your soul, and you have become purified from your sins, regenerate in all; the baa-lambs who breathed upon you are angels, and your good and pious teachers. The ill-fed cattle amidst the luxuriant grass means [Pg 94]that the avaricious, whilst surrounded by plenty, even begrudge themselves food; they will be misers even in the other world: they will have plenty to eat and drink, they will partake of both, and still will be eternally hungry and thirsty. Those beasts who fed in the barren field, and were so fat, means that those who have given from their little to the poor in this world, and have not chastised their bodies with hunger and thirst, will feed heartily in the other world out of little food, and will never know hunger or thirst. That the young birds cried so mournfully in the woods, my son, means that those mothers in this world who do not have their children baptised, but have them buried without, will, in the other world, eternally weep and cry. The two dogs who fought so in the garden means that those relatives who in this world fight and squabble over property will eternally fight in the other world, and never come to terms. That woman who was fishing in a lake so busily for something with a spoon, and could not catch it, is he who in this world adulterates milk with water and sells it in this state to others; he will in the other world continually be in a lake, and will eternally fish about with a spoon, in order to fish the milk out of the water, and will never succeed. That you saw a pretty clear brook and did not drink of it, but went to the spring where the water flowed out of the mouth of a dead dog, that means, my dear son, the beautiful sermons of the clergy and their holy prayers. The dead dog from whose mouth the clear water flowed represents the priests who preach pious and wise lessons, but never keep them themselves. The garden into which you went is Heaven. Those who live without sin in this world will come into such a beautiful garden in the other world. But now, my dear son, can you show me some proof that you have really been in that garden?"

The lad quickly took from his bag the white pigeon's feather, and handed it to him, saying, "Look here, my old father, I shot this from a white pigeon there." The old man took the pigeon's feather, and said to him, "You see, my son, I was that white [Pg 95]pigeon, and I have been following you all the journey through, and always kept watch over you, to see what you did. So God also follows man unknown to him, to see what he does. The feather you shot away was one of my fingers; look here, I have not got it!" and as he looked he saw that the little finger was missing from the old man's hand; with this, the old man placed the feather there, blew upon it, and the finger was once more all right. In the meantime the year came to an end—for if I may mention it here the year consisted of but three days then—so the old man said to the lad: "Well, my son, the year is now ended; hand me over the bag, and then you can go. But first let me ask you would you rather have heaven, or so much gold as you can carry home?" To this the lad replied that he did not wish for gold, but only desired to be able to go to heaven. Thereupon the old man at once filled a sack with gold for him, lifted it upon the lad's back, and sent him home. The lad thanked the old man for his present, betook himself home with his sack of gold, and became such a rich farmer with six oxen that not in the whole village, nay, not even in the whole neighbourhood, was there such a one who came near him. He also took to himself a suitable girl as his wife, who was as pretty as a flower; he is alive to this very day, if he has not died since. May he be your guest to-morrow!

FAIRY ELIZABETH.

There was once somewhere, I don't know where, beyond seven times seven countries, and even beyond them, a poor man who had a wife and three children. They were awfully poor. One day the eldest son said: "Dear mother, bake me some ash-cake and let me go into [Pg 96]service." His mother at once baked the cake, and the lad started, and went on and on till he came to a high snow-clad mountain, where he met a grey-haired man and greeted him: "May the Lord bless you, my good old father." "The Lord bless you, my son. What are you after?" asked the old man. "I am going out to service, if the Lord will help me to some place." "Well, then, come to me," said the old man, "I will engage you." So they went to the house of the grey-haired old man, and the very next day they went out ploughing but they only ploughed up some grass-land, and sowed it with seed. Now let me tell you, that the old man promised him a bushel of seed for sowing. Two days passed, and at dawn of the third day the old man said: "Well, my son, to-day you can go out ploughing for yourself; get the plough ready, yoke the oxen in, and in the meantime I will get the bushel of wheat I promised." So the lad put the oxen to the plough and the old man got the bushel of wheat and placed it on the plough. They started, the old man accompanying him. Just at the end of the village he said to the lad: "Well, my son, can you see that place yonder covered with shrubs? Go there, and plough up as much of it for yourself as you think will be enough for the bushel of wheat." The lad went, but was quite alarmed at the sight of the shrubs, and at once lost heart. "How could he plough there? Why, by the time he had grubbed up the shrubs alone it would be night." So he ran off home, and left the plough there, and the oxen then returned of their own accord to the old man's place—if I may interrupt myself, they were the oxen of a fairy. When the lad arrived at his father's house, his other brothers asked him: "What sort of a place have you found?" "What sort of a place!" replied he, "go yourself, and you will soon find out." The middle son set out, and just as he was going over the snow-clad mountain he met the old man, who engaged him on the spot as his servant, and promised him a bushel of wheat, as he had done before. They went to the old man's home, and he [Pg 97]fared just as his elder brother had done. At dawn on the third day, when he had to plough for himself, he got frightened at the sight of the vast number of shrubs, which no human being could have ploughed up in the stated time. So he went home too, and on his way he met his younger brother, who asked him: "What sort of a place have you found, my dear elder brother?" "What sort of a place had I? Get up out of the ashes, and go yourself, and you will soon find out." Now let me tell you that this boy was continually sitting among the ashes. He was a lazy, ne'er-do-weel fellow; but now he got up, and shook the ashes from him and said: "Well, my mother, bake me a cake also: as my brothers have tried their fortune let me try mine." But his brothers said: "Oh! you ash-pan! Supposing you were required to do nothing else but eat, you would not be good enough even for that." But still he insisted, that his mother should bake something for him. So his mother set to work and baked him a cake of some inferior bran, and with this he set out. As he went over the boundless snow-clad mountain, in the midst of it he met the old man and greeted him: "The Lord bless you, my old father!" "The Lord bless you, my son! Where are you going?" "I am going out to service, if I can find an employer." "Well, you are the very man I want; I am in search of a servant." And he engaged him on the spot, promising to make him a present of a bushel of wheat for sowing. They went home together, and after they had ploughed together for two days, the lad set out on the third day to plough up the land allotted to him for his own use: while the youngster was putting the oxen to the plough the old man got the wheat and placed it on the plough. On the dyke there was a big dog, who always lay there quietly; but this time he got up, and started off in front of him. The old man also accompanied him as far as the end of the village, from whence he showed him where to go ploughing. The youngster went on with the plough, and soon saw that he was not able to [Pg 98]plough a single furrow, on account of the thick bushes. After considering what to do, he bethought himself, and took his sharp hatchet and began to cut down a vast quantity of shrubs and thorns, the dog carrying them all into a heap. Seeing that he had cut enough, he began to plough. The two oxen commenced to drag the plough and cut up the roots in a manner never seen before. After he had turned three times, he looked round and said: "Well, I'm not going to plough any more, but will begin to sow, so that I may see how much seed I've got." He sowed the seed, and noticed that it was just sufficient, and therefore he had to plough no more. In great joy he set the plough straight and went home. The old man met him and said: "Well, my son, thanks to the Lord, you have now finished your year, and in God's name I will let you go. I do not intend to engage any more servants." Before I forget to tell you, I may mention it here, that the year had three days then. So the lad went home, and his brothers asked him: "Well, then, what sort of a place have you found?" "Well, I believe I've served my master as well as you did."

One day, a year after, he went into the field to look at his wheat crop. There he saw an old woman reaping some young wheat, so he went home and said to his father: "Well, my father, do you know what we have to do? let's go reaping." "Where, my son?" "Well, father, for my last year's service I had a bushel of wheat given to me for sowing, it has got ripe by this time, so let us go and reap it." So all four (his father, his two brothers, and himself) went; when they came to the spot they saw that it was a magnificent crop, a mass of golden ears from root to top, ready and ripe; so they all started to work and cut down every head.

They made three stacks of it, each stack having twenty-six sheaves. "Well my son," said the father, "there are three stacks here and there are three of you to guard them, so while I go home to hire a cart, guard them well, so that the birds may not carry [Pg 99]away a single stem." The father went home, and the three sat down (one at the foot of each stack) to watch them, but the youngest was the most anxious, as it was his own, and ran to and fro continually to prevent his brothers falling asleep. Just as he had awakened them and was going back to his own stack he saw a woodpecker dragging away, by jerks, a golden ear along the ground, so he ran after it in order to get it back, but just as he was on the point of catching it the woodpecker flew off further and further, and enticed him, until at last it got him into the very midst of the boundless snow-clad mountains. All of a sudden the youngster discovered where he was, and that it was getting dusk. "Where was he to go? and what was he to do?" So he thought he would go back to the stacks, but as he had kept his eye on the woodpecker and the wheat-ear, he had taken no notice of the surroundings, and knew not which way he had come. So he determined to climb the highest tree and look round from there: he looked about and found the highest tree, climbed it, and looked East but saw nought, South and saw nought: North, and far, very far away he saw a light as big as a candle; so he came down, and started off in the direction in which he had seen the light and went straight over ditches, woods, rocks, and fields till at last he came to a large plain, and there he found the fire which he had seen before, and lo! it was such a heap of burning wood that the flames nearly reached heaven: he approached it and when he drew near the burning heap he saw that a man was lying curled round the fire, his head resting on his feet, and that he was covered with a large cloak: then thought the lad, "Shall I lie down inside or outside of the circle formed by the body of the man?" If he lay outside he would catch cold; if he lay inside he would be scorched, he thought; so he crept into the sleeve of the cloak, and there fell asleep. In the morning when the sun arose, the big man awoke, he yawned wide, and got up from the fire; as he rose the youngster dropt out of his sleeve on to the ground: the giant [Pg 100]looked at him (because I forgot to tell you it wasn't a man, it was a giant), and was very much pleased at the sight; he quickly picked him up, took him into his arms, and carried him into his palace, (and even there put him into the best room) and put him to bed, covered him up well, and crept out of the room on tiptoe lest he should wake him. When he heard that the youngster was awake, he called to him through the open door, "Don't be afraid, my dear son, I am a big man it is true, but notwithstanding I will be to thee like thy father, in thy father's place; like thy mother, in thy mother's place." With this he entered the room, and the poor lad stared into the giant's eyes, as if he were looking up to the sky. Suddenly the giant asked him how he got there, and the lad told him the whole tale. "Well, my dear little son, I will give you everything that your heart can think of, or your mouth name, I will fulfil your every wish, only don't worry yourself;" and he had all sorts of splendid clothes made for him, and kept him on costly food; and this lasted till the lad became twenty years of age, when one day the lad became very sad, and his giant father asked him, "Well, my dear son, tell me why you are so sad, I will do all your heart can think of, or your mouth name; but do tell me what's the matter with you?" So the lad said, after hesitation, "Well! well! well! my dear father, I am so sad because the time has come when I ought to get married, and there's nobody here to get married to." "Oh! my son, don't worry yourself over that, such a lad as you has but to wish and you will find plenty of womankind, the very prettiest of them, ready to have you; you will but have to choose the one your heart loves best." So saying he called the lad before the gate and said: "Well, my son, you can see that great white lake yonder: go there at noon prompt and hide yourself under a tree, for every noon three lovely fairy girls come there who are as handsome as handsome can be: you*can* look at the sun, but you can't look at them! They will come disguised [Pg 101]as pigeons, and when they arrive on the bank they will turn somersaults, and at once become girls: they will then undress, and lay their dresses on the bank: you must then glide up, and steal the dress of the one your heart loves best, and run away home with it, but be careful not to look back, however they may shout: because if you do, believe me, she will catch you, box your ears, and take her clothes from you."

So he went to the lake and hid himself under an oak, and all at once three white pigeons came flying, their wings flapping loudly as they came, they settled down on the bank, and went to take a bath. The lad wasn't slow to leave his hiding-place, and pick up the dress of the eldest fairy girl and run away with it; but she noticed it at once, rushed out of the lake, and ran after him, shouting: "Stop! sweet love of my heart. Look at me; see how beautiful my skin is; how pretty my breasts are. I'm yours, and you're mine!" So he looked round, and the fairy snatched her dress away in a moment, slapped his face, and returned to the others in the lake. Poor lad! he was very sad, and went back and told his giant father all that had happened, and his giant father answered, "Well; wasn't I right? Didn't I tell you not to look back? But don't fret; three in number are the divine truths, and three times also will you have to try. There are two yet left, go again to-morrow at noon. Take care you don't look back, or pick up the same dress that you picked up yesterday, because, believe me, if you do, there will be the mischief to pay." So he went early next day (he couldn't wait till noon) and hid himself under a tree, when all of a sudden the pigeons appeared, turned somersaults, and became three beautiful fairy girls. They undressed, laid their dresses on the bank, and went into the lake; in short, the lad fared with the second as with the first—he couldn't resist the temptation of looking back when the beautiful fairy kept imploring him, as the sweet love of her heart, to gaze at her beautiful skin and breasts. He looked back, was slapped in the face as before, and lost the fairy dress. He went [Pg 102]home again, very sad, to his giant father, and told him how he had fared; and the giant said in reply: "Never mind, don't bother yourself, my son, three are the divine truths; there is one more left for you; you can try again to-morrow, but only be very careful not to look back this time." Next day he couldn't wait till noon, but went and hid himself under the oak very early, and had to wait a long, long time. At last the white pigeons arrived, turned somersaults as before, and put their dresses on the bank, whilst they themselves went into the lake. Out he rushed from his hiding-place, snatched up the youngest's dress, and ran away with it. But the fairy noticed that her dress was gone, and rushed out of the lake after him like a hurricane, calling out incessantly: "Stop! sweet love of my heart, look how beautifully white my skin is! See how beautifully white are my breasts. I am yours, and you are mine." But the lad only ran faster than ever, and never looked behind once, but ran straight home to his giant father, and told him that he had got the dress this time. "Well, my dear son," said he, "didn't I tell you not to worry yourself in the least, and that I would do all for you that your heart could desire, or your mouth name?" Once after this the lad was very sad again, so his giant father asked him: "Well, my son, what's the matter this time, that you are so sad?" "Well, my dear father, because we have only got a dress, and that is not enough for a wedding. What's the use of it? What can I do with it?" "Never mind, don't worry about that. Go into the inside closet, and on a shelf you will find a walnut, bring it here." So the lad went and fetched the nut, and the giant split it neatly in two, took out the kernel, folded up the dress (and I may mention it here the dress consisted of only one piece), put it inside the nut-shell, fitted the two halves together, and said to the lad: "Well, my son, let me have your waistcoat, so that I may sew this nut into the pocket; and be careful that no one opens it, neither thy father, nor thy mother, nor any one in this [Pg 103]world, because should any one open it your life will be made wretched; you will be an outcast."

With this, the giant sewed the nut into the pocket, and put the waistcoat on him. As they finished this, they heard a great clamping noise, and a chinking (as of coins) outside. So the giant bade him to look out of the window, and what did he see? He saw that in the courtyard there was a lovely girl sitting in a carriage drawn by six horses, and about her beautiful maids and outriders, and the giant said, "You see, it is Fairy Elizabeth, your ladylove." So they went out at once, and helped Fairy Elizabeth out of her carriage, then she ordered the carriage and horses to go back, at once, to where they had come from, and in a moment they disappeared, and there was no trace of them left. They then went into the house, but the giant remained outside, and he drew in the dust figures of a priest, and a cantor, and guests, and they appeared at once. All went into the house, and the young folks got wed, and a great wedding feast was celebrated. There was the bridegroom's best man, and the groom's men, and the bride's duenna, and all her bridesmaids, and the wedding feast lasted three full days. They ate, drank, and enjoyed themselves, and when all was over the young couple lived together in quiet happiness. Once more, however, the lad became very sad, and the giant asked him: "Well, my dear son, why are you sad again? You know that I will do all your heart can desire, or your mouth name." "Well, my dear father," replied he, "how can I help being sad; it is true we live together happily, but who knows how my father and mother and brothers and sisters are at home? I should like to go to see them."

"Well, my dear son," said the giant, "I will let you go; you two go home, and you will find your relations keeping the third anniversary of your death: they have gathered in all the golden corn, and become so rich that they are now the greatest farmers in the village: each of your brothers have their own home and they have become great men (six-ox farmers) and have a whole flock of [Pg 104]sheep." So the giant went outside, and drew in the dust the figures of horses and carriage, coachman, footmen, outriders, and court damsels, and they at once appeared; the young couple sat in the carriage, and the giant told the lad if ought happened to him he had only to think of one of these horses, and it would at once bring him back here. With this they started, and they arrived at home and, saw that the courtyard of his father's house was full of tables, crowded with people sitting round them, but no one spoke a word; they all were speechless so that you could not even hear a whisper. The couple got out of the carriage, in front of the gate, walked into the yard, and met an old man; it happened to be his father. "May the Lord give you a good day, Sir!" said he; and the old man replied, "May the Lord bless you also, my lord!" "Well sir," asked the young man, "what is the meaning of all this feasting that I see, all this eating and drinking, and yet no one speaks a word; is it a marriage or a funeral feast?" "My lord, it is a burial feast," replied the old man; "I had three sons, one was lost, and to-day we celebrate the third anniversary of his death." "Would you recognise your son if he appeared?" Upon hearing this his mother came forward and said, "To be sure, my dearest and sweetest lord, because there is a mark under his left armpit." With this the lad pulled up his sleeve and showed the mark, and they at once recognised him as their lost son; the funeral feast, thereupon, was at once changed into a grand wedding festival. Then the lad called out to the carriage and horses "Go back where you have come from," and in a moment there was not a trace of them left. His father at once sent for the priest and the verger and they went through all the ceremonies again, and whether the giant had celebrated them or not, certainly the father did: the wedding feast was such a one as had never been seen before! When they rose from the table they began the bride's dance: in the first place they handed the bride to the cleverest dancer, and whether he danced or not, most certainly the bride did: as she danced her feet never touched the ground, and everyone who was there looked at the bride only, and all whispered to each other, [Pg 105]that no man had ever seen such a sight in all his life. When the bride heard this she said, "Hum, whether I dance now or whether I don't, I could dance much better if anyone would return to me the dress I wore in my maiden days." Whereupon they whispered to each other, "Where can that dress be?" When the bride heard this she said, "Well, my souls, it is in a nut-shell, sewn into my husband's waistcoat pocket, but no one will ever be able to get it." "I can get it for you," said her mother-in-law, "because I will give my son a sleeping-draught in wine and he will go to sleep," and so she did, and the lad fell on the bed fast asleep; his mother then got the nut from his pocket and gave it to her daughter-in-law, who at once opened it, took the dress out, put it on, and danced so beautifully, that, whether she danced the *first* time or not, she certainly danced this time; you could not imagine anything so graceful. But, as it was so hot in the house, the windows were left open, and Fairy Elizabeth turned a somersault, became a white pigeon, and flew out of the window. Outside there was a pear tree, and she settled upon the top of it, the people looking on in wonder and astonishment; then she called out that she wanted to see her husband as she wished to say a word or two to him, but the sleeping draught had not yet lost its power, and they could not wake him, so they carried him out in a sheet and put him under the tree and the pigeon dropped a tear on his face; in a minute he awoke. "Can you hear me, sweet love of my heart?" asked the pigeon, "if you ever want to meet me seek for me in the town of Johara, in the country of Black Sorrow," with this she spread her wings and flew away. Her husband gazed after her for a while and then became so grieved that his heart nearly broke. What was he to do now? He took leave of all and went and hid himself. When he got outside of the gate he suddenly remembered what the giant had told him about calling to memory one of the horses; he no sooner did so than it appeared all ready saddled; he jumped upon it and thought he would like to be at [Pg 106]the giant's gate. In a moment he was there and the giant came out to meet him. "Well, my dear son, didn't I tell you not to give that nut to anyone?" The poor lad replied, in great sorrow, "Well, my dear father, what am I to do now?" "Well, what did Fairy Elizabeth say when she took leave of you?" "She said that if ever I wished to meet her again I was to go to the town of Johara, in the country of Black Sorrow." "Alas, my son!" said the giant, "I have never even heard the name, so how could I direct you there? Be still, and come and live with me, and get on as well as you can." But the poor lad said that he would go, and he must go, in search of his wife as far as his eye could see. "Well, if you wish to go, there are two more children of my parents left, an elder brother and an elder sister. Take this; here's a mace. We three children couldn't divide it amongst us, so it was left with me. They will know by this that I have sent you; go first to my elder brother, he is the king of all creeping things; perhaps he may be able to help you." With this he drew in the dust the figure of a colt three years old, and bade him sit on it, filled his bag with provisions, and recommended him to the Lord. The lad went on and on, over seven times seven countries, and even beyond them; he went on till the colt got so old that it lost all its teeth; at last he arrived at the residence of the king of all creeping things, went in, and greeted him, "May the Lord give you a good day, my dear father!" And the old man replied, "The Lord has brought you, my son. What is your errand?" And he replied, "I want to go to the country of Black Sorrow, into the town of Johara if ever I can find it." "Who are you?" asked the old man. With this he showed him the mace, and the king at once recognised it and said, "Ah, my dear son, I never heard the name of that town. I wish you had come last night, because all my animals were here to greet me. But stay, I will call them together again to-morrow morning, and we shall then see whether they can give us any information." Next morning the old man got up very early, took a whistle and blew it three times, and, in the twinkling [Pg 107]of an eye all the creeping things that existed in the world came forward. He asked them, one by one, whether they knew aught of the town of Johara in the country of Black Sorrow. But they all answered that they had never seen it, and never even heard its name. So the poor lad was very sad, and did not know what to do. He went outside to saddle his horse, but the poor brute had died of old age. So the old man at once drew another in the dust, and it was again a colt three years old. He saddled it for him, filled his bag with provisions, and gave him directions where to find his elder sister. With this the lad started off, and went over seven times seven countries, and even beyond them, till at last, very late, he arrived at the elder sister's of the giant and greeted her. She returned it; and asked him, "What is your errand?" he replied that he was going to the town of Johara in the country of Black Sorrow. "Well, my son," said the old woman, "and who has sent you to me?" "Don't you know this mace?" and she recognised it at once, and said, "Alas! my dear son, I am very pleased to see you, but I cannot direct you, because I never even heard of the place. Why did you not come last night, as all the animals were here then. But as my brother has sent you, I will call them all together again to-night, and perhaps they will be able to tell you something." With this, he went out to put his horse in the stable, and found that it had grown so old that it hadn't a single tooth left; he himself, too, was shrivelled up with age, like a piece of bacon rind, and his hair was like snow. At eve the old woman said to him, "Lie down in this bed!" when he lay down she put a heavy millstone upon him; she then took a whip, went outside the door, and cracked it. It boomed like a gun and the poor man inside was so startled that he lifted up the millstone quite a span high. "Don't be afraid, my son," called out the old woman, "I'm only going to crack it twice more," and she cracked it again; whether it sounded the first time or not, it certainly did this time, so that the poor man inside lifted the millstone quite a yard high, and [Pg 108]called out to the old woman not to crack that whip again, or he should certainly die on the spot. But she cracked it again, notwithstanding, and it sounded so loud, that whether the first two sounded or not, this time it sounded so loud that the poor man kicked the millstone right up to the ceiling. After that the old woman went in and said to him, "You can get up now, as I am not going to crack my whip any more." So he got up at once, and she went and opened the window, and left the door wide open too. At once it became quite dark, the animals came in such clouds that they quite obscured the sunlight; she let them in one by one through the window, and read out the name of each one of them from a list, and asked them if they knew where the country of Black Sorrow was, but nobody knew it; so she dismissed them and shut the window and door. The poor man was very sad now; he didn't know what to do next or where he was to go. "There is nothing more to be done," said the old woman; "but I will give you a colt, and fill your bag full of provisions, and in heaven's name go back where you have come from." They were still consulting when somebody knocked at the window and the old woman called out, "Who's that?" "It is I, my dear queen," replied a bird; and she began to scold it for being so late; but still she let it in, hoping that it might tell them something. Lo! it was a lame woodpecker. "Why are you so late?" she demanded, and the bird replied that it was because it had such a bad foot. "Where did you get your leg broken?" inquired the old woman. "In Johara, in the country of Black Sorrow." "You are just the one we want," said the old woman; "I command you to take this man on your back without delay and to carry him to the very town where you have come from." The woodpecker began to make excuses and said that it would rather not go there lest they should break the other leg also; but the old woman stamped with her foot, and so it was obliged to obey and at once set off with the man on its back, whose third horse had already died; on they went over seven times seven countries, and even beyond them, till they [Pg 109]came to a very high mountain, so high that it reached to heaven.

"Now then," said the woodpecker, "you had better get down here, as we cannot get over this." "Well, but," said the poor man, "how did *you* get over it?" "I? Through a hole." "Well then, take me also through a hole." Then the woodpecker began to make excuses, that it could not take him, first urging this reason and then that; so the poor man got angry with the woodpecker, and began to dig his spurs into the bird's ribs saying, "Go on, you must take me, and don't talk so much; it was you who stole the golden wheat-ear from my stack." So what could the poor woodpecker do but carry him. They arrived in the country of Black Sorrow, and stopped in the very town of Johara. Then he sent the woodpecker away, and went straight into the palace where Fairy Elizabeth lived. As he entered Fairy Elizabeth sat on a golden sofa; he greeted her, and told her he had come to claim her as his wife. "Is that why you have come?" replied she. "Surely you don't expect me to be *your* wife; an old bent, shrivelled-up man like you. I will give you meat and drink, and then in heaven's name go back to where you have come from." Hearing this the poor man became very sad and didn't know what to do, and began to cry bitterly; but in the meantime (not letting him know) Fairy Elizabeth had ordered her maids to go out at once and gather all sorts of rejuvenating plants, and to bring some youth-giving water, and to prepare a bath for him as quickly as possible. Then she turned to the old man again, and, in order to chaff him, said, "How can you wish a beautiful young girl like me to marry such an ugly old man as you? Be quick, eat, drink, and go back to where you have come from." In his sorrow the poor man's heart was nearly broken, when all at once Fairy Elizabeth said to him, "Well, dearest love of my youth, so that you may not say that I am ungrateful to you for having taken the trouble to come to me, and made all this long journey for me, I will [Pg 110]give you a bath." She motioned to the maids, they at once seized him, undressed him, and put him into the tub; in a moment he was a young man again a hundred times handsomer than he was in his youth; and while they were bathing him they brought from a shop numerous costly dresses and clothed him with them and took him to Fairy Elizabeth; man and wife embraced and kissed each other again and again, and once more celebrated a grand marriage festival, going through all the ceremonies again; after all this was over they got into a carriage drawn by six horses, and went to live with the giant, their father, but they never went again, not even once, to the place where he had been betrayed. The giant received them with great joy, and they are still alive to this-day, if they haven't died since. May they be your guests to-morrow!

THE THREE PRINCES.

There was once, I don't know where, beyond seven times seven countries, and at a cock's crow even beyond them—an immense, tall, quivering poplar tree. This tree had seven times seventy-seven branches; on each branch there were seven times seventy-seven crow-nests, and in each nest seven times seventy-seven young crows. May those who don't listen attentively to my tale, or who doze, have their eyes pecked out by all those young crows; and those who listen with attention to my tale will never behold the land of the Lord! There was once, I don't know where, a king who had three sons who were so much like each other that not even their mother could distinguish them from each other. The king sent his three sons wandering; the three princes went, and went, and, on the third day, they arrived at a vast forest, where [Pg 111]they first met a she-wolf with three whelps. "What are you doing here, princes, where not even the birds ever come?" asked the wolf, "you can go no further, because I and my whelps will tear you in pieces." "Don't harm us, wolf!" said the princes, "but rather, let's have your whelps to go as our servants." "I *will* tear you to pieces," howled the wolf, and attacked them; but the princes overcame the wolf, and took the three whelps with them. They went and went further into the vast forest and met a bear with three cubs, the next day. "What are you doing here, princes, where not even a bird comes?" asked the bear; "you can go no further, because I and my cubs will tear you in pieces." "Don't harm us, bear," said the princes, "but rather let's have your three cubs to come as our servants." "I *will* tear you in pieces," roared the bear, and attacked them, but the princes overcame the bear, and took the three cubs with them. Again they went into the vast forest, and met a lioness and her three cubs, on the third day. "What are you doing here, princes, where not even a bird comes? you can go no further, because I and my cubs will tear you in pieces." "Don't harm us, lioness," said the princes, "but let's have your three cubs to come as our servants." "I *will*tear you in pieces," roared the lioness, and attacked them, but the princes overcame the lioness, and took the three cubs as their servants: and thus each prince had three servants, a lion, a bear, and a wolf. At last they reached the outskirts of the vast forest, where the road divided into three, under a tree, and here the eldest said, "Let us stick our knives into the tree, and each start in a different direction; in a year hence we will be back again, and whosoever's knife is covered with blood, he is in danger, and the others must go in search of him." "Agreed," said the others, and, sticking their knives into the tree, started off in different directions.

After long wanderings the eldest came to a town which was wholly covered with black cloth, and here he took lodgings with an old woman. "Why is this town hung with black?" asked [Pg 112]the prince. "Alas, we live in great danger here!" said the old woman, "in the lake near the town lives the dragon with seven heads, who vomits fire, and to him we have to give a virgin every week, and to-morrow it is the king's daughter's turn, and she has to go, and this is the reason why our town is covered with black." "And is there no man who can help?" inquired the prince. "We have not found one yet," said the old woman, "although our king has promised his daughter, and after his death his realm, to the one who kills the dragon." The prince did not say another word, but took a rest and, afterwards, went towards the lake, and as he passed the royal palace he saw the princess in the window weeping. The royal princess was so beautiful that even the sun stopped before the window, in his course, to admire her beauty. At last he reached the lake, and could already hear, even at a distance, the dragon with seven heads roaring, so loudly that the ground trembled. "How dare you approach me? You must die, even had you seven souls!" roared the dragon, but instead of an answer the prince threw his mace at him, with such force that it smashed one of his heads on the spot, thereupon he attacked him with his sword, and also set his dogs at him, and while he cut the dragon's heads off one by one, his servants bit him to pieces, and thus killed the dragon, whose blood formed a brook seven miles long. After this he drew a tooth out of each head of the dragon and put them into his sabretache, and, as he was very tired, he lay down amongst the bulrushes and went fast asleep with his dogs. The Red Knight was watching the whole light from amongst the bulrushes, and, seeing that the prince was asleep, he crept to him and killed him, and quartered him, so that he might not revive, and, picking up the dragon's seven heads, went off towards the town. As soon as the Red Knight had gone the three dogs woke, and, seeing that their master had been murdered, began to howl in their sorrow. "If we only had a rope, so that we could tie him together. I know of a weed which would bring him [Pg 113]to life again," said the wolf. "If we only knew how to tie him together, I would soon get a rope," said the lion. "I would tie him together if I had a rope," said the bear; whereupon the lion ran to the town, the wolf went in search of the weed, and the bear remained behind to guard his master's body. The lion rushed into a ropemaker's and roared, "Give me a rope, or I will tear you in pieces." The ropemaker, in his fright, produced all the rope he had, and the lion rushed off with a coil. In the meantime the wolf also returned with the weed, and the bear tied the prince's body together, and the wolf anointed him. When, all at once, the prince woke, and, rubbing his eyes, stood up. "Well, I have slept a long time," said the prince, and as he saw that the sun was setting he returned to the town with his servants, and, as he again passed in front of the royal palace, he saw the princess once more, who looked at him, smiling this time. The prince again took his night's lodging with the old woman, and, as he got up next morning, the whole town was covered with red cloth. "Why is the whole town covered with red, now?" asked the prince. "Because the Red Knight killed the dragon, and saved the royal princess, and he is to be married to her to-day," replied the old woman. The prince thereupon went into the palace, into which crowds of people were streaming. The king was just leading the Red Knight to his daughter, and said, "Here, my daughter, this is the hero who killed the dragon, and only the hoe and the spade will separate him from you from this day." "My royal father," said the princess, "that isn't the man that killed the dragon, and therefore I cannot be his wife." "He did kill him," shouted the king, "and, in proof of it, he brought the dragon's seven heads with him, and therefore you have to be his wife, according to my promise." And there was a great feast after this, but the princess sat crying at the table, and the prince went home very downcast. "Give me some food, master, I'm hungry," said the wolf, when his master came home. "Go to the king and get some food from his table," and the [Pg 114]wolf went. The Red Knight sat on seven red pillows, between the king and his daughter, but when he saw the wolf enter, in his fright a pillow dropped from under him, and the wolf took a full dish, and went away, and told his master what had happened. "Give me some food, master. I'm hungry too," said the bear; and his master sent him also to the palace, and as he entered the Red Knight in his fright again dropped a pillow from under him. When the bear arrived at home with the food, he told this to his master. And as the lion got hungry too, he had to go for his food; and this time the Red Knight dropped a third pillow, and could hardly be seen above the table. Now the prince went to the palace himself, and as he entered every one of the pillows dropped from under the Red Knight in his fright. "Majesty," said the prince, "do you believe that the Red Knight has killed the dragon with seven heads?" "Yes," answered the king, "and he brought the seven heads with him, they are here." "But look, majesty, whether there is anything missing out of every head." The king examined the dragon's heads, and exclaimed in astonishment: "Upon my word there is a tooth missing from every head." "Quite so," said the prince, "and the seven dragon teeth are here," and, taking them from his sabretache, he handed the teeth to the king. "Your Majesty, if the Red Knight has killed the dragon, how could I have obtained the teeth?" "What's the meaning of this?" inquired the king, in anger, of the Red Knight; "who killed the dragon?" "Pardon!" implored the knight. In his fear he confessed all, and the king had him horsewhipped out of the palace, and sent the dogs after him.

He bade the prince sit down at once by the side of his daughter, as her bridegroom; and in joyful commemoration of the event they celebrated such a wedding that the yellow juice flowed from Henczida to Bonczida. And the prince and princess lived happily afterwards as man and wife.

However, it happened once that as the prince went hunting with [Pg 115]his three servants, and after a long walk strolled into the wood, he became tired and hungry; so he made a fire under a tree, and sat down at it, and fried some bacon; when suddenly he heard some one call out with a trembling voice in the tree: "Oh! how cold I am." The prince looked up, and saw an old woman on the top of the tree shivering. "Come down, old mother," said he. But the old woman said, still shivering with cold, "I'm afraid to come down, because your dogs will kill me; but if you will strike them with this rod, which I throw down to you, they will not touch me." And the good prince, never thinking that the old woman was a witch, struck his servants with the rod, who, without him noticing it, turned into stone. Seeing this, the old woman came down from the tree, and, having prepared a branch as a spit, she caught a toad. She drew it on the spit, and held it to the fire, close to the bacon; and when the prince remonstrated and tried to drive the old woman away, she threw the toad into his face, whereupon the prince fainted. As his servants could not assist him, the witch killed him, cut him up in pieces, salted him, and put him into a cask. The princess was waiting for her husband in great sorrow; but days passed, and still he did not come, and the poor princess bewailed him day and night.

In the meantime, the second prince returned to the tree in which they had stuck their knives; and, finding that his elder brother's knife was covered with blood, started in search of him. When he came to the town, it was again covered with black. He also took lodgings for the night with the old woman, and on inquiring she told him the whole story of the first prince, and also informed him that the town was draped in black because the prince was lost while hunting. The second prince at once came to the conclusion that it could be no one else but his elder brother, and went to the palace. The princess, mistaking him for her husband in her joy, threw her arms round his neck. "Charming princess, I am not your husband," said the prince, "but your husband's younger brother." The princess, however, would not believe him, as she [Pg 116]could not imagine how one man could so resemble another; therefore she chatted with him the whole day, as if with her husband, and, night having set in, he had to get into the same bed with her. The prince, however, placed his unsheathed sword between himself and his sister-in-law, saying: "If you touch me, this sword will at once cut off your hand." The princess was very sorry on hearing this, but, in order to try, she threw her handkerchief over the prince, and the sword cut it in two at once, whereupon the princess burst out crying, and cried the whole night. Next morning the prince went out in search of his brother, and went out hunting in the same wood where he had heard his brother was lost. But, unfortunately, he met the witch, and was treated in the same way as his brother. She killed and salted him also.

After this the youngest prince returned to the tree in which the knives were, and, finding both his brothers' knives covered with blood, went in the direction in which his eldest brother had gone. He came to the town, which was still draped in black, and learned all from the old woman; he went to the palace, where the princess mistook him too for her husband. He had to sleep with her, but, like his brother, placed a sword between them, and, to the great sorrow of the princess, he, too, went out hunting the next morning. Having become tired, he made a fire, and began to fry some bacon, when the witch threw him the rod; but the prince luckily discovered in the thicket the six petrified dogs, and instead of touching his own dogs with the rod, he touched those which had been turned into stone, and all six came to life again. The witch was not aware of this and came down from the tree, and the brutes seized her on the spot, and compelled her to bring their masters to life again. Then the two princes came to life again. In their joy all three embraced each other, and their servants tore the witch in pieces. Whereupon they went home, and now the joy of the princess was full, because her husband and her brothers-in-law [Pg 117]had all returned, and she had no longer any fear that the sword would be placed in the bed. On account of the joyful event the town was again draped in red cloth. The eldest prince lived happily with his wife for a long time, and later on became king. His two brothers went home safely.

THE THREE DREAMS.

There was once, I don't know where, even beyond the Operencziás Sea, a poor man, who had three sons. Having got up one morning, the father asked the eldest one, "What have you dreamt, my son?" "Well, my dear father," said he, "I sat at a table covered with many dishes, and I ate so much that when I patted my belly all the sparrows in the whole village were startled by the sound." "Well, my son," said the father, "if you had so much to eat, you ought to be satisfied; and, as we are rather short of bread, you shall not have anything to eat to-day." Then he asked the second one, "What have you dreamt, my son?" "Well, my dear father, I bought such splendid boots with spurs, that when I put them on and knocked my heels together I could be heard over seven countries." "Well, my good son," answered the father, "you have got good boots at last, and you won't want any for the winter." At last he asked the youngest as to what he had dreamt, but this one was reticent, and did not care to tell; his father ordered him to tell what it was he had dreamt, but he was silent. As fair words were of no avail the old man tried threats, but without success. Then he began to beat the lad. "To flee is shameful, but very useful," they say. The lad followed this good advice, and ran away, his father after him with a stick. As they reached the street the king was just passing [Pg 118]down the high road, in a carriage drawn by six horses with golden hair and diamond shoes. The king stopped, and asked the father why he was ill-treating the lad. "Your Majesty, because he won't tell me his dream." "Don't hurt him, my good man," said the monarch; "I'll tell you what, let the lad go with me, and take this purse; I am anxious to know his dream, and will take him with me." The father consented, and the king continued his journey, taking the lad with him. Arriving at home, he commanded the lad to appear before him, and questioned him about his dream, but the lad would not tell him. No imploring, nor threatening, would induce him to disclose his dream. The king grew angry with the lad's obstinacy, and said, in a great rage, "You good-for-nothing fellow, to disobey your king, you must know, is punishable by death! You shall die such a lingering death that you will have time to think over what disobedience to the king means." He ordered the warders to come, and gave them orders to take the lad into the tower of the fortress, and to immure him alive in the wall. The lad listened to the command in silence, and only the king's pretty daughter seemed pale, who was quite taken by the young fellow's appearance, and gazed upon him in silent joy. The lad was tall, with snow-white complexion, and had dark eyes and rich raven locks. He was carried away, but the princess was determined to save the handsome lad's life, with whom she had fallen in love at first sight; and she bribed one of the workmen to leave a stone loose, without its being noticed, so that it could be easily taken out and replaced; and so it was done!

And the pretty girl fed her sweetheart in his cell in secret. One day after this, it happened that the powerful ruler of the dog-headed Tartars gave orders that seven white horses should be led into the other king's courtyard; the animals were so much alike that there was not a hair to choose between them, and each of the horses was one year older than another; at the same time the despot commanded that he should choose the youngest from [Pg 119]among them, and the others in the order of their ages, including the oldest; if he could not do this, his country should be filled with as many Tartars as there were blades of grass in the land; that he should be impaled; and his daughter become the Tartar-chief's wife. The king on hearing this news was very much alarmed, held a council of all the wise men in his realm, but all in vain: and the whole court was in sorrow and mourning. The princess, too, was sad, and when she took the food to her sweetheart she did not smile as usual, but her eyes were filled with tears: he seeing this inquired the cause; the princess told him the reason of her grief, but he consoled her, and asked her to tell her father that he was to get seven different kinds of oats put into seven different dishes, the oats to be the growths of seven different years; the horses were to be let in and they would go and eat the oats according to their different ages, and while they were feeding they must put a mark on each of the horses. And so it was done, The horses were sent back and the ages of them given, and the Tartar monarch found the solution to be right.

But then it happened again that a rod was sent by him both ends of which were of equal thickness; the same threat was again repeated in case the king should not find out which end had grown nearest the trunk of the tree. The king was downcast and the princess told her grief to the lad, but he said, "Don't worry yourself, princess, but tell your father to measure carefully the middle of the rod and to hang it up by the middle on a piece of twine, the heavier end of it will swing downwards, that end will be the one required." The king did so and sent the rod back with the end marked as ordered. The Tartar monarch shook his head but was obliged to admit that it was right. "I will give them another trial," said he in a great rage; "and, as I see that there must be some one at the king's court who wishes to defy me, we will see who is the stronger." Not long after this, an arrow struck the wall of the royal palace, which shook it to its very foundation, like an earthquake; and great was the terror [Pg 120]of the people, which was still more increased when they found that the Tartar monarch's previous threats were written on the feathers of the arrow, which threats were to be carried out if the king had nobody who could draw out the arrow and shoot it back. The king was more downcast than ever, and never slept a wink: he called together all the heroes of his realm, and every child born under a lucky star, who was born either with a caul or with a tooth, or with a grey lock; he promised to the successful one, half of his realm and his daughter, if he fulfilled the Tartar king's wish. The princess told the lad, in sad distress, the cause of her latest grief, and he asked her to have the secret opening closed, so that their love might not be found out, and that no trace be left; and then she was to say, that she dreamt that the lad was still alive, and that he would be able to do what was needed, and that they were to have the wall opened. The princess did as she was told; the king was very much astonished, but at the same time treated the matter as an idle dream in the beginning. He had almost entirely forgotten the lad, and thought that he had gone to dust behind the walls long ago. *But in times of perplexity, when there is no help to be found in reality, one is apt to believe dreams*, and in his fear about his daughter's safety, the king at last came to the conclusion that the dream was not altogether impossible. He had the wall opened; and a gallant knight stepped from the hole. "You have nothing more to fear, my king," said the lad, who was filled with hope, and, dragging out the arrow with his right hand, he shot it towards Tartary with such force that all the finials of the royal palace dropped down with the force of the shock.

Seeing this, the Tartar monarch was not only anxious to see, but also to make the acquaintance of him who did all these things. The lad at once offered to go, and started on the journey with twelve other knights, disguising himself so that he could not be distinguished from his followers; his weapons, his armour, and everything on him was exactly like those around him. This [Pg 121]was done in order to test the magic power of the Tartar chief. The lad and his knights were received with great pomp by the monarch, who, seeing that all were attired alike, at once discovered the ruse; but, in order that he might not betray his ignorance, did not dare to inquire who the wise and powerful knight was, but trusted to his mother, who had magic power, to find him out. For this reason the magic mother put them all in the same bedroom for the night, she concealing herself in the room. The guests lay down, when one of them remarked, with great satisfaction, "By Jove! what a good cellar the monarch has!" "His wine is good, indeed," said another, "because there is human blood mixed with it." The magic mother noted from which bed the sound had come; and, when all were asleep, she cut off a lock from the knight in question, and crept out of the room unnoticed, and informed her son how he could recognise the true hero. The guests got up next morning, but our man soon noticed that he was marked, and in order to thwart the design, every one of the knights cut off a lock. They sat down to dinner, and the monarch was not able to recognise the hero.

The next night the monarch's mother again stole into the bedroom, and this time a knight exclaimed, "By Jove! what good bread the Tartar monarch has!" "It's very good, indeed," said another, "because there is woman's milk in it." When they went to sleep, she cut off the end of the moustache from the knight who slept in the bed where the voice came from, and made this sign known to her son; but the knights were more on their guard than before, and having discovered what the sign was, each of them cut off as much from their moustache as the knight's who was marked; and so once more the monarch could not distinguish between them.

The third night the old woman again secreted herself, when one of the knights remarked, "By Jove! what a handsome man the monarch is!" "He is handsome, indeed, because he [Pg 122]is a love-child," said another. When they went to sleep, she made a scratch on the visor of the knight who spoke last, and told her son. Next morn the monarch saw that all visors were marked alike. At last the monarch took courage and spoke thus: "I can see there is a cleverer man amongst you than I; and this is why I am so much more anxious to know him. I pray, therefore, that he make himself known, so that I may see him, and make the acquaintance of the only living man who wishes to be wiser and more powerful than myself." The lad stepped forward and said, "I do not wish to be wiser or more powerful than you; but I have only carried out what you bade me do; and I am the one who has been marked for the last three nights." "Very well, my lad, now I wish you to prove your words. Tell me, then, how is it possible there can be human blood in my wine?" "Call your cupbearer, your majesty, and he will explain it to you," said the lad. The official appeared hastily, and told the king how, when filling the tankards with the wine in question, he cut his finger with his knife, and thus the blood got into the wine. "Then how is it that there is woman's milk in my bread?" asked the monarch. "Call the woman who baked the bread, and she will tell," said the lad. The woman was questioned, and narrated that she was nursing a baby, and that milk had collected in her breasts; and as she was kneading the dough, the breast began to run, and some milk dropped into it. The magic mother had previously informed her son, when telling him what happened the three nights, and now confirmed her previous confession that it was true that the monarch was a love-child. The monarch was not able to keep his temper any longer, and spoke in a great rage and very haughtily, "I cannot tolerate the presence of a man who is my equal: either he or I will die. Defend yourself, lad!" and with these words he flashed his sword, and dashed at the lad. But in doing so, he accidentally slipped and fell, and the lad's life was saved. Before the former had time to get on his [Pg 123]feet, the lad pierced him through, cut off his head, and presented it on the point of his sword to the king at home. "These things that have happened to me are what I dreamt," said the victorious lad; "but I could not divulge my secret beforehand, or else it would not have been fulfilled." The king embraced the lad, and presented to him his daughter and half his realm; and they perhaps still live in happiness to-day, if they have not died since.

CSABOR UR.

There was once a young prince who was, perhaps, not quite twenty-five years old, tall, and his slim figure was like a pine tree; his forehead was sorrowful, like the dark pine; his thunder-like voice made his eyes flash; his dress and his armour were black, because the prince, who was known all over the world simply as Csabor Ur (Mr. Csabor), was serving with the picked heroes of the grand king, and who had no other ornaments besides his black suit but a gold star, which the grand king had presented to him in the German camp for having saved his life. The fame of Csabor Ur's bravery was great, and also of his benevolence, because he was kind to the poor, and the grand king very often had to scold him for distributing his property in a careless way. The priests, however, could not boast of Csabor Ur's alms, because he never gave any to them, nor did he ever give them any money for masses, and for this reason the whole hierarchy was angry with him, especially the head priest at the great king's court; but Csabor Ur being a great favourite of the great king, not even a priest dared to offend him openly, but in secret the pot was boiling for him. One cold autumn the great king arrived at the royal palace from the camp with Csabor Ur, the [Pg 124]palace standing on the bank of a large sheet of water, and before they had taken the saddles off the stallions the great king thus addressed Csabor Ur: "My lad, rest yourself during the night, and at dawn, as soon as day breaks, hurry off with your most trusty men into Roumania beyond the snow-covered mountains to old Demeter, because I hear that my Roumanian neighbours are not satisfied with my friendship, and are intriguing with the Turks: find out, my lad, how many weeks the world will last there (what's the news?) and warn the old fox to mind his tail, because I may perhaps send him a rope instead of the archiepiscopal pallium." Csabor Ur received the grand king's order with great joy, and, having taken leave of Dame Margit (Margaret), dashed off on his bay stallion over the sandy plains to the banks of the Olt, and from there he crossed over during a severe frost beyond the snow-covered mountains; he arrived at the house of Jordán Boer, the king's confidential man, whose guest he was, and here he heard of old Demeter's cunning in all its details, and also that he was secretly encouraged by the great king's head priest to plot against the sovereign; hearing this, Csabor Ur started on his journey, and arrived on the fourth day in Roumania, where he became the bishop's guest, by whom he was apparently received cordially; the old dog being anxious to mislead with his glib tongue Csabor Ur, about the events there, but it was very difficult to hoodwink the great king's man. Csabor Ur never gave any answer to the bishop's many words, and therefore made the bishop believe that he had succeeded in deceiving Csabor Ur; but he was more on his guard than ever and soon discovered that every night crowds of people gathered into the cathedral; therefore one night he also stole in there dressed in the costume of the country, and to his horror heard how the people were conspiring with the bishop against the great king, and how they were plotting an attack with the aid of the Turkish army.

Csabor Ur listened to these things in great silence and sent [Pg 125]one of his servants with a letter to the great king next day, in which he described minutely the whole state of affairs. The spies, however, laid in ambush for the servant, attacked and killed him, took Csabor Ur's letter from him, and handed it to the bishop, who learnt from its contents that Csabor Ur had stolen into the cathedral every night. He, therefore, had the large oak doors closed as soon as the congregation had assembled on the same night, and in an infuriated sermon he informed the people that there was a traitor among them. Hearing this everybody demanded his death, and they were ready to take their oath on the Holy Cross that they were not traitors. Whereupon the bishop ordered a stool to be placed on the steps of the altar, sat down, and administered the oath to all present. Only one man, in a brown fur-cloak, did not budge from the side of the stoup. The bishop, therefore, addressed him thus: "Then who are you? Why don't you come to me?" But the dark cloak did not move, and the bishop at once knew who it was and ordered the man to be bound; whereupon the multitude rushed forward to carry out his command. Thereupon the man dropped his brown cloak; and, behold, Csabor Ur stood erect—like a dark pine—with knitted brows and flashing eyes, holding in his right hand a copper mace with a gilt handle, his left resting on a broad two-edged sword. The multitude stopped, shuddering, like the huntsman, who in pursuit of hares suddenly finds a bear confronting him; but in the next moment the crowd rushed at their prey. Csabor Ur, after cutting down about thirty of them, dropped down dead himself. His blood spurted up high upon the column, where it can still be seen in the cathedral—to the left of the entrance—although the Roumanian priests tried their best to whitewash it. The great king heard of this, had the head priest imprisoned, and went with an immense army to revenge Csabor Ur's murder. With his army came also Dame Margit, dressed in men's clothes, who wept at the foot of the blood-bespurt column till one day after mass they picked her up dead from the flags.

|Pg 126|

THE DEVIL AND THE THREE SLOVÁK LADS.

There was once, I don't know where, in Slavonia, a man who had three sons. "Well, my sons," said he one day to them, "go to see the land; to see the world. There is a country where even the yellow-hammer bathes in wine, and where even the fence of the yards is made of strings of sausages; but if you wish to get on there you must first learn the language of the country." The three lads were quite delighted with the description of the wonderful country, and were ready to start off at once. The father accompanied them as far as the top of a high mountain; it took them three days to get to the top, and when they reached the summit they were on the border of the happy land: here the father slung an empty bag on every one of the lads' shoulders, and, pointing out to the eldest one the direction, exclaimed, "Ah! can you see Hungary?" and with this he took leave of them quite as satisfied as if he had then handed them the key of happiness. The three lads went on and walked into Hungary; and their first desire was to learn Hungarian, in accord with their father's direction. The moment they stepped over the border they met a man, who inquired where they were going? They informed him, "to learn Hungarian." "Don't go any further, my lads," said the man, "the school year consists of three days with me, at the end of which you will have acquired the requisite knowledge." The three lads stayed; and at the end of the three days one of them had happily learned by heart the words "we three"; the other, "for a cheese"; and the third, "that's right." The three Slovák lads were delighted, and wouldn't learn any more; and so they continued on their journey. They walked till they came to a forest, where they found a murdered man by the road-side; they looked at him, and to their astonishment they recognised the murdered man as their late master whom they had just left; |Pg 127|and while they were sighing, not knowing what to do, the rural policeman arrived on the spot. He began to question them about the murdered man, saying, "Who killed him?" The first, not knowing anything else, answered, "We three." "Why?" asked the policeman. "For a cheese," replied the second. "If this is so," growled the policeman, "I shall have to put you in irons." Whereupon the third said, "That's right." The lads were escorted by the policeman, who also intended to get assistance to carry away the dead man; but the moment they left, the dead man jumped up, shook himself, and regained his ordinary appearance, and became a sooty devil, with long ears and tail, who stood laughing at the lads, being highly amused at their stupidity, which enabled him to deceive them so easily.

THE COUNT'S DAUGHTER.

There was once, I don't know where, an old tumble-down oven, there was nothing left of its sides; there was also once a town in which a countess lived, with an immense fortune. This countess had an exceedingly pretty daughter, who was her sole heiress. The fame of her beauty and her riches being very great the marrying magnates swarmed about her. Among others the three sons of a count used to come to the house, whose castle stood outside the town in a pretty wood. These young men appeared to be richer than one would have supposed from their property, but no one knew where and how the money came to them. The three young men were invited almost every day to the house, but the countess and her daughter never visited them in return, although the young lady was continually asked by them. For a long time the girl did not accept their invitation, till one day she was preparing for a walk into the wood, in which the young counts' |Pg 128|castle was supposed to be: her mother was surprised to hear that she intended to go into the wood, but as the young lady didn't say exactly where she was going her mother raised no objection. The girl went, and the prettiness of the wood, and also her curiosity enticed her to go in further and further till at last she discovered the turrets of a splendid castle; being so near to it her curiosity grew stronger, and at last she walked into the courtyard. Everything seemed to show that the castle was inhabited, but still she did not see a living soul; the girl went on till she came to the main entrance, the stairs were of white marble, and the girl, quite dazzled at the splendour she beheld, went up, counting the steps; "one hundred," said the girl, in a half whisper, when she reached the first flight, and tarried on the landing. Here she looked round when her attention fell on a bird in a cage. "Girl, beware!" said the bird. But the girl, dazzled by the glitter, and drawn on by her curiosity, again began to mount the stairs, counting them, without heeding the bird's words. "One hundred," again said the girl, as she tarried on the next landing, but still no one was to be seen, but thinking that she might find some one she opened the first door, which revealed a splendour quite beyond all she had ever imagined, a sight such as she had never seen before, but still no one appeared. She went into another room and there amongst other furniture she also found three bedsteads, "this is the three young men's bedroom," she thought, and went on. The next room into which she stepped was full of weapons of every possible description; the girl stared and went on, and then she came to a large hall which was full of all sorts of garments, clerical, military, civilian, and also women's dresses. She went on still further and in the next room she found a female figure, made up of razors, which, with extended arms as it seemed, was placed above a deep hole. The girl was horror-struck at the sight and her fear drove her back; trembling she went back through the rooms again, but when she came into the [Pg 129]bedroom she heard male voices. Her courage fled and she could go no further, but hearing some footsteps approach she crept under one of the beds. The men entered, whom she recognised as the three sons of the count, bringing with them a beautiful girl, whom the trembling girl recognised by her voice as a dear friend; they stripped her of all, and as they could not take off a diamond ring from her little finger, one of the men chopped it off and the finger rolled under the bed where the girl lay concealed. One of the men began to look for the ring when another said "You will find it some other time," and so he left off looking for it. Having quite undressed the girl they took her to the other room, when after a short lapse of time she heard some faint screaming, and it appeared to her as if the female figure of razors had snapped together, and the mangled remains of the unfortunate victim were heard to drop down into the deep hole. The three brothers came back and one of them began to look for the ring: the cold sweat broke out on the poor girl hiding under the bed. "Never mind, it is ours new and you can find it in the morning," said one of the men, and bade the others go to bed; and so it happened: the search for the ring was put off till next day. They went to bed and the girl began to breathe more freely in her hiding-place; she began to grope about in silence and found the ring and secreted it in her dress, and hearing that the three brothers were fast asleep, she stole out noiselessly leaving the door half ajar. The next day the three brothers again visited the countess when the daughter told them that she had a dream as if she had been to their castle. She told them how she went up a flight of marble stairs till she counted 100, and up the next flight when she again counted 100. The brothers were charmed and very much surprised at the dream and assured her that it was exactly like their home. Then she told them how she went from one room to another and what she saw, but when she came in her dream as far as the razor-maid they began to feel uneasy and grew [Pg 130]suspicious, and when she told them the scene with the girl, and in proof of her tale produced the finger with the ring, the brothers were terrified and exclaiming, "We are betrayed!" took flight; but everything was arranged, and the servants, who were ordered to watch, caught them. After an investigation all their numberless horrible deeds were brought to light and they were beheaded.

THE SPEAKING GRAPES, THE SMILING APPLE, AND THE TINKLING APRICOT.

There was once, I don't know where, beyond seven times seven countries, a king who had three daughters. One day the king was going to the market, and thus inquired of his daughters: "What shall I bring you from the market, my dear daughters?" The eldest said, "A golden dress, my dear royal father;" the second said, "A silver dress for me;" the third said, "Speaking grapes, a smiling apple, and a tinkling apricot for me." "Very well, my daughters," said the king, and went. He bought the dresses for his two elder daughters in the market, as soon as he arrived; but, in spite of all exertions and inquiries, he could not find the speaking grapes, the smiling apple, and tinkling apricot. He was very sad that he could not get what his youngest daughter wished, for she was his favourite; and he went home. It happened, however, that the royal carriage stuck fast on the way home, although his horses were of the best breed, for they were such high steppers that they kicked the stars. So he at once sent for extra horses to drag out the carriage; but all in vain, the horses couldn't move either way. He gave up all hope, at last, of getting out of the position, when a dirty, filthy pig came that way, and grunted, [Pg 131]"Grumph! grumph! grumph! King, give me your youngest daughter, and I will help you out of the mud." The king, never thinking what he was promising, and over-anxious to get away, consented, and the pig gave the carriage a push with its nose, so that carriage and horses at once moved out of the mud. Having arrived at home the king handed the dresses to his two daughters, and was now sadder than ever that he had brought nothing for his favourite daughter; the thought also troubled him that he had promised her to an unclean animal.

After a short time the pig arrived in the courtyard of the palace dragging a wheelbarrow after it, and grunted, "Grumph! grumph! grumph! King, I've come for your daughter." The king was terrified, and, in order to save his daughter, he had a peasant girl dressed in rich garments, embroidered with gold, sent her down and had her seated in the wheelbarrow: the pig again grunted, "Grumph! grumph! grumph! King, this is not your daughter;" and, taking the barrow, it tipped her out. The king, seeing that deceit was of no avail, sent down his daughter, as promised, but dressed in ragged, dirty tatters, thinking that she would not please the pig; but the animal grunted in great joy, seized the girl, and placed her in the wheelbarrow. Her father wept that, through a careless promise, he had brought his favourite daughter to such a fate. The pig went on and on with the sobbing girl, till, after a long journey, it stopped before a dirty pig-stye and grunted, "Grumph! grumph! grumph! Girl, get out of the wheelbarrow." The girl did as she was told. "Grumph! grumph! grumph!" grunted the pig again; "go into your new home." The girl, whose tears, now, were streaming like a brook, obeyed; the pig then offered her some Indian corn that it had in a trough, and also its litter which consisted of some old straw, for a resting-place. The girl had not a wink of sleep for a long time, till at last, quite worn out with mental torture, she fell asleep.

Being completely exhausted with all her trials, she slept so [Pg 132]soundly that she did not wake till next day at noon. On awaking, she looked round, and was very much astonished to find herself in a beautiful fairy-like palace, her bed being of white silk with rich purple curtains and golden fringes. At the first sign of her waking maids appeared all round her, awaiting her orders, and bringing her costly dresses. The girl, quite enchanted with the scene, dressed without a word, and the maids accompanied her to her breakfast in a splendid hall, where a young man received her with great affection. "I am your husband, if you accept me, and whatever you see here belongs to you," said he; and after breakfast led her into a beautiful garden. The girl did not know *whether it was a dream she saw or reality*, and answered all the questions put to her by the young man with evasive and chaffing replies. At this moment they came to that part of the garden which was laid out as an orchard, and the bunches of grapes began to speak "Our beautiful queen, pluck some of us." The apples smiled at her continuously, and the apricots tinkled a beautiful silvery tune. "You see, my love," said the handsome youth, "here you have what you wished for—what your father could not obtain. You may know now, that once I was a monarch but I was bewitched into a pig, and I had to remain in that state till a girl wished for speaking grapes, a smiling apple, and a tinkling apricot. You are the girl, and I have been delivered; and if I please you, you can be mine for ever." The girl was enchanted with the handsome youth and the royal splendour, and consented. They went with great joy to carry the news to their father, and to tell him of their happiness.

[Pg 133]

THE THREE ORANGES.

There was once, I don't know where, a king, who had three sons. They had reached a marriageable age, but could not find any one who suited them, or who pleased their father. "Go, my sons, and look round in the world," said the king, "and try to find wives somewhere else." The three sons went away, and at bed-time they came to a small cottage, in which a very, very old woman lived. She asked them about the object of their journey, which the princes readily communicated to her. The old woman provided them with the necessaries for the journey as well as she could, and before taking leave of her guests, gave them an orange each, with instructions to cut them open only in the neighbourhood of water, else they would suffer great, very great damage. The three princes started on their way again, and the eldest not being able to restrain his curiosity as to what sort of fruit it could be, or to conceive what harm could possibly happen if he cut it open in a place where there was no water near: cut into the orange; and lo! a beautiful girl, such as he had never seen before, came out of it, and exclaimed, "Water! let me have some water, or I shall die on the spot." The prince ran in every direction to get water, but could not find any, and the beautiful girl died in a short time, as the old woman had said. The princes went on, and now the younger one began to be inquisitive as to what could be in his orange.

They had just sat down to luncheon on a plain, under a tall, leafy tree, when it appeared to them that they could see a lake not very far off. "Supposing there is a girl in the fruit, I can fulfil her wish," he thought to himself, and not being able to restrain his curiosity any longer, as to what sort of girl there could be inside, he cut his orange; and lo! a girl, very [Pg 134]much more beautiful than the first, stepped out of it, and called out for water, in order to save her life. He had previously sent his brother to what he thought was a lake; and, as he could not wait for his return with the water, he ran off himself, quite out of breath, but the further he ran the further the lake appeared to be off, because it was only a mirage. He rushed back to the tree nearly beside himself, in order to see whether the girl was yet alive, but only found her body lifeless, and quite cold.

The two elder brothers, seeing that they had lost what they had been searching for, and having given up all hope of finding a prettier one, returned in great sorrow to their father's house, and the youngest continued his journey alone. He wandered about until, after much fatigue, he came to the neighbourhood of some town, where he found a well. He had no doubt that there was a girl in his orange also, so he took courage, and cut it; and, indeed, a girl, who was a hundred times prettier than the first two, came out of it. She called out for water, and the prince gave her some at once, and death had no power over her. The prince now hurried into the town to purchase rich dresses for his love; and that no harm might happen to her during his absence, he made her sit up in a tree with dense foliage, the boughs of which overhung the well.

As soon as the prince left, a gipsy woman came to the well for water. She looked into the well, and saw in the water the beautiful face of the girl in the tree. At first she fancied that she saw the image of her own face, and felt very much flattered; but soon found out her mistake, and looking about discovered the pretty girl in the tree. "What are you waiting for, my pretty maid?" inquired the gipsy woman with a cunning face. The girl told her her story, whereupon the gipsy woman, shamming kindness, climbed up the tree, and pushed the pretty girl into the well, taking her place in the tree, when the pretty girl sank. The next moment a [Pg 135]beautiful little gold fish appeared swimming in the water; the gipsy woman recognised it as the girl, and, being afraid that it might be dangerous to her, tried to catch it, when suddenly the prince appeared with the costly dresses, so she at once laid her plans to deceive him: the prince immediately noticed the difference between her and the girl he had left; but she succeeded in making him believe that for a time after having left the fairy world, she had to lose her beauty, but that she would recover it the sooner the more he loved her: so the prince was satisfied and went home to his father's house with the woman he found, and actually loved her in hopes of her regaining her former beauty. The good food and happy life, and also the pretty dresses, improved the sunburnt woman's looks a little: the prince imagining that his wife's prediction was going to be fulfilled, felt still more attached to her, and was anxious to carry out all her wishes.

The woman, however, could not forget the little gold fish, and therefore feigned illness, saying that she would not get better till she had eaten of the liver of a gold fish, which was to be found in such and such a well: the prince had the fish caught at once, and the princess having partaken of the liver, got better, and felt more cheerful than before. It happened, however, that one scale of the fish had been cast out in the courtyard with the water, and from it a beautiful tree began to grow; the princess noticed it and found out the reason, how the tree got there, and again fell ill, and said that she could not get better until they burnt the tree, and cooked her something by the flames. This wish also was fulfilled, and she got better; it happened, however that one of the woodcutters took a square piece of the timber home to his wife, who used it as a lid for a milk jug: these people lived not very far from the royal palace, and were poor, the woman herself keeping the house, and doing all servants' work.

[Pg 136]One day she left her house very early, without having put anything in order, and without having done her usual household work; when she came home in the evening, she found all clean, and in the best order; she was very much astonished, and could not imagine how it came to pass; and it happened thus on several days, whenever she had not put her house in order before going out. In order to find out how these things were accomplished, one day she purposely left her home in disorder, but did not go far, but remained outside peeping through the keyhole, to see what would happen. As soon as everything became quiet in the house, the woman saw that the lid of the milk jug which was standing in the window, began to move with gentle noise, and in a few moments a beautiful fairy stepped out of it, who first combed her golden tresses, and performed her toilet, and afterwards put the whole house in order. The woman, in order to trap the fairy before she had time to retransform herself, opened the door abruptly. They both seemed astonished, but the kind and encouraging words of the woman soon dispelled the girl's fear, and now she related her whole story, how she came into the world, how she became a gold fish, and then a tree, and how she used to walk out of the wooden lid of the milk jug to tidy the house; she also enlightened the woman as to who the present queen was. The woman listened to all in great astonishment, and in order to prevent the girl from slipping back into the lid, she had previously picked it up, when she entered, and now threw it into the fire. She at once went to the prince, and told him the whole story.

The prince had already grown suspicious about his wife's beauty, which had been very long in returning, and now he was quite sure that she was a cheat: he sent for the girl and recognised her at once as the pretty fairy whom he had left in the tree. The gipsy woman was put into the pillory, and the prince married the pretty girl, and they lived ever after in happiness.

[Pg 137]

THE YOUNGEST PRINCE AND THE YOUNGEST PRINCESS.

There was once, I don't know where, an old petticoat a hundred years old, and in this petticoat a tuck, in which I found the following story. There was once a king who had seven sons and seven daughters: he was in great trouble where to find princesses of royal blood as wives for his sons and princes as husbands for his daughters. At last the idea struck him that the seven sons should marry the seven daughters. They all consented to their father's wish with the exception of the youngest son and daughter: "Well, if you won't," said the father, "I will give you your inheritance and you can go and try your fortune, and get married as best you can." The two children went, and came to a strange land, where they were overtaken by darkness in a wood. They chose a bushy tree for their resting place, whose leafy boughs bent down to the ground and afforded shelter. When they woke next morning, the girl told her brother that she had dreamt that there was a town not far off, where a king lived who had been ill for a long time, and thousands upon thousands of doctors had failed to cure him. He again dreamt that an old man with snow-white hair told him that the tree under which they slept gave water: in this water the king was to be bathed, and he would be cured. They at once examined the tree, and from a crack in the bark sap as clear as crystal was dripping; they filled their flasks with the fluid and continued their journey. When they reached the outskirts of the forest, they saw a town in front of them.

Having arrived there they went into an inn to find out whether their dream was true, and asked the host what the [Pg 138]news was in the town; he, in his conversation, mentioned the illness of the king, and the many unsuccessful attempts of men to cure him, and that he had strict orders, under a heavy penalty, to report at once every doctor that came to his inn. "I also am a doctor," said the prince, "and this youth is my assistant," he continued, pointing to his sister, who was dressed in male attire. The innkeeper at once reported them, and they went to court to try their remedy on the king. The king's body was covered with sores, and the doctor bathed his hand with the juice of the tree. To his great joy, the king discovered next morning that the place which had been bathed was visibly improving; he therefore, the very same night, sent a huge wooden vessel on a cart to the tree, to bring him sufficient water for a bath. After a few baths the king actually recovered; and the doctor, having received a handsome present, requested a favour of the king, viz., to pay him a visit and to do him the honour of dining with him. The king cordially granted the request, and the prince received him with great splendour in his spacious apartments, which were decorated with a lavishness becoming a sovereign. As the king found the doctor alone, he inquired after his assistant, and at this moment a charming pretty girl stepped from one of the side rooms, whom the king at once recognised as the doctor's assistant. The strangers now related to him their story, and the king became more affable, especially towards the pretty assistant, who at once gained possession of his heart and soul, and the short acquaintance ended with a wedding. The prince, not forgetting the object of his journey, started soon after the wedding festivities were over.

He passed on till he came to the boundary of the king's realm, and then went on as far as the capital of the next country. He was riding about the streets on a fine horse, when he heard a voice coming from a window close by, "Hum, you, too, won't get on without me," and looking in the direction from which the voice came, he discovered an old man looking out of the window. [Pg 139]He didn't take any notice of the voice, but went on; and, having arrived at an inn, made sundry inquiries, when he was told that adventurous young men in this town might either meet with great fortune or with a great misfortune; because the king had a daughter whom no one had as yet seen, with the exception of her old nurse. The girl had three marks on her, and whoever found out what they were, and where they were, would become her husband; but whosoever undertook the task and failed, would be impaled, and that already ninety-nine young fellows had died in this manner.

Upon hearing this, it became clear to the prince what the meaning of the old man's saying was; he thought, that no doubt the old man took him for another adventurer, and the thought struck him that the old man must be acquainted with the secret, and that it would be advantageous to make his acquaintance. He found a plea at once; the old man was a goldsmith, and, as the prince had lost the rowel of his golden spur on the road, he called on him, and, having come to terms about the spur, the prince inquired of him about the princess, and the old man's tale tallied with that of the innkeeper. After a short reflection, the prince told the old man who he was, and, with a look full of meaning, inquired if the goldsmith could help him in case he tried his luck. "For a good sum with pleasure," replied the goldsmith. "You shall have it," said the prince; "but tell me how, and I will give you this purse on account." The old man, seeing that there was good opportunity for gain, said, "I will construct a silver horse in which you can conceal yourself, and I will expose it for sale in the market. I am almost sure that no one will buy it but some one attached to the royal court, and if once you get in there, you can get out of the horse by a secret opening and go back whenever you like and, I think, you will succeed."

And so it happened; on the following market-day a splendid silver horse was exhibited in the vicinity of the royal palace: there were a good many admirers, but on account of the great [Pg 140]price there was no buyer, till at last a person belonging to the royal court enquired the price; after a few moments he returned and bought the horse for the king, who presented it to his daughter, and thus the prince managed to get into the chamber of the princess, which was the most difficult of all things, and he listened amidst fear and joy to the silvery voice of the pretty girl, who amused herself with the horse—which ran on wheels—and called it her dear pet.

Evening drew on, and the mysterious girl went to rest; everything became quiet, and only her old nurse was sitting up not far from her bed; but about midnight she, too, fell asleep; hearing that she was fast asleep, the prince got out of the horse and approached the girl's bed, holding his breath, and found the mark of the sun shining on the girl's forehead, the moon on the right breast, and three stars on the left. Having found out the three secret marks, the prince was about to retire to his hiding-place when the princess woke. She tried to scream, but at an imploring gesture of the youth she kept silence. The girl could not take her eyes off the handsome prince, who related to her how and for what reason he had dared to come. The girl, being tired of her long seclusion, consented to his scheme, and they secretly plotted how the prince should get out of the palace; whereupon he went back to his hiding-place. In accord with the plot, next morning the girl broke one of the horse's ears off, and it was sent back to the goldsmith's to be repaired, and the prince was thus able to leave his dangerous position.

Having again splendidly remunerated the goldsmith, he returned to his new brother-in-law, so that he might come back with a splendid suite and royal pomp, and appear as a king to try his fortune. The prince returned with many magnificently-clad knights and splendid horses, and reported himself to the king, and informed him by message that he was anxious to try his luck for the possession of his daughter. The king was very much pleased with the appearance of the youth, and therefore [Pg 141]kindly admonished him not to risk his life, but the prince seemed quite confident, and insisted on carrying out his wishes; so a day was fixed for carrying out the task. The people streamed out to the place where the trial was to take place, like as to a huge festival. And all pitied the handsome youth, and had sad misgivings as to his fate.

The king granted three days to those who tried their fortune, and three guesses. On the first and second day, in order not to betray the plot, and in order to increase the éclat the prince guessed wrongly on purpose; but on the third day, when everyone was convinced that he must die, he disclosed in a loud voice the secret marks of the princess. The king declared them to be right, and the prince was led to his future wife, amidst the cheers of the multitude and the joyous strains of the band. The king ordered immense wedding festivities all over the town, and resigned his throne in favour of his son-in-law, who reigned happy for many years after!

THE INVISIBLE SHEPHERD LAD.

There was once, I don't know where, a poor man who had a very good son who was a shepherd. One day he was tending his sheep in a rocky neighbourhood, and was sending sighs to Heaven as a man whose heart was throbbing with burning wishes. Hearing a noise as of some one approaching he looked round and saw St. Peter standing in front of him in the guise of a very old grey man. "Why are you sighing, my lad?" inquired he, "and what is your wish?" "Nothing else," replied the lad, respectfully, "but to possess a little bag which never gets full, and a fur cloak which makes me invisible when I put it on." His wish was [Pg 142]fulfilled and St. Peter vanished. The lad gave up shepherding now and turned to the capital, where he thought he had a chance of making his fortune. A king lived there who had twelve daughters, and eleven of them wanted at least six pairs of shoes each every night. Their father was very angry about this, because it swallowed up a good deal of his income; he suspected that there was something wrong, but couldn't succeed by any traps to get to the bottom of it. At last he promised the youngest princess to him who would unveil the secret.

The promise enticed many adventurous spirits to the capital, but the girls simply laughed at them, and they were obliged to leave in disgrace. The shepherd lad, relying on his fur cloak, reported himself; but the girls measured him, too, with mocking eyes. Night came, and the shepherd, muffling himself in his fur cloak, stood at the bedroom door where they slept, and stole in amongst them when they went to bed. It was midnight and a ghost walked round the beds and woke the girls. There was now great preparation. They dressed and beautified themselves, and filled a travelling bag with shoes. The youngest knew nothing of all this, but on the present occasion the invisible shepherd woke her—whereupon her sisters got frightened; but as she was let into their secret they thought it best to decoy her with them, to which, after a short resistance, the girl consented. All being ready, the ghost placed a small dish on the table. Everyone anointed their shoulders with the contents, and wings grew to them. The shepherd did the same: and when they all flew through the window, he followed them.

After flying for several hours they came to a huge copper forest, and to a well, the railing round which was of copper, and on this stood twelve copper tumblers. The girls drank here, so as to refresh themselves, when the youngest, who was here for the first time, looked round in fear. The lad, too, had something to drink after the girls had left and put a tumbler, together with [Pg 143]a twig that he broke off a tree, in his bag; the tree trembled, and the noise was heard all over the forest. The youngest girl noticed it and warned her sisters that some one was after them, but they felt so safe that they only laughed at her. They continued their journey, and after a short time came to a silver forest, and to a silver well. Here again they drank, and the lad again put a tumbler and a silver twig into his bag. In breaking off the twig the tree shook, and the youngest again warned her sisters, but in vain.

They soon came to the end of the forest and arrived at a golden forest, with a gold well and tumblers. Here again they stopped and drank, and the lad again put a gold tumbler and twig in his bag. The youngest once more warned her sisters of the noise the quivering tree made, but in vain. Having arrived at the end of the forest they came to an immense moss-grown rock, whose awe-inspiring lofty peaks soared up to the very heavens. Here they all stopped. The ghost struck the rock with a golden rod, whereupon it opened, and all entered, the shepherd lad with them. Now they came to a gorgeous room from which several halls opened, which were all furnished in a fairy-like manner. From these twelve fairy youths came forth and greeted them, who were all wonderfully handsome. The number of servants increased from minute to minute who were rushing about getting everything ready for a magnificent dance. Soon after strains of enchanting music were heard, and the doors of a vast dancing hall opened and the dancing went on without interruption. At dawn the girls returned—also the lad—in the same way as they had come, and they lay down as if nothing had happened, which, however, was belied by their worn shoes, and the next morning they got up at the usual hour.

The king was impatiently awaiting the news the shepherd was to bring, who came soon after and told him all that had happened. He sent for his daughters, who denied everything, but the tumblers and the twigs bore witness. What the [Pg 144]shepherd told the youngest girl also confirmed, whom the shepherd woke for the purpose. The king fulfilled his promise with regard to the youngest princess and the other eleven were burnt for witchcraft.

THE THREE PRINCESSES.

There was once, I shan't tell you where, it is enough if I tell you that there was somewhere a tumble-down oven, which was in first-rate condition barring the sides, and there were some cakes baking in it; this person (the narrator points to some one present) has eaten some of them. Well then, on the mountains of Komárom, on the glass bridges, on the beautiful golden chandelier, there was once a Debreczen cloak which had ninety-nine tucks, and in the ninety-ninth I found the following tale.

There was once a king with three daughters, but the king was so poor that he could hardly keep his family; his wife, who was the girls' stepmother, therefore told her husband one night, that in the morning she would take the girls into the wood and leave them in the thicket so that they might not find again their way home. The youngest overheard this, and as soon as the king and queen fell asleep she hurried off to her godmother, who was a magic woman, to ask her advice: her godmother's little pony (tátos) was waiting at the front gate, and taking her on its back ran straight to the magic woman. She knew well what the girl needed and gave her at once a reel of cotton which she could unwind in the wood and so find her way back, but she gave it to her on the condition that she would not take her two elder sisters home with her, because they were very bad and proud. As arranged next morning the girls were led out by their stepmother [Pg 145]into the wood to gather chips as she said, and, having wandered about a long time, she told them to rest; so they sat down under a tree and soon all three went to sleep; seeing this, the stepmother hurried home.

On waking up, two of the girls, not being able to find their mother, began to cry, but the youngest was quiet, saying that she knew her way home, and that she would go, but could not take them with her; whereupon the two elder girls began to flatter her, and implored her so much that she gave in at last. Arriving at home their father received them with open arms; their stepmother feigned delight. Next night she again told the king that she would lead them deeper still into the wood: the youngest again overheard the conversation, and, as on the night before, went on her little pony to her godmother, who scolded her for having taken home her bad sisters, and on condition that this time she would not do so, she gave her a bag full of ashes, which she had to strew over the road as they went on, in order to know her way back; so the girls were led into the wood again and left there, but the youngest again took her sisters home, finding her way by the ashes, having been talked over by many promises and implorings. At home, they were received, as on the first occasion; on the third night their stepmother once more undertook to lead them away; the youngest overheard them as before, but this time, she had not courage to go to her godmother, moreover she thought that she could help herself, and for this purpose she took a bag full of peas with her, which she strewed about as they went. Left by their mother, the two again began to cry, whereas the youngest said laughing, that she was able to go home on this occasion also; and having again yielded to her sisters she started on her way back, but to her astonishment could not find a single pea, as the birds had eaten them all. Now there was a general cry, and the three outcasts wandered about the whole day in the wood, and did not find a spring till sunset, to quench their thirst; they also [Pg 146]found an acorn under an oak under which they had lain down to rest; they set the acorn, and carried water in their mouths to water it; by next morning it had grown into a tree as tall as a tower, and the youngest climbed up it to see whether she could not discover some habitation in the neighbourhood; not being able to see anything, they spent the whole day crying and wandering about. The following morning, the tree was as big as two towers, but on this occasion too the youngest girl looked in vain from its summit: but at last, by the end of the third day, the tree was as tall as three towers, and this time the youngest girl was more successful, because she discovered far away a lighted window, and, having come down, she led her sisters in the direction of the light. Her sisters, however, treated her most shamefully, they took away all her best clothes, which she thoughtfully had brought with her, tied up in a bundle, and she had to be satisfied with the shabbiest; whenever she dared to contradict them they at once began to beat her; they gave her orders that wherever they came she had to represent them as daughters of rich people, she being their servant. Thus, they went on for three days and three nights until at last they came to an immense, beautiful castle.

They felt now in safety, and entered the beautiful palace with great hopes, but how frightened were they when they discovered a giantess inside who was as tall as a tower, and who had an eye in the middle of her forehead as big as a dish, and who gnashed her teeth, which were a span long. "Welcome, girls!" thus spoke the giantess, "What a splendid roast you will make!" They all three were terrified at these words, but the youngest shewed herself amiable, and promised the giantess that they would make all kind of beautiful millinery for her if she did them no harm; the woman with the big teeth listened, and agreed, and hid the girls in a cupboard so that her husband might not see them when he came home; the giant, who was even taller than his wife, however, at once began to sniff about, [Pg 147]and demanded human flesh of his wife, threatening to swallow her if she did not produce it. The girls were fetched out, but were again spared, having promised to cook very savoury food for the grumbling husband.

The chief reason of their life having been spared, however, was because the husband wanted to eat them himself during the absence of his wife, and the woman had a similar plan in her mind. The girls now commenced to bake and roast, the two eldest kneaded the dough, the youngest making the fire in the oven, which was as big as hell, and when it got red hot, the cunning young girl called the giant, and having placed a pot full of lard into the oven, asked him to taste it with his tongue to see whether the lard was hot enough, and if the oven had reached its proper heat. The tower of flesh tried it, but the moment he put his head inside the oven, the girl gave him a push and he was a dead man in the fiery oven; seeing this, the giantess got in a rage, and was about to swallow them up, but, before doing so, the youngest induced her to let herself be beautified, to which she consented; a ladder was brought, so that the young girl might get on to her head to comb the monster's hair; instead of combing, however, the nimble little girl knocked the giantess on the head with the huge iron comb, so that she dropped down dead on the spot. The girls had the bodies carted away with twenty-four pair of oxen, and became the sole owners of the immense castle. Next Sunday, the two eldest dressed up in their best, and went for a walk, and to a dance in the royal town.

After their departure their youngest sister, who remained at home to do servants' work, examined all the rooms, passages, and closets in the castle. During her search she accidentally found something shining in a flue. She knocked it off with a stone, and found that it was a most beautiful golden key. She tried it in every door and cupboard, but only succeeded, after a long search, in opening a small wardrobe with it; and, how great was her surprise to find that it was full of ladies' dresses [Pg 148]and millinery, and that every thing seemed made to fit her. She put on a silver dress in great haste, and went to the dance. The well-known little pony was outside waiting for her, and galloped away with her like a hurricane. The moment she entered the dancing hall all eyes were fixed on her, and the men and youths of the highest dignity vied with each other as to who should dance with her. Her sisters who, till her arrival, were the heroines of the evening and the belles of the ball, were quite set aside now. After a few hours' enjoyment the young lady suddenly disappeared; and, later on, received her sisters on their return in her servant's clothes. They told her that they had enjoyed themselves very well at first, but that later on some impudent female put them in the back-ground. The little girl laughed and said, "Supposing that I was that lady;" and she was beaten by her sisters, and called some not very polite names for her remark. Next Sunday the same thing happened again, only this time the young girl was dressed in gold. Everything happened the same, and she was again beaten at home.

The third Sunday the little girl appeared in a diamond dress. At the dance, again, she was the soul of the evening; but this time the young men wanted her to stay to the end of the ball, and watched her very closely, so that she might not escape. When, therefore, she tried to get away, she was in such a hurry that she had no time to pick up a shoe she accidentally dropped in the corridor; she was just in time to receive her sisters. The shoe came into the possession of the prince, who hid it carefully. After a few days the prince fell very ill, and the best physicians could not find a cure for him; his father was very nearly in despair about his only son's health, when a foreign doctor maintained that the patient could only be cured by marrying, because he was love-sick. His father, therefore, implored him to make him a full confession of his love, and, whoever the person whom he wished might be, he should have [Pg 149]her. The prince produced the shoe, and declared that he wanted the young lady to whom the shoe belonged. So it was announced throughout the whole realm, that all the ladies of the country should appear next Sunday to try on the shoe, and whosoever's foot it fitted she should become the prince's wife. On Sunday the ladies swarmed in crowds to the capital. Nor were the two eldest of the three sisters missing, who had had their feet previously scraped with a knife by their youngest sister, so that they might be smaller. The youngest sister also got ready after their departure, and, having wrapped the mate of the lost shoe in a handkerchief, she jumped on the pony's back in her best dress, and rode to the appointed place. She overtook her sisters on the road, and, jumping the pony into a puddle, splashed them all over with mud. The moment she was seen approaching 100 cannons were fired off, and all the bells were rung; but she wouldn't acknowledge the shoe as her own without a trial, and, therefore, tried it on. The shoe fitted her exactly, and when she produced its mate, 300 cannons greeted her as the future queen. She accepted the honour upon one condition, namely, that the king should restore her father's conquered realm. Her wish was granted, and she became the prince's wife. Her sisters were conducted back to their royal father, who was now rich and powerful once more; where they live still, if they have not died since.

CINDER JACK.

A peasant had three sons. One morning he sent out the eldest to guard the vineyard. The lad went, and was cheerfully eating a cake he had taken with him, when a frog crept up to him, and asked him to let it have some of his cake. "Anything else?" asked the [Pg 150]lad angrily, and picked up a stone to drive the frog away. The frog left without a word, and the lad soon fell asleep, and, on awaking, found the whole vineyard laid waste. The next day the father sent his second son into the vineyard, but he fared like the first.

The father was very angry about it, and did not know what to do; whereupon his youngest son spoke up, who was always sitting in a corner amongst the ashes, and was not thought fit for anything, and whom for this reason they nicknamed Cinder Jack. "My father, send me out, and I will take care of the vineyard." His father and his brothers laughed at him, but they allowed him to have a trial; so Cinder Jack went to the vineyard, and, taking out his cake, began to eat it. The frog again appeared, and asked for a piece of cake, which was given to him at once. Having finished their breakfast, the frog gave the lad a copper, a silver, and a gold rod; and told him, that three horses would appear shortly, of copper, silver, and gold, and they would try to trample down the vineyard; but, if he beat them with the rods he had given him they would at once become tame, and be his servants, and could at any time be summoned to carry out his orders. It happened as the frog foretold; and the vineyard produced a rich vintage. But Cinder Jack never told his master or his brothers how he had been able to preserve the vineyard; in fact, he concealed all, and again spent his time as usual, lying about in his favourite corner.

One Sunday the king had a high fir pole erected in front of the church, and a golden rosemary tied to the top, and promised his daughter to him who should be able to take it down in one jump on horseback. All the knights of the realm tried their fortune, but not one of them was able to jump high enough. But all of a sudden a knight clad in copper mail, on a copper horse, appeared with his visor down, and snatched the rosemary with an easy jump, and quickly disappeared. When his two [Pg 151]brothers got home they told Cinder Jack what had happened, and he remarked, that he saw the whole proceeding much better, and on being asked "Where from?" his answer was, "From the top of the hoarding." His brothers had the hoarding pulled down at once, so that their younger brother might not look on any more. Next Sunday a still higher pole, with a golden apple at the top, was set up; and whosoever wished to marry the king's daughter had to take the apple down. Again, hundreds upon hundreds tried, but all in vain; till, at last, a knight in silver mail, on a silver horse, took it, and disappeared. Cinder Jack again told his brothers that he saw the festivities much better than they did; he saw them, he said, from the pig-stye; so this was pulled down also. The third Sunday a silk kerchief interwoven with gold was displayed at the top of a still higher fir pole, and, as nobody succeeded in getting it, a knight in gold mail, on a gold horse, appeared; snatched it down, and galloped off. Cinder Jack again told his brothers that he saw all from the top of the house; and his envious brothers had the roof of the house taken off, so that the youngest brother might not look on again.

The king now had it announced that the knight who had shown himself worthy of his daughter should report himself, and should bring with him the gold rosemary, the apple, and the silk kerchief; but no one came. So the king ordered every man in the realm to appear before him, and still the knight in question could not be found; till, at last, he arrived clad in gold mail on a gold charger; whereupon the bells were at once rung, and hundreds and hundreds of cannons fired. The knight, having handed to the princess the golden rosemary, the apple, and the kerchief, respectfully demanded her hand, and, having obtained it, lifted his visor, and the populace, to their great astonishment, recognised Cinder Jack, whom they had even forgotten to ask to the king's presence. The good-hearted lad had his brothers' house rebuilt, and gave them presents as well. He took [Pg 152]his father to his house, as the old king died soon after. Cinder Jack is reigning still, and is respected and honoured by all his subjects!

THE THREE BROTHERS.

There was once a poor man who had three sons. "My sons," said he to them one day, "you have not seen anything yet, and you have no experience whatever; it is time for you to go to different countries and try your luck in the world; so get ready for the journey, and go as far as your eyes can see." The three lads got ready, and, having filled their bags with cakes specially prepared For the occasion, they left home. They went on and on till at last they got tired and lay down,—the two elder then proposed that, as it became good brethren, they should all share equally, and that they should begin with the youngest's provisions, and when they were finished should divide those of the second, and lastly those of the eldest. And so it happened; on the first day the youngest's bag was emptied; but the second day, when meal-time came, the two eldest would not give the youngest anything, and when he insisted on receiving his share, they gouged out his eyes and left him to starve. For the present let us leave the two eldest to continue their way, and let's see what became of the poor blind lad. He, resigning himself to God's will, groped his way about, till, alas! he dropped into a well. There was no water in it, but a great deal of mud; when he dropped into it the mud splashed all over his body, and he felt quite a new man again and ever so much better. Having besmeared his face and the hollows of his eyes with the mud he again saw clearly, because the healing power of the miracle-working mud [Pg 153]had renewed his eyes once more, and his whole face became of a beautiful complexion.

The lad took as much mud in a flower pot with him as he could carry and continued his journey, when suddenly he noticed a little mouse quite crushed, imploring him for help; he took pity on it, and, having besmeared it with the miraculous mud, the mouse was cured, and gave to his benefactor a small whistle, with the direction that if anything happened to him he had to blow the whistle, and the mouse, who was the king of mice, would come to his help with all his mates on earth. He continued his way and found a bee quite crushed and cured it too with the mud, and obtained another whistle, which he had to blow in case of danger, and the queen of the bees would come to his aid. Again going on he found a wolf shockingly bruised; at first he had not courage to cure it, being afraid that it would eat him; but the wolf implored so long that at last he cured him too, and the wolf became strong and beautiful; the wolf, too, gave him a whistle to use in time of need.

The lad went on till at last he came to the royal town, where he was engaged as servant to the king. His two brothers were there already in the same service, and, having recognised him, tried in every way to destroy him. After long deliberation as to how to carry out their plan they went to the king and falsely accused their brother of having told them that he was able to gather the corn of the whole land into the king's barn in one night; the lad denied it, but all in vain. The king declared that if all the corn was not in the barn by the morning he would hang him. The lad wept and wailed for a long time, when suddenly he remembered his whistles, and blew into the one that the mouse had given him and when the mice came he told them his misfortunes: by midnight all the corn of the country was gathered together. Next day his brothers were more angry still, and falsely said to the king that their brother was able to build a beautiful bridge of wax from the royal castle to the market place [Pg 154]in one night; the king ordered him to do this too, and having blown his second whistle the bees, who appeared to receive his command, did the task for him. Next morning from his window the king very much admired the beautiful arched bridge; his brothers nearly burst in their rage, and spread the report that their brother was able to bring twelve of the strongest wolves into the royal courtyard by the next morning. They firmly believed that on this occasion they were quite sure of their victory, because either the wolves would tear their brother in pieces, or if he could not fulfil the task the king would have him executed; but again they were out of their reckoning: the lad blew his third whistle and the king of wolves arrived to receive his orders. He told him his misfortune, and the wolf ordered not only twelve, but all his mates in the country, into the royal courtyard. The lad now sat on the back of the king of wolves, and drove with a whip the whole pack in front of him, who tore everything in pieces that crossed them. There was a great deal of weeping, imploring, and wailing in the royal palace, but all in vain; the king promised a sack full of gold, but all in vain. The king of the wolves, heedless of any words, urged on the pack by howling at them continually: "Drive on! Seize them!" The king promised more; two sacks, three sacks, ten, or even twenty sacks full of gold were offered but not accepted; the wolves tore everyone in pieces; the two brothers perished, and so did the king and all his servants, and only his daughter was spared; the lad married her, occupied the king's throne, and lives happily to this day if he has not died since. In his last letter he promised to come and see us to-morrow.

[Pg 155]

THE THREE VALUABLE THINGS.

There were once two kings who lived in great friendship; one had three sons, the other a daughter. The two fathers made an agreement, that in case of either of them dying, the other should become guardian of the orphans; and that if one of the boys married the girl he should inherit her property. Very soon after the girl's father died, and she went to live with her guardian. After a little time the eldest boy went to his father and asked the girl's hand, threatening to commit suicide if his request was refused; his father promised to give him a reply in three weeks. At the end of the first week the second son asked the girl's hand, and threatened to blow out his brains if he could not wed her; the king promised to reply to him in a fortnight. At the end of the second week, the youngest asked for the girl, and his father bade him wait a week for his answer. The day arrived when all three had to receive their reply, and their father addressed them thus: "My sons, you all three love the girl, but you know too well that only one can have her. I will, therefore, give her to the one who will show himself the most worthy of her. You had better go, wherever you please, and see the world, and return in one year from this day, and the girl shall be his who will bring the most valuable thing from his journey." The princes consented to this, and started on their journey, travelling together till they came to a tall oak in the nearest wood; the road here divided into three branches; the eldest chose the one leading west, the second selected the one running south, and the third son the branch turning off to the east. Before separating, they decided to return to the same place after the lapse of exactly one year, and to make the homeward journey together.

[Pg 156]

The eldest looked at everything that he found worthy of note during his travels, and spared no expense to get something excellent: after a long journey hither and thither, he at last succeeded in getting a telescope by the aid of which he could see to the end of the world; so he decided to take it back to his father, as the most valuable thing he had found. The second son also endeavoured to find something so valuable that the possession of it should make him an easy winner in the competition for the girl's hand: after a long search he found a cloak by means of which, when he put it on and thought of a place, he was immediately transported there. The youngest, after long wandering, bought an orange which had power to restore to life the dead when put under the corpse's nose, provided death had not taken place more than twenty-four hours before. These were the three valuable things that were to be brought home; and, as the year was nearly up, the eldest and the youngest were already on their way back to the oak: the second son only was still enjoying himself in various places, as one second was enough for him to get to the meeting place. The two having arrived at the oak, the middle one appeared after a little while, and they then shewed each other the valuables acquired; next they looked through the telescope, and to their horror they saw that the lady for the possession of whom they had been working hard for a whole year, was lying dead; so they all three slipped hurriedly into the cloak, and as quick as thought arrived at home; the father told them in great grief that the girl could belong to no one as she was dead: they inquired when she died, and receiving an answer that she had been dead not quite twenty-four hours, the youngest rushed up to her, and restored her to life with his magic orange. Now there was a good deal of litigation and quarrelling among the three lads: the eldest claimed the greatest merit for himself, because, he said, had they not seen through his telescope that the girl was dead they would have been still lingering at the oak, and the orange would have been of no avail; the second maintained that [Pg 157]if they had not got home so quickly with his cloak the orange would have been of no use; the third claimed his orange as the best, for restoring the girl to life, without which the other two would have been useless. In order to settle the dispute, they called all the learned and old people of the realm together, and these awarded the girl to the youngest, and all three were satisfied with the award, and the two others gave up all idea about suicide. The eldest, by the aid of his telescope, found himself a wife who was the prettiest royal princess on earth, and married her: the second heard of one who was known for her virtue and beauty, and got into his cloak, and went to her, and so all three to their great satisfaction led their brides to the altar, and became as happy as men can be.

THE LITTLE MAGIC PONY.

Once a poor man had twelve sons, and, not having sufficient means to keep them at home, he sent them into the great world to earn their bread by work and to try their fortunes. The brothers wandered twelve days and nights over hills and dales till at last they came to a wealthy king, who engaged them as grooms, and promised them each three hundred florins a year for their wages. Among the king's horses there was a half-starved looking, decrepit little pony; the eleven eldest boys continually beat and ill-treated this animal on account of its ugliness, but the youngest always took great care of it, he even saved all the bread crumbs and other little dainties for his little invalid pony, for which his brothers very often chaffed him, and in course of time they treated him with silent contempt, believing him to be a lunatic; he bore [Pg 158]their insults patiently, and their badgering without a murmur, in the same way as the little pony the bad treatment it received. The year of service having come to an end, the lads received their wages, and as a reward they were also each allowed to choose a horse from the king's stud. The eleven eldest chose the best-looking horses, but the youngest only begged leave to take the poor little decrepit pony with him. His brothers tried to persuade him to give up the foolish idea, but, all in vain, he would have no other horse.

The little pony now confessed to his keeper that it was a magic horse, and that whenever it wanted it could change into the finest charger and could gallop as fast as lightning. The twelve brothers then started homewards; the eleven eldest were proudly jumping and prancing about on their fine horses, whereas the youngest dragged his horse by its halter along the road: at one time they came to a boggy place and the poor little decrepit pony sank into it. The eleven brothers who had gone on before were very angry about it, as they were obliged to return and drag their brother's horse out of the mud: after a short journey the youngest's again stuck in the mud, and his brothers had to drag it out again, swearing at him all the time. When at last it stuck the third time they would not listen any more to their brother's cries for help. "Let them go," said the little pony, and after a short time inquired if they had gone far? "They have," answered the lad. Again, after a short time, the pony inquired whether he could still see them. "They look like flying crows or black spots in the distance," replied his master. "Can you see them now?" asked the pony in a few minutes. "No," was the reply; thereupon the pony jumped out of the mud and, taking the lad on its back, rushed forth like lightning, leaving the others far behind. Having arrived at home the pony became poor and decrepit as before, and crawled on to the dung heap, eating the straw it found there, the lad concealing himself behind the oven. The others having arrived showed their wages and horses to [Pg 159]their father, and being asked about their brother they replied that he had become an idiot, and chosen as his reward an ugly pony, just such a one as the one on the dung heap, and that he stuck fast in a bog, and perhaps was now dead. "It is not true," called out the youngest from behind the oven, and stepped forth to the astonishment of all.

Having spent a few days in enjoying themselves at their father's house, the lads again started on a journey to find wives. They had already journeyed over seven countries and seven villages as well, and had not as yet been able to find twelve girls suitable for them, till at last, as the sun was setting, they came across an old woman with an iron nose, who was ploughing her field with twelve mares; she asked of them what they sought, and, having learned the object of their wanderings, she proposed that they should look at her twelve daughters: the lads having consented, the old woman drove her twelve mares home and took the lads into her house and introduced them to her daughters, who were none others than the twelve mares they saw before. In the evening she bade each lad go to bed with one of the girls; the eldest lad got into bed with the eldest girl and so on, her youngest, who was the favourite daughter and had golden hair, becoming the youngest lad's bedfellow.

This girl informed the lad that it was her mother's intention to kill his eleven brothers; and so, in order to save them, on their all falling asleep, the youngest lad got up and laid all his brothers next to the wall, making all the girls lie outside, and having done this, quietly crept back into his bed.

After a little while, the old woman with the iron nose got up and, with a huge sword, cut off the heads of the eleven sleepers who were lying outside, and then she went back to bed to sleep. Thereupon the youngest lad again got up, and, waking his brothers, told them how he had saved them, and urged them to flee as soon as possible. So they hurried off, their brother remaining there till daybreak. At dawn he noticed that the old [Pg 160]woman was getting up, and that she was coming to examine the beds, so he, too, got up, and sat on his pony, taking the little girl with the golden hair with him. The old woman with the iron nose, as soon as she found out the fraud, picked up a poker, turned it into a horse, and flew after them; when she had nearly overtaken them, the little pony gave the lad a currycomb, a brush, and a piece of a horse-rug, and bade him throw first the currycomb behind him, and in case it did not answer, to throw the brush, and as a last resource the piece of horse-rug; the lad threw the currycomb, and in one moment it became a dense forest, with as many trees as there were teeth in the comb; by the time that the old woman had broken her way through the wood, the couple had travelled a long distance. When the old woman came very near again, the lad threw the brush behind him, and it at once became a dense forest, having as many trees as there were bristles in the brush. The old woman had the greatest difficulty in working her way through the wood; but again she drew close to their heels, and very nearly caught them, when the lad threw the horse-rug away, and it became such a dense forest between them and the old woman, that it looked like one immense tree; with all her perseverance, the old woman could not penetrate this wood, so she changed into a pigeon to enable her to fly over it; but as soon as the pony noticed this he turned into a vulture, swooped down on the pigeon, and tore it in pieces with his claws, thus saving both the lad and the pretty girl with the golden hair from the fury of the hateful old woman with the iron nose.

While the eleven elder brothers were still out looking after wives, the youngest married the pretty little girl with the golden hair, and they still live merrily together, out of all danger, if they have not died since.

[Pg 161]

THE BEGGAR'S PRESENTS.

There was once a very poor man, who went into the wood to fell trees for his own use. The sweat ran down his cheeks, from his hard work, when all at once an old beggar appeared and asked for alms. The poor man pitied him very much, and, putting his axe on the ground, felt in his bag, and, with sincere compassion, shared his few bits of bread with the poor old beggar. The latter, having eaten his bread, spoke thus to the wood-cutter: "My son, here! for your kindness accept this table-cloth, and whenever hereafter you feel need and are hungry, say to the cloth, 'Spread thyself, little cloth,' and your table will be laid, and covered with the best meats and drinks. I am the rewarder of all good deeds, and I give this to you for your benevolence." Thereupon the old man disappeared, and the wood-cutter turned homewards in great joy.

Having been overtaken by night on his way, he turned into a hostelry, and informed the innkeeper, who was an old acquaintance, of his good fortune; and, in order to give greater weight to his word, he at once made a trial of the table-cloth, and provided a jolly good supper for the innkeeper and his wife, from the dainty dishes that were served up on the cloth. After supper he laid down on the bench to sleep, and, in the meantime, the wicked wife of the innkeeper hemmed a similar cloth, and by the morning exchanged it for that of the woodcutter. He, suspecting nothing, hurried home with the exchanged cloth, and, arriving there, told his wife what had happened; and, to prove his words, at once gave orders to the cloth to spread itself; but all in vain. He repeated at least a hundred times the [Pg 162]words "Little cloth, spread thyself," but the cloth never moved; and the simpleton couldn't understand it. Next day he again went to the wood, where he again shared his bread with the old beggar, and received from him a lamb, to which he had only to say, "Give me gold, little lamb," and the gold coins at once began to rain. With this the woodcutter again went to the inn for the night, and showed the present to the innkeeper, as before. Next morning he had another lamb to take home, and was very much surprised that it would not give the gold for which he asked. He went to the wood again, and treated the beggar well, but also told him what had happened to the table-cloth and lamb. The beggar was not at all surprised, and gave him a club, and said to him, "If the innkeeper has changed your cloth and lamb, you can regain them by means of this club: you have only to say, 'Beat away, beat away, my little club,' and it will have enough power to knock down a whole army." So the woodcutter went to the inn a third time, and insisted upon his cloth and lamb being returned; and, as the innkeeper would not do so, he exclaimed, "Beat away, beat away, my little club!" and the club began to beat the innkeeper and his wife, till the missing property was returned.

He then went home and told his wife, with great joy, what had happened; and, in order to give greater consequence to his house, he invited the king to dinner next day. The king was very much surprised, and, about noon, sent a lackey to see what they were cooking for him; the messenger, however, returned with the news that there was not even a fire in the kitchen. His majesty was still more surprised when, at meal-time, he found the table laden with the finest dishes and drinks. Upon inquiry where all came from, the poor woodcutter told him his story, what happened in the wood, about the lamb and cloth, but did not mention a word about the club. The king, who was a regular tyrant, at once claimed the cloth and the lamb; and, as the man would not comply, he sent a few lackeys to him, to [Pg 163]take them away; but they were soon knocked down by the club. So the king sent a larger force against him; but they also perished to a man. On hearing this the king got into a great rage, and went in person with his whole army against him; but on this occasion, too, the woodcutter was victorious, because the club knocked down dead every one of the king's soldiers; the king himself died on the battle-field and his throne was occupied by the once poor woodcutter. It was a real blessing to his people; because, in his magnanimity, he delighted to assist all whom he knew to be in want or distress; and so he, also, lived a happy and contented man to the end of his days!

THE WORLD'S BEAUTIFUL WOMAN.

In the most beautiful land of Asia, where Adam and Eve may have lived, where all animals, including cows, live wild, where the corn grows wild, and even bread grows on trees, there lived a pretty girl, whose palace was built on a low hill, which looked over a pretty, a very pretty valley, from which one could see the whole world. In the same country there lived a young king who decided not to get married till he succeeded in finding the prettiest woman or girl in the world. The pretty maid lived with her old father, and with only two servant girls. The young king lived and enjoyed himself amongst the finest young aristocrats. One day it struck the young king that it would be a good thing to get married; so he instructed his aristocratic friends to go all over his vast realm, and to search about till they found the prettiest girl [Pg 164]in the land: they had not to trouble whether she was poor or rich; but she must be the prettiest. Each of them was to remain in the town where he found the girl that he deemed was the prettiest and to write and let the king know, so that he might go and have a look at all of them and choose for himself the prettiest amongst all the beauties, the one he liked best. After a year he received letters from every one of his seventy-seven friends, and extraordinarily all the seventy-seven letters arrived from the same town, where, on a low hill above a pretty little valley, there stood a golden palace, in which there lived a young lady with a nice old man and two maids, and from the four windows of which palace the whole world could be seen. The young king started with a large retinue of wedding guests to the place where the prettiest girl in the world lived: he found there all his seventy-seven friends, who were all fever-stricken with love, and were lying about on the pavement of the palace, on hay which was of a very fine silk-like grass; there they lay every one of them. The moment the young king saw the beautiful girl he cried: "The Lord has created you expressly for me; you are mine and I am yours! and it is my wish to find my rest in the same grave with you."

The young lady also fell very much in love with the handsome king; in her fond passion she could not utter a word, but only took him round his slender waist[1]and led him to her father. Her old father wept tears of joy, that at last a man was found whom his daughter could love, as she had thought every man ugly hitherto. The ceremony of betrothal and wedding was very short; at his pretty wife's wish, the king came to live on the beautiful spot, than which there was not a prettier one in the whole world! By the side of the palace there was an earth-hut, in which lived an old witch who knew all the young lady's secrets, and who helped her with advice whenever she needed it. The old witch praised the young lady's beauty to all she met, and it was she [Pg 165]who had gathered the seventy-seven young aristocrats into the palace. On the evening of the wedding she called upon "the world's beautiful lady" and praised the young king to her, his handsomeness and riches, and after she had praised him for an hour or two she sighed heavily: the pretty young lady asked her what troubled her, as she had this very moment spoken of her husband as being a handsome, rich, and worthy man? "Because, my pretty lady, my beautiful queen, if you two live sometime here, you will not long be the prettiest woman in the world; you are very pretty now, and your husband is the handsomest of all men; but should a daughter be born to you, she will be more beautiful than you; she will be more beautiful than the morning star—this is the reason of my sadness, my beautiful lady." "You are quite right, good old woman, I will follow any advice; if you tell me what to do, I will obey you. I will do anything to remain the most beautiful woman in the world." This was what the old witch said to the beautiful lady: "I will give you a handful of cotton wool; when your husband sleeps with you, put this wool on your lips, but be careful not to make it wet, because there will be poison on it. When your husband arrives at home all in perspiration from the dance, he will come to you and kiss you, and die a sudden death." The young lady did as the witch told her, and the young king was found dead next morning; but the poison was of such a nature that the physicians were not able to find out what the king had died of.

The bride was left a widow, and again went to live with her maid and her old father, and made a solemn vow that she would never marry again. And she kept her word. As it happened, however, by some inexplicable circumstance, or by some miracle, after a few months she discovered that she was with child; so she ran to the old witch and asked her what to do. The witch gave her a looking-glass and the following advice: "Every morning you have to ask this mirror whether there is a more beautiful woman than yourself in existence, and if it says that there is not, there [Pg 166]really won't be one for a long time, and your mind may be at ease; but should it say that there is one, there will be one, and I will see to that myself." The beautiful lady snatched the mirror from the witch in great joy, and as soon as she reached her dressing-room she placed the little mirror on the window ledge and questioned it thus: "Well, my dear little mirror, is there a more beautiful woman in the world than I?" The mirror replied: "Not yet, but there will be one soon, who will be twice as handsome as you." The beautiful woman nearly lost her wits in her sorrow, and informed the witch what the mirror had replied. "No matter," said the old hag, "let her be born, and we shall soon put her out of the way."

The beautiful lady was confined, and a pretty little daughter was born, and it would have been a sin to look at her with an evil eye. The bad woman did not even look at the pretty little creature, but fetched her mirror and said: "Well, my dear little mirror, is there a more beautiful creature than I?" and the looking-glass replied: "You are very beautiful, but your little daughter is seven times prettier than you." So as soon as she left her bed she sent for the old witch to ask her advice, who, when she took the babe in her arms, exclaimed that she had never seen such a beautiful creature in all her life. While she gazed at the beautiful child she spat in her eyes and covered her face, telling the beautiful woman to look at the child again in three hours, and when she uncovered it she would be surprised to find what a monster it had become. The beautiful lady felt very uneasy, and asked the witch whether she was allowed to question the mirror again? "Certainly," replied the witch, "for I know that at this moment you are the most beautiful woman in existence." But the mirror replied, "You are beautiful, but your daughter is seventy-seven times more beautiful than you." The beautiful woman nearly died of rage, but the old witch only smiled, being confident of her magic power.

[Pg 167]The three hours passed, the little girl's face was uncovered, and the old witch fainted away in her rage; for the little girl had become not only seven times, but seventy-seven times more beautiful than ever from the very same thing that usually disfigured other babies: when she recovered she advised the beautiful lady to kill her baby, as not even the devil himself had any power over it. The old father of the beautiful woman had died suddenly, broken hearted by his daughter's shame! The beautiful woman was nearly killed by sorrow over the loss of her father, and in order to forget her troubles, she spared her daughter till she was thirteen: the little girl grew more beautiful every day, so that the woman could not bear her daughter's beauty any longer, and handed her to the old witch to be killed. The witch was only too glad to avail herself of the opportunity, and took her into a vast forest, where she tied the girl's hands together with a wisp of straw, placed a wreath of straw on her head, and a girdle of straw round her waist, so that by lighting them she would burn to death the most beautiful masterpiece of the Lord. But all of a sudden a loud shouting was heard in the forest, and twelve robbers came running as swift as birds towards the place where the old witch and the pretty girl were standing. One of the robbers seized the girl, another knocked the old witch on the head, and gave her a sound beating. The witch shammed death, and the robbers left the wicked old wretch behind, carrying off the pretty girl (who had fainted in her fright) with them. After half an hour the old witch got up, and rushed to the castle where the beautiful woman lived, and said, "Well, my queen, don't question your mirror any more, for you are now the most beautiful creature in the world, your beautiful daughter lies under ground." The beautiful lady jumped for joy, and kissed the ugly old witch.

The pretty girl upon her recovery found herself in a nice little house, in a clean bed, and guarded by twelve men, who praised her beauty in whispers, which was such as no human eye [Pg 168]had seen before. The innocent little thing, not thinking of any harm, looked at the men with their great beards, who stared at her with wide open eyes. She got up from her soft bed, and thanked the good men for having delivered her from the clutches of the awful old witch, and then inquired where she was, and what they intended to do with her; if they meant to kill her, she begged them do it at once, as she would die with pleasure, and was only afraid of being killed by that horrible old witch, who was going to burn her to death. None of the robbers could utter a word, their hearts were so softened by her sweet words: such words as they had never before heard from human lips, and her innocent look which would have tamed even a wild bull. At last one of the robbers, who was splendidly dressed, said: "You pretty creature of the Lord, you are in the midst of twelve robbers, who are men of good hearts, but bad morals; we saved you from the hands of the ugly old witch whom I knocked down, and killed I believe; we would not kill you, for the whole world; but, on the contrary, would fight the whole world for you! Be the ornament of our house and the feast of our eyes! Whatsoever your eyes or your mouth may desire, be it wherever man exists, we will bring it to you! be our daughter, and we will be everything to you! your fathers! brothers! guardians! and, if you need it, your soldiers!" The little girl smiled, and was very pleased: she found more happiness among the robbers than she ever did in her mother's palace; she shook hands with all, commended herself to their protection, and at once looked after the cooking. The chief of the robbers called three strong maidens, dressed in white, from a cave, and ordered them to carry out without delay the orders of their queen, and if he heard one word of complaint against any of them, they should die the death of a pig. The young girl spoke kindly to the three maids, and called them her companions.

The robbers then went out on to the highway in great joy—to [Pg 169]continue their plundering—singing and whistling with delight, because their home and their band had the most beautiful queen in the world. The beautiful woman, the girl's mother, one day felt weary, and listless, because she had not heard any one praise her beauty for a very long time. So in her ennui she took her mirror and said to it: "My dear, sweet little mirror, is there a more beautiful creature in all the world, than I?" The little mirror replied, "You are very beautiful, but your daughter is a thousand times handsomer!" The woman nearly had a fit, in her rage, for she had not even suspected that her hateful daughter was yet alive: she ran to the old witch like one out of her mind, to tell what the mirror had said. The witch at once disguised herself as a gipsy, and started on her journey, and arrived at the fence of the place where the pretty girl lived; the garden was planted with flowers and large rose bushes; among the flower beds she could see the pretty girl sauntering in a dress fit for a queen. The old witch's heart nearly broke when she saw the young girl, for never, not even in her imagination, had she ever seen any one so beautiful. She stole into the garden among the flower beds, and on approaching saw that the young girl's fingers were covered with the most precious diamond rings: she kissed the girl's beautiful hand, and begged to be allowed to put on a ring more precious than any she had; the girl consented, and even thanked her for it. When she entered the house, she all at once dropped down as if dead; the witch rushed home, and brought the good news to the beautiful queen, who at once questioned the mirror, whether there was yet any one who was prettier than she, and the mirror replied, that there was not.

The pretty woman was delighted, and nearly went mad with joy on hearing that she was once more the most beautiful creature in existence, and gave the witch a handful of gold.

At noon the robbers dropped in one after another from their plundering, and were thunderstruck when they saw that the glory of their house and the jewel of their band lay dead. [Pg 170]They bewailed her with loud cries of grief, and commanded the maidens with threats to tell them who had done it, but they were even more stunned with grief, and bewailed the good lady, and could not utter a single word, till one of them said that she saw the pretty girl talking with a gipsy woman for a while, and that the moment the woman left she suddenly dropped down dead. After much weeping and wailing the robbers made preparations for the laying out of their adored queen; they took off her shoes in order to put more beautiful ones upon her pretty feet: they then took the rings off her fingers in order to clean them, and as at the very last one of the robbers pulled off the most precious ring from her little finger, the young girl sat up and smiled, and informed them that she had slept very well, and had had most beautiful dreams; and also that if they had not taken off that very ring (which the gipsy woman had put on that day) from her little finger she would never have waked again. The robbers smashed the murderous ring to atoms with their hatchet-sticks, and begged their dear queen not to speak to anyone, except themselves, as all others were wicked, and envious of her on account of her beauty, while they adored her. Having partaken of a good supper, the robbers again went out to their plunder singing, and quite at rest in their minds, and for a couple of weeks nothing happened to the young lady; but after a fortnight her mother again felt ennui and questioned her mirror: "Is there any one living being on this earth more beautiful than I?" The mirror replied: "You are very beautiful, but your daughter is one thousand times more beautiful." The beautiful lady began to tear her hair in rage, and went to complain to the witch that her daughter was alive still, so the witch again went off and found the young lady, as before, among the flower-beds. The witch disguised herself as a Jewess this time, and began to praise the gold and diamond pins with which the young lady's shawl was fastened, which she [Pg 171]admired very much, and begged the young lady's leave to allow her to stick another pin amongst those which she had already in her bosom, as a keepsake. Among all the pins the prettiest one was the one which the witch disguised as a Jewess stuck in the young lady's bosom. The young lady thanked her for it, and went indoors to look after the cooking, but as soon as she arrived in the house she gave a fearful scream and dropped down dead.

The joy of her mother was great when the witch arrived home in great delight and the mirror again proved that the girl was dead. The robbers were full of joy, in anticipation of the pleasure of seeing again their pretty young girl, whose beauty was apparently increasing daily; but when they heard the cries of sorrow of the three servant maids and saw the beautiful corpse stretched out on the bier, they lost all their cheerfulness and began to weep also. Three of the robbers carried in all the necessaries for the funeral, while the others undressed and washed the corpse, and as they were drawing out from her shawl the numerous pins, they found one amongst them which sparkled most brilliantly, whereupon two of them snatched it away, each being anxious to replace it in the girl's bosom when redressing her for burial, when suddenly the virgin queen sat up and informed them that her death was caused by a Jewess this time. The robbers buried the pin five fathoms deep in the ground, so that no evil spirit might get it. There is no more restless being in the world than a woman; it is a misfortune if she is pretty, and the same if she is not: if she be pretty she likes to be continually told of it, if she be not she would like to be. The evil one again tempted the beautiful lady, and she again questioned her mirror whether any living being was prettier than she: the mirror replied that her daughter was prettier.

Upon this she called the old witch all kinds of bad names in her rage, and threatened her that if she did not kill her daughter outright she would betray her to the world, and accuse her of having led her to all her evil deeds; that it was she who [Pg 172]induced her to kill her handsome husband, and that she had given her the mysterious mirror, which was the cause of her not being able to die in peace. The old hag made no reply, but went off in a boisterous manner: she transformed herself into a pretty girl and went straight into the house in which the young lady was dressing herself and falsely told her that she had been engaged by the robbers to wait always upon her while she dressed, because she had already been killed twice, once by a gipsy woman, and another time by a Jewess; and also that the robbers had ordered her not to do anything else but to help her in her toilet. The innocent girl believed all that the she-devil said. She allowed her to undo her hair and to comb it. The witch did her hair in accordance with the latest fashion, and plaited it and fastened it with all sorts of hair pins; while doing so she hid a hair-pin which she had brought with her among the girl's hair, so that it could not be noticed by anyone; having finished, the new lady's maid asked permission to leave her mistress for a moment, but never returned, and her young lady died, while all wept and sobbed most bitterly. The men and the maids had again to attend with tears to their painful duty of laying her out for her funeral; they took away all her rings, breast-pins, and hair-pins; they even opened every one of the folds of her dress, but still they did not succeed in bringing the young girl to life again. Her mother was really delighted this time, because she kept on questioning the mirror for three or four days, and it always replied to her heart's content. The robbers wailed and cried, and did not even enjoy their food; one of them proposed that they should not bury the girl, but that they should come to pray by the side of their dear dead; others again thought that it would be a pity to confide the pretty body to the earth, where it would be destroyed; others spoke of the terrible pang, and said that their hearts would break if they had to look at her dead beauty for any length of time. So they ordered a splendid coffin to be made of wrought gold. [Pg 173]They wrapped her in purple and fine linen; they caught an elk and placed the coffin between its antlers, so that the precious body might not decompose underground: the elk quietly carried the precious coffin about, and took the utmost care to prevent it falling from its antlers or its back. This elk happened to graze in Persia just as the son of the Persian king was out hunting all alone. The prince was twenty-three years old; he noticed the elk and also the splendid coffin between its antlers, whereupon he took a pound of sugar from his bag and gave it to the elk to eat. Taking the coffin from its back the Persian king's son opened the gold coffin with fear and trembling, when, unfolding the fine linen, he discovered a corpse, the like of which he had never seen before, not even in his dreams.

He began to shake it to wake her: to kiss her, and at last went down upon his knees by her side to pray to God fervently to restore her to life, but still she didn't move. "I will take her with me into my room," he said, sobbing. "Although it is a corpse that must have been dead for some time, there is no smell. The girl is prettier in her death than all the girls of Persia alive." It was late at night when the prince got home, carrying the golden coffin under his cloak. He bewailed the dead girl for a long time and then went to supper. The king looked anxiously into his son's eyes, but did not dare to question him as to the cause of his grief. Every night the prince locked himself up, and did not go to sleep until he had, for a long time, bemoaned his dead sweetheart; and whenever he awoke in the night he wept again.

The prince had three sisters, and they were very good girls, and very fond of their brother. They watched him every night through the keyhole, but could see nothing. They heard, however, their brother's sobbing and were very much grieved by it. The Persian king had war declared against him by the king of the neighbouring country. The king, being very advanced in age, asked his son to go in his place to fight the [Pg 174]enemy. The good son promised this willingly, although he was tortured by the thought of being obliged to leave his beautiful dead girl behind. As, however, he was aware that he would again be able to see and weep over his dear one when once the war was over, he locked himself in his room for two hours, weeping all the time, and kissing his sweetheart. Having finished, he locked his room and put the key in his sabretache. The good-hearted princesses impatiently waited till their brother crossed the border with his army, and so soon as they knew that he had left the country they went to the locksmith of the castle and took away every key he had, and with these tried to unlock their brother's room, till at last one of the keys did fit. They ordered every servant away from the floor on which the room was situated and all three entered. They looked all round, and in all the cupboards, and even took the bed to pieces, and as they were taking out the planks of the bed they suddenly discovered the glittering gold coffin, and in all haste placed it on the table, and having opened it found the sleeping angel. All three kissed her; but when they saw that they were unable to restore life, they wept most bitterly. They rubbed her and held balsam under her nose, but without avail. Then they examined her dress, which was very far superior to their own. They moved her rings and breast-pins, and dressed her up like a pretty doll. The youngest princess brought combs and perfumed hair-oils in order to do the hair of the dear dead. They pulled out the hair-pins and arranged them in nice order, so as to be able to replace them as before. They parted her golden hair, and began to comb it, adorning each lock with a hair-pin. As they were combing the hair at the nape of the neck the comb stuck fast, so they looked at once for the cause of it, when they saw that a golden hair-pin was entangled in the hair, which the eldest princess moved with the greatest care. Whereupon the beautiful girl opened her eyes and her lips formed themselves into a smile; and, as if awakening from a long, long dream, [Pg 175]she slightly stretched herself, and stepped from the coffin. The girls were not afraid at all, as she, who was so beautiful in her death, was still more beautiful in life. The youngest girl ran to the old king and told him what they had done, and that they had found out the cause of their brother's grief, and how happy they were now. The old king wept for joy and hastened after his daughter, and on seeing the beautiful child exclaimed: "You shall be my son's wife, the mother of my grandchildren!" And thereupon he embraced and kissed her, and took her into his room with his daughters. He sent for singing birds so that they might amuse his dear little new daughter. The old king inquired how she made his son's acquaintance and where she first met him. But the pretty princess knew nothing about it, but simply told him what she knew, namely, that she had two enemies who sooner or later would kill and destroy her; and she also told him that she had been living among robbers, to whom she had been handed over by an old witch who would always persecute her till the last moment of her life. The old king encouraged her, and bade her not to fear anyone, but to rest in peace, as neither her mother nor the old witch could get at her, the Persian wise men being quite able to distinguish evil souls from good ones. The girl settled down and partook of meat and drink with the king's daughters, and also inquired after the young prince, asking whether he was handsome or ugly; although, she said, it did not matter to her whether he was handsome or ugly; if he was willing to have her, she would marry him. The princesses brought down the painted portrait of the prince and the young girl fell so deeply in love with it that she continually carried it with her kissing it. One morning the news spread over all the country that the young king had conquered his enemy and was hurrying home to his residential city. The news turned out to be true, and clouds of dust could be seen in the distance as the horsemen approached. The princesses requested their pretty new [Pg 176]sister to go with them into the room which adjoined their brother's, where her coffin was kept under the bed.

The moment the prince arrived, he jumped off his horse, and, not even taking time to greet his father, he unlocked his room and began to sob most violently, dragging out the coffin gently from under the bed, placing it on the bed with great care, and then opening the lid with tears; but he could only find a hair-pin. He rushed out of the room like a madman, leaving the coffin and the door open, crying aloud, and demanding what sacrilegious hand had robbed his angel from him. But his angel, over whom he had shed so many tears, stood smiling before him. The youth seized her and covered her with as many kisses as there was room for. He took his betrothed, whom Providence had given to him, to his father and told him how he had found the pretty corpse on the back of an elk; and the girl also told the whole story of her life; and the princesses confessed how they had broken into their brother's room, and how they restored his sweetheart to life again. The old king was intoxicated with joy, and the same day sent for a priest, and a great wedding feast was celebrated. The young folks whom Providence had brought together lived very happily, when one day the young queen, who was as beautiful as a fairy, informed her husband that she was being persecuted, and that while her mother lived she could never have any peace. "Don't fear, angel of my heart," said the young king, "as no human or diabolic power can harm you while you are here. Providence is very kind to us. You seem to be a favourite and will be protected from all evil." The young queen was of a pious turn of mind and believed the true words of her husband, as he had only spoken out her own thoughts. About half a year had passed by and the beautiful woman of the world was still happy. Her mirror was covered with dust, as she never dreamt for a moment that her daughter was yet alive; but being one day desirous to repeat [Pg 177]her former amusement she dusted her mirror, and, pressing it to her bosom, said: "Is there a prettier living creature in the world than myself?" The mirror replied: "You are very pretty, but your daughter is seventy-seven thousand times more beautiful than you." The beautiful woman, on hearing the mirror's reply, fainted away, and they had to sprinkle cold water over her for two hours before she came round. Off she set, very ill, to the old witch and begged her, by everything that was holy, to save her from that hateful girl, else she would have to go and commit suicide. The old witch cheered her, and promised that she would do all that lay in her power.

After eight months had elapsed the young prince had to go to war again; and, with a heavy heart, took leave of his dear pretty wife, as—if one is obliged to tell it—she was *enceinte*. But the prince had to go, and he went, consoling his wife, who wept bitterly, that he would return soon. The young king left orders that as soon as his wife was confined a confidential messenger was to be sent without delay to inform him of the event. Soon after his departure two beautiful boys with golden hair were born and there was great joy in the royal household. The old king danced about, like a young child, with delight. The princesses wrapped the babies in purple and silk, and showed them to everybody as miracles of beauty.

The old king wrote down the joyful news and sent the letter by a faithful soldier, instructing him that he was not to put up anywhere under any pretence whatever. The old soldier staked his moustache not to call anywhere till he reached the young king.

While angels were rejoicing, devils were racking their brains and planning mischief!

The old witch hid a flask full of spirits under her apron and hurried off on the same road as the soldier, in order to meet him with his letter. She pitched a small tent on the road-side using some dirty sheets she had brought with her, and, placing [Pg 178]her flask of spirits in front of her, waited for the passers-by. She waited long, but no one came; when all of a sudden a huge cloud gathered in the sky, and the old witch was delighted. A fearful storm set in. As the rain poured down, the old witch saw the soldier running to escape the rain. As he ran past her tent, the wicked old soul shouted to him to come in and sit down in her tent till the rain was over. The soldier, being afraid of the thunder, accepted her invitation, and sat musingly in the tent, when the old woman placed a good dose of spirits in front of him, which the soldier drank; she gave him another drop, and he drank that too. Now there was a sleeping-draft in it, and so the soldier fell fast asleep, *and slept like a fur cloak*. The old woman then looked in his bag for the letter, and, imitating *the old king's* hand-writing to great perfection, informed the young prince that a great sorrow had fallen upon his house, inasmuch as his wife had been delivered of two puppies. She sealed the letter and woke the soldier, who began to run again and did not stop until he reached the camp. The young prince was very much upset by his father's letter, but wrote in reply that no matter what sort of children his wife had borne they were not to touch but to treat them as his own children until he returned. He ordered the messenger to hurry back with his reply, and not to stop anywhere; but the old soldier could not forget the good glass of spirits he had, and so went into the tent again and had some more. The witch again mixed it with a sleeping-draught and searched the bag while the soldier slept. She stole the letter, and, imitating the young prince's hand-writing, wrote back to the old king that he was to have his wife and the young babes killed, because he held a woman who had puppies must be a bad person. The old king was very much surprised at his son's reply but said nothing to anyone. At night he secretly called the old soldier to him and had his daughter-in-law placed in a black carriage. The old soldier sat on the box and had orders to take the woman and her two children into the middle of the forest and brain them there. The carriage stopped in the [Pg 179]middle of the forest, the old soldier got down and opened the door, weeping bitterly. He pulled out a big stick from under his seat and requested the young queen to alight. She obeyed his orders and descended holding her babes in her arms.

The old soldier tried three times to raise the stick, but could not do so; he was too much overcome by grief. The young queen implored him not to kill her, and told him she was willing to go away and never see anyone again. The old soldier let her go, and she took her two babes and sheltered in a hollow tree in the forest: there she passed her time living on roots and wild fruit.

The soldier returned home, and was questioned by the old king as to whether he had killed the young queen, as he didn't like to disappoint his son, who was to return from the camp next day. The old soldier declared on his oath that he had killed her and her babes too, and that he had thrown their bodies into the water. The young king arrived at home in great sorrow, and was afraid to catch sight of his unfortunate wife and her ugly babes.

The old king had left his son's letter upon his desk by mistake; the prince picked it up, and was enraged at its contents: "This looks very like my writing," he said, "but I did not write it; it must be the work of some devil." He then produced his father's letter from his pocket, and handed it to him. The old king was horrified at the awful lie which some devil had written in his hand. "No, my dear son," said the old father, weeping, "this is not what I wrote to you; what I really did write was, that two sons with golden hair had been born to you." "And I," replied the young king, "said that whatsoever my wife's offspring was, no harm was to happen to them till I returned. Where is my wife? where are my golden-haired children?" "My son," said the old king,

"I have carried out [Pg 180]your orders; I sent them to the wood and had them killed, and the corporal belonging to the royal household had their bodies cast into the water." The old soldier listened, through a crack in the door, to the conversation of the two kings, who both wept bitterly. He entered the room without being summoned, and said: "I could not carry out your orders, my lord and king; I had not the heart to destroy the most beautiful creature in the world; so I let her go free in the forest, and she left, weeping. If they have not been devoured by wild beasts, they are alive still." The young king never touched a bit of supper, but had his horse saddled at once, and ordered his whole body-guard out. For three days and three nights they searched the wood in every direction, without intermission: on the fourth night, at midnight, the young king thought he heard, issuing from a hollow tree, a baby's cry, which seemed as harmonious to him as the song of a nightingale. He sprang off his horse, and found his beautiful wife, who was more beautiful than ever, and his children, who were joyfully prattling in their mother's arms. He took his recovered family home, amidst the joyous strains of the band, and, indeed, a high festival was celebrated throughout the whole realm.

The young woman again expressed her fears with trembling, that, while her mother and that she-devil were alive, she could not live in peace.

The young king issued a warrant for the capture of the old witch; and the old soldier came, leading behind him, tied to a long rope, an awful creature, whose body was covered all over with frightful prickles, and who had an immense horn in the middle of her forehead. The young queen at once recognised her as the old witch, who had been captured in the act of searching the wood in order to find her, and slay her and her two babes. The young queen had the old witch led into a secret room, where she questioned her as to why she had persecuted her all her life. "Because," said the old witch, "I am the daughter of your grandfather, and the sister of your mother! When I was [Pg 181]yet but a suckling babe, your grandmother gave orders that I was to be thrown into the water; a devil coming along the road took me and educated me. I humoured your mother's folly because I thought she would go mad in her sorrow that a prettier creature than herself existed; but the Lord has preserved you, and your mother did not go mad till I covered her with small-pox, and her face became all pitted and scarred. Her mirror was always mocking her, and she became a wandering lunatic, roaming about over the face of the land, and the children pelting her with stones. She continually bewails you."

The young queen informed her husband of all this, and he had the old witch strangled, strung up in a tree, and a fire made of brimstone lighted under her. When her soul (pára-animal soul) left her wicked body, a horse was tied to each of her hands and feet, and her body torn into four, one quarter of her body being sent to each of the points of the compass, so that the other witches might receive a warning as to their fate.

The "most beautiful woman in the world" was now very ugly, and happened by chance to reach the palace where the pretty queen lived. Her daughter wept over her, and had her kept in a beautiful room, every day showing her through a glass door her beautiful children. The poor lunatic wept and tortured herself till one day she jumped out of the window and broke her neck. The young king loved his beautiful wife as a dove does its mate; he obeyed her slightest wish, and guarded her from every danger.

The two little sons with the golden hair became powerful and valiant heroes, and when the old king died he was carried to his vault by his two golden-haired grandchildren.

The young couple, who had gone through so many sad trials, are alive still, if they have not died since.

[1]The great pride of the Hungarian youth is to have a slender waist.

[Pg 182]

THE GIRL WITHOUT HANDS.

There was once, I don't know where, a king whose only son was an exceedingly handsome and brave fellow, who went far into the neighbouring country to fight. The old king used to send letters to his son into the camp, through an old faithful servant. Once it happened that the letter-carrying old servant took a night's lodging in a lonely house, which was inhabited by a middle-aged woman and her daughter, who was very pretty. The people of the house had supper prepared for the messenger, and during the meal the woman questioned him whether he thought her or her daughter to be the prettier, but the messenger did not like to state the exact truth, as he did not wish to appear ungrateful for their hospitality, and only said, "Well, we can't deny but must confess it that we old people cannot be so handsome as the young ones." The woman made no reply; but as soon as the messenger had left she gave her servant orders to take her daughter into the wood and kill her, and to bring her liver, lungs, and two hands back with him. The manservant took the pretty girl with him, and, having gone a good distance, he stopped, and told the girl of her mother's commands. "But," continued he, "I haven't got the heart to kill you, as you have always been very kind to me; there is a small dog which has followed us, and I will take his liver and lungs back to your mother, but I shall be compelled to cut off your hands, as I can't go back without them." The servant did as he proposed; he took out the small dog's lungs and liver, and cut off the girl's hands, much as it was against his wish. He carefully covered the stumps of her arms with a cloth, and sent the [Pg 183]girl away and went back to his mistress. The woman took the lungs and liver, put them into her mouth, and said, "You have come out of me, you must return into me," and swallowed them. The two hands she threw up into the loft. The servant left the woman's house in a great hurry at the earliest opportunity, and never returned again. In the meantime the girl without hands wandered about in unknown places. Fearing that she would be discovered in the daytime, she hid herself in the wood, and only left her hiding place at night to find food, and if she chanced to get into an orchard she ate the fruit she could reach with her mouth.

At last she came to the town where the king lived: the prince had by this time returned from the war. One morning, the king was looking out of his window, and to his great annoyance discovered that, again, there were less pears on a favourite tree in the orchard than he had counted the previous day. In a great rage he sent for the gardener, whose special business it was to take care of the orchard; but he excused himself on the ground that while he was watching the orchard at night an irresistible desire to sleep came over him, the like of which he had never experienced before, and which he was quite unable to shake off. The king, therefore, ordered another man to keep watch under the tree the next night, but he fared in the same way as the first; the king was still more angry. On the third night, the prince himself volunteered to keep watch, and promised to guard the fruit of the favourite tree; he laid down on the lawn under the tree, and did not shut his eyes. About midnight, the girl without hands came forth from a thicket in the garden, and, seeing the prince, said to him, "One of your eyes is asleep, the other one must go to sleep too, at once." No sooner had she uttered these words than the prince fell fast asleep, and the girl without hands walked under the tree, and picked the fruit with her mouth. But as there were only a few more pears left on the boughs which she could get at, she was obliged, in [Pg 184]order to satisfy her hunger, to step on a little mound, and stand on tiptoe that she might reach the fruit; whilst standing in this position she slipped, and, having no hands to hold on with, she fell on the sleeping prince.

The shock awoke the prince at once, and, grasping the girl firmly with his arms, he kept her fast. Next morning the king looking out of his window discovered to his astonishment that no pears were missing, and therefore sent a messenger into the garden to his son to inquire what had happened? As soon as dawn began to break, the prince saw the girl's beautiful face; the king's messenger had by this time reached the prince, who in reply to his query, said: "Tell my father that I have caught the thief, and I will take care not to let her escape. If my father, the king, will not give me permission to marry her, I will never enter his house again; tell him also, that the girl has no hands." The king did not oppose his son's desire, and the girl without hands became the prince's wife, and they lived happily together for a time. It happened, however, that war broke out again with the sovereign of the neighbouring country, and the prince was once more obliged to go with his army. While he was away the princess was confined, and bore two children with golden hair. The old king was highly delighted, and at once wrote to his son informing him of the happy event. The letter was again entrusted to the same man, who took the messages during the first war: he on his way remembered the house where he was so well received on a previous occasion, and arranged that he should spend the night there. This time he found the old woman only. He got into conversation with her, and she asked him where he was going, and what news he had from the royal town: the messenger told her how the prince had found a beautiful girl without hands, whom he had married, and who had had two beautiful children. The woman at once guessed that it was her own daughter, and that she had been deceived by her servant; she gave her guest plenty to eat and drink, till he [Pg 185]was quite drunk and went to sleep. Whereupon the woman searched the messenger's bag, found the king's letter, opened it and read it. The gist of the letter was this, "My dear son, you have brought to my house a dear and beautiful wife, who has borne you a beautiful golden-haired child."

The woman instantly wrote another letter, which ran thus: "You have brought to my house a prostitute, who has brought shame upon you, for she has been confined of two puppies." She folded the letter, sealed it as the first had been, and put it into the messenger's bag. Next morning the messenger left, having first been invited to spend the night at her house on his return, as the wicked mother was anxious to know what the prince's answer would be to the forged letter. The messenger reached the prince, handed him the letter, which gave him inexpressible grief; but as he was very fond of his wife he only replied, that, whatever the state of affairs might be, no harm was to happen to his wife until his return. The messenger took the letter back and again called upon the old woman, who was not chary to make him drunk again and to read the reply *clandestinely*. She was angry at the prince's answer, and wrote another letter in his name, in which she said, that if matters were as they had been represented to him in the letter, his wife must get out of the house without delay, so that he might not see her upon his return.

The messenger, not suspecting anything, handed the letter to the king, who was very much upset, and read it to his daughter-in-law. The old king pitied his pretty and good natured daughter deeply, but what could he do? They saddled a quiet horse, put the two golden-haired princes in a basket and tied it in front of the princess; and thus the poor woman was sent away amidst great lamentations.

She had been travelling without ceasing for three days, till on the third day she came into a country where she found a lake full of magic water, which had the power of reviving and making [Pg 186]good the maimed limbs of any crippled man or beast who bathed in it. So the woman without hands took a bath in the lake, and both her hands were restored. She washed her children's clothes in the same lake, and again continued her journey. Not long after this the war with the neighbouring king was over, and the prince returned home. On hearing what had happened to his wife he fell into a state of deep grief, and became so ill that his death was expected daily. After a long illness, however, his health began to improve, but only very slowly, and years elapsed before his illness and his great grief had so far been conquered that he had strength or inclination to go out. At last he tried hunting, and spent whole days in the forest. One day as he was thus engaged he followed a stag, and got deeper and deeper into the thick part of the wood; in the meantime the sun had set and darkness set in. The prince, having gone too far, could not find his way back. But as good luck would have it he saw a small cottage, and started in its direction to find a night's lodging. He entered, and found a woman with two children—his wife and two sons. The woman at once recognised the prince, who, however, did not even suspect her to be his wife, because her hands were grown again: but, at the same time, the great likeness struck him very much, and at first sight he felt a great liking for the woman. On the next day he again went out hunting with his only faithful servant, and purposely allowed darkness to set in so that he might sleep at the cottage. The prince felt very tired and laid down to sleep, while his wife sat at the table sewing, and the two little children played by her side.

It happened that in his sleep the prince dropped his arm out of bed; one of the children noticing this called his mother's attention to it, whereupon the woman said to her son, "Place it back, my son, place it back, it's the hand of your royal father." The child approached the sleeping prince and gently lifted his arm back again. After a short time the prince dropped his leg [Pg 187]from the bed while asleep; the child again told his mother of it, and she said, "Place it back, my son, put it back, it's your father's leg." The boy did as he was told, but the prince knew nothing of it. It happened, however, that the prince's faithful servant was awake and heard every word the woman said to the child, and told the story to his master the next day. The prince was astonished, and no longer doubted that the woman was his wife, no matter how she had recovered her hands. So the next day he again went out hunting, and, according to arrangement, stayed late in the wood and had to return to the cottage again. The prince, having gone to bed, feigned sleep, and dropped his arm over the bed; his wife, seeing this, again said, "Put it back, my son, put it back, it's your royal father's arm." Afterwards he dropped his other arm, and then his two legs purposely; and the woman in each case bade her son put them back, in the same words. At last he let his head hang over the bedside, and his wife said to her son, "Lift it back, my son, lift it back; it's your royal father's head." But the little fellow, getting tired of all this, replied, "I shan't do it; you better do it yourself this time, mother." "Lift it back, my son," again said the mother, coaxingly; but the boy would not obey, whereupon the woman herself went to the bed, in order to lift the prince's head. But no sooner had she touched him than her husband caught hold of her with both his hands, and embraced her. "Why did you leave me?" said he, in a reproachful tone. "How could I help leaving you," answered his wife, "when you ordered me out of your house?" "I wrote in the letter," said the prince, "this and this;" and told her what he had really written; and his wife explained to him what had been read to her from the letter that had been changed. The fraud was thus discovered, and the prince was glad beyond everything that he had found his wife and her two beautiful children.

He at once had all three taken back to the palace, where a [Pg 188]second wedding was celebrated, and a great festival held. Guests were invited from the 77th country, and came to the feast. Through the letter-carrying messenger it became known that the cause of all the mischief was no one else than the princess's envious mother. But the prince forgave her all at the urgent request of his wife; and the young couple lived for a great many years in matrimonial bliss, their family increasing greatly. At the old king's death the whole realm fell to the happy couple, who are still alive, if they have not died since.

THE KING AND THE DEVIL.

In the country where lions and bearded wolves live there was a king whose favourite sport was hunting and shooting; he had some hundred hounds or more, quite a house full of guns, and a great many huntsmen. The king had a steady hand, a sharp eye, and the quarry he aimed at never escaped, for the king never missed what he aimed at; his only peculiarity was that he did not care to go out shooting with his own people only, but he would have liked the whole world to witness his skill in killing game, and that every good man in the world should partake of it. Well then, whenever he made a good bag the cook and the cellarer had so much work to do that they were not done till dawn. Such was the king who reigned in the land where lions and bearded wolves live.

Once upon a time this king, according to custom, invited the sovereigns of the neighbouring lands to a great shooting party, and also their chief men. It was in the height of summer, just at the beginning of the dog-days. In the early morning, when they were driving out on to the pasture the sheep with the [Pg 189]silken fleece, the dogs could already be heard yelping, huntsmen blowing with all their might into the thin end of their horns, and all was noise and bustle, so that the royal courtyard rang out with the noise. Then the king swallowed his breakfast in a soldierlike fashion, and all put on their hunting hats adorned with eagle's feathers, buckled the shining straps under their chins, mounted their horses, and in a short time were off over hedges and ditches, plunging into the vast forest, as the heat was too great for them to hunt in the open country. Each king accompanied by his own men went in his own direction, and game was killed with lightning speed; but the king who owned the forest went by himself in order to show his friends how much game he could kill single handed. But by some strange chance—who can tell how?—no game crossed the king's track. He went hither and thither but found nothing; looking round he discovered that he had got into a part of the wood where not even his grandfather had ever been; he went forward but still was lost; sideways, but still did not know the way; to the right, and found that he was in the same predicament as the man in Telek, namely, that unless he was taken home he would never find it. He called upon God for help, but as he never did that before—for the king didn't like to go to church and never invited the priest, except upon All Souls' Day, to dinner—the Lord would not help him; so he called upon the Devil, who appeared at once, as he will appear anywhere, even where he is not wanted. "You need not tell me what you are doing here, good king," said the evil spirit, "I know that you have been out shooting and have found no game and that you have lost your way. Promise me that you will give me what you have not got in your house and you shall find plenty of game and I will take you home." "You ask very little, poor soul," said the king, "Your request shall be granted; moreover, I will give you something of what I have, whatever you may wish, if you will but take me home."

[Pg 190]Shortly afterwards the king arrived at home, and had so much game with him that his horse could scarcely stand beneath the weight; the other kings were quite impatient with waiting for him, and were highly delighted when he arrived. At last they sat down to supper and ate and drank heartily, but the devil ate nothing but the scrapings from the pots and pans, and drank no wine but the dregs that were left in the bottles. At midnight an old woman appeared before the company of jolly kings and shouted as loud as she could in delight because a beautiful little daughter had been born to the king. The devil jumped up and capered about in his joy; *standing on his toes and clapping his bony heels together, he spun the king round like a whirlwind* and shouted in his ear, "That girl, king, was not in your house to-day and I will come for her in ten years." The devil hereupon saddled midnight and darted off like lightning, while the guests stared at each other in amazement, and the king's face turned ghastly pale.

Next morning they counted the heads of game and found that the king had twice as much as all the rest put together: yet he was very sad; he made presents to all his guests, and gave them an escort of soldiers as far as the boundary of his realm.

Ten years passed as swiftly as the bird flies and the devil appeared punctually to the minute. The king tried to put him off, and walked up and down his room greatly agitated; he thought first of one thing and then of another. At last he had the swineherd's daughter dressed up like a princess, and placed her on his wife's arm, and then took her to the devil, both parents weeping most bitterly, and then handed the child over to the black soul. The devil carried her away in high glee, but when the pretty little creature was passing a herd of swine she said, "Well, little sucking pigs, my father won't beat me any more on your account, for I'm leaving you and going to the 77th country, where the angels live." The devil listened to the little girl's words and at last discovered that he had been [Pg 191]deceived; in a rage he flew back to the royal fortress, and dashed the poor child with such force against the gate-post that her smallest bone was smashed into a thousand atoms. He roared at the king in such a voice that all the window fittings dropped out and the plaster fell off the walls in great lumps. "Give me your own daughter," he screamed, "for whatever you promise to the devil you must give to him or else he will carry off what you have not promised." The king again tried to collect his wits and had the shepherd's daughter who tended the sheep with the golden fleece, and who was ten years old, dressed in the royal fashion and handed her to the devil amidst great lamentation. He even placed at the devil's disposal a closed carriage, "so that the sun might not tan his daughter's face or the wind blow upon her," as he said, but it was really to prevent the little girl seeing what was passing and so betraying herself. As the carriage passed by the silken meadow and the little girl heard the baaing of the lambs she opened the door and called to the little animals, saying, "Well, little baa-lambs, my father won't beat me any more on your account, and I won't run after you in the heat now, because the king is sending me to the 77th country, where the angels live." The devil was now in a towering passion, and the flame shot out of his nostrils as thick as my arm; he threw the little girl up into the clouds and returned to the royal palace.

The king saw the carriage returning and trembled like an aspen leaf. He dressed up his daughter, weeping bitterly as he did so, and when the devil stepped across the threshold of the palace he went to meet him with the beautiful child, the like of which no other mother ever bore. The devil, in a great rage, pushed the pretty lily into a slit of his shirt, and ran with her over hill and dale. Like a thunderstorm he carried off the little trembling Maria into his dark home, which was lighted up with burning sulphur, and placed her on a pillow stuffed with owl's feathers. He then set a black table before her, and on it mixed [Pg 192]two bushels of millet seed with three bushels of ashes, saying, "Now, you little wretch, if you don't clean this millet in two hours, I will kill you with the most horrible tortures." With this he left her, and slammed the door that it shock the whole house. Little innocent Maria wept bitterly, for she knew she could not possibly finish the work in the stated time. While she wept in her loneliness, the devil's son very quietly entered the room. He was a fine handsome lad, and they called him Johnnie. Johnnie's heart was full of pity at seeing the little girl's sorrow, and cheered her up, telling her that if she ceased crying he would do the work for her at once. He felt in his pocket, and took out a whistle; and, going into a side-room, he blew it, and in a moment the whole place was filled with devils, whom Johnnie commanded to clean the millet in the twinkling of an eye. By the time little Maria winked three times, the millet was not only cleansed, but every seed was polished and glittered like diamonds. Until the father's return Maria and Johnnie amused themselves in childish games. The old devil upon his return, seeing all the work done, shook his head so vehemently that burning cinders dropped from his hair. He gave the little girl some manna to eat and lay down to sleep.

Next day the ugly old devil mixed twice as much millet and ashes, as he was very anxious to avenge himself on the child whose father had taken him in twice; but, by the help of Johnnie's servants, the millet was again cleaned. The devil in his rage gnawed off the end of his beard and spat it out on the ground, where every hair became a venomous serpent. The little girl screamed, and at the sound of her voice all the serpents stretched themselves on the ground, and wriggled about before the little girl like young eels, for they were charmed, never having heard so sweet a voice before. The devil was very much enraged that all the animals and the devils themselves, with the exception of himself, were so fond of this pretty little girl. "Well, soul of [Pg 193]a dog, you little imp," said the devil, gnashing his teeth, "if by to-morrow morning you do not build from nothing, under my window, a church, the ceiling of which will be the sky, and the priest in it the Lord Himself, whom your father does not fear, I will slay you with tortures the like of which are not known even in nethermost hell."

Little Maria was terribly frightened. The old devil, having given his orders, disappeared amidst thunder. The kind-hearted Johnnie here appeared, blew his whistle, and the devils came. They listened to the orders, but replied, that no devil could build a church out of nothing, and that, moreover, they dare not go up to heaven and had no power over the Lord to make him become a priest; that the only advice they could give was, for Johnnie and the little girl to set off at once, before it was too late, and so escape the tortures threatened by the old devil. They listened to the advice of the devils, and Johnnie buried his whistle in a place where his father would not be able to find it, and send the devils after them. They hurried off towards Maria's father's land; when, all of a sudden, Maria felt her left cheek burning very much, and complained of it to Johnnie, who, looking back, found that his mother was galloping after them on the stick of a whitewashing brush. Johnnie at once saw their position, and told Maria to turn herself into a millet field, and he would be the man whose duty it was to scare away the birds. Maria did so at once, and Johnnie kept the sparrows off with a rattle. The old woman soon came up, and asked whether he had not seen a boy and girl running past, a few minutes before. "Well, yes," replied he, "there are a great many sparrows about, my good lady, and I can't guard my millet crop from them. Hush! Hush!" "I didn't ask you," replied she, "whether you had any sparrows on your millet field or not; but whether you saw a boy and girl running past." "I've already broken the wings of two cock [Pg 194]sparrows, and hanged them to frighten away the rest," replied the artful boy.

"The fellow's deaf, and crazy too," said the devil's wife, and hurried back to the infernal regions. The boy and girl at once retransformed themselves, and hurried on, when Maria's left cheek began to burn again, more painfully this time than before; and not without reason, for when Johnnie looked back this time, he saw his father, who had saddled the south wind, tearing after them, and great, awe-inspiring, rain-bearing clouds following in his track. Maria at once turned into a tumble-down church, and Johnnie into an aged monk, holding an old clasp-bible in his hand.

"I say, old fool, have you not seen a young fellow and a little wench run past? If you have, say so; if you have not, may you be struck dumb!" yelled the old devil to the monk with the Bible. "Come in," said the pious monk, "come in, into the house of the Lord. If you are a good soul pray to Him and He will help you on your journey, and you will find what you are so anxiously looking for. Put your alms into this bag, for our Lord is pleased with the offerings of the pure in heart." "Perish you, your church, and your book, you old fool. I'm not going to waste any money in such tomfoolery. Answer my question! Have you seen a boy and girl go past?" again inquired the devil, in a fearful rage. "Come back to your Lord, you old cursed soul," replied the holy father, "it's never too late to mend, but it's a sin to put off amending your ways. Offer your alms, and you will find what you seek!" The devil grew purple with rage; and, lifting up his huge mace, he struck like lightning at the monk's head, but the weapon slipped aside and hit the devil on the shin such a blow that made him and all his family limp; they would limp to this very day, if they had not perished since! Jumping on the wind with his lame leg, the devil rode back home. The young couple by this time had [Pg 195]nearly reached the land where Maria's father reigned; when, all of a sudden, both the girl's cheeks began to burn as they had never burnt before. Johnnie looked back and saw that both his father and his mother were riding after them on two dragons, who flew faster than even the whirlwind. Maria at once became a silver lake and Johnnie a silver duck. As soon as the two devils arrived they at once scented out that the lake was the girl and the duck the boy; because wherever there are two devils together nothing can be concealed. The woman began to scoop up the water of the lake, and the male devil to throw stones at the duck; but each scoop of water taken out of the lake only caused the water to rise higher and higher; and every stone missed the duck, as he dived to the bottom of the lake and so dodged them. The devil became quite exhausted with throwing stones, and beckoned to his wife to wade with him into the lake, and so catch the duck, as it would be a great pity for their son to be restored to earth. The devils swam in, but the water of the lake rose over their heads so quickly that they were both drowned before they could swim out, and that's the reason why there are no devils now left. The boy and the girl, after all their trials, at last reached the palace of Maria's parents. The girl told them what had happened to her since the devil carried her off, and praised Johnnie very highly, telling them how he had guarded her. She also warned her father, that he who does not love God must perish, and is not worthy of happiness. The king listened to his daughter's advice, and sent for a priest to the next village, and first of all married Maria to the son of the devil, and the young couple lived very happily ever after. The king gave up hunting, and sent messages to the neighbouring kings, that he was a happy father; and the poor found protection and justice in his land. The king and his wife both died at the same time, and, after that, Johnnie and his wife became rulers of the land inhabited by lions and bearded wolves.

[Pg 196]

THE THREE PRINCES, THE THREE DRAGONS, AND THE OLD WOMAN WITH THE IRON NOSE.

On the shores of the Blue Sea there was a land in which dragons grew. This land had a king whose court was draped in black, and whose eye never ceased to weep, because every Friday he had to send ninety-nine men to the dragons, who were the pest of the place, and who slew and devoured the ninety-nine human beings sent to them. The king had three sons, each of whom was handsomer and more clever than the other. The king was very fond of his sons, and guarded them most carefully. The eldest was called Andrew, the next Emerich, and the youngest Ambrose. There were no other lads left in the land, for the dragons fed on lads' flesh only. One day Andrew and Emerich went to their father and begged him to allow them to go and fight the dragons, as they were sure they could conquer them, and that the dragons would not want any more human flesh after they had been there. But the father would not even listen to his sons' request. As for Ambrose, he did not even dare so much as to submit such a request to his father. Andrew and Emerich, at length, by dint of much talking, prevailed upon their father to allow them to go and fight the dragons. Now, there were only three dragons left in the land: one had seven heads, another eight, and the third nine; and these three had devoured all the other dragons, when they found that there were no more lads to be had. Andrew and Emerich joyfully galloped off towards the copper, silver, and golden bridges in the neighbourhood of which the dragons lived, and Ambrose was left alone to console his royal father, who bewailed his other sons.

[Pg 197]Ambrose's godmother was a fairy, and as it is the custom for godmothers to give presents to their godchildren, Ambrose received a present from his fairy godmother, which consisted of a black egg with five corners, which she placed under Ambrose's left armpit. Ambrose carried his egg about with him under his left armpit for seven winters and seven summers, and on Ash Wednesday, in the eighth year, a horse with five legs and three heads jumped out of the egg; this horse was a Tátos and could speak.

At the time when the brothers went out to fight the dragons, Ambrose was thirteen years and thirteen days old, and his horse was exactly five years old. The two elder brothers had been gone some time, when he went into the stable to his little horse, and, laying his head upon its neck, began to weep bitterly. The little horse neighed loudly and said, "Why are you crying, my dear master?" "Because," replied Ambrose, "I dare not ask my father to let me go away, although I should like to do so very much." "Go to your royal father, my dear master, for he has a very bad attack of toothache just now, and tell him that the king of herbs sends word to him through the Tátos-horse with three heads, that his toothache will not cease until he gives you permission to go and fight the dragons; and you can also tell him that if you go, there will be no more dragons left on this earth; but if you do not go his two elder boys will perish in the stomachs of the dragons. Tell him, also, that I have assured you that you will be able to make the dragons vomit out, at once, all the lads whomsoever they have swallowed; and that his land will become so powerful when the lads, who have grown strong in the stomachs of the dragons, return, that, while the world lasts, no nation will ever be able to vanquish him." Thus spoke the Tátos colt, and neighed so loudly that the whole world rang with the sound. The little boy told his father what the Tátos colt had told him; but the king objected for a long time, and no wonder, as he was afraid lest evil might happen to [Pg 198]his only son: but at last his sufferings got the better of him, and, after objecting for three hours, he promised his son that if the Tátos were able to carry out its promise he would give him permission to go and fight the dragons.

As soon as he had uttered these words his toothache left him. The little lad ran off and told the message to his little horse, which capered and neighed with delight. "I heard you when you were bargaining," said the horse to its little master, who in his delight didn't know what to do with himself, "and I should have heard you even if you had been a hundred miles away. Don't fear anything, my little master; our ride, it is true, will be a long one, but in the end it will turn out a lucky one. Go, my great-great-grandmother's great-great-grandmother's saddle is there on that crooked willow; put it on me, it will fit me exactly!"

The prince ran, in fact he rushed like a madman, fetched the ragged old saddle, put it on his horse, and tied it to a gate-post. Before leaving his father's home, the little horse asked its little master to plug up one of its nostrils; the prince did so, and the little horse blew upon him with the other nostril which he had left open, when, oh, horror! the little boy became mangy like a diseased sucking pig. The little horse, however, turned into a horse with golden hair, and glistened like a mirror. When the little boy caught sight of his ugly face amidst the hair of his shining horse, he became very sad. "Plug up my other nostril, too!" said the horse with the golden hair. At first the little master would not do it, until the horse neighed very loudly and bade him do it at once, as it was very unwise to delay obeying the commands of a Tátos. So what could the poor lad do but plug up the other nostril of the horse. The horse then opened wide its mouth, and breathed upon the lad, who at once became a most handsome prince, worthy to be a fairy king. "Now sit on my back, my little master, my great king, we are worthy of each other; and there is no thing in the world that we cannot [Pg 199]overcome. Rejoice! You will conquer the dragons, and restore the young men to your father's realm; only do as I bid you, and listen to no one else."

In an hour's time they arrived on the shore of the Red Sea, which flows into the Blue Sea. There they found an inn, and close to the inn, within earshot, stood the copper bridge, on the other side of which the dragon with seven heads roamed about. Andrew and Emerich were already at the inn, and as they were very tired, they sat down and began to eat and drink: when the new guest arrived the knives and forks dropped from the two princes' hands; but when they learned that he, too, had come to fight the dragons they made friends with him. They could not, however, recognise him for all the world. Night set in, and Andrew and Emerich had eaten and drunk too much, and became decidedly drunk, and so slept very deeply. Ambrose ate little, drank nothing, and slept lightly. At dawn the Tátos-horse pulled his master's hair, in order to wake him; because it knew that the dragon had least strength at dawn, and that the sun increased his strength. Ambrose at once jumped on horseback and arrived at the copper bridge: the dragon heard the clattering of the horse's hoofs, and at once flew to meet him. "Pooh!" cried the dragon and snorted, "I smell a strange smell! Ambrose, is it you? I know you; may you perish, you and your horse! Come on!" They fought for one hour and three quarters. Ambrose, with two strokes, slashed six of the dragon's heads off, but could not, for a long time succeed in cutting off the seventh, for in it lay the dragon's magic power. But, at last, the seventh head came off too.

The dragon had seven horses, these Ambrose fastened together, and took them to the inn, where he tied them by the side of Emerich's horse. Andrew and Emerich did not awake till nine o'clock, when Emerich asked Andrew if he had killed the dragon, and Andrew asked Emerich if he had done so; at last Ambrose told them that he had killed the dragon with seven heads and [Pg 200]taken away his seven horses, which he gave to Emerich, who thanked him for them. The three then continued their journey together as far as the silver bridge: here again they found an inn, which stood close to the bridge. Emerich and Andrew ate and drank and went to sleep as before; the Tátos horse, as soon as day began to break, awoke his master, who cheerfully jumped up, dressed neatly, and left the princes asleep. The Tátos scented the dragon quite ten miles off, and growled like a dog, and the dragon in his rage began to throw his sparks at them when four German miles off; they rushed upon each other and met with a tremendous clash on the bridge; it was a very difficult task for Ambrose to conquer this huge monster, but at last, through the skilful manœuvring of his horse, he deprived the dragon of all his eight heads: the eight horses belonging to the dragon he tied to a post near the head of the eldest prince, Andrew. Andrew and Emerich did not awake till noon, and were astonished at the sight of the splendid horses, questioning each other as to who could have brought them there at such an early hour, and then came to the conclusion that the prince must have killed the dragon, and that these horses had belonged to the monster, for no such horses ever neighed under a man before. Ambrose again confessed that he had killed the dragon, and brought away his horses for them. He also urged his two companions to hurry on to kill the third dragon, or they would be too late. They all got on horseback, but in their joy two of them had had to eat and drink, till they had more than enough, but Ambrose, according to his custom, took but little; the two elder brothers again went to sleep and slept like tops; but again the little Tátos pulled Ambrose's hair, so soon as the morning star began to glimmer.

Ambrose got up at once, and dressed even more quickly than before; for the journey he took a small flask of wine, which he secured upon his saddle. The horse warned its master to approach the dragon with great caution, because it was a very [Pg 201]excitable one, and if he got frightened the least it would be very difficult to conquer the monster. Soon the monster with nine heads arrived, thumped once on the golden bridge, so that it trembled under the thump; Ambrose dashed at the dragon and fought with it, but they could not conquer each other, although they fought fiercely and long. At the last hug, especially, Ambrose grew so weak that, if he had not taken a long draught from his flask he would have been done for on the spot; the draught, however, renewed his strength, and they dashed at each other again, but still neither could conquer the other.

So the dragon asked Ambrose to change himself into a steel hoop and he, the dragon, would become a flint hoop, and that they should both climb to the top of yon rock, which was so high that the sun was only a good span above it; and that they should roll down together, and if, while running, the flint hoop left the rut, and, striking the steel hoop, drew sparks therefrom, that Ambrose's head should fall off; but if on the other hand, the steel hoop left the rut and struck the flint hoop so as to draw sparks, then all the dragon's heads should fall off. But they were both wise and stuck to their own ruts, rolling down in a straight course till they reached the foot of the mountain without touching each other, and lay down when they got to the bottom. As they could not manage in this way, the dragon proposed: "I will become a red flame and you will become a white one, and which ever flame reaches highest he shall be victor." Ambrose agreed to this also; while they were contending, they both noticed an old crow, which croaked at them from a hollow tree; the dragon was an old acquaintance of the aged crow, and requested it to bring in its beak as much water as would extinguish the white flame, and promised that if he won, he would give his foe's flesh to the crow, every bit of it.

Ambrose asked for a single drop of water, and promised the crow all the flesh of the big-bodied dragon. The crow helped [Pg 202]Ambrose: it soaked its crop full of water and spat it over the red flame; thus Ambrose conquered his last foe. He got on his horse, tied together the nine horses of the dragon with nine heads and took them to his brothers, who were still snoring loudly, although the sun had reached its zenith and was hot enough to make a roast. At last the two lazy people got up, and Ambrose divided the nine horses between them and took leave of them, saying, "Go in peace, I myself am obliged to run wherever my eyes can see." The two good-for-nothing brothers were secretly delighted, and galloped off homewards. Ambrose turned himself into a small rabbit, and as it ran over hill and dale it ran into a small hut where the three wives of the three dragons were seated. The wife of the dragon with seven heads took it into her lap and stroked it for a long time, and thus addressed it: "I don't know whether Ambrose has killed my husband; if he has, there will be a plague in the world, because I will turn into a great pear tree, and the odour of its fruit will be smelt seven miles off, and will be sweet to the taste but deadly poison. The tree which thus grows from me will not dry up till Ambrose plunge his sword into its root, then both it and myself will die." Then the wife of the dragon with eight heads also took the little rabbit in her lap, and spoke thus: "If Ambrose has killed my husband there will be a plague in the world, I can tell you! because in my sorrow I will change into a spring; there will be eight streams flowing out of this spring, each one of which will run eight miles, where it again will sub-divide into eight more branches. And whoever drinks of the water will die; but if Ambrose wash his sword in my blood—which is the water of the spring—all the water will at once dry up and I shall die." Then the wife of the dragon with nine heads spoke to the rabbit, saying, "If Ambrose has killed my husband, in my sorrow I will change into a huge bramble, and will stretch all over the world, all along the highroads. And whoever trips over me, will die; but if Ambrose cut my stalk in [Pg 203]two anywhere the bramble will dry up everywhere and I shall die."

Having listened to all this, the little rabbit scampered off out of the hut; but an old woman with an iron nose, the mother of the three dragons, chased him, and chased him over hill and dale: he ran, and rushed about, till at length he overtook his brothers; jumping on his little horse's back, he continued his journey at his leisure. As they travelled on, his eldest brother longed for some good fruit; just then they saw a fine pear tree, whereupon Ambrose jumped from his horse, and plunged his sword into the roots of the tree, and drew blood, and a moaning voice was heard. They travelled on for a few miles, when Emerich all of a sudden became very thirsty: he discovered a spring, and jumped off his horse in order to drink, but Ambrose was first to arrive at the water; when, plunging his sword into it, it became blood, and fearful screams were heard, and in one moment the whole of the water dried up. From this point Ambrose galloped on in front till he left his brothers two miles behind, because he knew that the bramble was stretching far along the country road; he cut it in two, blood oozed out, and the bramble at once dried up. Having thus cleared away all dangers from his brothers' way, he blest them and separated from them.

The brothers went home, but the old woman with the iron nose persecuted Ambrose more than ever, being in a great rage at his having killed her sons and her daughters-in-law. Ambrose ran as hard as he could, for he had left his horse with his brothers; but when he was quite exhausted and had lost all confidence in himself, he ran into a smithy, and promised the smith that he would serve him for two years for nothing if he would hide him safely and well. The bargain was soon struck, and no sooner had the smith hidden him than the old woman appeared on the spot and inquired after a youth: she described his figure, the shape of his eyes and mouth, height, colour of his moustache and hair, dress, and general appearance. But the smith [Pg 204]was not such a fool as to betray the lad who had engaged to work at his anvil for him for two years for nothing. So the old witch with the iron nose got to know nothing and left the place growling. One day Ambrose was perspiring heavily by the side of the anvil, so at eventide he went for a short walk in the road in order to get a mouthful of fresh air. When he had nearly reached the edge of the wood, which was only at a dog's trot from the smithy, he met a very old woman with wizened face, whose carriage was drawn by two small cats: the old woman began to ogle little Ambrose, making sheep's eyes at him, like fast young women do. "May hell swallow you, you old hag," said Ambrose to her angrily, "I see you have still such foolish ideas in your head, although you have grown so old!" Having said this he gave the carriage in which the witch sat, a kick, but poor Ambrose's right foot stuck fast to the axle, and the two cats scampered off over hill and dale with him until he suddenly discovered that he was trotting in hell, and saw old Pilate staring at him. The old witch with the iron nose—because it was she who had the carriage and pair of cats—fell over head and ears in love with the young lad, and at once asked him to marry her.

Ambrose shuddered when he heard this repulsive, unnatural request. "Very well," said the woman with the iron nose, "as you don't intend to marry me, into jail you go! twelve hundred-weight of iron on your feet!" Nine black servants seized hold of poor Ambrose, at once, and took him nine miles down into the bowels of the earth, and fastened a piece of iron weighing twelve hundred-weight on his feet and secured it with a lock. The poor lad wept and groaned, but no one had admission to where he was, with the exception of the old witch and one of her maids. The maid of the witch with the iron nose was not quite such an ugly fright as her wizened old mistress, in fact she was such a pretty girl that one would have to search far for a prettier lass. She commenced to visit Ambrose in his prison rather often, sometimes even when the old witch did not dream of [Pg 205]it—to tell the truth, she fell head over ears in love with the lad, nor did Ambrose dislike the pretty girl; on the contrary, he promised to marry her if she were able to effect his escape from his deep prison. The girl did not require any further coaxing, but commenced plotting at once. At last she hit upon a scheme, and thus spoke to her darling Ambrose: "You cannot get out of this place, unless you marry the old woman with the iron nose. She having once become your wife will reveal to you all her secrets; she will also tell you how she manages to keep alive so long, and by what ways and means she may be got rid of." Ambrose followed her instructions and was married to the old witch by a clergyman—there are clergy even in hell, as many as you want. The first night Ambrose, after having for a long time been kissing and making love to the old iron nose, asked her: "What keeps you alive for so long, and when do you think you will die? I don't ask these questions, my dearest love," he added, flatteringly, "as if I wished for your death, but because I should like to use those means myself which prolong your life and keep away everything from me which would shorten life, and thus preserve me, living long and happily with you." The old woman at first was half inclined to believe his words, but while meditating over what she had just heard, she suddenly kicked out in bed, and Ambrose flew three miles into hell in his fright.

But the result of all the questioning and flattering in the end was that the old woman confessed. She confided to him that she kept a wild boar in the silken meadow, and if it were killed, they would find a hare inside, inside the hare a pigeon, inside the pigeon a small box, inside the little box one black and one shining beetle: the shining beetle held her life, the black one her power; if those two beetles died then her life would come to an end, too. As soon as the old woman went out for a drive—which she had to do every day—Ambrose killed the wild boar, took out the hare, from the hare the pigeon, from the pigeon the [Pg 206]box, and from the box the two beetles: he killed the black one at once, but kept the shining one alive. The old witch's power left her immediately. When she returned home her bed had to be made for her. Ambrose sat by her bedside and looked very sad, and asked her with tears if she, who was the other half of his soul, died what would become of him, who was a man from earth and a good soul, who had no business there. "In case I die, my dear husband," said the doomed woman, in a mild voice, "open with the key which I keep in my bosom yon black closet in the wall. But you can't remove the key from my bosom until I am dead. In the closet you will find a small golden rod; with this rod you must strike the side of the castle in which we are, and it will become a golden apple. You, then, can get into the upper world by harnessing my two cats in my carriage, and by whipping them with the golden rod." Hereupon Ambrose killed the shining beetle too, and her pára (animal soul) left the old witch at once.

He then struck the castle side with the golden rod, and it turned into an apple; having harnessed the two cats and patted them with the golden rod, he bade the maid sit by him, and in a wink they reached the upper world. The maid had been kidnapped by the old witch with the iron nose from the king of the country in the upper world, in whose land the mouth of hell was situated. Ambrose placed the golden apple in the prettiest part of the country and tapped its side with the rod and it became a beautiful castle of gold, in which he married his sweetheart and lived with her happily. Some time after he returned to his father's land, where an immense number of strong soldiers had grown up since Ambrose had killed the dragons. The old king distributed his realm among his three sons, giving the most beautiful empires to Ambrose, who took his father to him and kept him in great honour. His wife bore pretty children who rode out every day on the Tátos.

[Pg 207]

THE WIDOWER AND HIS DAUGHTER.

I don't know in what country, in which county, in which district, in which village, in which street, in which corner, there lived a poor widower, and not far from him a rich widow. The widower had a beautiful daughter. The widow had two who were not very pretty, and were rather advanced in years. The widower married the widow and they combined the two households and lived together. The husband was as fond of his wife's daughters as of his own; but the woman liked her own daughters better than her husband's child, and the two older girls loved their parents truly but disliked their pretty sister very much. The poor man was very sad at this, but could not help it.

Once upon a time there was a fair held in the town, which was not far from the village, and the husband had to go to the fair. The two elder girls and their loving mother asked for no end of pretty dresses they wished their father to bring them from the fair: but the pretty girl of the poor man did not dare to open her mouth to ask for anything. "Well, my daughter, what shall I bring for you?" asked the poor man, in a sad voice; "why don't you speak? You shall have something, too." "Don't bring me anything," replied the pretty little girl, "but three walnuts, and I shall be satisfied; a little girl does not want any pretty dresses as yet." The poor man went to the fair and brought home many showy dresses, red shoes, and bracelets. The two girls rummaged among the heaps of pretty things; they threw about the coloured ribbons, golden rings, and artificial flowers; they tried on their heads the various Turkish shawls, and tried the effect of paints on their faces; they skipped about and sang in their joy; they cheerfully embraced their mother and highly praised their [Pg 208]father's choice. At last, having got tired of looking at the things, everyone put away her share into her closet. The pretty little girl placed the three walnuts in her bosom and felt very sad. The two elder girls could hardly wait for Sunday. They dressed up most showily; they painted their faces, and as soon as the bells began to ring ran to church and stuck themselves in the front pew. Before leaving home, however, they gave the pretty little girl some very dirty wheat and ordered her to clean it—about half a bushel full—by the time they came back from church. The little girl began to sort the wheat weeping, and her tears mingled with the wheat; but her complaining was heard in Heaven and the Lord sent her a flock of white pigeons who in a minute picked out the dirt and the tares from among the wheat, and in another minute flew back to where they had come from. The little girl gave thanks to Providence and cried no more. She fetched her three walnuts in order to eat them, but as she opened the first one a beautiful copper dress fell out of it; from the second a silver one; and from the third a glittering gold one. She was highly delighted, and at once locked the two walnuts in which the gold and silver dresses were, safely in a cupboard. She put on the copper dress, hurried off to church, and sat down in the last pew all among the old women: and lo! the whole congregation stood up to admire her, so that the clergyman was obliged to stop in his sermon: the two old maids looked back quite surprised and found that the new comer's dress was ever so much prettier than their own.

It happened that the king's son was also present in whose country the village was and in which village the poor man and his new wife lived. The beautiful girl dressed in the glittering copper dress was at once noticed by the king's son who was at that time looking for a wife all over the country. As soon as the pretty little girl noticed that the sermon was coming to an end she left her seat and ran home in order to get undressed before her step-mother and her two sisters got home. The king sent [Pg 209]a flunkey after her and gave him orders to note the door where the pretty girl entered; but the swift girl ran much quicker than the king's servant, and he lost her. She undressed in a great hurry, and by the time that her two sisters got home in company with their young men she had her copper dress put away in the walnut and locked it in a cupboard and donned her ordinary every-day dress, which was very clean, and was found in the act of fanning the fire under a pot full of cabbage, and making herself busy about the kitchen in general. "Poor orphan, you have not seen any thing," exclaimed the two eldest sisters, who were in high spirits. "The king's son was at church, he sat just opposite, for a while he kept his eyes fixed on us as if enchanted. You did not see that, did you? At the beginning of the sermon, however, such a beautiful girl, dressed in such a gorgeous dress, came in the like of which no human eye has ever seen before." "I did see that pretty girl as she turned the corner of the street." "From where did you see her?" at once asked the envious sisters. "I got on the ladder and went up to the chimney and saw her from there." "Indeed, then you spent your time gaping about. You will catch it when father comes home and finds the wheat unpicked." And they rushed to the place where the wheat was kept, but lo! the wheat was as clean as washed gold, and the tares and the dirt had been removed from the house.

In the afternoon the ladder was taken away from the front of the house, so that the orphan girl should not be able to get on it any more. In the afternoon the church bells were again heard ringing. The two elder girls dressed up even more showily than before and went to church. The prince also put in his appearance. The little orphan girl had twice as much wheat meted out to her, and they threatened that if it was not cleaned by the time they came home they would maltreat her. The little girl set to work in great sorrow, but white pigeons came, twice as many as in the morning. The wheat got cleaned like gold in [Pg 210]one minute. The little girl at once opened the second walnut, and the silver dress, shining like moonbeams, unfolded itself. She went to church and sat in the same seat where she sat in the morning. The prince took out his eyeglass and eyed the pretty girl in the silver dress. He nearly devoured her with his eyes. The girl did not stay long in her place, and at a moment when nobody was looking she stole out of the church and ran home. The king's flunkey again was unable to find out her abode. When the two sisters came home the little girl was filling the cleaned wheat into bags ready to be carried up into the loft. "Don't carry it up yet—wait a moment," said the two sisters to her. "You have never seen and will never behold in all your life what we saw to-day. The fairy girl of this morning came this afternoon to church dressed in pure silver; she gleamed like moonlight." "I've seen her," said the orphan girl, with a meek smile; "I got on the hoarding and stood on the top rail and saw her as she slipped out of church." "And how about the wheat; let's have a look at it. We suppose you spent all your time gaping again. Father will give it to you," said the two wicked girls. But the wheat was all clean, and would have been so if it had been as much more. They drove a lot of sharp nails into the top of the hoarding, in order to prevent the orphan girl getting on to it.

The two elder girls anxiously waited for the coming Sunday, as they were eager to show off some of their new dresses they had never had on before. Sunday at last arrived, and the two elder girls dressed up ever so much more gorgeously than before. They put on their rings; tied on many coloured bows; put on red shoes; and rouged their faces. They went off in great hurry as soon as the bells began. The prince again was present, and some of his friends with him. The two elder girls tried their best to look charming: they screwed up their mouths to make them look small; they piously bent their heads on one side, and kept on adjusting their ribbons and bows. Whenever the prince, [Pg 211]or any of his friends looked at them they coyly cast down their eyes and played with their nosegays. The little girl was again left at home; they gave her three times as much dirty wheat to pick as on the first occasion, and threatened her that if by the time they came home she did not get it picked her father would give her a sound thrashing. The pigeons again came to assist the pretty child, there were three times as many as at first, and her wheat was again picked in a minute. The little girl opened the third nut, and, dressed in the golden dress, went to church, and sat down in her usual place. The congregation was more astounded than ever; the women and girls jumped up from their seats. They did not listen to the sermon, but kept staring at the fairy little girl, and whispered to each other. The prince was determined that the girl must become his wife, whatever happened; but the fairy-like girl again slipped away, and the king's servant followed her, until he saw her run into a house, whereupon he marked it by sticking a gold rose into the gate-post. The little girl did not notice this. The elder girls came running home. "If you lived for another thousand years you would not see such a beauty as we saw to-day. We saw a pretty creature dressed in pure gold; we don't think there is another in the whole world like her." "I saw her," said the little girl, laughing; "I climbed on the mulberry tree and followed her with my eyes from the street corner all the way to church." "And how about the wheat; is it picked?" "The Lord has helped me," said the good little child, "as He always will help orphans." The mulberry tree was cut down the very same afternoon.

In the afternoon the girls did not bring home any more news from church; they did not inquire any more whether the wheat had been cleaned, because they noticed that their step-father was very angry with them for their having shown so much envy against their sister. The poor father led his little girl to the cottage of a widow who lived at the end of the village, and who [Pg 212]herself had no children. There she was kept for several weeks on rather scanty food. The prince had not come to church for several Sundays; but, after the lapse of three months, three weeks, and three days, at three in the afternoon, three quarters, and three minutes, he came on foot into the village, where he had seen the pretty girl. He had only his servant with him. They examined every gate-post, and at last found the golden rose which the servant had stuck there. They entered the cottage, wherein they found an old woman seated reading her prayers. "Is there a girl in this cot?" inquired the prince. "Yes, your highness," replied the old woman, "there are two, and either of them is well worthy of a prince's love." "Call them, my old mother, call them both; my heart will then recognise its choice."

"Here they are my lord and prince," said the mother with a joyful face, having in about half an hour got her two daughters dressed up as well as she could. "The choice of my heart is not among them;" said the prince, sadly, "have you no more daughters, good woman? call also the third if you value my happiness." "The Lord has not given me any more, these two are quite enough, you cannot find any prettier or better in the whole village." "Haven't you got a husband and hasn't he got a daughter?" asked the prince, in great sorrow. "My husband is dead," said the old hag, "it is three years since he was put into his grave." "Let us go on then, my lord and prince," said the servant, "and we shall find her if it please the Lord." As they passed through the gate the servant took the golden rose from the crack in the gate-post and threw it to the winds. The golden rose thereupon quietly floated in the air above the heads of the prince and his servant. The fortune-seekers followed the rose, mumbling prayers, till at the end of the village it dropped on the ground in front of the gate of the last cot. "Let's go in here, my lord and prince, as our prayer has brought us here." "If the Lord call us, let us enter, my faithful servant," replied the [Pg 213]prince. A cock crowed just as they stepped across the threshold, and a very poor old woman greeted the guests. "Have you a daughter, my old mother?" inquired the prince graciously. "No, my lord; I never had one," said the old woman sadly. "If not, don't you keep an orphan? The Lord will preserve the good mother who takes care of the orphan, as well as the orphan." "Yes, my lord, but she has no dress fit to appear in, and she is not a bit worthy of your looking at her; she is naughty and does not like work, and for this reason her step-mother has cast her off. Her father supplies in secret her daily food." "The Lord will provide for him who is in need," said the prince. "Call her; never mind how ugly she is, or how badly she is clad. I like to make orphans happy." After much pressing the wretch of an old woman at last produced the little girl, who looked very poor, but was very cleanly dressed; her face was as soft as dew. The prince recognised at the first glance the beautiful figure and the charming features.

"I'm not sorry for the trouble I have taken," said the prince, and embraced the pretty girl. He gave rich presents to the poor woman, and took his long-sought-for sweetheart with him. On his way home the servant reminded his master that it would not be the proper thing to bring the prince's bride home in such a sorry plight. The prince found his servant's remark correct. They had only to walk about three miles to reach the frontier of land where the prince's father reigned. They came to a round lake where they halted, and on its bank stood a large weeping willow, so they made the girl sit among the branches and advised her not to leave her place until they returned with the golden dresses and the royal carriage. Thereupon they left. The little girl had hidden the three walnuts in her bosom and in order to surprise her bridegroom she put on her golden dress and thus dressed awaited his return. No sooner had she finished her toilet than a whole troop of gipsy women arrived under the tree on which she sat in her golden dress. The gipsy [Pg 214]women at once questioned her, why she sat there? whom she expected? and where she was going! She, in her innocence, was not afraid of them, and told them of her descent, narrated them her past vicissitudes, her present good fortune, and also confided to them that she was preparing a joke for her royal bridegroom, and showed her walnuts and her glittering dresses in them. The prettiest of the gipsy women climbed on the tree and commenced to flatter her. She asked her to be allowed to see her walnuts, and in one moment, when the girl was off her guard, pushed her from the tree down into the lake. To the great amazement of the gipsies the girl transformed herself into a gold duck, and flew to the centre of the lake, and, alighting on the water, began to swim. Thereupon the gipsy women began to throw stones at her, which, however, she evaded by diving under water. The women at last got tired of throwing stones, and left the gold duck in the lake, and the gipsy woman among the branches of the weeping willow. The prince arrived at sunset at the tree where he had left his pretty *fiancée*. When lo! he discovered the woman in the golden dress. He admired her golden raiment, and begged her to tell him where she had got her golden dress. The gipsy told him what the girl had related to her, and asked him his forgiveness for not having mentioned it when she first saw him at the widow's cot, and made the prince believe that she had kept silence about it solely because she wished to find out whether he loved her in her poor dress. The prince believed every word the gipsy said, and begged her to come down and sit in his carriage, and to drive home with him to his royal father's palace. As the prince assisted the gipsy woman down from the willow, the tanned face of his *fiancée* looked to him as something most extraordinary. "You were not so sunburnt, my dear, when I left you; what made your skin get so discoloured?" "My tender skin got discoloured from the broiling rays of the sun," replied the wicked soul; "let me get into the shade and in a few days I shall [Pg 215]become pale again." The prince believed it and bade her sit in his carriage. "I can't leave here until you shoot that gold duck, I should like to have a bit of it at my wedding feast," said the false one. The bridegroom and his servants tried for a long time to hit the golden bird, they wasted a vast amount of powder and shot; but still the golden duck was unhurt because it always dived under the water.

The dusky woman looked very much disheartened when she took her seat in the prince's coach, but he soon revived her spirits by sweet and kind words, and in a short time they arrived at home. The old king did not at all like the looks of his future daughter-in-law, but on his son assuring him that in a few days she would regain her fairy-like beauty his mind was set at ease. They lived together for several months and the young wife was still sunburnt, and so the prince gradually got cool towards her. The gipsy woman noticed this, and in order to revive the spirits of her royal husband she announced it all over the town and in the adjacent villages that there would be a great feather-picking, held henceforth three times a week in the royal palace, and everybody rich and poor was invited, the queen being glad to see anyone. The golden duck had flown after the coach when the queen was driven home, and, having regained her girl-form, entered service not far from the royal mansion and worked diligently. She too went to the first feather-picking meeting, and, not saying a word to anyone, sat at the end of the table and made herself busy. "Well, my dear queen and wife," said the prince, "tell the good work-people here the pretty story which happened to you when your envious sisters would not let you go to church. Tell them also who helped you to clean the wheat." The gipsy did not know anything about these events; but still commenced to chatter away whatever came into her head first. She told them, among other things, that she had crept through the keyhole in the gate, and collected all the girls in the neighbourhood, with [Pg 216]whose help she finished her wheat-cleaning. "That wasn't so, most gracious queen," said a girl, with a pretty voice, who was very shabbily dressed but looked very clean; "it was from the chimney stack, and from the top of the hoarding, and from among the branches of the mulberry tree, from where the orphan girl did her peeping. But the poor orphan girl only told an innocent fib. It was the same girl with whom the prince fell in love, whom her half-sisters had cast off, for whom the prince searched with his servant, whom he seated in the willow tree, and whom you pushed into the lake, whom your husband tried to shoot. That orphan girl is nobody else but myself." The prince at once recognised his sweetheart. His wife thereupon fainted away. She soon recovered however.

The king made an example of the gipsy woman for her wicked deed: he had her quartered, and burnt, and then married the little orphan girl. He had her stepmother cast into prison, and her two daughters' hair cut, which he ordered to be burnt and cast to the winds: he also took the orphan girl's father to his court, and married him to the widow at whose cot he had found his wife. The poor little orphan girl's and her father's wedding were celebrated together. There was plenty to eat and drink, so that even the orphan children had rice to eat. Behind the door there stood a sack in which the Danube and the Theiss were kept. I too was among the dancing guests, and had a long spur made of straw on my boot; somebody pushed me by accident, and my spur knocked a hole in the sack in which the Danube and Theiss were kept; so the water all ran out and engulphed me, and washed me ashore, not far from here. If you don't believe my story, here I am!

[Pg 217]

THE WISHES.

There were 10,000 wagons rolling along the turnpike road, in each wagon there were 10,000 casks, in each cask 10,000 bags, in each bag 10,000 poppy seeds, in each poppy seed 10,000 lightnings. May all these thunderous lightnings strike him who won't listen to my tale, which I have brought from beyond the Operencian Sea!

There was once, it doesn't matter where: there was once upon a time, a poor man who had a pretty young wife; they were very fond of each other. The only thing they had to complain of was their poverty, as neither of them owned a farthing; it happened, therefore, sometimes, that they quarrelled a little, and then they always cast it in each other's teeth that they hadn't got anything to bless themselves with. But still they loved each other.

One evening the woman came home much earlier than her husband and went into the kitchen and lighted the fire, although she had nothing to cook. "I think I can cook a little soup, at least, for my husband. It will be ready by the time he comes home." But no sooner had she put the kettle over the fire, and a few logs of wood on the fire in order to make the water boil quicker, than her husband arrived home and took his seat by the side of her on the little bench. They warmed themselves by the fire, as it was late in the autumn and cold. In the neighbouring village, they had commenced the vintage on that very day. "Do you know the news, wife?" inquired he. "No, I don't. I've heard nothing; tell me what it is." "As I was coming from the squire's maize-field, I saw in the dark, in the distance, a black spot on the road. I couldn't make out what it was, so I went nearer, and lo! do you know what it was?—A beautiful [Pg 218]little golden carriage, with a pretty little woman inside, and four fine black dogs harnessed to it." "You're joking," interrupted the wife. "I'm not, indeed, it's perfectly true. You know how muddy the roads about here are; it happened that the dogs stuck fast with the carriage and they couldn't move from the spot; the little woman didn't care to get out into the mud, as she was afraid of soiling her golden dress. At first, when I found out what it was, I had a good mind to run away, as I took her for an evil spirit, but she called out after me and implored me to help her out of the mud; she promised that no harm should come to me, but on the contrary she would reward me. So I thought that it would be a good thing for us if she could help us in our poverty; and with my assistance the dogs dragged her carriage out of the mud. The woman asked me whether I was married. I told her I was. And she asked me if I was rich. I replied, not at all; I didn't think, I said, that there were two people in our village who were poorer than we. That can be remedied, replied she. I will fulfil three wishes that your wife may propose. And she left as suddenly as if dragons had kidnapped her: she was a fairy."

"Well, she made a regular fool of you!"

"That remains to be seen; you must try and wish something, my dear wife." Thereupon the woman without much thought said: "Well, I should like to have some sausage, and we could cook it beautifully on this nice fire." No sooner were the words uttered than a frying-pan came down the chimney, and in it a sausage of such length that it was long enough to fence in the whole garden. "This is grand" they both exclaimed together. "But we must be a little more clever with our next two wishes; how well we shall be off! I will at once buy two heifers and two horses, as well as a sucking pig," said the husband. Whereupon he took his pipe from his hatband, took out his tobacco-pouch, and filled his pipe; then he tried to light it with a hot cinder, but was so awkward about it that he upset [Pg 219]the frying-pan with the sausage in it. "Good heavens! the sausage; what on earth are you doing! I wish that sausage would grow on to your nose," exclaimed the frightened woman, and tried to snatch the same out of the fire, but it was too late, as it was already dangling from her husband's nose down to his toes. "My Lord Creator help me!" shouted the woman. "You see, you fool, what you've done, there! now the second wish is gone," said her husband, "what can we do with this thing?" "Can't we get it off?" said the woman. "Take off the devil! Don't you see that it has quite grown to my nose; you can't take it off." "Then we must cut it off," said she, "as we can do nothing else." "I shan't permit it: how could I allow my body to be cut about? not for all the treasures on earth; but do you know what we can do, love? there is yet one wish left; you'd better wish that the sausage go back to the pan, and so all will be right." But the woman replied, "How about the heifers and the horses, and how about the sucking pig; how shall we get those?" "Well, I can't walk about with this ornament, and I'm sure you won't kiss me again with this sausage dangling from my nose." And so they quarrelled for a long time, till at last he succeeded in persuading his wife to wish that the sausage go back to the pan. And thus all three wishes were fulfilled; and yet they were as poor as ever.

They, however, made a hearty meal of the sausage; and as they came to the conclusion that it was in consequence of their quarrelling that they had no heifers, nor horses, nor sucking pig, they agreed to live thenceforth in harmony together; and they quarrelled no more after this. They got on much better in the world, and in time they acquired heifers, horses, and a sucking pig into the bargain, because they were industrious and thrifty.

[Pg 220]

THE TWO ORPHANS.

There was once, I know not where, even beyond the Operencian Land, a village, and at the end of the village a little hovel. Within the tumble-down walls of this hovel a poor old woman was lying on some rotting straw, and two children were crying by her side. The elder was a pretty girl. The younger was her brother, a small boy with auburn hair. The old mother died. Her cold body was buried by the parish; but, as none offered themselves to take charge of the two orphans, they left the place. They went and went, over many a hill and dale, and had already covered a long distance when Jack felt burning thirst. They found in the road some turbid water in a rut, at the sight of which the thirsty little fellow shouted for joy. "My dear sister, I will drink from this rut." "Don't drink from it," said his thoughtful sister, "or you will turn into a cart-wheel if you do." Jack sighed, and they went on their way. They found some bears' tracks in which some stale rain-water was putrifying. "My dear sister, I'm thirsty, allow me to drink of this rain-water." "If you drink, my dear brother, you will become a bear." The little fellow began to cry, but obeyed, and they went on. In the road they found some footprints of a wolf. Jack again implored his sister, with tears, and repeated his former request. "Don't drink, my dear Jack, or else you will become a wolf." Jack, although his tongue was parched with burning thirst, obeyed, and they continued their walk quite exhausted. They found the footmarks of a roebuck in the road. Water clear as crystal shone in them, that invited him to drink. Jack's feet gave way under him when he reached the water, and, in spite of all warning, he drank of it with avidity. His sister, seeing her fear [Pg 221]realised, began to cry. The beautiful auburn locks of her brother suddenly turned to a soft grayish hair, and horns grew behind his ears. His legs and arms became the four legs of a roedeer, and the pretty little creature rubbed gently against his sister, who stroked him with her pretty hands. The little girl and her brother, the roebuck, continued their journey till at last they reached the king's palace, where the young monarch received them with smiles, and offered them a tidy little room. The little girl lived with her brother here, and, although she forbade him to speak before others, they would chat when left alone, their conversation turning mainly upon their deceased good mother, their journey, the handsome young king, and his frequent hunts. After several weeks the pretty girl received a royal splendid dress and was married to the young king.

The fame of their wedding travelled over seven countries. The loving couple lived contentedly together; the queen was pretty and good, and her husband was madly in love with her. The little deer kept continually by his sister's side; they ate from the same plate, and drank out of the same glass, and slept in the same room; but this happiness did not last long. There lived in the king's country an old witch, with iron teeth, who had a very ugly daughter, whose face was black, her eyes were yellow, her nose was full of warts, her teeth like hoes, her voice screeching, her waist crooked; and, besides all this, she was lame of one foot. It was the old witch's determination to make this creature the queen of the realm. As she was frustrated in her design she raved. In her fury she tore up bits of rocks, and dried up whole forests. She vowed death upon the poor orphan's head; and, in order to cheer up her ugly daughter's long forlorn hope, she prophecied the queen's death, and thus spoke: "Dear child, beloved Lucinda, would you like to be a queen? if so, go secretly into the king's palace, and when the king is out hunting, steal near the queen in her sleep, and cut off a large lock of her hair, and bring it to me. Mind where you step, and keep an [Pg 222]eye on every movement of hers." Lucinda dressed herself in a cloak with grey and red stripes, and at dead of night she reached the king's palace, and without arousing suspicion stole into the queen's bedroom. She spread her cloak on the floor, so that she might not awake the sleeping queen with its rustling as she moved about, and at her mother's sign she approached the queen's bed on tiptoe, and cut off a beautiful lock with a rusty old knife: the little deer did not wake. In the morning, the witch wrapt the beautiful auburn lock in the lungs of a toad, and roasted it over the embers of some yew boughs which were cut on Christmas night. After a while, with the ointment thus made, the old witch rubbed Lucinda from head to foot, who became the next moment an exact likeness of the young queen. Now the old witch began to ponder how to do away with the young queen, and at last she hit upon a plan. There lived at court a miserly gate-keeper, whom she bribed with gold, and with his assistance, in the absence of the king, they broke into the queen's bedroom at night, and dragged away by force the poor innocent woman; the little deer woke at the noise, and followed the murderers at a distance.

In a secluded corner of the courtyard there was an old disused stone-well, and in this well lived a huge whale; they threw the pretty queen to the bottom of this well, and in her now empty bed Lucinda was placed, whose outer appearance was not in the slightest different from that of the queen, so that when the king arrived at home he did not notice the awful fraud. The little deer henceforward spent all his days near the well, which circumstance did not escape the notice of the quick-eyed old witch. So she instructed her daughter to persuade her royal husband to have the deer killed, and in order to carry this out, she planned the following scheme. Lucinda shammed deadly illness, her mother having previously changed her red complexion to yellow; her husband sat every day and night by her bedside, while the little deer still spent all his time by the well. [Pg 223]They could not find any medicine which could give the patient relief, when Lucinda, as planned beforehand, expressed a desire to have the deer's heart and liver cooked for her. Her husband was horrified on hearing this unexpected wish, and began to suspect his wife. He could not believe that she could wish to have her dear little animal, which she idolized, killed; but Lucinda would not give in, until at last the king, being very much concerned about his wife's recovery, allowed himself to be persuaded, and gave orders to one of his cooks to have the deer killed. The deer heard quite well what Lucinda wished and what the orders were, but kept silence; and, in order not to arouse suspicion, went back to its favourite place, the well, where, in its deep grief, it thus spoke down into the whale's dwelling:

My little sister, my little sister,You dear little sister,Come out of the well,Out of the whale's stomach,Because they are whetting the knifeFor my gentle breast,They are washing the basinFor my beautiful red blood.

When the cook, clasping a long knife, stole up to the little animal in order to drag it to the slaughter-house, the deer repeated his mournful song, upon hearing which the cook got frightened and ran away and informed the king of what he had heard and seen. Thereupon the king determined to personally satisfy himself as to whether his tale was true. The little deer thereupon cried twice as mournfully as before, and amid tears sang out the same song as before.

The king now stepped forward from his hiding-place, and the deer, upon being questioned, told him the story how the witch and the gate-keeper dragged his sister out of bed, and how they threw her into the well. As soon as the pretty animal finished its tale, the huge whale was dragged out from the bottom of the well; they slit open its stomach, and the real [Pg 224]queen appeared, now seven times prettier than before; her husband himself assisted her and conducted her back to the palace in triumph.

Lucinda, her mother, and the gate-keeper were quartered, and their bodies exhibited at the four corners of the castle as a warning to everybody. The queen anointed her little brother with some ointment she had found in the whale's stomach, and he regained his old form. And so all three of them are alive to this very date, if they have not died since. May they get into an egg shell and be your guests to-morrow.

THE WONDERFUL FROG.

There was once, I don't know where, a man who had three daughters. One day the father thus spoke to the eldest girl: "Go, my daughter, and fetch me some fresh water from the well." The girl went, but when she came to the well a huge frog called out to her from the bottom, that he would not allow her to draw water in her jug until she threw him down the gold ring on her finger. "Nothing else? is that all you want?" replied the girl, "I won't give away my rings to such an ugly creature as you," and she returned as she came with the empty pitchers. So the father sent the second girl, and she fared as the first; the frog would not let her have any water, as she refused to throw down her gold ring. Her father gave his two elder daughters a good scolding, and then thus addressed the youngest: "You go, Betsie, my dear, you have always been a clever girl: I'm sure you will be able to get some water, and will not allow your father to suffer thirst; go, shame your sisters!" [Pg 225]Betsie picked up the pitchers and went, but the frog again refused the water unless she threw her ring down; but she, as she was very fond of her father, threw the ring in as demanded, and returned home with full pitchers to her father's great delight.

In the evening, as soon as darkness set in, the frog crawled out of the well, and thus commenced to shout in front of Betsie's father's door: "Father-in-law! father-in-law! I should like something to eat." The man got angry, and called out to his daughters; "Give something in a broken plate to that ugly frog to gnaw." "Father-in-law! father-in-law! this won't do for me; I want some roast meat on a tin plate," retorted the frog. "Give him something on a tin plate then, or else he will cast a spell on us," said the father. The frog began to eat heartily, and, having had enough, again commenced to croak: "Father-in-law! father-in-law! I want something to drink." "Give him some slops in a broken pot," said the father. "Father-in-law! father-in-law! I won't have this; I want some wine in a nice tumbler." "Give him some wine then," angrily called out the father. He guzzled up his wine and began again: "Father-in-law! Father-in-law! I would like to go to sleep." "Throw him some rags in a corner," was the reply. "Father-in-law! father-in-law! I won't have that; I want a silk bed," croaked the frog. This was also given to him; but no sooner has he gone to bed than again he began to croak, "Father-in-law! father-in-law! I want a girl, indeed." "Go, my daughter, and lie by the side of him," said the father to the eldest. "Father-in-law! father-in law! I don't want that, I want another." The father sent the second girl, but the frog again croaked: "Father-in-law! father-in-law! I don't want that, Betsie is the girl I want." "Go, my Betsie," said the father, quite disheartened, "else this confounded monster will cast a spell on us." So Betsie went to bed with the frog, but her father thoughtfully left a lamp burning on the top of the oven; noticing which, the frog crawled out of bed and blew the lamp out.

[Pg 226]The father lighted it again, but the frog put it out as before, and so it happened a third time. The father saw that the frog would not yield, and was therefore obliged to leave his dear little Betsie in the dark by the side of the ugly frog, and felt great anxiety about her. In the morning, when the father and the two elder girls got up, they opened their eyes and mouths wide in astonishment, because the frog had disappeared, and by the side of Betsie they found a handsome Magyar lad, with auburn locks, in a beautiful costume, with gold braid and buttons and gold spurs on his boots. The handsome lad asked for Betsie's hand, and, having received the father's consent, they hastened to celebrate the wedding, so that christening might not follow the wedding too soon.

The two elder sisters looked with invidious eyes on Betsie, as they also were very much smitten with the handsome lad. Betsie was very happy after, so happy that if anyone doubt it he can satisfy himself with his own eyes. If she is still alive, let him go and look for her, and try to find her in this big world.

THE DEVIL AND THE RED CAP.

There was once, I know not where, a soldier who was flogged many times, and who one night had to stand on sentry. As he paced up and down, a man with a red cap stopped in front of him and stared hard into his eyes. The soldier said not a word, but the stranger began: [Pg 227]"My dear son, I know what happens in your heart, you don't like this soldier's life, and your thoughts are at this very minute wandering to your sweetheart." The soldier at once concluded that he had to do with the devil, and so made his acquaintance. "Well, my dear son," said the devil, "undress quickly, and let's change our clothes; I will stand here on guard for you if you promise me that in a year hence, on this very day, at this very hour, to the very minute, you will be back here. In the meantime, go home to your native place, and don this red cap, as you can freely walk about and no one will see you as long as you have it on your head." The soldier went home to his native land, over seven times seven countries, and no one saw him as he reached his village. He walked into the garden and opened the door leading into his father's house and stood there listening. His friends were just then speaking of him. He was delighted to hear it, and gradually took the red cap from his head and suddenly appeared before them, who were very pleased to see him back. His sweetheart was also there; but no one would believe their own eyes, and thought that some sprite played them a trick. But the soldier explained it all; and, in order to prove the truth, he disappeared, and the next minute reappeared. All went well with the poor soldier until the time came when he had to start back. At the appointed hour and minute he took leave of his friends and sweetheart amid tears.

He put on his red cap and walked back unseen by any. "Bravo, my son," said the devil. "I see now that you are an honest man. A Magyar always keeps his word. You've returned to the very hour and minute. I've received a good many floggings, though, during your absence; but don't be afraid, we shall alter all this. You needn't be particular about your good conduct; nobody will touch you henceforth, as I've cast a spell and whenever they flog you the captain will feel the pain." The devil then changed his uniform, took back the red cap, and disappeared. The poor soldier—he couldn't help it, as he was tired of soldiering—again committed something wrong, the punishment for which was one hundred strokes. All the preparations to carry out the sentence had already been made, but before he was even touched the captain began to yell as he felt [Pg 228]quite sure that he would suffer under it. Therefore he deemed it more wise to recommend the dismissal of the useless fellow, instead of worrying about him. And so it happened, the soldier was dismissed and arrived home safely: but since this happened even the devil will not take pity on a poor soldier.

JACK DREADNOUGHT.

A poor widow had a son who was so courageous that not even the devil's mother would have frightened him, and therefore he was named in his childhood Jack Dreadnought. His mother was in continual terror lest something dreadful might happen to her son, as he was so plucky, nay foolhardy, and determined to use all possible means to teach him to fear. For this reason she sent him to the clergyman of the village as "mendicant," and requested the minister to use all his knowledge in trying to teach her son to fear. The clergyman left nothing untried to make the boy frightened; he told him all sorts of ghostly and horrible tales, but these, instead of frightening the lad, made him only more anxious to make the acquaintance of ghosts similar to those mentioned in the tales. The clergyman thereupon hit upon the idea of introducing some sham ghosts in order to break Jack Dreadnought's intrepidity.

He fixed upon the three nights before Christmas; on these nights the lad had to go to ring the bells at midnight in the tower that stood at the very end of the village, and the clergyman thought that he could find some opportunity of frightening Jack. He took an old cassock and stuffed it with straw and placed it before the tower door with one hand on the handle. Midnight came and Jack went to ring the bells and discovered the dummy in [Pg 229]the cassock. "Who are you?" he called out, but received no reply. "Very well," said the boy, "if you won't answer I will tell you this, that if you don't clear off from that door I'll kick you in the stomach that you will turn twelve somersaults." As there was no reply, Jack in his rage took hold of the dummy's collar and threw him on the ground with such violence that it rolled away three fathoms, and then, as if nothing had happened, went up into the tower, rang the bells, and went home. The clergyman, as his first experiment did not succeed, made two dummies the next day, which were exactly alike; one he placed in the same position as before at the door of the tower, the other near the bell ropes.

At midnight Jack again went to ring the bells and, as before, made short work of the first dummy; as he did not receive any reply he took him by the collar and threw him on the ground. When he went up into the tower and saw that the rope was held by another, he thought it was the first one, and thus addressed him, "Well, my friend, you've come here, have you? You hadn't enough with the first fall? Answer me or I will dash you on the ground so that you will not be able to get up again," and as the dummy did not reply Jack took it by the throat and pitched it from the window of the tower, and it whizzed through the air. The clergyman had had two unsuccessful experiments but he had great confidence in the third. He made three dummies this time, two were placed as before and the third he stood on the bell so that it might prevent it ringing. Jack Dreadnought dealt with the two first dummies as on the previous night, but as he was about to ring, to his astonishment, he discovered the dummy on the bell; he was not frightened, but when he saw that it would not come down, after a polite request, took it angrily by one leg and pitched it through the window like a cat. The clergyman had now come to the conclusion that he was unable to teach Jack fear, and now commenced to plan how he might get rid of him. The next morning he called [Pg 230]him, and thus spoke to him: "Jack, you are a fine courageous fellow; go, take my grey horse, and as much provisions as you think will last you three days, and go into the world and follow your nose; do not stop all day, but take up your night quarters wherever darkness finds you. Do this for three days, and settle down where you spend the third night, and you will be prosperous."

The clergyman thought that Jack would perish on the way; but we shall see whether he did. Jack started off the first day, and in the evening came to a narrow, round timber hut, which was rather high, and he decided to sleep there. As he found it empty he made a fire in its centre and commenced to fry some bacon; all of a sudden he felt something dripping, he looked up and saw something like a human form dangling in the air. "Well, upon my word," shouted he, "the devil won't leave me alone even here: get down from there, will you, or do you expect me to take you down?" No reply came, and Jack, with a clever jump, caught hold of one of his legs, and brought it down, but the head was torn off and fell down. Only then he discovered that it was a hanged man, but he did not think much of it, and stayed there all night. He travelled the whole of the next day; in the evening he reached an inn and asked for a room, and received in reply that they had an empty room on the upper floor, the only one vacant; but that no one could sleep there, as the place was haunted. "What!" shouted Jack; "Oh! I know those ghosts; let me have a dish of good food, a mouthful of good wine, and a burning candle in the upper room, and I will sleep there. I swear by Beelzebub that the ghosts will come no more!" The innkeeper tried to dissuade Jack from his foolhardy attempt, but he would not give way.

He was shown into the room; it was a large apartment on the upper floor. Jack placed the lighted candle in the middle; a dishful of food and a jug of wine by the side of it; and settled down in a chair, waiting for the awful ghosts. No sooner had [Pg 231]the clock struck midnight than, all of a sudden, a fearful chorus of animal noises was to be heard, like the howling of dogs, neighing of horses, bellowing of cattle, roaring of wild beasts, bleating of sheep and of goats, and also crying, laughing, and clanking of chains. Jack was quite delighted with the nocturnal concert; but, all of a sudden a big skull rolled in through the door and stopped by the side of the dish. Jack stared at it, and, instead of the skull, he saw an old monk standing before him with long heavy chains. "Good evening, brother friar!" shouted Jack, "pray have supper with me." "I'm going from here," said the friar, "and I want you to come too; I will show you something." "With pleasure," replied Jack, "will you lead the way, you devil, or you reverend gentleman?" Thereupon Jack followed the friar with the lighted candle. When they arrived at the stairs the friar insisted upon his going first, but Jack would not; and the friar was obliged to lead the way. Next they came to a narrow landing at the top of the cellar stairs. Here, again, the friar invited him to go first, but he would not; and so the apparition had to go first. But, as soon as he went down a few steps, Jack gave the friar such a push with such dexterity that he went head over heels down the steps and broke his neck. In the morning the innkeeper had the friar buried. He made Jack a handsome present, and the latter continued his journey.

Jack Dreadnought rode the whole next day, and in the evening again came to an inn, where he could not get any room except up stairs, where no one else would sleep, on account of ghostly visitors. Jack took the room and was again enjoying his supper in the centre, when the old clock struck midnight. The same sort of music struck his ear as on the previous night, and, amid a great crash, a human hand dropped from the ceiling to near his dish. Jack, in cold blood, took up the hand and threw it behind the door. Another hand fell and went the same way. [Pg 232]Now a leg came, and this, too, went behind the door. Then came its fellow, which was soon despatched to the rest. At last a big skull dropped right into the middle of the dish and broke it. Jack got into a rage, and threw the skull violently behind the door; and, on looking back, he found, instead of the limbs, an immense ghost standing behind the door, whom Jack at once taxed with the damage done to the dish, demanding payment. The ghost replied, "Very well; I will pay for it, if you come with me." Jack consented, and they went off together; as before, he always insisted on the ghost going first. They came to a long winding staircase, and down into a huge cellar. Jack opened his eyes and mouth wide when he found in the cellar three vats full of gold, six vats of silver, and twelve vats of copper coins. Then the ghost said to him, "There, choose a vat full of coins for your dish, and take it whenever you like." But Jack, however, did not touch the money, but replied, "Not I; do you suppose that I will carry that money? Whoever brought it here, let him take it away." "Well done," replied the ghost; "I see I've found my man at last. Had you touched the treasure you would have died a sudden death; but now, since you are such a fine courageous fellow, the like of whom I have never seen before, settle down in this place and use the treasure in peace; nobody will ever disturb or haunt you any more." After these words the ghost disappeared.

Jack became the owner of the immense treasure, and married the innkeeper's only daughter, who was very pretty, and lives with her to this day, if he has not died since, enjoying life and spending the money he found in the vats in the cellar.

[Pg 233]

THE SECRET-KEEPING LITTLE BOY AND HIS LITTLE SWORD.

There was once, I don't know where, beyond the seas, a little village, and in the village a widow. The widow had a pretty little son whose cheeks were as the rose; on the left side of the little boy a scabbard had grown, and as the boy grew the scabbard grew with him. On the same day on which the little boy was born the point of a sword appeared in the soil in their little garden, which kept pace with the growth of the scabbard on the little boy's side. When the boy was a year old he discovered the sword in the garden, and every evening at sunset he tried the sword in the scabbard. One evening after sunset the little boy lay down and fell fast asleep. Next morning he awaited dawn squatting by the side of the growing sword, which he passed seven times into the scabbard. He ran quite delighted to his mother, who got up as the morning bell began to ring. "Oh, my dear mother, I had such a nice dream. I wouldn't give my dream for the whole world." "Then what have you dreamt, my son?" queried the mother. "I wouldn't tell anyone till my dream has been realised." "Yes, but I want to know it," said his mother angrily, "and if you won't tell me, I will thrash you."

But the widow threatened her little son in vain; neither kind words nor threats could induce him to tell his secret. At last she thrashed him, but with no result; the little fellow went into the garden and knelt down by the side of his little sword, which had the peculiar feature that it continually revolved, and cut everyone's hand who touched it with the exception of that of the little boy. The little sword as soon as its point felt the touch of [Pg 234]the scabbard stopped and slid into the scabbard, and the little boy for a long time gazed at his weapon and wept bitterly. As he was thus weeping in his mother's garden, the king of the country passed outside the fencing; the king heard the sound of crying and stopped his carriage, and thus spoke to his footman: "My dear servant, go to see who is crying in that garden, and ask the cause of it?" The footman obeyed, and on his return gave the following reply to his royal master: "Your majesty, a child is kneeling among the flowers, and cries because his mother has cruelly beaten him." "Bring him here, my dear servant, tell him his king wants him, who has never cried in his life, and cannot bear to hear anyone else cry." The footman brought the child back with him, wiped away his tears, and the king asked the dear little boy whether he would like to go with him as he was willing to adopt him as his son. "I would like to go, majesty, if my mother would let me." "Go, my servant, to this little fellow's mother," said the king to his footman, "and tell her that the king will take her pretty son to his palace and if he behave well will give him half of his realm, and also his prettiest daughter."

The widow, who only a moment ago was so angry, commenced to cry for joy, and placed her son with her own hands into the king's lap, and kissed the monarch's hand. "Don't be so stubborn when you are at your royal father's court as you were at your widow-mother's house," she said to him, and with these words the old woman ran away from her pretty little son, who again cried bitterly. Then the dear little prince begged leave to get down from the carriage; he pulled the little sword up out of the ground, and placed it in the scabbard, where it rattled unceasingly. They had driven a good distance, and the boy had had his cry, when the king said, "Why did you cry so bitterly in the little garden, my dear son?" "Because" replied the little boy "my mother continually scolded me, and also thrashed me cruelly." "And why did your mother thrash you cruelly and scold you?" [Pg 235]asked the king. "Because I wouldn't tell her my dream." "And why would you not tell your dream to your poor mother?" "Because I will not tell it to anyone till it is fulfilled." "And won't you tell it to me either?" asked the king in astonishment. "No, nobody shall know it but God, who knows it already." "I'm sure you will tell me when we get home," said his royal father smiling. After three days' journey they arrived at the king's town: the queen with her three daughters were greatly delighted that their royal husband and father had brought them such a pretty boy. The girls offered all sorts of things to their pretty brother.

"Don't love him so much," said the wise king, "as he does not deserve it; he harbours some secret in his heart which he will not tell anyone." "He will tell me," said the eldest girl, but the little boy shook his head. "He will tell it me," said the second. "Not I," said the little boy angrily. "You won't keep it from me," said the youngest coaxingly. "I will not tell my secret to anyone till it is realised, and I will punish anyone who dares to inquire," threatened the little boy. The king in his great sorrow looked at his wife and daughters; he summoned his servants, handed the little boy to them, and said, "Take away this stubborn child, take him to your house, he's not fit for a royal palace." The sword at the little boy's side clanked loudly; the servants obeyed their royal master's orders, and took the boy to the place where they lived. The pretty child cried upon being taken away from the gorgeous palace, and the servants' children consoled him, offered him fruits and toys, and thus brought back his spirits in a few hours; the children got used to each other, and the little boy lived with them until he became seventeen years of age. The elder daughters of the king married kings of countries beyond the seas, and the youngest one has also grown old enough to be married. One day she ran from the lofty palace into the servants' house, where she saw the little boy, who had grown so handsome that there wasn't a more [Pg 236]handsome lad to be seen over seven times seven countries. The king's daughter was very much struck as she had never before seen so fine a lad, and thus spoke to him: "If you, handsome lad, will reveal your secret to me I will become yours, and you will be mine, and not even the coffin shall separate us." The lad thrashed the inquisitive princess as he had promised of yore; the pretty girl wept bitterly and ran to her royal father and complained about the lad's cruelty. The old king was very angry and uttered an oath, adding, "If he had a thousand souls he will have to die; his very memory must die out in my country."

On the same day on which the widow's son had beaten the king's daughter, lofty gallows were erected on the western side of the royal town, and the whole population went out to the place where the execution was to take place. The hangman tied the handsome lad's hands behind his back, when the sword again clanked at the lad's side. The assembled people, who a moment ago were so noisy, grew silent, when the king's preacher read out the sentence. Suddenly a great hubbub arose, and a gorgeous coach, from which a white flag was waving, was seen driving rapidly up to the gallows; in the coach sat the King of the Magyars. The coach stopped underneath the gallows, and the King of the Magyars jumped out and asked for the handsome lad's reprieve, who was blindfolded. The angry king informed him that he had great reason to have the scoundrel hanged, because he thrashed his daughter for no other cause than her asking him to reveal his secret. The secret was a dream which he could only tell when it was realised. "My royal colleague, hand the culprit over to me," said the king of the Magyars, "I'm sure he will tell me his secret. I have a pretty daughter who is like the Morning Star, and she will get it out of him." The sword again clanked at the side of the handsome lad. The king handed the prisoner to the Magyar king, who bade him sit in his carriage, and asked him his secret. [Pg 237]"It is impossible, my king and master," said the sad lad, "until the dream is fulfilled." "You will tell my daughter," said the Magyar king smiling. "To none!" said the lad resolutely, and his sword gave a terrific clank. The king and the handsome lad arrived at Buda in a few days. The king's daughter was just promenading in the garden when her father arrived with the handsome lad. The pretty girl hurried to her father, and as she kissed his hand she noticed the handsome lad, the like of whom she had never seen before. "Have you brought him for me?" inquired the love-sick maid, "from fairy land? No woman has yet carried, has yet borne, such a child in her arms!"

"My dear daughter, I've brought him not from fairy land, but from the gallows," replied the king, who was vexed with his daughter for having so quickly fallen in love with him, although she had never spoken to a man before. "I don't care, my dear father," said the blushing maid, "even if you brought him from the gallows, he's mine, and I am his, and we shall die together." The last words were addressed by the king's daughter to the handsome lad, who smothered the pretty princess with kisses. "You will soon be angry with him, my dear daughter," said the sorrowful king, "if you ask his secret; he's a coarse fellow, he's of no royal blood, his place is among the servants." "If he killed me, if he gouged out my eyes, or bit off my nose, I couldn't get angry with him," said the princess. "He will tell me his secret, his lodging will be in the room set apart for my guests, and he will find a place in the middle of my heart!"

But the king shook his head, and sent the lad down into the summer-house, where he could amuse himself with reading. No sooner had a week passed than the girl, who was as pretty as a fairy, put her best dress on and went to the summer-house to pay a visit to the lad who lived secluded there, to get his secret out of him. When the young lad saw the pretty girl and had examined her beautiful dress, the book dropped from his hand, and he stared but could not utter a single word. The princess thereupon [Pg 238]addressed him in such a beautiful voice as his ear had never heard before, "Tell me, my handsome lad, why have I come to see you, if you guess it I will be yours?" "My dove, my angel!" said the lad with glowing cheeks, "I won't tell you my secret, and if you wish to get back safely to your royal father's palace you had better not ask any more questions about the matter." But the girl would not listen to the lad's warning but pressed for an answer more urgently and embraced him and kissed him. The lad at last got so angry that he slapped the princess's face and made her nose bleed. The princess ran screaming back to the palace, where her father was waiting for her answer; when the king beheld the blood running down upon the pretty girl's beautiful dress, he yelled down from the window into the garden, "I will starve you to death, you son of a dragon!" and began to wash his daughter's cheek and nose.

The very same day the king summoned all the masons and bricklayers in the town, and gave them orders to run up in all haste a square building in which there was to be just room for a stool and a small table, the table to be so small that only a prayer book could find room on it. In two hours a small tower was built; the masons had already left off work, and were going to inform the king that the structure was finished. They met the king's daughter, who asked one of the masons to stay, the one who appeared to be the eldest, and asked him whether he could make so small a hole in the tower that a plate of food and a bottle of wine could be passed through, and which could not be noticed by any one. "To be sure," said the grey old mason, "I can and I will make it." The hole was ready in a quarter of an hour; the king's daughter paid the mason handsomely and hurried home.

At sunset, among a large crowd of people, the secret-keeping lad was conducted into the stone structure, and after all his misdeeds had been once more enumerated he was walled in. But the king's daughter did not allow him to suffer either hunger or [Pg 239]thirst, she visited her sweetheart three times every day; and brought him books for which he asked. The king sent every third day his secretary to look after the prisoner and to see if he were dead, but the scribe found him still alive, and the king was very much astonished. One day the Turkish Sultan sent a letter to the Magyar king; the messenger bearing the letter brought with him also three canes; the Turkish Sultan wrote in the letter, that if the king could not tell him which of the three canes grew nearest the root, which in the middle, and which at the top, he would declare war against him. The king was very much alarmed, and became sad. His daughter noticed her father's sorrow, and inquired,

"Why are you so downcast, my royal father?" "How can I be otherwise, my dear daughter," said the good king; "look here, the Turkish Sultan has sent me three canes, and writes, that if I cannot tell him which is the cane's root-end, middle-part, and top-end, he will send his army against my country." "*The God of the Magyar's* will help you, my dear father," said the girl; and hurried to the tower, and informed her sweetheart through the secret hole of the Turkish Sultan's message, and of her father's sorrow. "Go home, my love, my sweetheart; go to bed and sleep, and when you wake tell your royal father that you have dreamt that the canes have to be placed in lukewarm water, and he will then be able to tell on which part of the plant the canes grew: the one that sinks to the bottom is the one from nearest the root; the one which does not sink and does not float on the surface, comes from the middle; and the one that remains on the surface is from the top." The girl ran home, went to bed and slept, and told her father her dream, as her sweetheart had instructed her. The king did as his daughter advised him, and marked the three canes, namely, with one notch the root-piece, the middle-piece with two notches, and the top-piece with three, and sent the explanation to the Sultan; and, actually, the canes had grown [Pg 240]as the Magyar king had picked them out; and the Sultan did not declare war against the Magyar.

After a year the Sultan wrote another letter to the Magyar king and sent him three foals; in the letter he asked him to guess which of the three animals was foaled in the morn, which at noon, and which in the evening, and threatened with war in case a correct guess was not forthcoming. The king was again sorrowful, and his daughter asked him the reason. "How should I not be sorrowful, my pretty sweet daughter," said the old king, "I had another letter from the Sultan, and he sent me three foals, and if I cannot tell him which was foaled in the morn, noon, and even, he will declare war against me." "The Lord will again help you, my dear royal father," said the girl quite joyfully. In half an hour she was again with her sweetheart, and communicated to him her father's trouble and sorrow. "Go home, idol of my heart," said the captive lad; "go to bed and sleep. In your dream scream out, and when your father asks you what is the matter, tell him that you dreamt that the Sultan had sent some Turks in order to carry your father off to captivity, as he was not able to guess when the foals were born; but just as they were pinioning him, you dreamt that the lad who had slapped your face got out somehow from his prison, and told you which of the foals was foaled in the morning, which at noon, and which in the evening." The king's daughter ran home and did exactly as the immured lad had told her. Next morning the tower was pulled down and the handsome lad conducted before the king. "The Lord has preserved you in your long captivity, my son, and I also feel inclined to grant you pardon. But before doing this you will have to help me in an important matter. I hand you here the Sultan's letter, read it; the three foals are in my stables; can you answer his query?" "I can, my king and master," said the liberated lad, "but I must ask you some questions. Have you got three exactly similar troughs?" "No, but I will get [Pg 241]some," replied the king. In a quarter of an hour three troughs of the same size and colour were ready. "Give orders, my king," said the lad, "to have some oats put into one, some live coals in the other, and some dry coal in the third: the foal which goes to the oats was foaled in the morning, the one to the live coals, at noon, and the one which goes to the dry coals, in the evening." The king did as the lad advised him. He marked the foals and sent them home. The Sultan was satisfied and did not send any troops against the Magyar king.

The Sultan had an aunt who was a witch, whom he consulted what to do in order to get possession of Hungary, and to tell him how he could get to know who was the man who answered all his questions so cleverly. "Alas! my dear relative," said the witch, "it isn't the Magyar king who answered all your queries: he has a lad who is the son of a very poor woman, but who will become king of Hungary; so long as you do not kill him you will covet Hungary in vain." Another letter came to the king of Hungary, in which it was written that if the lad who was kept by the king, and who was the brat of a poor woman, be not sent to Turkey, war shall be declared against the king. The king shewed the letter to the good lad in great sorrow, who, after having read the haughty monarch's lines, spoke thus: "I'm not afraid of bald-headed dogs, and I will cut to pieces the whole lot of them." At these words the sword clanked as it never did before. "I do not want anything save two lads; they must be both alike, and I will paint a mask resembling their features, and if we three look alike I'm not afraid of the whole world."

In the royal town were two brothers who were exactly alike, and the handsome lad painted himself a mask and put it on, and all three went to Turkey. The witch smelt the strangers' approach from a great distance. When they arrived in the Sultan's palace they all three saluted him, and all three bowed simultaneously; they answered the Sultan's questions all together; they sat down to supper all together; they all conveyed their [Pg 242]food to their mouths at the same time; they all got up at the same time; after supper they all three bowed, and at the signal from the Sultan all three went to bed. The Sultan could not see any difference between the three, but he did not like to kill all three. The witch, however, recognised the lad, and explained to her nephew his distinguishing feature, but the Sultan could not understand her explanation. "Well, you will know to-morrow morning, my Sultan and relative, which is the one whom we intend to kill," said the witch; "you will know him by his shirt-collar, which will have a scissors-cut in it; he is the Magyar king's man." An hour before midnight, at the time the witches are invisible, and when they are able to pass through the eye of a needle, the old witch glided through the keyhole into the bedroom where the youths soundly slept. All three were lying in the same bed, the handsome lad on the outside. The witch produced a pair of small scissors, and clipped out a piece of his shirt-collar, and then crept out of the room. But the handsome lad, when dressing in the morning, noticed in the looking-glass the damaged shirt-collar and marked his two mates' collars the same way. The Sultan asked the three lads to breakfast. The old witch stood in the window, and was very much surprised that the shirt-collars of all three were marked in the same way. After breakfast, they bowed and retired, and were allowed to return home. The king's daughter was very anxious until her sweetheart returned, but when she saw him one evening in her father's palace in good health and safe she was greatly delighted, and begged her father's permission to marry him. The king, however, made no reply, and the girl was very vexed with her father. One evening when she was again pleading on his behalf she suddenly fainted away; her eye fell on a letter sent by the Turkish Sultan asking her Father to send him this strange lad alone, because he was a dangerous man to Hungary. The old king sent the letter to the lad by his daughter, which the girl handed to him with tears. "Do not weep, love of my heart. [Pg 243]God is with me, and his power." Thus he consoled her. "I will start at sunrise to-morrow, and in a year's time we shall be each other's." The brave hero went alone to the Sultan; he met the old witch in the courtyard, who whispered to him, "It is the last time you will come to beautiful Turkey." The sword clanked, and the youth would not even listen to the old woman's words. When he stepped across the Sultan's threshold, fifteen armed Turks confronted him: the sword darted forth from its scabbard, and cut up the Turks into pulp. It did not touch the Sultan, but went back into its scabbard. At night the old witch tried to steal the lad's sword, but the sword jumped out and chopped off the witch's iron nose. Next morning the Sultan arrayed an enormous army against the lad, but the sword did its work so swiftly that not a sword, nor an arrow even so much as scratched the lad, and all the Turks were killed in a heap.

The daughter of the Magyar king was nearly in despair, because her sweetheart did not return on the appointed day, and she bothered her father with her requests until he led an army against Turkey. The girl led the troops herself in military uniform, but the troops had not to march more than a mile, as the lad was already on his way home with his little sword. The king's daughter and the army conducted him to the royal palace, and proclaimed him viceroy. The young hero with a few thousand soldiers returned to the country where he was born. His mother was very much frightened when she saw the soldiers approach, as she thought that they had come to destroy the town; and was still more frightened when she discovered that, while other courtyards were free from soldiers, her own was full of them, so full that one could not even drop a needle among them. She trembled, when a handsome fellow got off his horse, and approached her, but was very much surprised when the same handsome fellow took hold of her hand and kissed it, saying: "Well, my dear mother, I will now tell you what I have dreamt. I dreamt that I should become king of Hungary, my dream has [Pg 244]become true, and I may tell you now what it was, because it is an accomplished fact, and I am king of Hungary. I wouldn't tell you in my childhood when you asked me, because had I told you my dream the Magyar king would have killed me. And now may the Lord bless you that you did beat me; had you not beaten me the king would not have taken me; had he not taken me he would not have sentenced me to the gallows; had the king not sentenced me to the gallows the other king would not have carried me off.... I am now off to get married." And so it happened; he went home with his soldiers, and married the daughter of the Magyar king. He is still alive if he has not died since!

SHEPHERD PAUL.

There was once, I don't know where, a shepherd, who one day found a little boy in a meadow; the boy was not more than two days old, and so the shepherd took him to an old ewe and it nursed the child. The little boy was suckled by it for seven years, his name was Paul; and he grew so strong that he was able to uproot good-sized trees. The old shepherd kept the boy another seven years on the old ewe's milk, and after that he grew so strong that he could pull up oak-trees like weeds. One day Paul betook himself into the world in order to see countries, to get to know something of life, and try his luck. He went on and on, and on the very first day he met a man who was combing huge trees like one does flax. "Good day, my relative," said Paul; "upon my word, you are very strong! my Koma!" "I am Tree-Comber," said the man, "and am very anxious to wrestle with Shepherd Paul." "I'm the man you name; come along and let us wrestle," exclaimed Paul. And thereupon he seized Tree-Comber and threw [Pg 245]him to the ground with such force that he sunk into the ground as far as his knees. But he soon recovered, jumped up, seized Paul, and threw him to the ground, so that he went in as far as his waist; and then Paul again caught him, and put him in as far as his neck. "That will do!" called out Tree-Comber; "I can see that you are a smart fellow, and should be glad to become your ally." "Well and good," said Paul, and they continued their journey together.

They went on and soon after found a man who was crushing stones to powder with his hands, as if they were clods. "Good day," said Paul; "you must be a strong chap, my Koma." "I am Stone-Crusher, and should like to wrestle with Shepherd Paul." Thereupon Paul wrestled with him too, and defeated him the same way as he had done Tree-Comber; and he too became an ally, and all three continued their journey. After a short time, they came across a man who was kneading hard iron, as if it were dough. "Good day," said Paul; "you must have the strength of a devil, Koma." "I am Iron-Kneader, and should like to fight Shepherd Paul," answered this man. Paul wrestled with him and defeated him, and they all four became allies, and continued their journey. About noon they settled down in a forest, and Paul thus addressed his mates: "We three are going to look for some game, and you, Koma Tree-Comber, will stop here in the meantime and prepare a good supper for us." The three went hunting, and Tree-Comber in the meantime commenced to boil and roast, until he had nearly got the meal ready, when a little dwarf with a pointed beard came to the place, and said, "What are you cooking, countryman? Give me some of it." "I'll give you some on your back if you like," replied Tree-Comber. The little dwarf made no reply, but waited till the sauerkraut was done, and then, suddenly seizing Tree-Comber by the neck and pulling him on his back, he placed the saucepan on his belly, ate the sauerkraut, and disappeared. Tree-Comber was rather ashamed of this, and in order to hide the real facts from [Pg 246]his friends, commenced working afresh; however, the vegetable was not done by the time his mates returned, but he did not tell them the cause of it.

Next day, Stone-Crusher remained behind, while the others went hunting; he fared like Tree-Comber with the dwarf with the pointed beard, and the same thing happened to Iron-Kneader on the third day. Thereupon, Paul spoke thus: "Well, my Komas, there must be something behind all this, I think; none of you have been able to do the work while the rest of us were hunting. I propose that you three go hunting, while I remain and prepare the food." They went in high glee, chuckling that the little dwarf would teach Shepherd Paul a lesson also. Paul hurried on with the cooking, and had nearly finished, when the little fellow with the pointed beard came and asked for something to eat. "Be off," shouted Paul, and picked up the saucepan, so that the little fellow could not get it. The dwarf tried to get hold of his collar, but Paul swiftly seized him by his beard and tied him to a big tree, so that he could not move. The three mates returned early from their hunting, but Paul had the supper ready, and thus spoke to the three astonished men: "You, my Komas, are a fraud, you weren't able even to outwit that little dwarf with the pointed beard. Now let us have our supper at once, and then I will show you what I have done with him." When they finished, Paul took his mates to the place where he had fastened the dwarf, but he was gone, and so was the tree, as he had pulled it up by its roots and run away. The four fellows thereupon decided to give chase to him, and they followed the track made by the tree, and thus arrived at a deep hole, and as the track of the tree stopped here they came to the conclusion that the dwarf must have for a certainty got down into the deep hole. They held a short consultation and came to the resolution that they would lower Paul in a basket, and that they would remain above until Paul should pull the rope, and thus give them a signal to haul him up with all haste. So they [Pg 247]lowered Paul, and deep below in the earth among beautiful valleys he found a splendid castle, into which he at once entered. In the castle he found a beautiful girl who at once warned him to run away as fast as possible if he valued his life, because the castle belonged to a dragon with six heads, who had kidnapped her from earth, taken her to this underground place, and made her his wife; but Paul decided to await the dragon's return, as he was desirous of liberating the pretty girl. The monster with six heads soon arrived and angrily gnashed his teeth at the foolhardy Paul, who thus addressed him, "I am the famous Shepherd Paul, and I've come to fight you." "Well done," replied the dragon; "so, at least, I shall have something for supper, but first, let's have something to whet our appetites." Whereupon he commenced to devour a few hundredweights of huge round boulders, and, after he had satisfied his hunger, offered Paul one. Paul took a wooden knife and cut in two the stone offered to him, which weighed one hundredweight, and took up both halves and launched them with such power at the dragon that two of his heads were smashed to pulp. The dragon thereupon got into an awful rage, and made a furious onslaught on Paul, but he with a clever sword-cut slashed off two more of the monster's heads, and took him round the waist, and dashed him against the rock with such force, that the brains splashed out of the remaining two heads. The pretty girl thereupon with tears in her eyes thanked Paul for his services, for having liberated her from her ugly tormentor, but at the same time informed him, that two younger sisters of hers were languishing in the possession of two more powerful dragons.

Paul thereupon at once made up his mind to liberate the other two, and to take the girl with him. The girl handed him a golden rod, with which he struck the castle; and it became a golden apple, which he put in his pocket and went on. Not far off in a gorgeous castle he found the second girl, whose husband and tormentor was a dragon with twelve heads. This girl gave [Pg 248]Paul a silk shirt in order to make him more fit for the struggle with her husband. The shirt made Paul twice as strong. He had dinner with the twelve-headed dragon, and after a long struggle succeeded in defeating him, and took away all his twelve heads; he then transformed the castle with a golden rod into a golden apple, and continued his way with the two girls. Not far off in a castle they found the third girl, who was the youngest and the prettiest, and whose husband was a dragon with eighteen heads, who, however, assumed the shape of a little dwarf with a pointed beard whenever he went on his expeditions on the surface of the earth.

Paul longed more than ever to be at him, and in order the better to fortify him for the struggle with the awful monster, the pretty girl dressed him in a silk shirt which made him ten times stronger, and she also gave him some wine which doubled his power again. When the huge dragon with the eighteen heads arrived, Paul at once accosted him, saying, "Well, my Koma, I'm Shepherd Paul, and I've come to wrestle with you, and to liberate that pretty girl from your claws." "I'm glad I've met you," replied the dragon, "it's you who killed my two brothers, and you'll have to pay for that with your life, for it is only your blood that can repay me for the loss." Thereupon the monster went into the next room, to put on the fortifying shirt, and to drink the strengthening wine; but there was no shirt, and no wine in the cask, because the pretty girl had allowed what Paul could not drink to run out. The dragon became very angry and began to pace up and down, being rather nervous as to the issue. But Paul was not long before he set at him, and with one stroke slashed off six of his heads, and, after a short struggle, either broke or cut off the rest; and having thus liberated the third girl, he transformed the castle, like the previous two, into a golden apple, hid it in his pocket, and started with the three girls towards the opening at the top of which his mates awaited him.

Having got there, as there was no room for all four in the [Pg 249]basket, Paul bade the three girls to get in, and pulled the rope, whereupon his three mates hastily drew up the basket. Seeing the three pretty girls, they forgot all about hauling up Paul; each chose a girl and hastily left the forest, and settled down with them beyond the seventh country. Paul seeing that he was deceived by his faithless friends, began to swear in his rage, and vowed by heaven and earth that so soon as he should get out he would take bloody revenge on his deceitful mates, even if they had hidden themselves at the end of the world. Thereupon, he walked about aimlessly underground, and cogitated how to get out. After long wanderings he came to the nest of the huge griffin, in which he found several small griffins, and as the old bird was away, and it was hailing fire, he covered the nest with his cloak, and thus saved the little griffins. The old bird, in order to reward him, took him upon its back to carry him up to the surface. It took with it some provisions for the way, which consisted of a roast bullock hanging on one side, and a cask of wine on the other, and gave Paul directions that whenever it turned its head to the bullock he was to cut off a piece, and put it in its mouth, and whenever it turned its head to the cask, to pour a pint of wine down its throat. The griffin started off with Paul on its back, and flew three days and three nights, and on the morning of the fourth day it alighted with Paul outside the very town where his three faithless mates lived, put him down, and returned to its nest. Paul, as soon as he had rested from his fatigues, started off in search of his three mates, who were dreadfully frightened when they saw Shepherd Paul appear, who they thought was dead long ago. Paul gave them a severe scolding for their faithlessness, and then quietly killed all three. He placed the three apples in the prettiest part of the town, side by side, tapped them with the golden rod, and they became three splendid castles. He placed the three girls in them, married the youngest, and lives with her still in the middle castle, if he hasn't died since!

[Pg 250]

THE PELICAN.

There was once, I don't know where, there was in the world an old king; one of whose eyes always wept, and the other always smiled. He had three sons. The youngest was twelve, the eldest twenty, and the middle one sixteen. These three sons got talking together one spring morning about different things: the eldest of his sweetheart, the middle one of his saddle-horse, and the youngest one of his birds. Their conversation at last turned upon more serious matters, and they wished to know why their father's one eye always wept and why the other always smiled; so they decided to go and ask him the reason at once. The father was at luncheon. The eldest son knocked; and, after greeting his father, kissed his hand, and asked him why the one eye always wept and the other always smiled? The father looked very angrily at his son, and beckoned him to go. The boy became very frightened at seeing his father grow angry so suddenly, and ran away. Just as he ran through the door he heard a noise at his heels, and found that his father had thrown his knife and fork after him. The terrified lad brought the disappointing news to his brothers. "Then I'll ask him, if no one else will," said the middle son, who, for his chivalrous deeds, was his father's favourite. The king still sat at lunch, and the second son, like his elder brother, also asked his father why one eye always wept, whilst the other always smiled. The father then threw knife and fork after him, and the fork stuck fast in the heel of the lad's shoe. The lad was very frightened, and told his brothers what had happened, at which they were much disappointed, as they had every confidence in him. "It is of no use your going," said the second eldest to the youngest, "because our royal father dislikes you on account of your bird-catching habits."

[Pg 251]But still the little boy went in, and in a trembling but confident voice asked his father why one eye always wept, whilst the other always smiled. The king, who had just finished his lunch, no sooner heard the boy's question than he threw his knives and forks at him, and the blade of one knife lodged in the boy's thigh, so that the blood spurted out; but the little boy was not frightened, and, amid his tears, drew the knife out from his thigh, and having wiped it, took it back to his father, and repeated his question. The father lovingly stroked the little fellow's hair and bade him sit on a low chair, and told him the secret, saying: "One eye always laughs because you three boys are very handsome children; and when I die you will make three brave kings for any three countries. My other eye always weeps because once upon a time I had a beautiful pelican, whose song was so charming, that whosoever heard it was at once transformed into a youth seventeen years of age. That bird was stolen from me by two men dressed in black. That is the reason why one eye always weeps, and why my soul is vexed within me." The little fellow kissed his father's hand and hurried off to his brothers, who received him with a mocking smile, but soon felt ashamed of themselves, when the child, with his wounded thigh, brought the reply to their question. "We will try to console our father, and make him young again," said the three brothers all together; "We will endeavour to find that pelican, if it be yet alive, whether it be on land or sea." Having thus spoken, they at once got ready for the journey.

The eldest and the middle sons went to their father's stables, saddled the finest horses, and put a great deal of treasure in their sabretaches, and set forth: so that the youngest son was left without a horse, as his elder brothers had taken away the horses that would have suited him.

When they came to the end of the village, an old beggar met them, and asked them for a coin or a bit of bread: the two elder lads took no notice of him, but galloped on, the beggar [Pg 252]shouting mocking words after them. The youngest lad arrived half an hour later, and shared half his cake with the beggar. "As you have helped me, prince," said the beggar, "I will help you. I know where you are going, and what you are seeking. You would need the lives of three men if you went on foot, or on the back of an ordinary horse, for the church in which your pelican sings now is beyond the Operencian Sea. The saddle-horse which can go there must have been brought up on dragon's milk, to prevent its hoofs being worn away on the long journey; but for a good deed you may expect a good one in return. You have helped me, and I will help you, with my advice at least, and that is all a poor beggar can offer. Five miles from this bridge where we stand lives an old witch who has two horses. If you serve her for a year (her year has three days) she will give you as much money as you ask for; but if you do not serve your whole year she will chop off your head. The man has not yet been found who can serve her a whole year, for her horses are her two daughters, and so soon as the groom falls asleep, they either disappear into the clouds or the sea; or slip under ground, and do not reappear until the groom's head is impaled. But I trust that you will be able to take care of them. Take this whistle; it has three holes. If you open the first hole the King of the Gnats will appear at your command; if the second, the King of the Fishes; if the third, the King of the Mice. Take great care of this whistle, and when you have done your year, don't ask for money, cattle, clothes, lands, or suchlike things (the old witch will offer you all these), but ask for the half-rotten foal which lies buried seven fathoms deep in the dung-heap. There is a hen-coop, and on the top of it a saddle and a bridle; put these on the foal just after you have dug it out. It will be too weak to walk, therefore you must take it on your back, and carry it to the end of the village. There you will find a bridge. Place it under the bridge, in the water, for one hour, and then wash it. I won't tell you any more."

[Pg 253]The same evening, just after the cows had been driven home, the lad was to be seen sitting on the threshold of the witch's door. The old witch was at the same hour driving her horses home from the field. Sometimes they jumped about on the ground; sometimes they flew in the air; but the old witch was after them everywhere, riding a-straddle on a saddled mopstick. "Good evening, my dear old mother," said the lad, in a confidential voice. "Good fortune has brought you, my dear son," commenced the witch, "it's lucky that you called me your mother, for see! there are ninety-nine human heads impaled, and yours would have been the hundredth. What's your errand, my dear son?" "I'm looking for a situation, my dear old mother!" "Good fortune has brought you, my dear son; the year lasts three days with me, and during that time you will have to take care of my two horses. Your wages will be whatever you ask, and as much as you desire. But if you don't take care of those two horses, you must die!" "The Lord will help me." "Come in to supper, for you will have to take the horses out into the Silken Meadow for the night." The prince went in, and after supper the witch poured a sleeping draught into the new groom's drinking-cup. Supper over the prince went into the stables and stroked the horses. He then prepared two halters from a piece of rope that the beggar had given him, threw them over their heads, and jumped on the back of the finer horse. The horse, which had become quite tame with the unusual halter, walked along peaceably with the prince on its back, to the great surprise of the witch. "Well, that fellow must know a thing or two!" sighed the old witch as she looked after him, and slammed the door behind her. As soon as the prince arrived in the Silken Meadow with the horses a heavy sleep seized him, and he slept soundly all night. The sun was high in the heavens when he woke, rubbing his sleepy eyes, and began to call for his horses, which would not come. He was in great despair until, fumbling in his pockets, he found the little whistle, which he immediately [Pg 254]blew, leaving the first hole open. The King of the Gnats appeared! "We wait your orders," said a huge gnat: "speak and tell us what you require. If it be anything in the air we will find it for you." "I had to take care of two horses, and I cannot find them. If I do not take them home, death will be my doom." Gnats went flying forth in all directions at their king's singing, and in less than half an hour two griffins alighted in front of the lad. He struck them on the heads with a halter, and they became horses, and the little groom went home in great joy. "So you have brought them home safely, my son; your breakfast is ready; eat it and then go to sleep. By-and-by your dinner will be ready. You have nothing else to do to-day." So saying, the old witch gave her horses a sound thrashing with a peel, and then, giving them some burning cinders to eat, went back to the house, and, sitting in a corner, threaded beads until noon.

In the evening the old woman again mixed some sleeping draught into the little groom's drink, making it stronger than before. He took out his horses, and when he had gone a little way on the road he fell off the saddle, and slept till noon the next day. When he awoke his horses were gone, and so he blew his whistle, leaving the second hole open, and the King of the Fishes appeared. "We wait your orders," said a mighty whale; "speak and tell us. If it is to be found in or above the ocean we will find it." "I had to guard two horses, and I can't find them anywhere, and if I don't take them back I must die." Fishes swam forth in every river and sea at the command of their king, and in an hour they drove a big pike to shore, which had two little gold fish in its inside. The whale ordered a sword-fish to rip open the pike's belly. The little lad struck the gold fishes on the head with his halter, and they became horses once more. Late in the afternoon the little groom arrived in the courtyard with the horses. "Go inside, my son, and have something to eat, you have nothing more to do until the [Pg 255]evening," said the witch, who then thrashed her horses with a huge poker, and, having given them some burning cinders to eat, hobbled back into the house and began to count her gold coins. The prince had to spend another night with the horses; and in the evening the old witch went to the horses, and, having scolded them well, declared that if they would not hide themselves properly this time she would punish them horribly. She gave her little groom drink until he was half drunk, and also three pillows which were stuffed with owl's feathers, which would make him sleep sounder. And he did go to sleep until the midday sun awoke him next day in the Silken Meadow. But the little whistle again came to his aid; he opened the lowest hole and blew the whistle, and the King of all the Mice appeared. "We wait your orders," said a rat with a big moustache. "Whatever is to be found on earth or under its crust we will bring to you, if you order us to do so." "I had to guard two horses and can't find any trace of them; if I don't take them home I must die." The mice came forth from every wall and every hole in the ground at the squeak of their king. After an hour and a half they drove two rats from a granary to the lad, who struck them on the head with his halter, and changed them back into his horses.

On his arrival at home the witch said to the prince, "So you have guarded them well, my dear son. Your year of service is over. Ask what you like. Here are three keys, one of which opens a cellar where there are vats full of gold and silver, take as much as you like. The second key opens a wardrobe, from which you may choose either royal dresses, or if you like magic garments, which will change into anything you like. The third key opens the stables, where you will find horses with golden or silver hair; take which you like best, and as many as you like, it is all the same to me." The prince looked at the treasures, clothes, and horses, but chose none of them, and returned the keys, looking very downcast.

[Pg 256]"My father the king has horses, costly garments, and gold; I have no need for any of these things."

"Ask, then, whatever you like; ask my life, because whosoever has served a year with me well deserves his wages."

"I don't want your life or your death, my dear old mother; but under your dung-heap there lies buried seven fathoms deep a wretched foal, and on the top of your hen-coop there's a worn-out old saddle very much soiled. These are the things I want; give them to me."

"You're in league with the devil, my dear son, take care that you don't get into hell."

The witch tried to put him off, and made all manner of excuses, but at last she brought a golden spade and traced a triangle on the dung-heap which pointed to where, without fail, the wretched foal was to be found. The prince dug without ceasing for seven days and seven nights, and on the dawn which followed the eighth night the ground began to move under his spade and the Tátos foal showed its hoofs. The prince dug it out, scraped the dirt from it, and, having fetched the saddle from the hen-coop, put it on the foal; and having taken leave of his witch mistress he took the foal on his back and carried it as far as the bridge. While the foal was soaking in the water the old beggar appeared on the bridge and received a piece of bread from the prince.

"Prince, when you sit on your horse's back," said the beggar, "take care of yourself. It will carry you through clouds and over waters; it knows well the way to the country where the pelican lives, so let it go wherever it pleases. When you arrive at the shore of the Operencian Sea leave your horse there, for you will have to walk three hundred miles further. On your way go into every house and make inquiries. A man who knows how to use his tongue can get far, and one question is worth more than a hundred bad guesses. On the shore of the Operencian Sea there are two trees, one on this side and one on [Pg 257]the opposite shore; you cannot get over the sea unless you climb the trees when they kiss each other, and this only happens twice a year, at the end of the summer and at the beginning of spring. More I will not tell you. Good-bye."

Their conversation had lasted a whole hour, and behold! the wretched foal had become such a beautiful horse with golden hair and three legs, that one could not find another to match it.

The little prince got into the saddle, which had also become gold, and rode leisurely over the bridge. At the other end his steed spoke thus: "I shall now be able to see, my little master, whether we can start at once;" and thereupon darted into the clouds; from thence to the moon; from thence to the sun; and from the sun to the "hen and chickens" (the Pleiades); and from thence back to the bridge.

"I have lived for many a thousand years, but such a rider as you has not sat on my back before." And again it darted off over seven times seven countries, and in half an hour the prince reached his brothers, who had been galloping for the last three days and three nights. They rode together for a little while when the eldest thus spoke: "My younger brothers, if we all three keep together we shall never be able to find the pelican. The road divides into three branches here. Let each of us go into a different country, and let us mark this finger-post, and in one year's time meet here again. Should blood ooze out of the post it will be a sign that the brother who is absent is in misery or captivity; but if milk flow out of it, then he is well." This proposal was accepted. The two eldest took the roads on the right and the youngest the one on the left. But the two eldest were wicked. They did not look for the pelican but got into bad habits and spent their time in making love to young ladies. They did not trouble themselves very much about their father's rejuvenescence. The youngest prince went on steadily and covered a thousand miles a day; till at last he reached the Operencian Sea. The two trees which stood on its shores were [Pg 258]just then kissing each other. The prince slackened the girth of his horse, jumped on the tree, ran along its upper branches, which touched the tree on the other side of the sea, and in an hour gained the opposite shore. He had left his horse in a silken meadow, the grass standing as high as the horse's knees. His horse neighed after him and urged him to make haste.

On the opposite shore of the sea there was a golden forest. He had a small hand-adze with him and with it he notched the stems of the trees so that he might not miss his road upon his return. Beyond the golden forest there stood a small cottage where an aged woman a hundred years old lived.

"Good day, my dear old mother."

"Good fortune has brought you, my dear son. What are you doing here, whither not even a bird ever comes? What do you want here, my dear son?"

"I am trying to find the pelican, my dear old mother."

"Well, my son, I do not know where it is, but I have heard of it. Go a hundred miles beyond yonder silver forest, and ask my grandmother. If she does not know anything about it, nobody does. On your way back with your bird come and see me, my dear son, and I will give you a present. Life is worth living."

The old woman sent her cat with the prince, which accompanied him as far as the right road, mewed once, and turned back. The wandering prince, after a journey which lasted for weeks, got through the silver forest and found a cottage where the old woman lived, who was so much bent from age that her nose touched the ground.

"Good evening, my grandmother."

"Good fortune has brought you, my dear son. What are you doing here, whither not even a bird ever comes? What do you want, my dear son?"

"I seek the pelican, my dear mother, whose song makes old people young again. The Jesuits have stolen it from my father."

[Pg 259]"Well, my son, I know nothing of it. But fifty miles beyond yonder copper-forest lives my mother, and if she knows nothing about your bird, then nobody does. On your way back with the bird call upon me, my dear son, and I will give you a good present for your trouble. Life is still very pleasant, even to me."

The prince again continued his journey in company with a red cock, which took him as far as the right road. There it crowed once, and flew back. After a journey of days and weeks the prince discovered on the borders of the copper-forest a little cottage, in which the old woman sat, whose eyelids were quite covered with moss. "Good day, my dear old mother!" "Good fortune has brought you, my dear son. What do you want?"

"I am looking for the pelican." "You are on the right spot, my dear son. Though I have never seen it; because when it was brought hither I could use my legs no longer. Step across the threshold, and within a gun-shot you will see an old tumble-down church; the pelican is kept in there. By the side of the church there is a beautiful mansion, in it live the two old Jesuits who brought the bird from some foreign land; but the bird will not sing to them. Go and tell them that you think you will be able to make the bird sing, as perhaps it will sing to you as you come from a foreign land."

The prince, however, didn't dare to go to see the friars, but waited for the evening or the morning bell to be rung, and then stole into the church. He had to wait for seven days, and still he did not succeed in hearing the pelican sing, as on each occasion a deep sleep overcame him. The two friars had become youths of seventeen years of age during the last two days.

No one knew why the bird did sing on the third day. On this day, the prince, as soon as he had stepped into the church, made his nose bleed, and this kept him awake, and he heard the bird's song, and saw the friars caper round the cage and throw sugar into it. The prince hid himself under a chair, and when [Pg 260]every one had retired to rest after evening prayers he let the bird out of its cage, hid it under his cloak, and went back to the first old woman and made her young again. The old woman jumped with delight, and gave him as much gold and silver as he liked. In a few weeks he got back to the other old women who lived in the gold and silver forests, and they regaled him in a royal manner.

When he reached the sea-shore the two trees were kissing again, so he ran across them with the bird and appeared by the side of his horse, which had eaten so much of the fine grass that it had become so fat that the girth had quite cut into its belly. He made the horse young too, and sat on its back, and in a short time returned to the post where he had left his brothers. Lo! blood was flowing on that side on which his brothers had gone. His sensitive heart was quite overcome with sorrow, because his brothers were either in danger or misery. So he went on the same road on which the poor fellows had departed. He had not gone more than a couple of miles before he came to an inn. Adjoining the inn was a garden, where his two brothers were working in irons, because they had squandered their all, including their horses, and had got into debt for drink. After scolding the innkeeper the little prince bought his brothers off and repurchased their horses.

They then started home all together, and he related all his adventures, and how he had got possession of the favorite pelican. At last they came to the outskirts of a forest about three miles from home, and at this place the two elder brothers attacked him from behind, cut off his hands and feet, took his little bird from him, and hurried home in order to lengthen their father's life by means of the song of the dear bird that had been brought back from so far off. The poor little prince began to cry bitterly with pain and fear. His cries were heard by a swine-herd who was tending his herd in the same forest in which the wicked brothers had maimed the little prince.

[Pg 261]The swine-herd picked up the poor boy without hands and feet and carried him to his hut. "He will do to take care of the hut," said the swine-herd, "poor wretch!" In the evening, the little crippled boy related all about his brothers' cruelty, and the poor swine-herd's heart was filled with pity for the boy's misfortune. Next morning just as he was going to look after his hogs the little prince called him back with fearful screams, and to his surprise he saw something that looked like a human skull wriggle out of the ground. He quickly knocked off the top of the skull with his hatchet, and the remainder slipped back into the ground. From the part cut off, blood flowed on to the ground. Somehow or other his maimed finger came in contact with the mud formed out of the blood and the dust and to his astonishment it was healed. Great was the simple swine-herd's joy! He rubbed the boy's stumps with the mud, and lo! his hands and feet grew again!

As soon as the news had spread in the royal town that the pelican had come back all the old men gathered together and many brought presents to the princes, and took out their horses and dragged their carriage along the streets. At ten o'clock the next morning the church was crowded, and the pelican was reinstalled in its old place. The organ began to play but the bird would not sing. The king had it proclaimed through the length and breadth of his kingdom that any one who could make the pelican sing should have half his realm. The swine-herd heard the news and told it to his helpmate. "Take me, my brother, under your cloak," said the little prince, "as I do not wish my brothers to see me, lest they kill me. Let us then go into the town, and, as you are very old, I will induce the pelican to sing and make you young." So they set off together and the swine-herd sent word into the crowded meeting that he had confidence in the Lord, and thought he would be able to make the bird sing. The people crowded round the swine-herd, who had a handsome, well-built boy hidden under his cloak. They conducted him into the [Pg 262]church, where he at once took off his great cloak, and no sooner did the pelican see its liberator than it at once began to sing most beautifully, and all the old men who were there assembled in great numbers became seventeen years old. The king recognised his son and made him tell all about his journey. When he came to the incident of the savage attack by his brothers the people began to hiss and groan, and resolved to draw and quarter the two villains, to tie them to horses' tails, drag them over the town, and hang them on the four corners of the fortress. The resolution was at once carried into effect. In vain did the kind-hearted lad beg for their lives. They had to die. The old king gave half of the realm to the young prince. The swine-herd was dressed up in velvet and purple, and they all are alive to this day, if they have not died since.

THE GIRL WITH THE GOLDEN HAIR.

There was once, I do not know where, in the world an old man who had twelve sons; the eldest of whom served the king for twenty-four years. One day the old man took it into his head that all his sons should get married, and they all were willing to comply with their father's wish, with the exception of the eldest son, who could not on any account be coaxed into matrimony. However the old man would not give in, and said, "Do you hear me, my son? the eldest of you must marry at the same time as the youngest; I want you all to get married at the same time."

So the old man had a pair of boots made for himself with iron soles and went in search of wives for his twelve sons. He [Pg 263]wandered hither and thither over several countries until the iron soles of his boots were worn into holes; at last, however, he found at a house twelve girls, who, he thought, would do.

The eleven younger lads made great preparations and went to the fair to buy themselves saddle-horses; but the eldest, who was serving the king, did not concern himself about anything, and turned out the king's horses to grass as usual. Among the animals there was a mare with a foal, and Jack—this was the name of the eldest lad—always bestowed the greatest care upon the mare. One day, as the whole stud were grazing in the fields, the mare neighed and said to the lad, "I say, Jack, I hear that you are thinking of getting married; your eleven brothers have already gone to the fair to purchase riding-horses for the wedding; they are buying the finest animals they can get; but don't you go and purchase anything: there is a foal of mine that was foaled last year, go and beg the king to let you have it, you will have no cause to repent your choice. The king will try to palm off some other animal on you, but don't you take it. Choose the foal as I tell you."

So it happened Jack went up stairs and saw the king and spoke to him thus: "Most gracious Majesty! I have now served you for twenty-four years and should like to leave this place, because my eleven brothers are already on their way to get themselves wives; the tips of my moustache too reach already to my ears, the days fly fast, and it is high time for me to find a wife too; I should be much obliged if you would pay me my wages." "You are perfectly right, my dear son, Jack," replied the king, "it is high time that you too get married; and, as you have so faithfully served me, I will give orders for your wedding to be celebrated with the greatest pomp. Let me know your wishes! would you like to have so much silver as you can carry, or would you prefer as much gold?" "Most gracious Majesty, I have only one desire, and that is to be allowed to take with me from your stud a certain foal that belongs to a certain mare that [Pg 264]is with foal again this year." "Surely you don't want to make an exhibition of yourself on that wretched creature?" "Aye, but I do, your Majesty, and I do not want anything else."

Our Jack was still fast asleep when his eleven brothers set out on the finest horses to fetch their girls. Jack did not get up till noon, at which hour the king ordered out a coach and six, together with a couple of outriders, and thus addressed the lad: "Well, Jack, my boy, I have no objection, you can take your foal, but don't reproach me hereafter." Jack thereupon had plenty to eat and drink, and even took out a bucketful of wine to his foal and made it drink the whole. He then took his goods and chattels and sat in the coach, but the king would not allow the foal to run along with the coach, and said: "Not that way, if I know it; put the ugly creature up on the box! I should feel ashamed if anybody saw the ugly brute running alongside my coach." So the foal was tied up to the box, and they set off till they reached the outskirts of the town. By this time the foal, which was in a most uncomfortable position, presented a most pitiful sight; for by rubbing against the box the whole of one of its sides had become raw. So they stopped, and it was taken down and placed on the ground. Jack got out, and, the coach having set out for home, he sat on the foal's back, his feet touching the ground. The foal gazed round to see whether anybody was looking on, and, not seeing a soul, it flew up high into the air and thus addressed the lad: "Well, my dear master, at what speed shall we proceed? Shall we go like the hurricane or like a flash of thought?" "As quick as you can, my dear horse," was his reply.

They flew along for a while, when the foal again spoke, asking: "Is your hat tied on, my dear master?"

"Yes, it is, my dear horse."

Again they flew along, and again the little foal said: "Well, my dear master, your hat that you have bought for your wedding is gone. You have lost it. We have left it some seven [Pg 265]miles behind, but we will go back to fetch it; nobody has as yet picked it up." So they returned and picked up the hat, and the little foal again flew high up into the air. After proceeding for three hours they reached the inn where his brothers had decided to take up their night's lodgings. The other lads had started at dawn, he not till noon, after his midday meal, and still he left them behind. Having got within a short distance of the inn, the foal alighted on the ground with Jack, and addressed him in these words: "Well, my dear master, get off here and turn me out on to that heap of rubbish and weeds yonder, then walk into the inn and have plenty to eat and drink; your eleven younger brothers will also arrive here shortly." So Jack entered the inn, ordered a bottle of wine, made a hearty meal, and enjoyed himself heartily. He took out a bucketful of wine to his foal and gave it to drink; time passed on ... when, at last his brothers arrived. They were still at some distance when the youngest caught sight of the foal, and exclaimed: "Oh, look at that miserable screw! Surely it is our eldest brother's steed." "So it is! So it is!" exclaimed all the others, but at the same time they all stared at each other, and could not explain how it came to pass that, although they had started much earlier than their brother, they had been outdistanced by him, notwithstanding the fact that his animal could not be compared with their own horses. The brothers put their steeds into the stables and placed plenty of hay and corn before them, then they walked into the tap-room and found Jack already enjoying himself.

"So you have got here, brother," they remarked. "As you behold, youngsters, though I had not left home when the clock struck twelve." "Certainly it is a mystery how you have got here on that thorough-bred of yours, a wolf could swallow the creature at a bite."

They sat down and ate and drank; so soon as it became dark, the lads went out to look after the horses.

[Pg 266]"Well then, where will you put your horse over night?" they inquired of the eldest.

"I will put it into the same stables with yours."

"You don't mean that, it will barely reach to the bellies of our horses, the stables are too big for that steed of yours."

But Jack took his foal into the stables and threw his cloak over its back. In the meantime his brothers had returned to the tap-room and were holding council as to what was to be done with their eldest brother.

"What shall we do with him? what indeed? what can we do under the circumstances but kill him? It will never do to take him with us to the girls, they will laugh at us and drive us off in disgrace."

At this the foal began to speak, and said: "I say, dear master, tie me near the wall, your brothers will come to kill you, but don't do anything in the matter, leave it to me; join them, eat and drink, and then come back and lie down at my feet, I will do the rest."

Jack did as he was told; upon leaving the tap-room he returned to the stables and lay down at the feet of his foal, and as the wine had made him a bit drowsy he soon fell asleep. Ere long his brothers arrived with their hatchet-sticks which they had purchased for the wedding.

"Gee-up, you jackass," they shouted, and all eleven were about to attack the poor little foal, when it kicked out with such force that it sent the youngest flying against the wall.

"Get up, dear master, they have come." Jack thereupon woke, and his little foal asked him, "What shall I do with them?"

"Oh! knock them all against the wall."

The foal did as it was told, and the lads dropped about like crab-apples. It collected them all into a heap, when Jack, seeing their condition, became frightened, so he hurriedly picked up a bucket, ran to the well, fetched some water and poured it [Pg 267]over the eleven. They managed, with some difficulty, to get on to their feet and then showered reproaches upon him, complaining bitterly about his unbrotherly conduct in ordering his foal to handle them so roughly as it had done.

The eleven then left the inn without a moment's delay, and toiled along the whole night and the next day, until at last, on the following evening, they reached the home of the twelve girls. But to get in was not such an easy task, for the place was fenced round with strong iron rails, the gate was also very strong and made of iron, and the latch was so heavy that it took more than six powerful men to lift it. The eleven brothers made their horses prance about and bade them to kick against the latch, but all their manoeuvres were of no avail—they could not move the latch.

But what has become of Jack? where did he tarry? His foal knew only too well where the girls could be found, and how they could be got at; so he did not budge from the inn until late in the afternoon, and spent his time eating and drinking. His brothers were still busily engaged with the latch, hammering at it and kicking, when at last, just when the people were lighting the candles at dusk, the brothers discovered Jack approaching high up in the air on his foal. As soon as he reached the gate he wheeled round, the foal gave a tremendous kick at the latch, whereupon the gate, and with it a portion of the railing, heeled over into the dust. The landlady, a diabolical old witch, then came running to the gate with a lamp in her hand, and said: "I knew Jack that you had arrived, and I have come and opened the gate." This statement was of course not true.

The lads entered the house, where they found the twelve girls all standing in a row. With regard to the age of the maidens they corresponded to those of the lads; and when it came to choice, the eldest lad fell in love with the eldest girl, the [Pg 268]youngest lad with the youngest maid, and so on, every lad with the girl of his own age. They sat down to supper, each girl by the side of her beau; they ate and drank, enjoyed themselves, and the kissing had no end. At last they exchanged handkerchiefs. As it was getting late, and the young folks became sleepy, they all retired to rest. Beds were prepared for all twenty-four in a huge room; on one side stood the beds for the girls, on the other those for the lads. Just then the mischievous old witch, who was the girls' mother, walked out of the house, and muttered to herself:

"Now I have got you all in my net, you wretched crew, we shall see which of you will leave this place alive!"

It so happened that Jack went out to look after his foal; he took a bucketful of wine with him and gave his animal a drink, whereupon the foal spoke to him thus:

"I say, dear master! we have come to an awful place; that old witch intends to kill you all. At the same time don't be frightened, but do what I am about to tell you. After everybody has gone to bed, come out again and lead us horses out from these stables, and tie twelve horses belonging to the old witch in our places. With regard to yourselves, place your hats on to the girls' heads, and the old witch will mistake the maids, and slay them in your stead. I will send such a deep slumber over them that even a noise seven times as loud as you will make cannot wake them."

In conformity with the advice thus received, Jack re-entered the bedchamber, placed the twelve men's hats on to the heads of the girls; he then exchanged the horses, and went back to bed. Soon after the old witch commenced to whet a huge knife, which sent forth a shower of vivid sparks: she then approached the beds, groped about, and as soon as she discovered a hat, snap! off went a head, and so she went on until she had cut off all the girls' heads. Then she left the house, fetched a broad axe, [Pg 269]sharpened it and went into the stables. Snap! off came the head of the first horse, then the next, till she had killed all twelve.

The foal then stamped upon the ground, whereupon Jack went out, and was thus spoken to by his foal:

"Now then, dear master! rouse up all your brothers, and tell them to saddle their horses! and let them get away from this place without a moment's delay. Don't let dawn overtake them here, or they are lost. You yourself can go back and finish your sleep."

Jack rushed in and with great difficulty roused them; and then informed them of the dangerous position they were in. After a great deal of trouble, they got up and left the place. Jack himself laid down and had a sound sleep. As soon as the first streaks of dawn appeared, the foal again stamped; Jack went out, sat upon it, and as they flew through the gate the foal gave the railing such a powerful kick that even the house tottered and fell. The old witch hereupon jumped up in great hurry, sat a-straddle an iron pole, and rode in pursuit of Jack.

"Stop Jack, you deceitful lad!" she shouted; "you have killed my twelve daughters, and destroyed my twelve horses. I am not sure whether you will be able to come again hither or not!"

"If I do, I shall be here; if not, then I shan't."

Poor Jack got weary of his life, not having been able to get himself a wife. He did not return to his native town, but went into the wide, wide world. As he and his foal were proceeding on their journey, the steed said to him: "Look, dear master! I have stept on a hair of real gold; it is here under my hoof. It would bring ill luck if we picked it up, but it would equally be unlucky to leave it; so you had better take it with you." Jack picked up the golden hair, and re-mounted his foal, and continued his journey. After a while the foal again spoke, saying: "My dear master! now I have stept on a half [Pg 270]horse-shoe of pure gold, it is here under my hoof. It would be unlucky to take it with us, but we should not fare better if we left it; so you had better take it." Jack picked up the half horse-shoe of pure gold, put it into his bag, and they again flew like lightning. They reached a town just as the evening bell rang, and stopped in front of an hostelry; Jack got off, walked in and asked the innkeeper:

"Well, my dear host, what is the news in this town?"

"Nothing else, my kinsman, but that the king's coachman, who drove his state-coach, is lying on his death-bed; if you care for the situation, you had better take it."

So Jack at once made up his mind, and went to see the king—who was then still a bachelor—and was at once engaged by him to drive the state-coach. He did not ask for any wages, but only stipulated that his foal should be allowed to feed with the coach-horses from the same manger. To this the king agreed, and Jack at once proceeded to the stables. In the evening the other grooms (there were some fifty or sixty of them) raised a great cry, and all asked for candles from the woman who served out the stores. But Jack did not want any, so he did not ask for any, and still his horses were in better condition, and were better groomed than the rest. All the other grooms used a whole candle a head every night. This set the storekeeper woman thinking; she could not imagine how it could be that, whereas all the other men wanted a whole candle a head every blessed night, the man who drove the state-coach did not want any, and still his horses looked a hundred times better than the others. She told the strange discovery to the king, who immediately sent for all the men with the exception of Jack.

"Well, my sons, tell me this: How is it that every one of you burns a whole candle every night, whereas my state-coachman has never asked for any, and still his horses look seven times better than yours?"

[Pg 271]"Oh, your majesty, he has no need to ask for any; we could do without them, if we were in his position."

"How is that, explain yourselves."

"Because, sir, he does his work one morning by the light of a golden hair, and every other morning by the rays of half a horse-shoe of pure gold."

The king dismissed the grooms, and the next day at dawn concealed himself, and watched Jack, and satisfied himself with his own eyes that his men had spoken the truth. So soon as he got back into his rooms, he sent for Jack, and addressed him thus:

"I say, my boy, you were working this morning by the light of a hair of real gold."

"That is not true, your majesty; where on earth could I get a hair of real gold?"

"Don't let us waste any words! I saw it with my own eyes this morning. If the girl to whom that golden hair belonged is not here by to-morrow morning you forfeit your life! I'll hang you!"

Poor Jack returned to the stables and wept like a child. "What is the matter?" inquired his foal; "Why do I see those tears? what makes you cry?"

"How could I help crying and weeping? the king has just sent for me and told me that if I can't produce the girl to whom the golden hair belonged he will hang me."

"This is indeed a very serious look-out, my dear master, because you must know that the old witch whose twelve girls we have slain has yet another most beautiful daughter; the girl has not yet been allowed to see daylight, she is always kept in a special room which she has never yet left, and in which six candles are kept burning day and night—that is the girl to whom that golden hair once belonged. But never mind, eat and drink to your heart's content, we will go and fetch her. But be [Pg 272]cautious when you enter the house where the daughter of the old witch is guarded, because there are a dozen bells over the door, and they may betray you."

Jack therefore ate and drank, and took a bucketful of wine to his foal too, and gave it a drink. Then they started and went and went, until after a while they reached the dwelling of the old witch. Jack dismounted, cautiously approached the door, carefully muffled the dozen bells, and gently opened the door without making the slightest noise. And lo! inside he beheld the girl with the golden tresses, such a wonderfully pretty creature the like of which he had not set his eyes upon before during all his eventful life. He stole up to her bedside on tiptoe, grasped the girl round the waist, and in another second was again out of the house, carrying her off with him. He ran as fast as he could and mounted his steed. The foal gave a parting kick to the house that made the roof tumble in, and the next moment was off, high up in the air like a swift bird. But the old witch was not slow either, the moment she was roused she mounted a long fir-pole and tore after Jack like forked lightning.

"It is you, Jack, you good-for-nothing, deceitful fellow! My twelve daughters have perished by your hand, and now you carry off my thirteenth! You may have been here before, but I'll take care that you don't come again."

"If I do, I do; if I don't, I don't."

Jack went and went, and by dawn had already reached home; he conducted the girl into the king's presence, and lo! no sooner had the monarch caught sight of her than he rushed forward and embraced her, saying: "Oh, my darling, my pretty love, you are mine and I am yours!" But the girl would not utter a single word, not for the whole world. This made the king question her: "What is the matter, my love? Why are you so sad?"

"How can I help being sad? Nobody can have me until [Pg 273]some one brings hither all my goods and chattels, my spinning-wheel and distaff, nay, the very dust in my room."

The king at once sent for Jack.

"Well, my boy, if the golden-haired girl's goods and chattels, spinning-wheel, distaff, and the very dust in her room, are not here by to-morrow morning, I will hang you."

Jack was very much downcast and began to cry. When he reached the stables his foal again asked him: "What's the matter with you, my dear master? Why all this sorrow?"

"How can I help weeping and crying, my dear horse; the king has sent for me and threatened to hang me if the golden-haired girl's goods and chattels, nay, the very dust of her room, be not here by to-morrow morning."

"Don't fret, my dear master, we will go and fetch them too. Get a table-cloth somewhere, and when you enter her room spread out the cloth on the floor and sweep all her paraphernalia into it."

Jack got ready and started on his errand. Within a short time he reached the dwelling of the old witch, entered the room, and spread out his cloth. But, would anybody believe it, the glare of the place very nearly blinded him; the very dust on the floor was pure gold. He swept everything he could find into the table-cloth, swung the bundle on his back, and ran out; having got outside, the foal at his bidding gave the building a powerful kick that demolished its very foundations. This woke the old witch, who immediately mounted a red-hot broom and tore after him like a whirlwind.

"Confound you, deceitful Jack! after you have robbed me of all my thirteen daughters, you now come and steal the chattels of the youngest girl. I warrant that you won't return hither any more."

"If I do, I do; if I don't, I don't."

Jack went home with the luggage and handed it to the king.

[Pg 274]"Well, my darling, my pretty love! your wish is now fulfilled, and nothing can prevent you from becoming mine."

"You shall have me, but only on one condition. Somebody must go for my stud with golden hair, which is to be found beyond the Red Sea. Until all my horses are here nobody can have me."

The king again sent for Jack.

"Listen to this, my boy; the girl with the golden hair has a golden-haired stud beyond the Red Sea; if you don't go at once to fetch them, you forfeit your life."

Jack went down stairs in great trouble, bent over his foal, buried his face in his hands, and wept most bitterly, and as he sobbed and moaned the little foal asked: "What are you crying about now?" Jack told the foal what the king had ordered him to do, and what the punishment would be if the order were not obeyed.

"Don't weep, dear master, don't fret; the thing can be done if you follow my directions. Go up stairs to the king and beg of him twelve buffalo-hides, twelve balls of twine, a grubbing-hoe, and an ordinary hoe, besides a stout awl to sew the buffalo-hides together with."

Jack went to the king and declared himself willing to carry out his order if he would let him have these things, to which the king replied: "Go and take anything that you may require, there must be some sixty buffalo-hides still left hanging in the loft."

Jack went up to the loft and took what he wanted; then he ate and drank, gave his foal a bucketful of wine, and set out in search of the horses with the golden hair.

He journeyed on till, after a short lapse of time, he reached the Red Sea, which he crossed on the back of his foal. As soon as they emerged from the water and gained the opposite shore, the foal said: "Look, my dear master; can you see the pear-tree [Pg 275]on that hill yonder? Let's go up on the hill, take your hoe and dig a hole big enough to hold me; and as soon as you have dug the hole sew the twelve buffalo-hides together and wrap them round me, as it would not be advisable for me to get into the hole without them. As soon as I have got in, blow this whistle and the stallion will appear; and the moment you see it touching the buffalo skins, throw a halter over its head."

Jack tucked up his shirt-sleeves, dug the hole, sewed the twelve buffalo-hides on to the foal, and his steed got into the hole. Then he blew the whistle, and lo! a fine stallion, with golden hair, and almost entirely covered with golden froth, jumped out of the ground; it pranced about, and kicked out in all directions, whereupon Jack's foal said: "Now then, my dear master, throw that halter over its head and jump on its back." Jack did as he was told; when, no sooner was he on its back, than the stallion gave a tremendous neigh that rent all the mountains asunder. At its call a vast number of golden-haired horses appeared; so many, that Jack was not able to count them. The whole herd immediately took to their heels, and galloped off with the speed of lightning. The king had not yet finished dressing in the morning when the whole stud with golden hair stood arrayed in his courtyard. So soon as he caught sight of them he rushed off to the girl with the golden hair and exclaimed: "Well, my love, the golden horses are all here, and now you are mine." "Oh, no! I shan't be yours. I won't touch either food or drink until the lad who has fetched my animals milks the mares."

The king sent for Jack.

"I say, my boy, if you do not at once milk the mares, I'll play the hangman with you."

"How can I milk them, sir? Even as they are, I find it difficult to save myself from being trampled to death."

"Do not let us waste any words; it must be done!"

Jack returned to the stables, and looked very sad; he would [Pg 276]not touch any food or drink. His foal again addressed him and asked: "Why all this sorrow, dear master?"

"How could I help being sad? The king has ordered me to milk the mares no matter what happens, whether I get over it dead or alive."

"Don't fret. Ask him to lend you the tub up in the loft, and milk the mares. They won't do you the least harm."

And so it happened. Jack fetched the tub and milked the mares. They stood all the time as quietly as the most patient milch-cows. The king then said to the girl with the golden hair, "Well, my darling; your wish is fulfilled, and you are mine."

"I shan't be yours until the lad who milked the mares has bathed in the milk."

The king sent for Jack.

"Well, my boy, as you have milked the mares, you had better bathe in the milk."

"Gracious majesty! How could I do that? The milk is boiling hot, and throws up bubbles as high as a man."

"Don't talk; you have to bathe in the milk or you forfeit your life."

Jack went down and cried, and gave up all hope of life; he was sure of death on the gallows. His foal again spoke, and said: "Don't cry, dear master, but tell me what is the matter with you." Jack told him what he had to do under penalty of death.

"Don't fret, my dear master; but go to the king and ask his permission to allow you to lead me to the tub, and be present when you take your bath. I will draw out all the heat, and you can bathe in the milk without any fear."

So Jack went to the king, and said, "Well, gracious majesty, at least grant me the favour of allowing my foal to be present when I am having my bath, so that it may see me give up the ghost."

[Pg 277]"I don't care if there be a hundred foals present."

Jack returned to the stables, led his foal to the tub, who began to sniff. At last it took a deep breath, and beckoned to Jack not to jump in yet. Then it continued drawing in its breath, and suddenly at a sign Jack jumped into the tub, and had his bath. When he finished and got out of the tub he was three times more handsome than before; although he was a very handsome lad then. When the king saw this he said to the lad: "Well, Jack, you see you would not have the bath at first. I'm going to have one myself." The king jumped in, but in the meantime the foal had sent all the heat into the milk back again, and the tyrant was scalded to death. The heat was so intense that nothing was left of his body except a few bits of bone, as big as my little finger, which were every now and then brought up by the bubbles. Jack lost not a moment, but rushed up to the girl with the golden hair, embraced and kissed her, and said: "Well, my pretty darling, love of my heart, you are now mine, and I am yours; not even the spade and the hoe shall separate us one from another." To which she replied: "Oh, my love, Jackie, for a long time this has been one of my fondest wishes, as I knew that you were a brave lad."

The wedding was celebrated with great pomp, that gave people something to talk about over seven countries. I, too, was present at the banquet, and kept on shouting: "Chef! Cook! let me have a bone," till, at last, he did take up a bone and threw it at me. It hit me, and made my side ache ever since.

[Pg 278]

THE LOVER'S GHOST.

Somewhere, I don't know where, even beyond the Operencian Seas, there was once a maid. She had lost her father and mother, but she loved the handsomest lad in the village where she lived. They were as happy together as a pair of turtle-doves in the wood. They fixed the day of the wedding at a not very distant date, and invited their most intimate friends to it; the girl, her godmother—the lad, a dear old friend of his.

Time went on, and the wedding would have taken place in another week, but in the meantime war broke out in the country. The king called out all his fighting-men to march against the enemy. The sabres were sharpened, and gallant fellows, on fine, gaily-caparisoned horses, swarmed to the banners of the king, like bees. John, our hero, too, took leave of his pretty *fiancée*; he led out his grey charger, mounted, and said to his young bride: "I shall be back in three years, my dove; wait until then, and don't be afraid; I promise to bring you back my love and remain faithful to you, even were I tempted by the beauty of a thousand other girls." The lass accompanied him as far as the frontier, and before parting solemnly promised to him, amidst a shower of tears, that all the treasures of the whole world should not tempt her to marry another, even if she had to wait ten years for her John.

The war lasted two years, and then peace was concluded between the belligerents. The girl was highly pleased with the news, because she expected to see her lover return with the others. She grew impatient, and would sally forth on the road by which he was expected to return, to meet him. She would go out often ten times a day, but as yet she had no tidings of her John. Three years elapsed; four years had gone by, and [Pg 279]the bridegroom had not yet returned. The girl could not wait any longer, but went to see her godmother, and asked for her advice, who (I must tell you, between ourselves) was a witch. The old hag received her well, and gave her the following direction: "As it will be full moon to-morrow night, go into the cemetery, my dear girl, and ask the gravedigger to give you a human skull. If he should refuse, tell him that it is I who sent you. Then bring the skull home to me, and we shall place it in a huge earthenware pot, and boil it with some millet, for, say, two hours. You may be sure it will let you know whether your lover is alive yet or dead, and perchance it will entice him here." The girl thanked her for her good advice, and went to the cemetery next night. She found the gravedigger enjoying his pipe in front of the gate.

"Good evening to you, dear old father."

"Good evening, my lass! What are you doing here at this hour of the night?"

"I have come to you to ask you to grant me a favour."

"Let me hear what it is; and, if I can, I will comply with your request."

"Well, then, give me a human skull!"

"With pleasure; but what do you intend to do with it?"

"I don't know exactly, myself; my godmother has sent me for it."

"Well and good; here is one, take it."

The girl carefully wrapped up the skull, and ran home with it. Having arrived at home, she put it in a huge earthenware pot with some millet, and at once placed it on the fire. The millet soon began to boil and throw up bubbles as big as two fists. The girl was eagerly watching it and wondering what would happen. When, all of a sudden, a huge bubble formed on the surface of the boiling mass, and went off with a loud report like a musket. The next moment the girl saw the skull balanced on the rim of the pot. "He has started," it said, in a [Pg 280]vicious tone. The girl waited a little longer, when two more loud reports came from the pot, and the skull said, "He has got halfway." Another few moments elapsed, when the pot gave three very loud reports, and the skull was heard to say, "He has arrived outside in the yard." The maid thereupon rushed out, and found her lover standing close to the threshold. His charger was snow-white, and he himself was clad entirely in white, including his helmet and boots. As soon as he caught sight of the girl, he asked: "Will you come to the country where I dwell?" "To be sure, my dear Jack; to the very end of the world." "Then come up into my saddle."

The girl mounted into the saddle, and they embraced and kissed one another ever so many times.

"And is the country where you live very far from here?"

"Yes, my love, it is very far; but in spite of the distance it will not take us long to get there."

Then they started on their journey. When they got outside the village, they saw ten mounted men rush past, all clad in spotless white, like to the finest wheat flour. As soon as they vanished, another ten appeared, and could be very well seen in the moonlight, when suddenly John said:

"How beautifully shines the moon, the moon;"How beautifully march past the dead."Are you afraid, my love, my little Judith?"

"I am not afraid while I can see you, my dear Jack."

As they proceeded, the girl saw a hundred mounted men; they rode past in beautiful military order, like soldiers. So soon as the hundred vanished another hundred appeared and followed the others. Again her lover said:

"How beautifully shines the moon, the moon;"How beautifully march past the dead."Are you afraid, my love, my little Judith?"

"I am not afraid while I can see you, my darling Jack."

And as they proceeded the mounted men appeared in fast [Pg 281]increasing numbers, so that she could not count them; some rode past so close that they nearly brushed against her. Again her lover said:

"How beautifully shines the moon, the moon;"How beautifully march past the dead."Are you afraid, my love, my little Judith?"

"I am not afraid while I see you, Jack, my darling."

"You are a brave and good girl, my dove; I see that you would do anything for me. As a reward, you shall have everything that your heart can wish when we get to my new country."

They went along till they came to an old burial-ground, which was inclosed by a black wall. John stopped here and said to his sweetheart: "This is our country, my little Judith, we shall soon come to our house." The house to which John alluded was an open grave, at the bottom of which an empty coffin could be seen with the lid off. "Go in, my darling," said the lad. "You had better go first, my love Jack," replied the girl, "you know the way." Thereupon the lad descended into the grave and laid down in the coffin; but the lass, instead of following him, ran away as fast as her feet would carry her, and took refuge in a mansion that was situated a couple of miles from the cemetery. When she had reached the mansion she shook every door, but none of them would open to her entreaties, except one that led to a long corridor, at the end of which there was a dead body laid out in state in a coffin. The lass secreted herself in a dark corner of the fire-place.

As soon as John discovered that his bride had run away he jumped out of the grave and pursued the lass, but in spite of all his exertions could not overtake her. When he reached the door at the end of the corridor he knocked and exclaimed: "Dead man, open the door to a fellow dead man." The corpse inside began to tremble at the sound of these words. Again said Jack, "Dead man, open the door to a fellow dead man." Now the corpse sat up in the coffin, and as Jack repeated a third time the words "Dead man, open the door to a fellow dead man," [Pg 282]the corpse walked to the door and opened it.

"Is my bride here?"

"Yes, there she is, hiding in the corner of the fire-place."

"Come and let us tear her in pieces." And with this intention they both approached the girl, but just as they were about to lay hands upon her the cock in the loft began to crow, and announced daybreak, and the two dead men disappeared.

The next moment a most richly attired gentleman entered from one of the neighbouring rooms. Judging by his appearance one would have believed it was the king himself, who at once approached the girl and overwhelmed her with his embraces and kisses.

"Thank you so much. The corpse that you saw here laid out in state was my brother. I have already had him buried three hundred and sixty-five times with the greatest pomp, but he has returned each time. As you have relieved me of him, my sweet, pretty darling, you shall become mine and I yours; not even the hoe and the spade shall separate us from one another!"

The girl consented to the proposal of the rich gentleman, and they got married and celebrated their wedding-feast during the same winter.

This is how far the tale goes. This is the end of it.

SNAKE SKIN.

Far, very far, there was once, I do not know where, even beyond the frozen Operencian Sea, a poplar-tree, on the top of which there was a very old, tattered petticoat. In the tucks of this old petticoat I found the following tale. Whosoever listens to it will not see the kingdom of heaven.

[Pg 283]There was in the world a poor man and this poor man had twelve sons. The man was so poor that sometimes he had not even enough wood to make a fire with. So he had frequently to go into the forest and would pick up there what he could find. One day, as he could not come across anything else, he was just getting ready to cut up a huge tree-stump, and, in fact, had already driven his axe into it, when an immense, dread-inspiring serpent, as big as a grown-up lad, crept out of the stump. The poor man began to ponder whether to leave it or to take it home with him; it might bring him luck or turn out a disastrous venture. At last he made up his mind that after all was said and done he would take it home with him. And so it happened, he picked up the creature and carried it home. His wife was not a little astonished at seeing him arrive with his burden, and said, "What on earth induced you, master, to bring that ugly creature home? It will frighten all the children to death."

"No fear, wife," replied the man; "they won't be afraid of it; on the contrary, they will be glad to have it to play with."

As it was just meal-time, the poor woman dished out the food and placed it on the table. The twelve children were soon seated and busily engaged with their spoons, when suddenly the serpent began to talk from underneath the table, and said, "Mother, dear, let me have some of that soup."

They were all not a little astonished at hearing a serpent talk; and the woman ladled out a plateful of soup and placed it under the bench. The snake crept to the plate and in another minute had drunk up the soup, and said: "I say, father, will you go into the larder and fetch me a loaf of bread?"

"Alas! my son," replied the poor man, "it is long—very long—since there was any bread in the larder. I was wealthy then; but now the very walls of the larder are coming down."

"Just try, father, and fetch me a loaf from there."

[Pg 284]"What's the good of my going, when there is nothing to be found there?"

"Just go and see."

After a good deal of pressing the poor man went to the larder when—oh, joy!—he was nearly blinded by the sight of the mass of gold, silver, and other treasure; it glittered on all sides. Moreover, bacon and hams were hanging from the roof, casks filled with honey, milk, &c., standing on the floor; the bins were full of flour; in a word, there were to be seen all imaginable things to bake and roast. The poor man rushed back and fetched the family to see the miracle, and they were all astounded, but did not dare to touch anything.

Then the serpent again spoke and said "Listen to me, mother dear. Go up to the king and ask him to give me his daughter in marriage."

"Oh, my dear son, how can you ask me to do that? You must know that the king is a great man, and he would not even listen to a pauper like myself."

"Just go and try."

So the poor woman went to the king's palace, knocked at the door, and, entering, greeted the king, and said: "May the Lord grant you a happy good day, gracious king!"

"May the Lord grant the same to you, my good woman. What have you brought? What can I do for you?"

"Hum! most gracious king, I hardly dare to speak ... but still I will tell you.... My son has sent me to request your majesty to give him your youngest daughter in marriage."

"I will grant him the request, good woman, on one condition. If your son will fill with gold a sack of the size of a full-grown man, and send it here, he can have the princess at any minute."

The poor woman was greatly pleased at hearing this; returned home and delivered the message.

[Pg 285]"That can easily be done, dear mother. Let's have a wagon, and the king shall have the gold to a grain."

And so it happened. They borrowed a wagon of the king, the serpent filled a sack of the required size full of gold, and put a heap of gold and diamonds loose in the wagon besides. The king was not a little astonished, and exclaimed, "Well! upon my word, although I am a king I do not possess so much gold as this lad." And the princess was accordingly given away.

It happened that the two elder princesses were also to be married shortly, and orders were issued by the king that the wedding of his youngest daughter should take place at the same time. The state carriage was therefore wheeled out of the shed, six fine horses were put to it, the youngest princess sat in it and drove straight to the poor man's cottage to fetch her bridegroom. But the poor girl very nearly jumped out of the coach when she saw the snake approaching. But the snake tried to allay her fears and said, "Don't shrink from me, I am your bridegroom," and with this crept into the carriage. The bride—poor thing, what could she do?—put her arm round the snake and covered him with her shawl, as she did not wish to let the whole town know her misfortune. Then they drove to church. The priest threw up his arms in amazement when he saw the bridegroom approach the altar. From church they drove to the castle. There kings, princes, dukes, barons, and deputy-lieutenants of the counties were assembled at the festival and enjoying themselves; they were all dancing their legs off in true Magyar style, and very nearly kicked out the sides of the dancing-room, when suddenly the youngest princess entered, followed by her bridegroom, who crept everywhere after her. The king upon seeing this grew very angry, and exclaimed, "Get out of my sight! A girl who will marry such a husband does not deserve to stay under the same roof with me, and I will take care that you two do not remain here. Body-guards, conduct [Pg 286]this woman with her snake-husband down into the poultry-yard, and lock them up in the darkest poultry-house among the geese. Let them stay there, and don't allow them to come here to shock my guests with their presence."

And so it happened. The poor couple were locked up with the geese; there they were left crying and weeping, and lived in great sorrow until the day when the curse expired, and the snake—who was a bewitched prince—became a very handsome young man, whose very hair was of pure gold. And, as you may imagine, great was the bride's joy when she saw the change.

"I say, love," spoke her prince, "I will go home to my father's and fetch some clothes and other things; in the meantime, stay here; don't be afraid. I shall be back ere long without fail."

Then the prince shook himself and became a white pigeon, and flew away. Having arrived at his father's place he said to his parent, "My dear father, let me have back my former horse, my saddle, sword, gun, and all my other goods and chattels. The power of the curse has now passed away, and I have taken a wife to myself."

"The horse is in the stables, my son, and all your other things are up in the loft."

The prince led out his horse, fetched down his things from the loft, put on his rich uniform all glittering with gold, mounted his charger, and flew up into the air. He was yet at a good distance from the castle where the festivities were still going on, when all the loveliest princesses turned out and crowded the balconies to see who the great swell was whom they saw coming. He did not pass under the crossbeam of the gate, but flew over it like a bird. He tied his charger to a tree in the yard, and then entered the castle and walked among the dancers. The dance was immediately stopped, everybody gazed upon him and admired him, and tried to get into his favour. For amusement [Pg 287]several of the guests did various tricks; at last his turn came, and by Jove! he did show them things that made the guests open their mouths and eyes in astonishment. He could transform himself into a wild duck, a pigeon, a quail, and so on, into anything one could conceive of.

After the conjuring was over he went into the poultry-yard to fetch his bride. He made her a hundred times prettier than she already was, and dressed her up in rich garments of pure silver and gold. The assembled guests were very sorry that the handsome youth in rich attire, who had shown them such amusing and clever tricks, had so soon left them.

All at once the king remembered the newly-married couple and thought he would go to see what the young folks were doing in the poultry-yard. He sent down a few of his friends, who were nearly overpowered by the shine and glitter on looking into the poultry-house. They at once unlocked the door, and led the bride and bridegroom into their royal father's presence. When they entered the castle, every one was struck with wonder at discovering that the bridegroom was no one else than the youth who had amused them shortly before.

Then the bridegroom walked up to the king and said: "Gracious majesty, my father and king, for the past twelve years I lay under a curse and was compelled to wear a serpent's skin. When I entered, not long ago, your castle in my former plight, I was the laughing-stock of everybody, all present mocked me. But now, as my time of curse has passed, let me see the man who can put himself against me."

"There is, indeed, nobody, no man living," replied the king.

The bridegroom then led off his bride to the dance, and celebrated such a fine wedding, that it was talked of over seven countries.

[Pg 288]

THE FAIRIES' WELL.

Tale, tale, mate; a black little bird flew on the tree; it broke one of its legs; a new cloak, a shabby old cloak; it put it on.

Well, to commence! there was in the world a king, who was called the "Green King," and who had three daughters. He did not like them at all; he would have very much preferred if they had been boys. He continually scolded and abused them, and one day, in a fit of passion, the words slipped from his lips: "What *is* the good of all these wenches? I wish the devil would come and fetch them all three!" The devil wasn't slow; he took the king at his word and ran away with all three girls at once. The king's fondest wish was hereafter fulfilled; his wife bore him three sons, and he was very fond of them.

But the king grew old; his hair turned quite grey. So his sons set out for the fairies' well to fetch their father some youth-giving water. They wandered along till they came to a small road-side inn, where they had something to eat and drink, and gave their horses hay and corn. They tippled for some time, until the two elder princes got jolly, and commenced to dance in true style. The youngest one every now and then reminded them that it was time to continue the journey, but they would not listen to him. "Don't talk so much," they said, "if you are so very anxious to be off you had better leave us and go alone."

So the youngest saddled his horse and left his two brothers. He travelled along until all of a sudden he discovered that he had lost his way and found himself in a vast forest. In wandering hither and thither, he came to a small hut in which an old hermit dwelt. He at once went to it, knocked and entered, and [Pg 289]greeted the old man, saying, "May the Lord grant you a happy good day, my father."

"The Lord bless you, my son! where are you going?"

"Well, old father, I intend to go to the fairies' well for some youth-giving water, if I can the way thither."

"May the Lord help you, my son! I don't believe that you will be able to get there unaided, because it is a difficult journey. But I will tell you something. I have a piebald horse, that will carry you without mishap to the fairies' well. I will let you have it if you promise to bring me back some youth-giving water."

"I will bring you some with pleasure, old father. You are quite welcome to it."

"Very well, my son! Get on the piebald, and be off in the name of Heaven!"

The piebald horse was led out and saddled, the prince mounted, and in another second they were high up in the air, like birds, because the piebald was a magic horse that at all times grazed on the silken meadow, the meadow of the fairies. On they travelled, till all at once the piebald said:

"I say, dear master, I suppose you know that once you had three sisters, and that all three were carried off by the devil. We will go and pay a visit to the eldest. It is true, your brother-in-law is at this moment out rabbiting, but he will be back soon if I go to fetch him. He will ask you to bring him, also, some youth-giving water. I'll tell you what to do. He has a plaid which has the power of making the wearer invisible. If you put it on, nobody on this earth can see you. If he will give you that plaid you can promise him as much water as he likes; a whole tub full, if he wants it."

When they reached the house, the prince walked in; and the piebald horse immediately hurried off to the fields, and began to drive the devil so that his eyes sparkled. As the devil ran homewards, he passed a pair of gallows with a man hanging upon them; he lifted off the corpse, and ran away with it. Having [Pg 290]arrived at home, he called from the yard through the window: "Take this, wife! half of him roasted, the other half boiled, for my meal. Be sure to have him ready by the time I get inside." Thereupon he pitched the dead man through the window; the meal was ready in a minute and the devil walked in, sat down and ate him. Having finished, he happened to look towards the oven and caught sight of the prince.

"Halloo! is it you, brother-in-law? Why did you not speak? What a pity that I did not notice you sooner? You are just too late; you could have had a bit or two of my bonne-bouche."

"Thank you, brother-in-law. I don't care for your dainties."

"Well, then get him some wine, wife! perhaps he will have some of that?"

The wife brought in the wine and placed it on the table, and the two set to drinking.

"May I ask, what are you looking for in this strange part of the world?" inquired the devil.

"I am going to the fairies' well for some youth-giving water."

"Look here, my good man, I am a bit of a smart fellow myself, something better than you, and still I could not accomplish that journey. I can get to within about fourteen miles of the place, but even there the heat is so great that it shrivels me up like bacon-rind."

"Well, I will go all the same, if Heaven will help me!"

"And I will give you as much gold and silver as you can carry, if you will bring me back a gourdful of that water."

"I'll bring you back some, but for nothing less than for the plaid hanging on that peg. If you will give that to me you shall have the water."

At first the devil would not part with the plaid on any account; but the prince begged so hard that the devil at last yielded.

"Well, brother-in-law! This is such a plaid, that if you put it on nobody can see you."

[Pg 291]The prince was just going when the devil asked him, "Have you any money for the journey, brother?"

"I had a little, but I have spent it all."

"Then you had better have some more." Whereupon he emptied a whole dishful of copper coins into the prince's bag. The prince went out into the yard and shook the bridle; the piebald horse at once appeared, and the prince mounted. The devil no sooner caught sight of the piebald than he exclaimed, addressing the prince, "Oh, you rascally fellow! Then you travel on that villainous creature—the persecutor and murderer of our kinsfolk? Give me back at once my plaid and my gourd, I don't want any of your youth-giving water!"

But the prince was not such a fool as to give him back the plaid. In a minute the piebald was high up in the air and flew off like a bird. They travelled along until the horse again spoke and said, "Well then, dear master, we will now go and look up your second sister. True, your brother-in-law is out rabbiting, but he will soon be back if I go for him. He, too, will offer you all sorts of things in return for getting him some youth-giving water. Don't ask for anything else but for a ring on the window sill, which has this virtue, that it will squeeze your finger and wake you in case of need."

The prince went into the house and the piebald fetched the devil. Everything happened as at the previous house. The devil had his meal, recognised his brother-in-law, sent for wine, and asked the prince:

"Well, what are you doing in this neighbourhood?"

"I am going to the fairies' well for some youth-giving water."

"You don't mean that! You have undertaken a very difficult task. I am as good a man as a hundred of your stamp put together, and still I can't go there. The heat there is so great that it would shrivel me up like bacon-rind at a distance of fourteen miles. They boil lead there as we boil water here."

[Pg 292]"Still I intend to go, by the help of Heaven."

"Very well, brother-in-law. I will give you so much treasure that you can fill several wagons with it, if you will bring me a gourd full of that youth-giving water."

"I don't want anything, brother-in-law, but that ring in the window yonder."

"Of what use would it be to you?"

"Oh! I don't know; let me have it."

So after a good deal of pressing the devil gave him the ring and said:

"Well, brother-in-law, this is such a ring that it will squeeze your finger and wake you, no matter how sound you may be asleep."

By this time the prince had already reached the courtyard, and was ready to start, when the devil stopped him and said:

"Stop a bit, brother-in-law, have you any money for the journey?"

"I had a little, but it is all gone," replied the prince.

"Then you had better have some." Whereupon the devil emptied a dishful of silver money into the prince's bag. The prince then shook the bridle and the piebald horse at once appeared, which nearly frightened the devil into a fit.

"Oh, you rascally fellow!" he exclaimed. "Then you are in league with the persecutor of our kinsfolk? Stop! Give me back that ring and gourd at once. I don't want any of your youth-giving water!"

But the Green Prince took no notice of the devil's shouting and flew away on his piebald like a bird. They had been travelling for some distance when the horse said: "We shall now go to see your youngest sister. Her husband, too, is out at present rabbiting, but I shall fetch him in, in no time. He, also, will beseech you to get him some youth-giving water, but don't you yield, no matter how much wealth he promises you, [Pg 293]until he gives you his sword that hangs on the wall. It is such a weapon that at your command it will slay the populations of seven countries."

In the meantime they reached the house. The Green Prince walked in and the piebald went to look for the third devil. Everything happened as on the two previous occasions, and the devil asked his wife to send him in three casks of wine, and they commenced drinking. All of a sudden the devil asked, "Where are you going?"

"I am going to the fairies' well for some youth-giving water. My father has grown very old and requires some of the water to give him back his youth."

The devil replied that it was impossible to get there on account of the great heat. To which the prince said, that he was determined to go, no matter what might happen.

"Very well," continued the devil. "I will give you as much gold and silver as your heart can wish or your mouth name if you will bring me back a gourd full of the water."

"The gold is of no use to me; I have plenty of it at home; as much as I need. But if you will give me that sword on the wall, I will bring you some water from the fairies' well, with pleasure."

"Of what use would that sword be to you? You can't do anything with it."

"No matter. Let me have it."

The devil, at first, would not part with the sword; but, at last, he gave in. The Green Prince went into the yard, and was about to start, when the devil asked:

"Brother-in-law, have you any money left for the journey?"

"I had some; but it's nearly gone."

"Then you had better have some." And with this the devil put a plateful of gold coins into the prince's bag. The latter shook the bridle and his piebald appeared. The devil was very much alarmed at the sight, and exclaimed: "You rascal, then [Pg 294]you associate with our arch-persecutor. Let me have back my sword and the gourd, I don't want any of your water." But the prince did not listen to him; in fact he had no time to heed the devil's words even if he had any intention of doing so, as he was already high up in the air, and the piebald now questioned him: "How shall we go, dear master? shall we fly as fast as the whirlwind, or like a flash of thought?" "Just as you please, my dear horse."

And the piebald flew away, with the prince on its back, in the direction of the fairies' well. Soon they reached their goal, and alighted on the ground, whereupon the horse said: "Well, my dear master, we have reached our destination. Put on the plaid that the first devil gave you and walk into the fairy queen's palace. The queen has just sat down to supper. Eat, drink, and enjoy yourself. Don't be afraid, nobody will know that you are there. In the meantime I will go into the silken meadow and graze with the horses of the fairy over night. I shall return in the morning and we will then fill our gourd."

And so it happened. The Green Prince put on the plaid and walked into the fairy queen's dining-room, sat down and supped, and for every glass of wine consumed by the fairy he drank two. The supper over they enjoyed themselves. Suddenly the fairy queen felt a sensation as if she were touched by a man, although she could not see anybody. She thereupon exclaimed to her fairies: "Fairies, fairies, keep the bellows going under the boiling lead. Some calamity will befall us to-night."

In the morning the piebald appeared before the castle; the Green Prince was still fast asleep, but luckily the ring squeezed his finger and he awoke and so was saved. He lost no time in going down to his horse.

"I am glad to tell you, my dear master, that all is well. They have not yet been able to see you. Let us go and get the water at once. This is how you must proceed. Stick the gourd on the point of your sword and then dip it under. But, be [Pg 295]careful; the gourd must touch the water before my feet get wet, or else we must pay with our lives for our audacity."

The Green Prince did as he was told. He stuck the gourd on the point of the sword and dipped it into the well, before the piebald's hoofs touched the surface of the water.

"Well, my dear master, this has gone off without mishap. Let us at once go and liberate your sisters." First they visited the youngest. The Green Prince put on the plaid, and brought her away unnoticed. Then he rescued the second princess; and at last the eldest, by the aid of his plaid. And their diabolic husbands never noticed that they had been stolen. Having thus liberated his three sisters, he returned without delay to the hermit's hut.

"Well done, my son! Have you brought back any youth-giving water?" exclaimed the hermit, as he saw the prince approaching in the distance.

"To be sure, old father; I have brought plenty."

With these words the Green Prince approached the hermit, and allowed just one drop of the magic water drop on to the old man's hand; and oh, wonder! immediately a change came over him, and the old man instantly became young, and looked like a lad of sixteen.

"Well, my son; you have not made your journey in vain. You have secured the prize that you have striven for; and I shall always be deeply grateful to you until the end of my days. I won't take back the piebald from you, as I have another one exactly like it hidden away somewhere. True, it is only a little foal; but it will grow, and will then be good enough for me."

Then they parted, and the prince bent his way homewards. Having arrived at home he allowed a drop of the magic water drop on to his father's hand, and the old king immediately became a youth of sixteen. And he not only got younger, but also grew handsomer; and a hundred times better looking than he ever was before.

[Pg 296]But the Green Prince had been away for such a length of time on his journey to the fairies' well that not even his father could remember him. The king had completely forgotten that the prince was ever born. What was he to do? Nobody knew him at his father's palace, or would recognise him as his father's son; so he conceived the strange idea of accepting a situation as swineherd in his father's service. He found stables for the piebald in a cellar at the end of the town.

While he tended his father's pigs, and went through his duties as swineherd, the fairies travelled all over the world and searched every nook and corner for the father of the child of their queen. Among other places they also came to the town of the Green King, and declared that it was their intention to examine every prince, as the person for whom they searched could only be a prince. The Green King then suddenly remembered that he had once another son but did not know his whereabouts. Something or other, however, recalled to his mind the swineherd, so he at once took pen and paper and wrote a note to the swineherd. The purport of the writing was that the king was the real father of the swineherd, and that the prince should come home with the least possible delay. The Green King sealed the letter and handed it to a gipsy with strict instructions to at once deliver it to the swineherd. The gipsy went, and the swineherd read the note and handed it back to the messenger, saying:

"My good man, take the note back. They have sent you on a fool's errand. I am not the son of the Green King."

The gipsy took the letter back in great anger. The swineherd, again, ran as fast as his legs would carry him to the stables in the cellar at the outskirts of the town, saddled his piebald, and rode *ventre à terre* to the centre of the town, and pulled up in front of the king's palace. There was such a sight to be seen. A great number of wonderfully pretty fairies had congregated, and were fanning the fire under a huge cauldron of boiling lead, [Pg 297]which emitted such a heat that nobody could approach. The eldest prince came out and was about to try his fortune; he was gorgeously dressed, his garments glittering like a mass of gold. As he approached the cauldron full of boiling lead, a pretty fairy called out to him:

"Son of the Green King! are you the father of the child of the queen of fairies?"

"I am."

"Then jump into this seething mass of boiling lead."

He jumped in and was burnt, shrivelling up to the size of a crab-apple.

"You won't do," said the fairy.

Then the second prince stepped forth; his dress, too, was one mass of sparkling gold. As he approached the cauldron a fairy exclaimed:

"Son of the Green King! are you the father of the child of the queen of fairies?"

"I am."

"Then jump into this seething mass of boiling lead."

He jumped in and fared no better than his elder brother.

Now the swineherd rode forth on his piebald horse. His clothes were one mass of dirt and grease. To him, too, the fairy called out:

"Are you the father of the child of the queen of fairies?"

"I am."

"Then jump into this seething mass of boiling lead like the rest."

And, behold! he spurred the piebald horse, pulled tight the bridle, and again slackened it. The piebald shot up into the air like an arrow; and, having reached a good height, it came down with the swineherd on its back in one bold swoop, and jumped into the cauldron full of boiling lead without a single hair of him getting hurt. Seeing this, the fairies at once lifted [Pg 298]him out, tore his dirty clothes from him, and dressed him up in garments becoming a king.

He married the queen of fairies and a sumptuous wedding-feast was celebrated.

This is the end of my tale.

THE CROW'S NEST.

There was once in the world a poor man who had a wife and two children, the elder a girl, the younger a boy. The poor man went out one day ploughing with two wretched little oxen, his only property; his wife remained at home to do the cooking. The girl, being the older of the two children, was often sent out on short errands; upon the present occasion, too, she was away from the house, her mother having sent her out to borrow a peel, the dough for the bread being very nearly spoilt for having been kept too long in the trough.

Availing herself of the girl's absence, the mother killed the poor little boy and hid him in a pot of stewed cabbage. By the time that the girl returned her dear little brother was half stewed. When the mess was quite done, the woman poured it into a smaller pot, placed the small pot into a sling, and sent the food by her daughter to her husband who was in the field. The man liked the dish very much, and asked the girl:

"What kind of meat is this? It is very nice."

"I believe, dear father, mother had to kill a small lamb last night, and no doubt she cooked it for you," replied the girl.

But somehow or other the girl learned the true state of things, and the news nearly broke her heart. She immediately went back to the field, gathered up the bones of her little brother, carefully wrapped them into a beautiful piece of new white linen [Pg 299]and took them into the nearest forest, where she hid them in a hollow tree. Nobody can foretell what will happen, and so it came to pass that the bones did not remain very long in the hollow of the tree. Next spring a crow came and hatched them, and they became exactly such a boy as they were before. The boy would sometimes perch on the edge of the hollow, and sing to a beautiful tune the following words:—

"My mother killed me,"My father ate me,"My sister gathered up my bones,"She wrapped them in clean white linen,"She placed them in a hollow tree,"And now, behold, I'm a young crow."

Upon one occasion, just as he was singing this song, a man with a cloak strolled by.

"Go on, my son," he said, "repeat that pretty song for me! I live in a big village, and have travelled a good deal in my lifetime, but I have never heard such a pretty song."

So the boy again commenced to sing:—

"My mother killed me,"My father ate me,"My sister gathered up my bones,"She wrapped them in clean white linen,"She placed them in a hollow tree,"And now, behold, I'm a young crow."

The man with the cloak liked the song very much, and made the boy a present of his cloak; Then a man with a crutch-stick hobbled by. "Well, my boy," he said, "sing me that song again. I live in a big village, have travelled far, but have never heard such a pretty tune." And the boy again commenced to sing:—

"My mother killed me,"My father ate me,"My sister gathered up my bones,"She wrapped them in clean white linen,"She placed them in a hollow tree,"And now behold I'm a young crow."

The man with the crutch-stick, too, liked the song immensely, and gave the boy his crutch-stick. The next one to pass was a miller. He also asked the boy to repeat the pretty tune, and as the boy complied with his request the miller presented him with a millstone.

Then a sudden thought flashed across the boy's head and he flew to his father's house, settled on the roof, and commenced to sing:—

"My mother killed me,"My father ate me,[Pg 300]"My sister gathered up my bones,"She wrapped them in clean white linen,"She placed them in a hollow tree,"And now behold I'm a young crow."

The woman was terrified, and said to her daughter, "Go and drive away that bird, I don't like its croaking." The girl went out and tried to drive away the bird, but instead of flying away the young crow continued to sing the same song, and threw down the cloak to his sister. The girl was much pleased with the present, ran into the house and exclaimed: "Look here what a nice present that ugly bird has given to me!"

"Very nice indeed; very nice indeed. I will go out too," said her father. So he went out, and the bird threw down to him the crutch-stick. The old man was highly delighted with the gift; he was getting very weak, and the crutch-stick came in useful to him as a support.

"Look here what a strong crutch-stick he has given to me! It will be a great help to me in my old age."

[Pg 301]Then his mother jumped up from behind the oven and said, "I must go out too; if presents won't shower at least a few might drivel to me."

So she went out and looked up to the roof, and the boy gave her a present for which she had not bargained. He threw the millstone at her, which killed her on the spot.

Thus far goes our tale. Here it ends.

WOMAN'S CURIOSITY.

A shepherd saved the life of the daughter of the king of snakes, the princess narrowly escaping being burnt to death. To show him her gratitude she taught him the language of animals, and he was able to understand them. One day his donkey said something that made him smile; whereupon his wife commenced to tease him, and wanted to know the joke, but the shepherd was unable to gratify her wish, as his betraying the secret would have immediately been followed by the penalty of sudden death. However the wife would not give in and leave him in peace, but continued to torment her husband with so many questions that he at last determined to die rather than to bear his wife's ill-temper any longer. With this view he had his coffin made and brought to his house; he laid down in the coffin quite prepared for death and ready to divulge the secret. His faithful dog sat mournfully by his side watching, while the cock belonging to the house merrily hopped about in the room. The dog remonstrated with the cock and said that this was not the time for merriment, seeing how near their master was to death. But the cock replied quite curtly, "It's master's own fault! why is he such a great fool and coward? Look at me! I have fifty [Pg 302]wives, and they all do as I tell them to do! If I can get on with so many, surely he ought to be able to manage one!" Hearing this the shepherd jumped out of the coffin, seized a wet rope-end and gave the woman a sound thrashing.

Peace was restored, and they lived happily together ever after.

END OF THE TALES.

[Pg 303]

NOTES TO THE FOLK-TALES.

PRINCE CSIHAN. Kriza xvii.

In this tale and some others (*e.g.* "Fairy Elizabeth") it is said that in order to celebrate a wedding the clergyman and the *executioner* were sent for. Several of the clergy who live among the

Székely people on the very spot have been applied to for an explanation of the perplexing word, but they were unable to furnish any clue. The word is not given in Kriza's Glossary. It appears to be one of those curiosities of popular nomenclature so often found in Hungary, and may be a fanciful name for "sacristan," or sexton. One of the many names of this official is "harangozó," *i. e.* the bellringer; hence the individual who holds the corresponding office among the Jews is in small villages sometimes called "the Jewish bellringer," a clear case of *lucus a non lucendo.* A friend of the editors (who is a Székely) says that "hóhér" in his part means any one who torments, maltreats, or brutalises another. It is also made into a verb thus, "hóhérholja a lovat," "he maltreats the horse." He says that the hóhér is nearly always mentioned in fairy tales in connection with the priest, who was generally accompanied by him: but he does not think the word has any special significance in Folk-Lore.

Page 5. "Vasfogu Bába." Bába, in Magyar, as in Japanese, means a midwife: in Slavonic, an old woman. See Ralston's *Russian Folk Tales*: note, p. 137. "The French are coming." This must be unique. The usual exclamations are, "The Turks are coming," or "The Tartars are coming." The nurse will frighten a naughty child with Turks or Tartars. For the heroic deeds of a popular hero against the French, cf. "*Le Chevalier Jean*, Conte Magyar, par Alex. Petoefi ...traduit par A. Dozon." Paris. 18°.

The present story is one of a host wherein the gratitude of beasts is compared with the ingratitude of man; and is a more perfect version of the well-known Puss in Boots. Cf. Schiefner, *Avar Tales.* There is [Pg 304]a variant, "Madon linna" ("The Snake's Castle"), collected in Russian Karelia, where the hero is the only son of an old couple, the mother when dying tells her son not to be downhearted, as he still has his father to help him; soon after the father fell sick. "What shall I do, dear father, when you die?" asked the lad. "Go to the forest," replied the father, "and there you will find three traps, bring home alive whatever you find." Soon the father died, and the lad was left alone in his sorrow; after many days he suddenly remembered what his father had said, and set off to the forest, where he found the traps. In the first and second there was nothing, but in the third was a brown fox, which he brought home alive, thinking to himself, "There's not much to be got out of this beast; I shall soon die of hunger." When he got home, he put the fox on a bench and sat down, when, lo! the fox said, "Look here, Jussi Juholainen, wouldn't you like to get married?" The lad replied, "Why should I marry, poor fox? I couldn't live with a poor woman, and a rich one wouldn't have me." "Marry one of the royal family, and then you'll be rich." The lad said that it was all nonsense; but the fox declared he could do it, and then the story goes on very much like Prince Csihan, shewing the king how rich the suitor for his daughter's hand was, and frightening the dependents of the snake into declaring that they belonged to Jussi Juholainen. At last they reach the snake's castle, "the like of which is not in the whole country, nay, not in the wide world. An oak was growing by the wayside, and a holly tree in the courtyard, all the leaves were golden coloured, and golden feathered birds sang among the branches; and in the park was a magnificent elk with gold and silver hairs."

The fox frightens the snake by telling of the coming of a great king, saying, "O poor snake, the king is coming to destroy your house, and kill you." The snake at once hurried off to the store-house[1] where the linen was kept, and hid there, and in due course [Pg 305]was burnt up with the stores, by the fox, who set fire to the whole. The king was "giddy" with delight at his son-in-law's wealth, and stayed many days. When he prepared to return home, the fox proposed that Jussi Juholainen and his man should now visit the king, much to the king's chagrin, who tried to make excuses; but as this failed, calves and dog-like creatures, and so forth, were made to jump about the wayside, and in the courtyard, so as to be something like the palace of his son-in-law. But all failed; and the fox, having shown how much greater and wealthier a man Jussi Juholainen was, disappeared. See *Suomen Kansan Satuja ja Tarinoita.* Part ii. Helsingissä, 1873:[2] where, under head "Kettu kosiomiehenä" (the fox as wooer for some one), page 36, another variant (Kehnon koti), "the Evil One's home," is given.

In the Karelian story, "Awaimetoin Wakka" (the Keyless Chest), *S. ja T.* i. p. 151, a lad, when walking in the wood one day, heard his dog barking, and saw that it was a wood-grouse it had found. He drew his bow and was about to shoot when the bird begged him not to do so, and promised to reward him. The lad kept the bird for three years, and at the end of each year a feather fell from the bird's tail, first a copper one, then a silver one, and lastly a gold one; which feathers in the end brought wealth and greatness.

In the Finnish story of "the Golden Bird," a story very much like "Cinder Jack" (in this collection), p. 149, a wolf brings fortune and power to the hero because he fed her and her young ones.

In another Finnish story, "Oriiksi muutettu poika" (The Enchanted Steed), in *Suomalaisia Kansansatuja*, i. (Helsingissä, 1881), a fox assists the fugitives to defeat the devil, who pursues them. This tale is very much like the latter part of "Handsome Paul," p. 33. Compare also a variant from near Wiborg in *Tidskriften Suomi*, ii. 13, p. 120.

In a Lapp story a little bird helps. See "Jætten og Veslegutten," from Hammerfest. *Lappiske Eventyr og Folkesagn ved. Prof. Friis, Christiania*, 1871,[3] p. 52, &c.

It is a cat in "Jætten, Katten og Gutten," from Alten, *Friis*, 63; [Pg 306]and a fox in "Bondesønnen, Kongesønnen og Solens Søster," from Tanen, *Friis*, 140.

Mr. Quigstad reports another variant from Lyngen, in which also a cat helps the hero.

See also Steere's *Swahili Tales*: "Sultan Darai"; Dasent's *Tales from the Norse*: "Lord Peter," and "Well done, and ill-paid."

Old Deccan Days: "The Brahman." "The Tiger and the Six Judges."

Mitford's *Tales of Old Japan*: "The Grateful Foxes." "The Adventures of little Peachling"; and a Bohemian story of the Dog and the Yellow-hammer in Vernaleken's *In the Land of Marvels*.

Ralston's *Puss in Boots* in *XIXth Century, January*, 1883. A most interesting and exhaustive article.

Ralston's *Russian Folk Tales*: "The water King and Vasilissa the Wise." A story which in the beginning is very like "The Keyless Chest."

Benfey's *Pantschatantra*, i. 208, and *passim*.

Kletke, *Märchensaal aller Völker*: "Gagliuso."

Perrault, *Contes des Fées*: "Le maitre chat."

Hyltén-Cavallius and Stephens. *Svenska Folksagor*, i. *Stockholm*, 1844: "Slottet som stod på Guldstolpar."

Gubernatis, *Zoological Mythology*, vol. i. 193; vol. ii. 134, 157.

Grimm's *Household Tales*, Bohn's ed. vol. i. "the Golden Bird," p. 227; vol. ii. pp. 46, 154, 323, 427, 527.

Mentone Stories, in the *Folk-Lore Record*, vol. iii. part 1, 43.

Denton's *Serbian Folk-Lore*, 51, 296.

Naake's *Slavonic Tales*: "Golden Hair," p. 133, a Bohemian Tale.

Stokes's *Indian Fairy Tales*: "The Demon and the King's Son," 180.

Payne's *The Book of the Thousand Nights and One Night*, "Abou Mohammed," vol. iv. p. 10.[4]

STEPHEN THE MURDERER. Kriza, xviii.

The Hungarians have had a Dr. Faust in the person of Professor Hatvani, but in his case he got the best of the bargain; see [Pg 307]*A Magyar Fauszt*, by Maurus Jókai. The Hungarian professor is an historical personage, and only resembles Dr. Faust in having a compact with the devil.

Lad. Arany traces a resemblance between this tale and one in Benfey's *Pantschatantra*, where it is related how a poor Brahmin, in reward for his long penitence, has his bones thrown into the sacred waters of the Ganges.

There is a curious Finnish story which resembles this tale, "Ennustukset" (Predictions), from Ilomantsi in *S. ja T.* ii. 64-72. Two wise men (seers) were out walking, and came near a house where a ewe was just in the throes of parturition. The younger man wished the elder (and chief) to help it. "Why should I?" replied he, "a wolf will eat the lamb." "It is very sad; but still we ought to help the poor sheep." In a moment the lamb was born. Just then the cries of the mistress of the house were heard, for she was in travail. The young man again begged his companion to use his power. "Well! I will help her," said the old seer; "but would it be kind, for the boy, when born, will murder his father?" He gave his assistance, and in a moment the child was born. The master of the house, however, had overheard the conversation, and told it to his wife, who was horrified at the news. Upon talking it over, they decided to let the lamb and child live, as the men's words were most likely of no importance. In the autumn, at the feast of Keyri (the cattle-god), the lamb was slain and made into Keyri soup, according to the old custom. The broth was put on the table, and the meat in the window to cool;[5] and the couple laughed at the words of the men. After the broth was finished they went for the meat, and lo! it was all scattered on the ground, and a wolf was devouring the last pieces at its leisure.

They were terrified, and cried, "Well, then! the men's words were true." The man then snatched the child out of its cradle, and was about to cut its throat, when the woman cried, "Do not kill our own child! Let us fasten it on a plank, and put it to sea, so that it may die in that way." And so they did. Tossed by wind and waves, the [Pg 308]child chanced to come to the shore near a monastery, where a peasant found him and took him to the abbot, who brought him up. When he had grown up, he got tired of living there, and was sent to the mainland. He wandered on and on till he came to a house. The mistress only was in, the master being in the wood. Here the lad was engaged to go and look after the turnips, as some thieves had been stealing them; and the mistress gave him a bow and arrows, with strict orders to shoot any one who came. This just suited the lad, who went and hid himself behind a large stone in the middle of the field. Before long a man came over the fence and filled his arms with turnips. The lad drew his bow and shot, and the man fell. The lad returned home, and told what he had done; and the mistress said that she was glad that the thief had perished. They then waited for the master's return, but as he did not come, they went to look for him, and found that the lad had killed him. The lad stayed with the woman, and after a time married her, and all went well till one day they went to the bath[6] together; then she saw a red stripe on the man's chest, and asked, "What is this?" "I don't know," replied he, "I've had it ever since I was born." "Where were you born?" asked the woman. He then told her all he knew; and, to their horror, i they found out they were mother and son. The man at once set off to the wise men, to know what to do, and how to be forgiven. On the way he met a monk, with a book under his arm, and said, "I've killed my father, and married my mother! How can I be forgiven?" The monk looked through his book and said, "Poor man! your sins can never be forgiven; they are too awful." The man could not contain himself when he heard this, and struck the monk such a blow that he died.

He then went on and met an older monk and told him all. He looked through his book and said "There is no forgiveness." He [Pg 309]then killed this monk also. Going on he met a third monk with books under his arms, and cried, "I've killed my father, and married my mother, and murdered two old men who said there was no forgiveness. What do you think?" The old man looked through his books, thought a little, and said, "There is no crime so great but that it can be forgiven when man truly repents. You must go to a rock and dig a well in it. Wait till the water rises. And your mother must sit beside it with a black sheep in her arms until its wool becomes white." When the man heard this he thanked the monk, and returned and told his mother all. So they went to a rock, and the man began to dig with a chisel; and the woman sat beside him with the sheep in her arms. He worked for a long time, but with no success. Now the rock was close to the road, and good and bad passed by. One day a gentleman drove past gaily, the horse-bells tinkling as he went; he asked the man what he was doing, and was told all. "Who and what are you?" said the man. "O! I am a very clever man," replied the other. "I can make wrong right, and right wrong. I am going to the assizes, where I will help you if you pay me." This enraged the man, because he had to work so hard, whilst the other lived by trickery. Whilst he grumbled his old anger flared up, and he struck the gentleman in the forehead with his chisel and killed him. In a moment the rock opened and there was a well, and the black sheep became white. This they were exceedingly glad to see, but the man did not know what to do about killing the gentleman. So he went to the old monk again and told him all. "Well!" said the monk, "that's better. He has sinned much more against God than you; therefore your time of repentance has been shortened. Go in peace." Thus the sinners escaped judgment and continued to live together in peace. The one as mother, the other as son. So much for that! (The ordinary ending of Finnish tales.)

Another Finnish story, "Antti Puuhaara" (Andrew Tree Twig), *S. ja. T.* ii. 100, begins much in the same way, only in that case the child is to be heir of a rich merchant who happened to be in the house at the time and overheard all. He does his best to prevent the prediction coming true; which, however, spite of all, is fulfilled. [Pg 310]Cf. *Magyarische Sagen* von Mailáth. "Die Brüder." Also "*Die Thaten des Bogda Gesser Châns,*" *eine ostasiatische Heldensage aus dem mongolischen übersetzt von J. J. Schmidt, Petersburg* 1839. And *Folk-lifvet i Skytts härad i Skåne wid början af detta århundrade, Barndomsminnen utgifna af Nicolovius,Lund.* 1847. "Rike Pehr Krämare." Also *Dasent*, "Rich Peter the Pedlar"; *Grimm*, "The Devil with the Three Golden Hairs"; and *Sagas from the Far East*, in which the king fears when he hears the hermit's prophecy of his son's future, p. 268.

The bed that the devils so much dreaded occurs in the Polish tale, "Madey," Naake's *Slavonic Tales*, p. 220. A merchant being lost in a wood promises an evil spirit that he will give him something that he had not seen in his house if he will set him in the right road. This something turns out to be a son born in the merchant's absence. When the boy grows up he sets out to get the bond from the devil that his father gave when lost in the wood. As the lad goes on his journey he comes to the hut of a robber of the name of Madey. He had murdered his father, and only spared his mother to prepare his food. Here, as in the Magyar story, the lad is spared on condition that he finds out what sort of bed is prepared for the robber in hell. The lad enters hell by means of holy water and incense, and the lame demon Twardowski[7] is threatened with Madey's bed if he does not give up the bond, which he is loth to do. This at once produces the desired effect, and Madey was so horrified at the lad's account of the bed that he struck his murderous club into the ground, and vowed he would wait till the lad returned as a bishop. Years afterwards, when the little boy had become a bishop, he found a beautiful apple tree and an old man kneeling at its foot. The tree was the robber's club, the old man Madey. As Madey makes his [Pg 311]confession apple after apple becomes a dove and flies heavenward, till at last he confesses his father's murder, and then the last disappears; and, as the bishop pronounces the absolution, Madey crumbles to dust.

See, also, *Svenska Folksägner, af H. Hofberg, Stockholm*, 1882, p. 48. "Ebbe Skammelsson was a knight who was engaged to the beauteous Malfrid of Tiraholm. As they both were yet young, the knight set out for the Holy Land, promising to return in seven years. Soon after Ebbe's departure Malfrid's father died, and the maid remained with her mother. Years rolled on, but Ebbe did not return; and as the maid began to fade away, her mother promised her to another, thinking Ebbe must be dead. There was a splendid wedding; and just as the guests sat down to the table, a knight in golden armour galloped up to the house. The bride turned pale beneath her crown, and the mother, who recognised Ebbe, rushed out and reminded him that the seven years were past, and he was too late. In wild rage he struck off the lady's head; and then, dashing into the wedding hall, slew the bride and bridegroom. Filled with horror and remorse at his own deeds, he vaulted on to his horse, and rode into the wild woods. There he roamed in agony and despair. The pope's indulgence was obtained at the holy father's feet, but not peace; so, returning to the home of his old love, he begged the judge to sentence him to the severest punishment. After long deliberation the council determined that he should be loaded with the heaviest irons, and should pass a day and a night on each of the three hundred and sixty-five islands in Bolmen. This was carried out; and in his little boat he dragged himself from isle to isle. At length he reached the last, and crawled into a barn. His sad fate had made a deep impression on the people, and a minstrel wrote a song, which, a witch said, so soon as Ebbe heard, his irons would fall off and he would die. As he lay in the barn, a servant, who went to milk the cows, began to sing, 'Knight Ebbe's Song.' He listened with breathless attention, and then cried out: 'One part is true, one part is false.' The girl fled in terror. Soon the villagers gathered round to know who he was. He dragged himself to the hill, and, telling who he was, begged to be taken to the churchyard. Now, between the village of Angelstad and the church there is a large stone: mounting this, Ebbe cried, 'Am I worthy to [Pg 312]rest in consecrated ground? If so, let it be....' At that moment the irons dropped off, and he died. The people buried him in the path, outside the north wall of the church; but the wall fell down each night, until it was so built as to include the outlaw's grave. The crosses on the roof of the parish church are said to be made of Ebbe's fetters, which for a long time hung inside the sacred building." Cf. J. Allvin, *Beskrifning öfver Vestbo härad*, p. 147. The same story, with some slight difference, is current in Halland.[8] A comparison between this and the wild Finnish story is not without interest, as shewing the humanising influence which has toned down the rude and rugged teaching of the early ages.

Cf. Campbell, *Tales of the Western Highlands*, p. 19: "The Inheritance."

Baring Gould, *Curious Myths of the Middle Ages*. "The Mountain of Venus," p. 213.

Grimm, vol. ii. p. 366. "The Three Green Twigs."

Merényi, *Tales from the Banks of the Danube*, vol. ii. p. 7, in Hungarian.

There is an interesting Lapp variant, "Fattiggutten, Fanden og Guldbyen." *Friis*, p. 161.

THE LAMB WITH THE GOLDEN FLEECE. Kriza, ix.

Cf. *Round the Yule Log*. "Hans, who made the Princess laugh," p. 269.

Grimm, vol. ii. "The Jew among the Thorns," p. 97 and Notes, p. 410, in which the Jew is compelled to dance to the sound of the fiddler.

Engel's *Musical Myths*, vol. ii. "The Indefatigable Fiddler," p. 29, and the "Ratcatcher of Hamelin," p. 37. (Also, *Baring Gould's Curious Myths*, p. 417.)

Griechische und Albanische Märchen, von J. G. von Hahn, Leipzig, 1864, vol. i. p. 222, and vol. ii. p. 240.—*Ladislaus Arany*. "The Sad Princess" (in Hungarian).—*Gaal*, vol. iii. "The Powerful Whistle."

[Pg 313]

FISHER JOE. Kriza, xvi.

Page 16. *Grimm*, vol. i, "The Gold Children," p. 331, where a man draws a gold fish out of the water, which tells him if he will throw it back into the water he shall have a splendid castle. He throws it back, and all comes as the fish said. The fisher must not reveal how it has come about; but his wife's curiosity makes him break his word, and all disappears.[9] The man catches the fish once more, and the same things happen, wealth and destitution; and then the fish is caught a third time. This time the fish is cut into six pieces, two of which are put in the ground, and grow up as golden cities; two are given to the man's horse, which has two golden foals; and two to the man's wife, who bears two golden children. See *Grimm's* notes, p. 453. *Gubernatis*, vol. i. p. 249 (as to Phallic Significance), and vol. ii. sub. art. "Fish," p. 330. Also Caballero's (Spanish) *Fairy Tales*, "The Bird of Truth," p. 1, and the "Knights of the Fish," p. 29, where a poor cobbler, with no work, goes a-fishing as a last resource, catches a fish, and cuts it into six, with the same result as in the above tale. And *Portuguese Folk-Tales, Folk-Lore Society*, 1882; "The Baker's Idle Son," p. 72; Payne's *Arabian Nights*, vol. i. pp. 33-51.

Just as Fisher Joe lays his head on his wife's knee, and sleeps while wonders happen, so does the drummer rest, while the maiden does his tasks for him, in the story of the "Drummer," in *Grimm*, ii. 335.

Cf. also Dasent's *Tales from the Norse*. "The Mastermaid," p. 84, |Pg 314|and Denton's *Serbian Folk-Lore*. "The Golden Fleeced Ram," p. 71.

Page 18. The trouble that comes from the king (or lord) seeing the hero's wife, or bride, is a common incident in Folk-Tales.

See the Finnish "Leppäpölkky" (Alder Block). *S. ja T.* ii. p. 2, where the hero, after infinite trouble, secures the lovely Katherine, who is said to be so beautiful that—

"One can see her skin through her clothes,Her flesh through her skin,Her bones through her flesh,Her marrow through her bones!"

When he arrived at home with his lovely prize, the king wished to know the whole of his adventures. Now it so happened that Alder Block had during his travels changed himself to an ermine, and had heard Syöjätär—who was the mother of the snakes he and his comrades had killed—tell what plans she had for destroying her children's murderer, as in the Magyar tale of "The three Princes, the three Dragons, and the Old Woman with the Iron Nose," p. 202 of this collection. Syöjätär declared at the same time that whoever dared to repeat her words[10] would be changed into a blue cross. Alder Block saved his comrades from the snares till the last one, which took the form "of beds with feather pillows;" and this time his companions, before he could stop them, threw themselves down, and were caught. The king ordered him to explain why his companions were not with him; and as Alder Block did so, he changed into a blue cross, standing in the churchyard. The whole story is a most interesting one, weaving in materials that are ordinarily to be found, not in one, but in many folk tales. The end of all is, the king got the lovely Katherine, and "took her to his castle, where they still live to-day, and perhaps to-morrow also; and there came good sons and beautiful daughters. I was also at the wedding. They gave me a wax horse. The saddle was made of turnip and the whip of peas. The feast lasted for many days; and when I came from it I came to Riettilä's |Pg 315|corn kiln.[11] The kiln began to burn, and I to extinguish it. In the heat my horse began to melt, my saddle to roast, and the village's illegitimate children to eat it up. I began to drive them away, but the dogs were set at me; and when I began to whip them, they bit my whip to pieces. So all my things were destroyed, and poor me fell down. Perhaps I shall never be well again, it was so long." Compare this characteristic ending with that of the Magyar tales.

In the Finnish "Ei-niin-mitä" (Just nothing), *S. ja T.* ii. 53, a man catches a swan-maiden of great beauty. The king, so soon as he hears of her, determines to have her for his son, and the courtiers advise him to make the man procure—1st, "A table, on which is painted the moon and stars;" this his wife gets her husband while he is asleep; 2nd, "he was to go nowhere and fetch nothing." His wife again helps him, by sending him to a house where an old woman summons all her servants (Cf. "Fairy Elizabeth," p. 106). This time it is a frog who takes the man, and he at length comes to a palace; and as he paces the floor at night, he mutters to himself, "Just nothing." "Beg your pardon," says a voice; and he finds that he has an invisible companion, who obeys all his commands, and answers to the name of "Just Nothing." When he returns to the king, he finds they are just celebrating the wedding of the king's son with his own wife, who does not recognise him till he drops a ring into the empty goblet out of which he has drunk the corn brandy the bride had given him. By his new powers he soon upsets the bad king and his host, and then all is joy and happiness. Cf. *Musaeus, Volksmärchen der Deutschen von J. L. Klee. Leipzig*, 1842. "Der geraubte Schleier"; *Walachische Märchen von A. und A. Schott. Stuttgart*, 1845. "Der verstossene Sohn." Weil, *Tausend und eine Nacht*, vol. iv. "Geschichte des Prinzen Ojanschach;" *Irische Elfenmärchen, von Grimm. Leipzig*, 1826. "Die Flasche."

|Pg 316|Kletke, *Märchensaal aller Völker, für Jung und Alt. Berlin* 1845, vol. iii. "Der Wundermann."

Cf. "Bondesønnen, Kongesønnen og Solens Søster," *Friis*, p. 140; where the hero, by means of a fox, rescues the Sun's sister's sister, "Evening Red," from the giants who had stolen her, and who were turned into pillars of stone as soon as they caught sight of the Sun's sister, Dawn. So soon as the king heard of her, he determined to have her for his son's wife, and set heavy tasks for the hero to perform, which he does by means of his wife's power.

In another tale from Tanen, "Bæive Kongens eller Sol Kongens Datter," *Friis*, p. 152, the hero will insist upon the king knowing that he is going home with the Sun King's daughter, whom he has caught by stealing her swan dress, and so gets into trouble, as the king does all he can to get possession of the girl.

In "Gutten, som tjente hos Kongen," *Friis*, p. 167, from Tanen, the hero is to have the king's daughter in return for faithful service but at the last moment the king demands certain labours before he will allow the marriage to take place. In this case it is the Gieddegæs̃ old woman, that is, a wise or troll woman, who helps the hero.

A magic ship that can sail over land and sea is a favourite in Lapp stories, and is often one of the tasks set. Cf. "Ruobba[12] Jætten og Fanden," *Friis*, p. 67. Here the third son feeds axes, augurs, planes, and all sorts of tools,[13] which come and beg for food, and by their means builds the ship. See Finnish "Maan, meren, kulkija laiwa" ("The Ship that can Sail on Land and Sea"), from Ilomantsi. *S. ja T.* ii. p. 22.

Somewhat similar incidents occur in the tale "Seppo Ilmarisen kosinta" ("Smith Ilmarinen's Courtship"). *S. ja T.* i. p. 1, wherein Ilmarinen goes to woo fair Katherine, the Hiihto king's daughter. The first task was to plough the king's snake-field—where the snakes were crawling two yards deep—in bare feet and bare skin. Then he sang a lake full of fishes into the courtyard. Next he [Pg 317]went to bring a chest which had been covered for a long time, and which the old man, Untamoinen, had. When Ilmarinen asked for the beautiful Katherine's wedding chest the old man replied, "If you can stand on my tongue, jump and dance, then I will give it to you." The smith jumped on to his tongue, but the old man's mouth was so wide he swallowed Ilmarinen. The smith did not mind that; he made a smithy of his shirt, bellows of his trousers, used his left knee for an anvil, and his left hand for tongs. Of the copper buckle of his skirt he made a bird with claws of iron and bill of steel. He then sang a song and the bird became alive, and by its means he dug his way out of Untamoinen's stomach, got the chest, and after a great many troubles with fair Katherine at last got home.

In the latter part of the tale one is reminded of such stories as *Household Stories from the Land of Hofer*, "St. Peter's Three Loaves," p. 265; *Grimm*, vol. ii., "The Rich Man and the Poor Man," p. 1, and Notes, p. 373; Stokes's *Indian Tales*, "Rajah Harichand's Punishment," p. 224.

LUCK AND BLISS. Kriza, xii.

Cf. Caballero's *Spanish Tales*, "Dame Fortune and Don Money," p. 190, and "Fortune and Misfortune," p. 147.

Naake, "Wisdom and Fortune," p. 243, a Bohemian tale.

THE LAZY CAT. Kriza, xi.

This tale does not call for any special remark.

HANDSOME PAUL. Kriza, i.

Page 25. Old men in Hungary are always addressed as "my father," or "my elder brother," and in turn address their juniors as "my son," or "my younger brother." Women are also addressed as "mother," "daughter," "elder sister," or "younger sister." Cf. the "little father," in modern Russian; also *Reynard the Fox in South Africa*, by Dr. Bleek, "The Lion who took a Woman's Shape," [Pg 318]p. 50, where the lion calls a woman "my mother" and "my aunt," and she calls him "my uncle."

Fisk, *Myths and Myth-Makers*, pp. 166, 167, Zulu Uthlakanyana meets a cannibal, whom he calls "uncle," and is called "child of my sister." The Yakuts in Siberia call the bear "beloved uncle."

Tylor's *Primitive Culture*, vol. ii. p. 231.

Tylor's *Early History of Mankind*. pp. 130-49; 288-91.

Ibn Batuta, the Moorish traveller, mentions that in his time—about 1347—old men in Cansai, the modern Hangchenfu, were commonly addressed as "Atha," *i. e.*"Father" in Turkish. Cf. *The Travels of Friar Odoric* (Hakluyt Soc.), iv. p. 288.

Vide Giants in the Introduction to this collection.

The incident of finding the giant occurs in many stories, *e.g.* a Finnish tale relates how some sailors sailing along the coast near Wiborg saw a fire lighted on the shore, and, as they were nearly frozen, landed, and found to their horror a giant laid round it with his feet under his head (cf. Giant in "Fairy Elizabeth," p. 99 of this vol.) The giant awakes and asks where they are from, and hearing that they were from Wiborg, tells them he knows it well, and drinks with great gusto a tun of tar, remarking, "Ah! that's the old Wiborg drink!" Topelius, *Boken om vårt Land. Helsingfors*, 1875, p. 153.

See also a similar tale, "Glosheds Altare," from Bohuslän, *Hofberg*, p. 81. It is commonly reported in Bohuslän and Dal that the giants withdrew to Dovre in Norway, or else to some uninhabited island in the North Sea, and that they most anxiously inquired of any travellers they came across how things were going on in their native land. They are said to have left their homes "when modern mankind began to exist," in the Swedish stories. They often declare it was on account of the continued ringing that they left the land.

In "Ulfgrytstenarna," from Närike, the giant hearing the bells for the first time tells his wife to put a stone in her garter and sling it at the grey cow which is tinkling near Hjelmar, meaning the newly-built church at Örebro. The giantess threw the stone thirteen miles too far. The giant threw and missed, and the bells sounded with wondrous clearness. The giant then seized two enormous rocks, and set off to |Pg 319|crush the church; on the way an old man who had set out to stop him, showed him a pile of shoes worn out by his journey from Örebro. The giant threw the rocks down and went home. *Hofberg*, p. 132.

See also the story about the old man and Ragnar Lodbrok, who is said to have delivered Rome from the Norse men, by showing their worn-out iron shoes. Also Gibeonites and Joshua; Joshua, ix. 5.

Giants sometimes built instead of destroying religious houses. See *Afzelius, Svenska Folkets Sagohäfder*, v. p. 31, where the giant Rise is said to have built Riseberg Monastery and given it his own name; also "Skaluda-Jätten," a story from Vestergötland.

For a giant's appetite, *p. 26*, see "Vas Péter," a tale quoted by Kozma, in which Glutton eats 366 fat oxen in six hours, and Drunkard empties 366 casks of wine, each holding one hundred buckets, in the same time.

Big Mouth, in "Hidatsa," an Indian tale, drinks enormous draughts. *Folk-Lore Record*, vol. i. p. 140.

The horse in "Prince Mirkó," p. 65, like the giant in this tale, asks the hero what he sees, and then tells him to shut his eyes, whilst they go on.

Page 27. The king's daughter falling in love with one who acts as servant is a common incident in Finnish and Lapp tales. Generally, the hero is one who by wearing a cap on the pretext of having a sore head conceals his beauty, which the king's daughter by chance happens to see when the cap is off.

Cf. "Tuhkamo" from Sodan Kyla in North Finland, *S. ja T.* i. p. 35, where the hero is told to fell all the trees near a bay, and is assisted by his bride. The whip as a mode of summoning assistance is mentioned in "Fisher Joe," *supra*, p. 16.

For difficult tasks vide "Fisher Joe," *supra*, p. 18; "The Three Brothers," p. 153; "The King and the Devil," p. 192; "The Widower and his Daughter," p. 208; "The Girl with the Golden Hair," p. 271.

Cf. also *Malagasy Isùlakòlona*, in *Folk-Lore Journal*, 1884, p. 130.

Also *Verhandlungen der gelehrten Estnischen Gesellschaft zu Dorpat. Zweiter Band, drittes Heft*, p. 76. "Der dankbare Fürstensohn."

Stier, *Ungarische Märchen*, "Das kleine Zauberpferd."—Kletke, |Pg 320|*Märchensaal aller Völker*, "Die gläserne Hacke"; "Kojata"; "Der Orangenbaum und die Biene."

Polnische Volksagen und Märchen, by Woycicki, translated by Levestam, "Die Flucht."

Hyltén-Cavallius och Steffens. *Svenska Folksagor*. "Hafs-Firum."

Samlade Smärre Berättelser, af C. F. Ridderstad, *Linköping*, 1849. "Agnete lille Dei."

Winter, *Danske Folkeeventyr*. "Prindsen och Havmanden."

The reader need not be surprised to hear that the simple Magyar peasant uses classical names like Pluto, Furuzsina (Euphrosiné); for until 1848 Latin was the official language, and many of the scientific works were written in it, and so a great many words found their way into the vulgar tongue, such as: penna, calamus, bugyelláris (pugillares), jus, &c.

Page 32. The chase after the fugitives is a well-known folk-tale incident. See several instances in this collection. Generally the pursuer is stopped by something thrown down by the pursued. See "The Little Magic Pony," p. 160, and notes *infra*.

In other stories such as the present and "The King and the Devil," p. 193, the pursued change into all manner of wonderful things. Cf. *Grimm*, vol. i. "Fundevogel," p. 202, and "The Two King's Children," vol. ii. p. 113.

In a Portuguese Folk-Tale, "The Daughter of the Witch," F.L.S. 1882, p. 15, the boy becomes a public road, and the girl an old man with a sack on his back; then the boy becomes a hermitage and the girl a hermit; and lastly, when the mother comes, who, as usual, is the keenest witted, the lad becomes a river, and the girl an eel. The mother, as she cannot catch the eel, pronounces the curse of forgetfulness in case any one should kiss the hero, which one of his sisters does, while he sleeps. See also in the same collection, "May you vanish like the wind," p. 20.

In "Fairy Helena," a story quoted by Kozma in his paper read before the Hungarian Academy, the fairy's father blows across a wide river, and at once it is spanned by a golden bridge. The fairy then strikes a rusty table-fork with a *kourbash*, and it at once becomes a golden steed, upon which the lovers flee into Italy. When they |Pg 321|discover that they are followed,

Helena spits on the floor, the door-latch, and the hinge of the door, and each expectoration speaks, and so deludes the king's messengers, and allows the fugitives more time (Cf. Ralston's *Russian Tales*, p. 142; *Grimm*, i.: "Sweetheart Roland," p. 225, where one change of Roland is to a fiddler, who makes the witch dance till dead.) The king following in the form of a gigantic eagle, the tips of whose wings touch heaven and earth, reminds of such stories as the Lapp "Jaetten og Veslegutten," from Hammerfest, *Friis.* p. 49, where the giant is heard coming like a gust of wind; and in "Jaetten og Drengen hans," from Tanen, *id.* p. 58, where the giant and his wife pursue the lad, as he walks away, with his bag of silver coins.

See also Finnish "Oriiksi muntettu poika," *S. ja. T.* i. 142, and variants there given, in which the devil follows in the form of a storm-cloud.

Wonderful transformations of a like sort occur in Indian stories, *e.g.*, "The Phúlmati Ráni's arms and legs grew into four houses, her chest became a tank, and her head a house in the middle of the tank; her eyes turned into two little doves; and these five houses, the tank, and the doves, were transported to the jungle. The little doves lived in the house that stood in the middle of the tank. The other houses stood round the tank." Stokes' *Indian Tales*, "Phúlmati Ráni," p. 5, and "The Bél Princess," p. 148, where we read, "Then the girl took a knife in her own hand, and cut out her two eyes; and one eye became a parrot, and the other a *mainá*(a kind of starling). Then she cut out her heart, and it became a great tank. Her body became a splendid palace and garden; her arms and legs became the pillars that supported the verandah roof; and her head the dome on the top of the palace."

Page 34. For the curse of oblivion see Panch-Phul Ranee, *Old Deccan Days*, p. 143, where the conjurors throw some powder in the rice and fire, and no sooner did the rajah receive them than he forgot his wife, child, and all that had ever happened to him. In "Chandra's Vengeance," p. 260, forgetfulness is brought about by enchanted drink. Cf. *Grimm*, ii. "The Drummer," p. 338.

[Pg 322]In the romance of *Ogier le Danois*, Morgue la Faye, who had kissed Ogier at his birth, but had been forgotten by him, meets him when he is a hundred years old, and by means of a ring restores him to youth and beauty. When Ogier drew near to the castle of Avalon he was met by singing fays, and a glorious crown placed on his head, whereupon he instantly forgot all the past, and had no thought "ni de la dame Clarice, qui tant estoit belle et noble ... ne de creature vivante." See Keightley's *Fairy Mythology, Bohn's Library*, p. 48.

The Irish tale of "Grey Norris" from Warland, tells how a little dog jumps up and kisses the hero, and at once he forgets the poor princess who waits outside.*Folk-Lore Journal*, 1883, p. 323.

The Polish tale "Prince Unexpected," contains a similar incident. *Id.* 1884, p. 16.

THE TRAVELS OF TRUTH AND FALSEHOOD. Kriza, ii.

In another version three crows discuss the healing powers of the dew. Cf. also another version communicated by Kriza in the *Szépirodalmi Figyelö*. The tale is also found in Hungary Proper. Cf. Gaal, *Märchen der Magyaren*, "Die dankbaren Thiere."

Cf. Cruelty of sister or others: in "Envious Sisters," p. 50, "The Three Brothers," p. 152, and "The Girl without Hands," p. 182.

Steere's *Swahili Tales*, "Blessing or Property," p. 397.

Also Wagner's *Asgard and the Gods*, p. 113, where Holda's Quick-born (fountain of life) restores the crippled and aged. Spanish peasants believe in a mysterious herb, *pito-real*, invisible to men, and known to swallows only, which restores eyesight. See *Folk-Lore Record*, p. 295. 1883.

Page 37. Obtaining useful knowledge in secret. Cf. *Sagas from Far East*, xiv. "The Avaricious Brother," p. 151, in which the poor brother obtained precious gifts, which he saw the Dakinis (female genii) use; the rich brother when he heard of it went to see what he could get, and was seized by the enraged spirits, and after [Pg 323]due consultation punished, by having his nose pulled out five ells long, and nine knots tied in it.

In *Old Deccan Days*, "The Learned Owl," p. 74, tells how the birds in the tree tell secrets. In "The Wanderings of Vicram Maharajah," p. 121, it is two cobras, and in "Panch-Phul Ranee," p. 139, two jackals.

See also *Stories from Mentone*, "The Charcoal Burners," p. 41. *Folk-Lore Record*, vol. iii.; and Stokes' *Indian Tales*, "The Fair Prince," p. 198.

Cf. Finnish "Totuus ja walhe" (Truth and falsehood), and "Riuta ja Rauta;" under section 10 of *S. ja T.* ii. pp. 134-146, entitled "Paha on pettäjän perintö" (The Deceiver's part is a bad one).

Magyarische Sagen, by Mailáth, i. "Die Brüder," p. 169.

Gerle, *Volksmärchen der Böhmen. Prag.* 1819. "St. Walburgisnachttraum oder die drei Gesellen."

Volkslieder und Sagen der Wenden, von Haupt und Schmaler, *Grimma* 1843. "Recht bleibt immer Recht."

Old Deccan Days, "Truth's Triumph," p. 50.

Serbian Folk-Lore: "Justice or Injustice—which is best?" p. 83. Where the heroes are king's sons, and the just one is helped by fairies who come to the spring to bathe.

In "The two Travellers," *Grimm*, vol. ii. p. 81, the heroes are a sour-tempered shoemaker and a merry tailor. Two sinners hanging on the gallows talk, and thus the sightless tailor learns many secrets. So soon as he recovers his sight, he sets off, and arrives at the very town where the shoemaker has gone, who persuades the king to set the tailor terrible tasks to perform, which he does, by the aid of grateful animals, whose lives he spared. The cobbler has his eyes picked out by the crows that sit on the heads of the two hanged men. See notes, p. 408, and a fragmentary story of "The Men on the Gallows," p. 466, in the same volume.

In Naake's *Slavonic Tales*, "Right and Wrong," from the Servian, the Vilas, beings peculiar to Servia, female genii, come to the spring where the blind brother is, and talk.

Also Dasent's *Tales from the Norse*, "True and Untrue," p. 1.

[Pg 324]*Undvalgte Eventyr og Fortællinger* ved C. Molbech, *Kjöbenhavn*, 1843. "Godtro og utro, et Skaansk Folkesagn."

Sagen, Märchen und Lieder der Herzogthümer Schleswig—Holstein and Lauenburg vom R. Müllenhoff. *Kiel*, 1845. "Vom Bauernsohn der König ward."

Portuguese Stories. "Unless the Lord build the house, they labour in vain who build it." *Folk-Lore Record*, 1881, p. 157. The driver hears the devils talking on the top of the cave, where he shelters, and by means of which he obtains riches and honour. In this case, the gouging out of the eyes is omitted, and the whole story modified, and, if one may so say, Christianised.

THE HUNTING PRINCES. Kriza, iii.

Steel, flint, and tinder, form to this day the "Smoker's companion" in the rural districts of Hungary, although matches were invented more than half a century ago by a Hungarian.

Page 39. The youngest son in the Finnish story, "Ihmeellinen Sauwa," (The Wonderful Stick,) *S. ja T.* i. p. 158, is told to shoot at an oak, and if he hits it (which he does) he would find his mother who had been carried off one day whilst walking in the garden years before.

For other versions see "A Year Hence" in Gaal, vol. ii.; also "The Three Princes" in the present vol. p. 110, and "The Prince who tied the Dawn" in another collection of Erdélyi, entitled "*Magyar Népmesék*."

Dragons[14] appear at every turn in folk-lore, and therefore we can give but a short selection of comparisons out of the countless hosts of legends and tales. "At Lueska there is a dark cavern called the Dragon's Den, which was the terror of the country, and its legend is an interesting example of how old folk-tales are modified, as time rolls on; in this case, the burghers of the town can't tell what to do, and a little dwarf tinker declares he can kill the monster, but that he will [Pg 325]claim as his reward the hand of the burgomaster's daughter. The burgomaster is mightily indignant, but is obliged to give way to the force of popular opinion; and is surprised to find his daughter quite willing to make the sacrifice for the sake of her neighbours. The tinker confesses and communicates. He then sets off and gathers a herb called dragon's bane—a powerful narcotic—and makes a strong infusion of it. With this he sets out, driving two calves before him, and taking some of his tools, and his fire-pan full of hot embers. The dragon soon scents the cattle, and rushing out devours them. Meanwhile, the tinker views all from a tree. Soon the dragon rolls over and falls asleep. The tinker then pours a goatskin full of his infusion over the monster's head, who falls into a deep sleep. Down comes the tinker and settles him, cuts off his head, and carries it in triumph to the town, where the joyous crowd carry him shoulder-high to the burgomaster's. There the tinker declares that he will not accept the maiden's hand unless she accepts him freely and willingly. The young girl, won by his magnanimous conduct, declares he has won her heart. Whereat he flings off his disguise, and lo! the lord of Csicso, who confesses that he has long loved the beautiful maid. General happiness and joy. Curtain!" *Pictures of Hungarian Life*, p. 28.

Cf. "Grendel" in the "Lay of Beowulf"; "The Lambton Worm," in Surtees' *History of Durham*, ii. p. 173; Hardwick's *Traditions*, p. 40, and Henderson's *Folk-Lore of Northern Counties*, F.L.S., under "Worms." Nork, *Mythologie der Volksagen*, says, the dragon was sacred to Wodin, and that its image was placed over houses, &c. to keep away evil influences.

In *Tales from Hofer's Land*, "The Three Black Dogs," p. 214, the dogs kill the dragon, and Jössl marries the princess; in "Zovanin Senza Paura," p. 348, fearless Johnny kills the dragon that has taken possession of the fountains.

Baring Gould's *Curious Myths*. "St. George," and Brady's *Clavis Calendaria*, vol. i. p. 310.

In Denton's *Serbian Folk-Lore*, "True-steel," p. 146, an alligator replaces the dragon; the incidents are very like those in the Magyar tale, but the tale is longer, beginning with three sisters, as well as the brothers. The sisters are carried off, much the same as in [Pg 326]the Russian story "Marya-Morevna" (*Ralston*, p. 85); and, in seeking for the sisters, the Magyar incidents come in. The story continues to tell of the youngest son's entering the forbidden chamber, and letting loose a man, True-steel, who was confined there (cf. Payne's *Arabian Nights*, vol. i. p. 141, "Story of the Third Calender"), who runs away with his wife. His labours to regain her occupy the rest of the tale. True-steel is killed in the end, by the secret of his strength being destroyed, as in "Punchkin."

The tying up of Midnight and Dawn is a piece of primitive science that in one shape or other is to be found in many stories. Cf. Lapp stories, where "Evening Red," and the "Sun's Sister" are girls; *Friis*, No. 44; and in No. 45 Ashiepattle goes for a golden lasso, and has to go till the sunlight ceases; and then till the moonlight ceases; and then till starlight ceases. When he arrives in the regions of darkness he finds the golden lasso. The tale appears to be imperfect, and no use is made of the lasso. Guns and cannons appear beyond the land of the moonlight!

The Finnish "Leppäpölkky" tells how Alder Block goes to a castle, and is told "that a wicked one cursed the sunlight, and so a snake with nine heads has taken it; and when the snake goes to the sea, he takes the sun with him. When he is in the country it is day, when he is in the sea it is night. A wicked one has cursed the moonshine, and a snake with six heads has taken the moonshine. When he is on the land, it is light; but when he is in the sea, it is dark. The wicked one has also cursed the dawn, because it began to shine too soon, and he could not sleep; so the snake with three heads has taken the dawn. When he is on the land we have dawn, but when he is at sea we have no dawn." The heroes in turn destroy the snakes; and dawn, the moon, and the sun escape; and as each shines over the land, the people pray for blessings on the man's head, who has delivered the dawn, moon, and sun. This appears to be pretty clearly an attempt of early man to describe natural phenomena. The story goes on to tell how the king offered his daughters to the heroes, but they declined them, only asking for a little corn.

There is a most interesting myth of Dawn and Twilight, well worthy of notice, in the Esthonian "Koit ja Ämarik" (Dawn and [Pg 327]Twilight). In old times a mother had two daughters named Videvik (twilight) and Ämarik (evening twilight). Both were charming and beautiful in appearance, and in behaviour just as the song says:

"Pea valge, pôsld punasedSitik mustad silmakulmud.""Eyes white, cheeks red,Eyebrows black as a dung beetle."

When the sun went to its Creator (set), the elder sister came from the plough with two oxen, and led them, as an intelligent being ought, to the river's brink to drink. But, just as now, beauty is the first thing among girls, and the good-looking ones often gaze into the looking-glass. So, also, did she, the handsome Videvik. She let her oxen be oxen, and went to the river's edge; and lo! there on the silver looking-glass of the water lay reflected the eyebrows black as dung beetles, and the charming gold-coloured cheeks, and her heart was glad. The moon, who in accord with the Creator's command and ordinance, was going to light the land, in place of the sun, who had sunk to rest, forgot to attend to his duty, and threw himself, like an arrow, with loving desire into the earth's deep bosom, down to the bottom of the river; and there, mouth to mouth, and lip to lip, he sealed his betrothal to Videvik with a kiss, and claimed her as his bride. But, during this he had quite forgotten his duties; and, see! deep darkness covered the land whilst he lay on Videvik's bosom. Then occurred a sad misfortune. The forest robber, Wolf, who now had all his own way, as no one could see him, tore one of Videvik's oxen, which had gone to the forest to feed, and seized it as food for himself. Although the shrill nightingale was heard, and its clear song from the forest rang through the darkness:

"Lazy girl! lazy girl! the long night! the striped ox!To the furrows! to the furrows! fetch the whip! fetch the nag!Tsät! Tsät!""Laisk tüdruk, laisk tüdruk, ööpik! kiriküüt!Raule, raule, too püts, too püts!Tsät! Tsät!"

Yet Videvik heard not: she forgot all but love. Blind, deaf, and without understanding is love. Of the five senses but feeling is left! When Videvik at last woke from her love, and saw the Wolf's deed, [Pg 328]she wept bitterly, and her tears became a sea. The innocent tears did not fall unobserved by Vana-isa (the old father). He stepped down from his golden heaven to punish the evil-doers, and to set a watch over those who had broken his commands. He scolded the wicked Wolf, and the Moon received Videvik to wife. To this day Videvik's mild face shines by the Moon's side, longingly looking at the water where she tasted for the first time her husband's love. Then Vana-isa said, "In order that there may be no more carelessness about the light, and lest darkness grows in power, I command you, guardians, go each one to your place. And you, Moon and Videvik, take charge of the light by night. Koit and Ämarik I put daylight into your hands. Do your duty honestly. Daughter Ämarik in your care I place the setting sun. See that in the evening every spark be put out, so that no accident happen, and that all men be in peace! And you my son Koit take care when you light the new light of the new day that every place has its light." Both the Sun's servants honestly attended to their duty, so that he was never missing, even for a single day, from the heavens. The short summer nights now drew near, when Koit and Ämarik stretched hand and mouth to each other: the time when the whole world rejoices, and the little birds make the forests ring with their songs in their own language; when plants begin to bloom, and shoot forth in their beauty; when Vana-isa stepped down from his golden throne to keep Lijon's festival. He found all in order, and rejoiced greatly over his creation, and said to Koit and Ämarik, "I am pleased with your watchfulness, and wish you continued happiness! You may now become man and wife." But they both replied together, "Father, perplex us not. We are satisfied as we are, and wish to remain lovers: for in this we have found a happiness which never grows old, but is ever young." Vana-isa granted their wish, and returned to his golden heaven.

Cf. Castrén, *Finsk Mytologi*, p. 66, and "Kalevala," Run. 17, line 478. The Rev. Dr. Taylor kindly points out Dr. Donner's observation in his *Lieder der Lappen*, p. 55: "Diese Anschauung ist doch bekanntlich auch unter den arischen Völkern vielfach verbreitet."

For the discovery of the hero by his shooting, and the rest of the incidents of the story, cf. *Grimm*, ii. "The Skilful Huntsman," p. 103, [Pg 329]and notes, p. 412: and the marshal in "The Two Brothers," *Grimm*, i. p. 252. In the Lapp. *Friis*, No. 18, the Vesle boy compels the nobles who go out shooting with him to give him the rings they had received from the princesses they are betrothed to, before he will give them some ptarmigan he had shot, and which they are anxious to have, as they had been unsuccessful in their search for game; and this in order to prevent false boasting on the part of the nobles, as we find in other variants. Juanillo, in the Spanish tale, makes each of his brothers give him a golden pear, and then one of their ears; and next insists upon branding them on the shoulder, as if they were his slaves: and so in the end proves their treacherous conduct; see *Patrañas*, "Simple Johnny," p. 38.

In "Gutten, Havfruen, og Ridder Rød," from Lyngen, *Friis*, p. 131, Knight Red[15] acts the part of a traitor, and is shown to be so by the hero, who exhibits part of a ring, the other part of which the princess has, and which they broke when the lad entered the princess' tower to fetch the king's sword, which was hidden there. The reward for bringing it to the battle-field being the princess' hand.

See also Ritter Red in "Shortshanks," and the "Big Bird Dan," pp. 155, 443, in Dasent's *Tales from the Norse*.

In a Russian tale (*Afanassieff*, vi. 52), Ivan, by the help of his animals, kills the twelve-headed serpent that is killing all his people, and then goes to sleep on the princess's knees. A water-carrier passing cuts off Ivan's head, and presents himself as the hero. The beasts return, and find a crow upon Ivan's body, which they spare on condition that it brings the water of life and death. (This incident occurs in the Finnish "Golden Bird" a raven coming with its young ones to eat the corpse.) Ivan is resuscitated, and the water-carrier punished. *Gubernatis*, vol. i. 216. Dogs restore the dead hero to life in the story of "John and the Amulet."*Folk-Lore Record*, 1884, p. 197.

[Pg 330]The candle at the princesses' heads suggests the Indian stories which tell of sticks placed at the head or feet, and whilst they are there the girl cannot move. *Stokes*, pp. 54, 186.

THE LAZY SPINNING GIRL WHO BECAME A QUEEN. Kriza, iv.

The story of the mannikin who is clever at spinning or weaving is widespread. Thus, in a rubric of the "Catalan" map of the world, in the National Library at Paris, the date of which map has been fixed at A.D. 1375, we read, "Here [N.W. of Catayo] grow little men who are but five palms in length; and though they be little, and not fit for weighty matters, yet they be brave and *clever at weaving*, and at keeping cattle...." (Col. Yule's translation in *Cathay, and the Way Thither.*)

A Swedish story tells how a young newly-married girl is terribly upset by the constant calls of household work; and one morning, in despair at the many things to be done, she shut herself in the room, and, throwing herself on the couch, wept bitterly, saying, "Oh, unhappy me! Is there no one to help me, or comfort a poor woman?" "I can," said a voice; and lo! there was the old man of Hoberg, a good sprite, who had been a friend to the family for generations.

"You bewail your slave life," said the old man, "but that comes from your want of practice in real work. I will give you ten obedient servants who will faithfully assist you in all your doings." Just then he shook his coat, and ten droll little creatures sprang out, and began to put the room in order. "Stretch forth your hands to me," said the old man. Elsa tremblingly put out her hands to the old man, who said—

"Tummetott, HjertehandSlikepott, Lille Per Roligman."Långestång,[16]

[Pg 331]"Be quick and take your places!" In a moment the ministering spirits disappeared into Elsa's fingers, and the old man vanished.

The young wife sat staring at her hands for a time, but soon felt a strange desire to work.

"Here am I sitting dreaming," said she, with unwonted cheerfulness, "and it's already seven o'clock. Everyone is waiting for me," she continued; and, hurrying out, she began her work. From that time she was the model housewife of the district; see *Hofberg*, p. 58. "De tio tjenstandarna," from Småland.[117]

[Pg 332]Cf. the mannikin called "Panczimanczi," in Lad. Arany's "*Eredeti Népmesék*," p. 277. His height is half an ell, his moustache two ells, his beard three ells long. He is seen leaping merrily over a fire, and heard singing the following: "I am Panczimanczi; no one knows my name; I roast, I cook, I boil; the day after to-morrow I shall fetch my pretty bride home."

In Kriza's tale his name is Dancing Vargaluska. "How the name is held to be part of the very being of the man who bears it, so that by it his personality may be carried away, and, so to speak, grafted elsewhere, appears in the way in which the sorcerer uses it as a means of putting the life of his victim into the image upon which he practises;" *e.g.* the widespread making of wax images to represent certain persons, and then melting them, that the persons named may waste away. Magyar peasants say, that hair combings must not be thrown away, lest the birds get them, and build them in their nests; for whilst they are doing so, you will have headache; and again, if a young girl wishes to compel a young man to marry her she must steal something from the young man, and take it to a witch, who adds to it three beans, three bulbs of garlic, a few pieces of dry coal, and a dead frog. These are all put into an earthenware pot, and placed under the threshold, with the words, "Lord of the infernal regions and of the devils, and possessor of the hidden treasure, give to N. or M. some incurable illness (or inflame him with unquenchable love for N. or M.), and I will join you."

See also "The Two Orphans," where the witch's daughter steals a lock of the queen's hair, p. 222. Cf. the Finnish method of curing "knarr" (German "Knirrband"), a complaint that is common at harvest-time among those who are not used to the reaping-hook. Amongst its symptoms are curious crackings of the wrist. The sick one asks someone who is well "to chop his knarr" for him, which is done as follows. The patient lays his sick hand upon a chopping block, and three pieces of three-jointed straw are so laid, side by side, as to correspond joint for joint. The "doctor" then takes an axe, and chops with all his strength into the block through the first joint. "What are you chopping?" asks the sick one. "I'm chopping the [Pg 333]'knarr' out of your joint into the wood." The same question and answer is repeated after second blow; after the last blow the chopper cries "Now he's gone!" In North Germany the ceremony is performed on the threshold, and ends with the sign of the cross. Cf. *Finnish Folk-Lore* in "*Notes and Queries*," 6th S. xi. p. 23. Also, *Suomen Muinaismuisto-Yhdistyksen Aikakauskirja*, v. p. 103.

Algerian peasants have a great objection to their portraits being taken; and Holderness folks rub warts with stolen beef, &c., and let it rot, saying the warts will disappear with the decaying of the meat, &c., &c. "A similar train of thought shows itself in the belief that the utterance of the name of a deity gives to man a means of direct communication with the being who owns it, or even places in his hands the supernatural power of that being, to be used at his will." Tylor's *Early History of Mankind*, pp. 124, 129, and Lubbock's *Origin of Civilisation*, p. 245.

Cf. Swedish "Jätten Finn och Lunds domkyrka." *Hofberg*, p. 12. The giant promises to build a church for the white Christ if Laurentius can find out his name, and if not he must forfeit his eyes—

"Helt visstÄr hvite kristEn gud, som sitt temple är värdig.Jag bygger det jag, om du säger mig blottHvad namn jag fått,Se'n kyrkan är murad och färdig.Men kan du ej säga mitt namn, välan,Du vise man!Gif akt på hvad vite jag sätter:Då måste du ge mig åt mina småDe facklor två,Som vandra på himmelens slätter."[118]

Laurentius found out that the giant's name was "Finn" by hearing the giantess hush her crying child.

Similar tales are told of many churches. *E.g.* Drontheim Cathedral, where the giant is called "Skalle"; see Sjöborg, *Collections*, Part ii. [Pg 334]p. 182. Of Eskilssäter's Church, where the giant's name was "Kinn," see Fernow, *Verml. Beskr*, i. p. 318.

Also of a church in Norrland, where St. Olaf found out the troll's name, "Wind and Weather," see *Iduna*, vol. iii. p. 60; and about Kallundborgs Church, in Själland, cf. Thiele, *Danske Folkesagn*, i. p. 43.

Tales from the Land of Hofer, "The Wild Jäger and the Baroness"; secret name, "Buzinigala," p. 110.

In the *Land of Marvels*, Vernaleken, "Winterkolble," p. 24; and "Kruzimügeli," p. 28.

Grimm. vol. i. "Rumpelstiltskin," pp. 221, 412.[119]

The tale appears to be confused towards the end, the three deformed beggars being the three aunts of the Norse; see *Dasent*, p. 222. The ordinary story has no dwarf or secret name in it; cf. Spanish tale of "Guardian Spirits," in *Caballero*, p. 64.

Also, *Patrañas*, "What Anna saw in the Sunbeam," p. 193.

And in *Portuguese Folk-Tales*. "The Aunts." *Folk-Lore Soc.* p. 79.

On the other hand, in the Swedish story from Upland the girl who could spin gold from clay and long straw was helped by a dwarf whose name turned out to be "Titteli Ture!". See Thorpe's *Yule Tales*, p. 168.

See also, *Grimm*, ii. p. 163, "The Lazy Spinner," in which the woman by her wit contrives to evade her spinning; notes, p. 428. The Finnish story of "The Old Woman's Loom," from Korpo, is almost identical with Grimm's.

[Pg 335]

THE ENVIOUS SISTERS. Kriza, v.

Cf. the beginning of the tale "The Three Princesses," in the present volume, p. 144. The tale is frequently found in Hungary, also amongst the Germans and Servians.

For cruelty towards the best (generally the youngest), cf. pp. 36, 152, 182 in this collection; *Chaucer* and *Boccacio*; *Grimm*, i. "The Girl without Hands," p. 127, and Notes, p. 378. The Finnish variant tells how there was once a brother and sister, and when the father was dying he said to his son, "Treat your sister well." All went on comfortably until the brother married a girl who was "the devil's wife's daughter," and before long, owing to her slanders, the sister was turned out. The girl then went to the king's castle, and lived there as a beggar. In the spring the king's son went to sow his field, and said: "Who first eats of these peas, she shall be my wife." This he said in a joke to the others. But the girl was there, behind the fence, and she heard and remembered it all.

Summer came—the peas were ripe. Then the girl dug a hole under the fence, and went and ate some peas. Suddenly the king's son remembered his pea-field, and thought, "I will go and see how the peas are getting on." He went and saw some one had been eating them, and so he watched for some time, and lo! a girl came cautiously through a hole and began to eat the peas. The king's son seized her and carried her home in a sheet. Then he dressed her in a royal dress, and made her ready to be his wife, as a king's bride ought to be. They lived together till the king's son made his wife pregnant, then he was obliged to go to the war, and he said to his wife, "If you have a boy send me a letter, and I will come back: if it is a girl, send me a letter, and I will come back when I can." Well! the wife had a son. She sent a letter asking her husband to come home at once, and sent a slave with it. The slave went to spend the night in the girl's home. When he had been there a little time the mistress said, "Would you like to sleep here?" "Yes," answered the messenger, and began to bathe; but the devil's daughter, in the meantime, opened his bag and changed the letter's [Pg 336]meaning, and put "a female child is born." The slave knew nothing of it, but set off with the letter to the king's son. When he read it he sent the same slave back with the answer, "I will come when I have time," and the slave returned. On his way he came to the same house, and the mistress in the same way sent him to the bath and opened the bag and changed the letter, "As the child is born, the woman must put off the royal dress and put on her own rags, and she may, with her child, go where she likes." The slave brought the letter to the wife, who did as the letter said, and set off begging and moaning. She began to be thirsty, and sought for water in the wood. In a little time she found a well, where there was wonderfully clear water and a beautiful golden ladle. She put down her child, and went a little way from the well. When the child was alone it stretched out to the ladle and fell head first into the well. The mother rushed to help him and got her child out before he was drowned. Wherever the water touched her she became much more beautiful and white. The child also became like no other in the world. The woman set off with her child, and at last came to her own home, where her brother was still living with his wife. She was not recognised, and asked for a night's lodging. The mistress shouted, "Outside the door is a good place for you." "Very well," said the woman, and stayed there with her child all night.

She sat there all night, and the king with his soldiers from the war came there. As the king walked in his room, the woman let her child crawl on the floor. It crawled to the king, who took it and said, "Who are you, poor woman, who are so beautiful, and have so handsome a child?" "I have been in this house before, but my sister-in-law hated me." "Hold your noise, you blackguard," shouted the woman, and wished to stop her. But the other went on, "My sister-in-law hated me, and thrashed me, and drove me away almost dead. I then went to the king's castle, and became the king's son's wife. When I was pregnant the king's son went to war, and I sent him a letter that I had got a boy; but he was so angry, that he ordered me and my child out; and so I had to leave a good home." "Hold your noise!" shouted the brother's wife again. But the king said, "I am lord here;" and the woman continued and explained all. [Pg 337]The brother's wife again shouted, "Hold your noise, you good-for-nothing!" Then the king seized her by the hair, and hanged her from the gutter, and took his wife and boy home, and they lived happily. If they are yet alive, I don't know. "Neitonen Hernemaassa."—"The maid in the pea-field," *S. ja T.* 1, p. 116.—Cf. "Neitonen Kuninkaan Sadussa," ("The maid in the king's garden,") *id.* 108; "Pigen uden Haender," in *Udwalgte Eventyr og Fortaellinger, en Laesebog for Folket og for den barnlige Werden*, (Copenhagen, 1843). No. 48, p. 258; "The Girl without Hands," p. 182, in this collection; and Steere's *Swahili Tales*. "Blessing and Property," p. 403.

The Finnish tale, "Tynnyrissä kaswanut Poika," ("The boy who grew in a barrel,") *S. ja T.* 1, 105, tells how a king's son heard the three daughters of a peasant woman talking. The eldest said, "I would like to make all sorts of foods and drinks out of one corn;" the middle one, "I would like to make all sorts of clothes out of one flax thread;" the youngest said, "I don't like work, but will bear children three times, and have three sons each time, who shall have:

"Kun kupeesta kuumottawi,Päiwyt ompi pääla' ella,Käet on kultaa kalwoisesta,Jal'at hopeiset polwista."

"The moon shining in the temples,The sun on the top of the head,Hands of gold to the wrist,Feet of silver from the knees."

The king's son marries the youngest girl and, when she is pregnant, goes to war. She bears three sons, which the midwife exchanges for three whelps; the same thing happens a second time; and also a third time, when the wife manages to save one son. The people insist upon her being sent away; and so she and her child (which she takes secretly in her bosom) are put in a barrel and thrown into the sea. The barrel grows too small, so the lad kicks the bottom out, and they land, and live in a hut, where the woman makes nine cakes of her milk, and finds her other eight boys. The king's son soon discovers them, and all goes well. The changed letter also occurs in Antti Puuhaara.

[Pg 338]Cf. Hahn, *Griechische Märchen*; "Sun, Moon, and Morning Star;" in which the king's son marries all the three girls.

Deccan Days, "Truth's Triumph," p. 54, where Guzra Bai had one hundred and one children, which the nurse threw out of the palace on the dust-heap, and substituted stones for them.

In the Land of Marvels, "The Blackbird," p. 34.

Stokes' *Indian Tales*. "The boy who had a moon on his forehead, and a star on his chin:" also Phúlmati Ráni who had on her head the sun; on her hands, moons; and her face was covered with stars.

Gonzenbach, *Sicilianische Märchen*, vol. i. p. 19.

Stier, *Ungarische Volksmärchen*: "Die verwandelten Kinder."

Stier, *Ungarische Sagen*: "Die beiden jüngsten Königskinder."

Schott, *Wallachische Märchen*: "Die goldenen Kinder."

Gubernatis, vol. i p. 412, says, "In the European story, when the beautiful princess, in the absence of the prince, her husband, gives birth to two beautiful sons, the witch induces the absent prince to believe that, instead of real sons, his young wife has given birth to pups. In the seventh story of the third book of Afanassieff, the young queen gives birth, during the king's absence, to two sons, of whom one has the moon on his forehead, and the other a star on the nape of his neck (the Açvinâu). The wicked sister of the young queen buries the children. Where they were buried a golden sprout and a silver one sprung up. A sheep feeds upon these plants, and gives birth to two lambs, having, the one the sun on its head, the other a star on its neck. The wicked sister, who has meanwhile been married to the king, orders them to be torn in pieces, and their intestines to be thrown out into the road. The good lawful queen has them cooked, eats them, and again gives birth to her two sons, who grow up hardy and strong, and who, when interrogated by the king, narrate to him the story of their origin: their mother is recognised, and becomes once more the king's wife. The wicked sister is put to death." In vol. ii. p. 30, another story of Afanassieff, bk. iii. 13, is quoted, which resembles the "Envious Sisters"; also a Servian story, p. 31, where the cut-off hands are replaced by golden ones, by means of the ashes of three burned hairs from the tails of a black stallion and a [Pg 339]white mare. Reference is also made to *Pentamerone*, bk. iii. No. 2; *Afanassieff*, bk. iii. No. 6; *the Mediæval Legends of St. Uliva*, by Prof. A. d'Ancona, Pisa, Nistri, 1863; and, *Figlia del Re di Dacia*, by Prof. A. Wesselofski, Pisa, Nistri, 1866.

Cf. Notes in *Stokes*, pp. 242, 250; *Grimm*, vol. i.: "The Gold Children," p. 333.

Portuguese Tales, by Pedroso: "The Maiden with the Rose on her Forehead," *F.L.S.* p. 65.

KNIGHT ROSE. Kriza vi.

In folk-stories we often find the heroes erecting some post or pole, or leaving some article behind them, which will tell of their danger. Cf. "The Three Princes," p.111 of this volume. In "The Two Brothers," (*Grimm*, vol. i. p. 244,) the foster-father gave to each of the boys a bright knife, and said, "If ever you separate, stick this knife into a tree at the place where you part, and then when one of you goes back, he will be able to see how his absent brother is faring, for the side of the knife which is turned in the direction by which he went will rust if he dies, but will remain bright as long as he lives." Cf. "The Gold Children," where death is shown by the drooping of the brother's gold lily: and notes, *ib.* p. 453.

In the Russian story "Ivan Popyalof" (*Afanassieff*, ii. 30), Ivan hung up his gloves, and said to his brothers, "Should blood drop from my gloves, make haste to help me."

In "Marya-Morevna" (*Afanassieff* viii. No. 8), the silver left by Prince Ivan turned black when evil befell him.

In "Koschei, the Deathless" (*Afanassieff*, ii. 24), Prince Ivan let some drops of blood run from his little finger into a glass, gave it to his brothers, and said "If the blood in this glass turns black, tarry here no longer; that will mean I am about to die."

See Ralston's *Russian Folk-Tales*, pp. 67, 88, 102.—The Serbian story of "The Three Brothers" tells how the brothers stuck their knives into an oak tree, and when a knife fell out it was a sign that the owner was dead. Vide *Denton*, p. 273.

[Pg 340]In "Five to One," *Sagas from the Far East*, p. 107, six youths set out and travelled till they came to where six streams met, and each planted a tree at the head of the stream he chose, and if any tree withered away it was a sign evil had befallen its planter.

In the Greek story, "Sun, Moon, and Morning Star," (Hahn, *Griechische Märchen*,) the brothers give their sisters two shirts, and if they become black it means misfortune.—Cf. also *Folk-Lore Record*, vol. i. p. 207.

In the curious Egyptian story of the "Two Brothers," the younger brother says to the elder one, "When thou shalt take a jug of beer into thy hand and it turns into froth, then delay not; for to thee of a certainty is the issue coming to pass." *Records of the Past*, vol. ii. p. 144.

See also Isìlakòlona in "Malagasy Folk-Tales," *Folk-Lore Journal*, 1884, p. 130.

In folk-stories the giants were gifted with a keen sense of smell; and no sooner did they enter the room where a man was than they knew of his being there. The Norwegians and Swedes have stories of beings, which are called "Trynetyrk," or "Hundetyrk," and so have the Lapps and Finns. The Lapps call them "Bædnag-njudne," *i.e.*, dog's nose; and the Finns, "Koiran-Kuonalanien," which means the same. These monsters were men who had noses like dogs, and so could track men by their scent. They were said to be enormously large, and to have had one eye in the middle of their forehead; and were much dreaded on account of their being cannibals. A Lapp story tells how once a Lapp girl got lost, and came to a Bædnag-njudne's house. He was not at home, but his wife was. The girl was little, poor, and quite benumbed by the cold, and looked so terrified that the wife thought it would be a sin for Bædnag-njudne to eat her when he came home. So she took her and hid her under her gown. When Bædnag-njudne came home, he at once began to sniff about, and said, "I smell some one." His wife said all sorts of things to make him believe it was not so; and, when she did not dare to conceal the girl any longer, she let her out of the house secretly, and told her to fly for her life. Meanwhile, Bædnag-njudne was long sniffing about the house; and when he could not find anyone [Pg 341]inside he went outside, and soon found the footprints. So soon as the girl saw the monster was after her, in her terror she sprang from a bridge and hid herself under it. So the monster lost the track, and the girl was saved. *Friis*, p. 43.—Cf. "Jack the Giant Killer," where the giant says,

"Fa, fe, fi, fo, fum,I smell the blood of an Englishman;Be he alive, or be he dead,I'll grind his bones to make my bread."*Grimm*, vol. ii. p. 504.

In the northern ballad we are told how a girl is carried off by the fairies. Two of her brothers set off to rescue her, but fail, because they do not carry out Merlin's instructions. The third one succeeds; and, while he sits talking to his sister, the hall doors fly open and the elf king comes in shouting:

"With *fi*, *fe*, *fa*, and *fum*,I smell the blood of a Christian man,Be he dead, be he living, with my brand,I'll clash his harns frae his harn pan."

See Dr. Jamieson's *Illustrations of Northern Antiquities*.

In the Eskimo story of "The Girl who fled to the Inlanders," (*Rink*, p. 218,) the inlanders know a coast woman has come, by the smell: In "Inuarutligak," we are told of singular people, whose upper parts are human, and lower little dogs: and are endowed with a keen sense of smell.—Cf. p. 199, in this collection.

The cutting up of the hero's body reminds us of the Egyptian story of Typhon cutting up Osiris, who is restored to life by Horus; see *Uarda*, note to cap. viii. Cf. also *Sagas from the Far East*, tale v. p. 75, and *Vernaleken*, "The Three White Doves," p. 269.

In the Eskimo stories the heroes are restored to life by the singing of certain mystic songs.

In the legend of Gurû Guggâ, the bullocks are restored to life by the singing of charms; Temple's *Legends of the Punjâb*, p. 124. Cf. *Grimm*, vol. ii. "Water of Life," and note, p. 399; Ralston's *Russian Tales*, p. 236.

[Pg 342]The "wound-healing grass"[20] is in all probability flixweed (*Sisymbrium Sophia*), the Magyar name for which signifies "wound-healing leaf;" see article on Székely Folk-Medicine in *Folk-Lore Record*, April, 1884, p. 98, and the Finnish story of "Golden Bird."

With regard to the passage "Rose ... was so beautiful that though you could look at the sun you could not look at him," cf. the reply of Curidach to Attila, as related by Priscus. "He, (Attila,) then invited Curidach, chieftain of the Akatziri, to come and celebrate their joint triumph at his court, but that chieftain, suspecting that his benefactor's kindness was of the same nature as the promised boon of Polyphemus to Ulysses, courteously declined, saying, 'It is hard for a man to come into the presence of a god, and if it be not possible to look fixedly even at the orb of the sun, how shall Curidach gaze undistressed upon the greatest of God's' (*i.e.*Attila)." *Italy and her Invaders*, by T. Hodgkin, London, 1880, vol. ii. p. 84.

The story of a girl assuming a snake's skin reminds us of the daughter of Ypocras, who dwelt at Lango, in the form of a great dragon; see *The Voyages and Travels of Sir John Maundeville*, cap. iv. See also, "Snake-skin," in this collection, p. 283.—A Snake Friend occurs in the Swahili "Blessing or Property," (*Steere*, p. 405); in the Finnish "Haastelewat Kuuset," ("The Talking Pines,"); in "Melusina," B. Gould's *Curious Myths*, p. 471, and in Keightley's *Fairy Mythology*, p. 480.—In the Norse story of the "Three Princesses of Whiteland," (*Dasent*, p. 210,) the princesses gradually rise out of the earth as the lad destroys the trolls. See also *Vernaleken*, "The Fisher's Son," p. 250.

In the Serbian tale of "The Three Brothers," *Denton*, p. 275, the witch destroys two of the brothers, having first persuaded them to throw one of her hairs on their animals. The third brother resuscitates them, and all goes well. Cf. "The Enchanted Doe," in *Pentamerone*.[21]

Cf. "To Lappepiger gifte sig med Stall," *Friis*, 106, and "Ivan, Kupiskas Son," *Friis*, p. 170. Cf. exhaustive note in Stokes's *Indian Tales*, pp. 163, 268; and the Portuguese tale, "Slices of Fish," in *Pedroso: Folk-Lore Society*, p. 102. For animals that help, cf. "The Three Princes," p. 113 of this volume.

[Pg 343]To defeat a witch by drawing her blood is well known in the lore of the people.

Cf. Lapp stories, "Ulta Pigen," where the lad catches an Ulta girl by pricking her in the hand with a pin, so as to draw blood. A similar incident occurs in "Goveiter Pige," from Næsseby. In "Bondesønnen, Kongesønnen og Solens Søster," from Tanen, the herd is told to prick his bride (who has gone from him on account of his looking behind) in her hand till blood comes, and then suck the drop off. He did so and secured his bride. *Friis*, pp. 23, 39, 140.

The same superstition is well known in the North of England. In Lincolnshire there is a tale still told (1888) of a farmer who could not get his horses to go past a certain cottage until he got down and thrashed the old woman, who lived there, till the blood came. Whereupon the horses went past without further ado. In Sykes's *Local Records* of Newcastle-upon-Tyne, under March 26th, 1649, we are told how it was decided that certain women were witches, because blood did not come when they were pricked with pins by the "witch-finder." See also *Witch Stories* by L. Linton, p. 260, &c.

We must not feel surprised when we learn that it is still customary among the Servians and other half-civilised nations to subject women who are suspected as witches to the trial by water, since there are still many persons living who can remember the same thing having been done in the Netherlands and Germany. Thus, in 1823, it went through all the papers that a middle-aged woman at Delten, in Guelderland, being suspected of being a witch, volunteered herself to prove her innocence by the trial of water, that the trial actually took place in broad daylight before a crowd of people in a neighbouring canal, and that the result of the trial turned out in her favour. The following case is more horrible. It happened about thirteen years after the above date on the Peninsula Hela, near Dantzic. A man living in the Cassubian village Ceynowa was taken ill with dropsy, and a quack pointed out a poor widow fifty-one years old, and mother of five young children, as the witch who had caused the man's illness. In order to force her to undo the charm, the quack beat her and jumped on her in a most brutal manner, and she was led to the bed [Pg 344]of the patient, who beat her with a stick until she was covered with blood. Not content with this, the quack and some fishermen took her into a boat and rowed out to sea twice; they tied her hands and threw her into the water. On the second occasion they towed her after the boat so long that the poor creature was drowned. The further particulars are so revolting that one is apt to think that one reads a description of a punishment among the cannibals. And this happened in the Prussian State in the month of August of the year 1836!—From *Die Gartenlaube*, December 1884.

See also *Folk-Lore Record*, vol. v. p. 156, and Feb. 1883, p. 58; and Henderson's *Folk-Lore of Northern Counties*, p. 181, and notes, which says, "In Brittany, if the lycanthropist be scratched above the nose, so that three drops of blood are extracted, the charm is broken. In Germany, the werewolf has to be stabbed with knife or pitchfork thrice on the brows before it can be disenchanted."

Restoration to Life. Cf. "Marya Morevna," *Ralston*, p. 91; Panch-Phul Ranee, *Frere*, p. 140; "Loving Lailí," *Stokes*, p. 83, where Majnún is restored to life by Lailí cutting her little finger inside her hand straight down from the top of her nail to her palm, out of which the blood gushed like healing medicine; and the Bél-Princess, where the blood of the little finger again comes in. Also "Golden Hair," *Nauké*, p. 108, and the Lapp story "Ivan," *Friis*, p. 176. Mr. Quigstad, of Tromsø, to whose courtesy and learning I am deeply indebted, says he has heard a similar incident in a Lapp story from Lyngen.

PRINCE MIRKÓ. Kriza, xiii.

Page 59. In the Finnish "Leppäpölkky" ("Alder Block"), *S. ja T.* ii. p. 2, one half of the castle laughs and one half cries. The crying being on account of a great three-headed snake which arose from the sea, and would devour half the castle, half the men, and half the precious stones if the king did not give his eldest daughter in their stead.

[Pg 345]*Page 63.* The Tátos is a mythic horse possessed of the most marvellous powers. It is generally represented (as in the present tale) as being a most wretched creature to begin with. Cf. "The Little Magic Pony," p. 157; "The Three Princes, &c.," p. 197, where it is hatched from a five-cornered black egg; "the wretched foal which lies seven fathoms deep in the dung-heap," in "The Pelican," p. 256; the ugly creature in "The Girl with the Golden Hair," p. 264; and the piebald in the "Fairies' Well," p. 289. It feeds on burning cinders, and its breath changes the most wretched things into the most glorious. Sometimes, however, the first breath has an extraordinary effect, as *e.g.* p. 198, where Ambrose becomes like "a diseased sucking pig." The name is still a favourite one among the peasants for their horses. The word Tátos also meant a priest in the old pagan days, but it never has this meaning in the folk-tales.

The Tátos also appears in "Die Königstöchter," in Mailáth's *Magyarische Sagen*, vol. i. p. 61. See also "Zauberhelene," vol. ii. of the same collection, where we are told "Taigarot war ein wunderbares Pferd; es verstand die Reden der Menschen, antwortete auch und hatte neun Füsze." The whole story tells how Argilus carries off his wife, Helen, from the power of Holofernes, the fire-king, who has got her in his underground home. Taigarot belongs to Holofernes, and tells him where Helen is carried off, and so he recovers her. Argilus hears that the magic horse has a younger brother still more powerful although possessing but four legs. This horse belongs to one Iron nose, a witch, and so Argilus enters her service in order to obtain it. His duties are, first to control the witch's stud of brazen horses; next to look after her twelve black mares, who are her daughters, and then to milk them, and make a bath of their milk. He manages to do all by means of a magic staff, and so obtains the horse; whilst the witch is burnt to death in the bath which she thinks will make her young. The horse tells Argilus to wash it in the bath, and it at once becomes the colour of gold, and from every hair hangs a golden bell. With this horse Argilus carries off his wife. Holofernes follows on Taigarot, and not being able to overtake them, digs his spurs into Taigarot, [Pg 346]who in his indignation at such treatment kicks Holofernes off, and so breaks his neck.

For magic horses in other lands cf. the following tales:—the Finnish "Oriiksi Muntettu Poika;" "The Little White Horse" in "Ferdinand the Faithful," *Grimm*, ii. p. 156; Katar, in "The Bay with a Moon and Star," *Stokes*, p. 131, which becomes changed by twisting his right ear; "Weisnittle," in Stier's *Ungarische Volksmärchen*, p. 61; Sleipnir, Odin's eight-legged horse that used to carry the father of the gods as swift as the wind over land and sea, in Wagner's *Asgard and the Gods;* and "Bayard, Faithful Bayard!" the good steed in the Carolingian Legends in Wagner's *Epics and Romances of the Middle Ages*, pp. 367-396; "the shaggy dun filly" in "The Young King of Easaidh Ruadh," in *Campbell's Tales of the Western Highlands*, vol. i. p. 4; and the "steed," in "The Rider of Grianaig," vol iii. p. 14 of the same book.

A magic horse appears in the Lapp story "Jætten og Veslegutten," (The Giant and the Vesle Boy), from Hammerfest; *Friis*, p. 48. In this case it assists the boy to escape from the giant, and to marry a king's daughter; and finally becomes a prince when its head is cut off. "A winged horse" appears in "Ivan, Kupiskas Søn," a story from Akkala, in Russian Finland; *Friis*, p. 170. In "Jætten Katten og Gutten" (the Giant, the Cat, and the Boy), from Alten, *Friis*, p. 63, the boy saves the giant's son from a troll cat, and is told by the lad he saves, that his father will offer him a gold horse and "a miserable one," and he is to be sure and choose the miserable one; and in like manner he was to choose a miserable box, and a miserable flute, in preference to golden ones, which would be offered to him. There is a somewhat similar Finnish story, "Paholaisen antamat Soittoneuwot" (Musical Instruments Given by the Devil), *S. ja T.*, vol. i. p. 181, where the hero, when in the woods, sees the devil[122] running for his life, with [Pg 347]a pack of wolves at his heels. The lad shoots into the pack, killing one wolf, and thus terrifying the rest. The grateful devil promises the lad whatever he wishes. Acting on the advice of a maid in the devil's house, he asks "for the mare which is in the third stall, on the right-hand side of the stable." The devil is very loath to give this, but is obliged to do so, and gives the boy a kantele, a fiddle, and a flute besides. The mare acts the part of a Tátos for part of the tale, and then changes into a woman, being the wife of the king, who appears at the latter part of the story, and who orders the hero to perform difficult tasks. The kantele is like the fiddle in the "Jew in a thicket" (*Musical Myths*, vol. ii. p. 122; *Grimm*, vol. ii. p. 97), it makes every one dance that hears it. The woman drops out of the story, and the persecuting king is kicked up into the clouds by the irate devil who comes to help the hero, and is never heard of again.

A horse that can talk plays a prominent part in another Finnish tale, "The Golden Bird."—"Dapplegrim" is the magic foal in the Norse; see *Dasent*, pp. 313 and 367. See also the "brown foal" in *Grimm*, "Two Brothers," No. 107, and the "white horse," in "Ferdinand the Faithful," No. 126, and *note*.

Note also horses in "Der goldne Vogel," "Das Zauberross," and "Der Knabe und der Schlange," in Haltrich's, *Siebenbuergische Märchen*; "La Belle aux cheveux d'or," in *Contes des Fées*, par Mme. D'Aulnoy; "Schönchen Goldhaar," *Märchensaal aller Völker für Jung und Alt*, Dr. Kletke, i. p. 344; "Der goldne Apfelbaum," in Kaiadschitsch, *Volksmärchen der Serben*, p. 33; and Denton, p. 43. Enchanted horses play a prominent part in "Simple Johnny," p. 36, and "The Black Charger of Hernando," p. 292, in *Patranas or Spanish Stories*.—Cf. "The little Mare" from Mentone, *F. L. Record*, vol. iii. p. 44. The Russians tell of "a sorry colt rolling in the muck," which possesses marvellous powers in "Marya Morevna," *Ralston*, p. 94; and in "Koshchei, the Deathless," there is an heroic steed, *ibidem*, p. 101. See also "Ivan Kruchina," *Naake*, p. 124. "The marvellous white horse" appears also in Austria; see *Land of Marvels*, pp. 48, 256, 260, 272, 342.

In the story of the third royal mendicant, in the *Arabian Nights*, Agib mounts a black horse and flies through the air. Similar incidents [Pg 348]will be found in Nos. 1, 2, 4, 10, 17 of Dietrich's *Runische Volksmärchen*. Several variants, together with the author's view of their significance, are to be found in *Gubernatis*, vol. i., chap. ii.

The following, quoted from Stokes's *Fairy Tales*, p. 278, is worthy of notice:—

"On the morning of the day which was to see his last fight, Cúchulainn ordered his charioteer, Loeg, to harness the Gray to his chariot. 'I swear to God what my people swears' said Loeg, 'though the men of Conchobar's fifth (Ulster) were around the Gray of Macha, they could not bring him to the chariot.... If thou wilt, come thou, and speak with the Gray himself.' Cúchulainn went to him. And thrice did the horse turn his left side to his master.... Then Cúchulainn reproached his horse, saying that he was not wont to deal thus with his master. Thereat the Gray of Macha came and let his big round tears of blood fall on Cúchulainn's feet. The hero then leaps into his chariot and goes to battle. At last the Gray is sore wounded, and he and Cúchulainn bid each other farewell. The Gray leaves his master; but when Cúchulainn, wounded to death, has tied himself to a stone pillar to die standing, then came the Gray of Macha to Cúchulainn to protect him so long as his soul abode in him, and the 'hero's light' out of his forehead remained. Then the Gray of Macha wrought the three red routs all around him. And fifty fell by his teeth and thirty by each of his hooves. This is what he slew of the host. And hence is (the saying) 'Not keener were the victorious courses of the Gray of Macha after Cúchulainn's slaughter.' Then Lugaid and his men cut off the hero's head and right hand and set off, driving the Gray before them. They met Conall the Victorious, who knew what had happened when he saw his friend's horse. And he and the Gray of Macha sought Cúchulainn at the pillar-stone. Then went the Gray of Macha and laid his head on Cúchulainn's breast. And Conall said, 'A heavy care to the Gray of Macha is that corpse.' Conall himself, in the fight he has with Lugaid, to avenge his friend's slaughter, is helped by his own horse, the Dewy-Red. When Conall found that he prevailed not, he saw his steed, the Dewy-Red, by Lugaid. And the steed came to Lugaid and tore a piece out of his side."

[Pg 349]("Cúchulainn's Death," abridged from the "Book of Leinster," in *Revue Celtique*, Juin, 1877, pp. 175, 176, 180, 182, 183, 185).

See also, Grimm's *Teutonic Mythology*, Stallybrass, vol. i. pp. 328, 392; McGregor's *Folk-Lore of the North-East of Scotland*, p. 131; and Belludo, the goblin horse of Alhambra. Nor must we forget "Phooka," the wild horse of Erin's isle.

Note also the "Iliad"; cf. book ii. 760, book viii. 157, book x. 338, 473; specially Xanthus and Balius who talk, book xix. 440; and, Martial's splendid epigram, beginning "Phosphore redde diem, cur gaudia nostra moraris?"

Thus on every side we find this noble creature entwined in the lore of the people, from the peasants' dull superstition to great Milton's song,—

"Of the wondrous horse of brass,On which the Tartar king did ride."

The horse still plays an important part in the folk-lore. Thus *e.g.* Yorkshire people say, that if you see a piebald horse, and do not look at his tail, or think of a fox, whatever you wish for will be granted; also, that you must spit over your finger for luck when you see a white horse. The four black horses and chariot still rush through Penzance streets in the night, according to some, and the white horse is carried by the Christmas mummers in various parts of England and Germany. In the Midlands a horse's head and skin is dragged about on Christmas eve; a simulacrum, as some think, of Odin's heroic steed. Cf. *Henderson*, p. 70, also F. Finn and Magyar Songs on St. Stephen's Day. *Academy* 1884. pp. 150, 315.

Page 63. For breathing on old things and causing them to change, see p. 92, where the baa-lambs restore the lad's body by blowing; and a Finnish tale tells how a snake commands the hero to create with his clean breath a copper battlefield that they may fight, and is told by the man to create an iron one with his heathen breath, which he does; and other snakes come in the story who in turn create copper and silver battlefields, see Leppäpölkky, *S. ja T.* 2.

Sometimes the change is effected by a bath, as in "Fairy Elizabeth," p. 110, *supra.*

[Pg 350]Cf. *Grimm*, "Iron John," vol. ii. p. 195.

Page 65. A glass mountain appears in the "Iron Stove," *Grimm*, vol. ii. p. 161; "the princess on the glass mountain" in Thorpe's *Yule-Tide Stories*, p.86; and "The crystal mountain" in *Vernaleken* p. 276. It occurs also in a Lincolnshire story, where the forsaken wife sits at her husband's door and sings:

"Bare bull of orange return to me,For three fine babes I bore to thee,And climbed a glass hill for thee,Bare bull of orange return to me."*Folk-Lore Journal*, 1885, p. 188.[23]

See also notes to "The Little Magic Pony," *infra.*

The giant in "Handsome Paul," p. 26, like the Tátos in the present tale, tells his friend to shut his eyes and open them at intervals on account of the great speed they are going at; just as in the Finnish "Golden Bird," the young man on the wolf's back is obliged to rub his eyes with his handkerchief because the pace they are going at makes them water. In the hurry he drops it and asks the wolf to stop a minute to pick it up and is told it is already 1,000 miles behind them.

Page 66. Knight Mezey's wonderful sword is one of a numberless group of incidents wherein the sword plays an important part; in this story Mirkó ordered out his magic sword to protect him while he slept, and then to join with Knight Mezey's in mowing down the enemies. When he met Doghead (p. 73), their swords in like manner flew out of the scabbards and fought their masters' battles; and in the "Secret-keeping little Boy," p. 233, in this collection, the hero is born with a scabbard at his side, whilst a sword point appeared in the garden and grew as the scabbard grew; this sword cut up into pulp any one who came near its master on mischief bent. Alderblock's sword in the Finnish story in like manner flew out and cut Syöjätär into mincemeat. The Greeks told of "Harpé," the sword Hermes lent to Perseus, and of the honoured swords of Ulysses and Achilles.

Norse legends tell of wondrous swords, such as Odin's "Gram" that [Pg 351]he drove into an ash tree there to remain till the man should be found strong enough to draw it out.[24] Cheru's sword, forged by the dwarfs, "shone every morning on the high place of the sanctuary, sending forth its light afar when dawn arose like a flame of fire;" then there is Heimdal, born of nine mothers, the sword "Ase" of the Edda, who with his mighty sword made even cunning Loki cry for mercy.

In the Niebelungen there is "Balmung," craftily made by the dwarfs and tempered in dragons' blood, wherewith Siegfried smote the giants, and did mighty wonders, yea, even after its master's death slaying his enemies, till at last it rested on his grave by Brunhild's side. Roland wielded his good sword "Durindart," the gift of an angel, against the Paynim foe and did great wonders.

Dietrich in terrible conflict won "Eche-sax": Flammberg and the good horse Bayard wrought wonders in the days of Haymon and his children: Hunford's token of reconciliation to Beowulf, was the gift of "Hrunting" hardened in dragon's blood: Nägling, Nagelring, and Rosen, too, smote their worms, whilst "Mimung," good trusty Mimung, in the hands of heroes, did mighty wonders, even splitting asunder a floating pack of wool; and was so keen that Amilias did not know that Mimung had cut him in two till he shook himself; and lo! he fell into two pieces. Wayland Smith laboured in our own land, and brought forth a wondrous sword.

"Bitterfer, the sword hight,Better swerde bar never knight.Horn, to thee ich it thought,Is nought a knight in InglondSchal sitten a dint of thine hand;Forsake thou it nought."

[Pg 352]Charlemagne had his "Joyeuse"; Roland his "Durendal"; Arthur his "Excalibur"—

"All the haft twinkled with diamond sparks,Myriads of topaz-lights, and jacinth workOf subtlest jewellery."

A wondrous thing that "rose up out of the bosom of the lake," held by an arm "clothed in white samite, mystic and wonderful;" and when the sword was thrown back to the lake (its master's life being well nigh run) by the bold Sir Bedivere—

"behold an armClothed in white samite, mystic and wonderful,That caught him by the hilt, and brandish'd himThree times, and drew him under in the mere."

Cf. Wagner's *Epics and Romance; Asgard and the Gods; Morte d'Arthur*, book 1, cap. xxiii. and book 21, cap. v.; *Mythical and Mediæval Swords*, by Lady Verney, in *Contemporary Review*, October, 1880; *The Seven Champions of Christendom;* and Payne's *Arabian Nights*, vol. xi. pp. 129, 164.

In the Finnish "Oriiksi muutettu poika," the devil has a wonderful sword, which the hero obtains by the help of the horse: see also "The Water Smith," Keightley's*Fairy Mythology*, p. 260.—"Shortshanks," in *Dasent*, p. 153, gets possession of the only eye an old hag had, and so obtained "a sword, such a sword! It would put a whole army to flight, be it ever so great;" and certainly it chopped up sundry ogres later on in the tale; cf. p. 188 in the same collection.

The trap-door by which Mirkó entered the nether world appears in many stories, such as "St. Patrick's Purgatory"; see Baring Gould's *Curious Myths*, p. 230, and note to "Shepherd Paul" in this collection, *infra*.

Page 68. In the Lapp stories it is said that if Stallo's[25] dog is [Pg 353]not killed as well as the monster himself, that it will lick its master's blood and then Stallo will come to life again, just as the witch in this story is evolved out of the morsels of unburnt ribs. See "Stallo" and "Fogden i Vadsø, som gjorde sig til en Stallo," in *Friis*, pp. 74, 97.

Page 71. The flashing eyes of the princess remind us of the Gorgons. Her repentance is like that of the queen in the Russian story, who slays and restores the hero; *Ralston*, p. 235.

The "strength-giving fluid" occurs in numerous stories, *e.g.*, in the Finnish stories, "Alder Block," *S. ja T.*, ii., p. 2, and the "Enchanted Horse," where the hero cannot move an immense sword until he wets his head with the blood that is in a tub in the middle of the forbidden room in the devil's house. Cf. also *Ralston*, p. 237; *Dasent*, "The big bird Dan," pp. 445, 459; *Folk-Lore Record*, 1879, p. 99; and, "Irish Folk-Tales," *ibidem*, 1883, p. 55.

Sometimes it is a belt or ointment that gives strength, as in "The Blue Belt" and "The Three Princesses of Whiteland," in *Dasent*, pp. 178, 209. Cf. *ante*, p. 248.

A daughter explains to the hero how to conquer her father, in Brockhaus, *Märchensammlung des Somadeva Bhatta*, vol. i., p. 110.

Page 72. In the Karelian story "Awaimetoin Wakka," *S. ja T.* i., p. 151, the lad threw a great iron pole against Vääräpyärä's castle, in order to let the inmates know he was coming. In the Finnish "Alder Block," *S. ja T.* ii. p. 2, the hero throws or kicks off one of his shoes, and it flies to his comrades, and they come and help him.

In "The History of Gherib and his brother Agib," Terkenan threw an iron mace at his son with such power that it smote three stones out of a buttress of the palace; Payne's *Arabian Nights*, vol. vi., p. 152. See also "Story of Vasilisa" in Naake's *Slavonic Tales*, p. 57; and "Sir Peppercorn," in Denton's *Serbian Folk-Lore*, p. 128: where Peppercorn hurls the giant's mace back to him just as Mirkó did; and *Roumanian Fairy Tales*, p. 64.

As to the name "Doghead," see Notes to "The Three Dreams," *infra*, p. 377.

Page 74. The castle that collapses into an apple also appears in "The Three Princes," p. 206, in this collection.

[Pg 354]For a variant of Knight Mezey cf. "Zöldike," a Magyar tale, in *Gaal*, vol. iii., in which the beautiful meadow, the tent, the sleeping knight, and the witch weaving soldiers, all occur.

THE STUDENT WHO WAS FORCIBLY MADE KING. Kriza vii.

Page 77. Heroes of folk-tales often attain wealth, &c., by picking up some apparently useless thing on the road. See Halliwell, *Nursery Rhymes*, "The Three Questions;" "The Princess of Canterbury," pp. 153-155.

Oriental writers, Indian and Persian, as well as Arab, lay great stress upon the extreme delicacy of the skin of the fair ones celebrated in their works, constantly attributing to their heroines, bodies so sensitive as to brook with difficulty the contact of the finest shift, and we may fairly assume that the skin of an Eastern beauty, under the influence of constant seclusion and the unremitting use of cosmetics and the bath, would in time attain a pitch of delicacy and sensitiveness such as would in some measure justify the seemingly extravagant statements of their poetical admirers, of which the following anecdote (quoted by Ibn Khellikan from the historian Et Teberi) is a fair specimen. Ardeshir Ibn Babek (Artaxerxes I.), the first Sassanian King of Persia (A.D. 226-242), having long unsuccessfully beseiged El Hedr, a strong city of Mesopotamia, belonging to the petty king Es Satiroun, at last obtained possession of it by the treachery of the owner's daughter, Nezireh, and married the latter, this having been the price stipulated by her for the betrayal of the place to him. It happened afterwards that one night as she was unable to sleep and turned from side to side in the bed, Ardeshir asked her what prevented her from sleeping. She replied, 'I never yet slept in a rougher bed than this; I feel something irk me.' He ordered the bed to be changed, but she was still unable to sleep. Next morning she complained of her side, and on examination a myrtle leaf was found adhering to a fold of the skin, from which it had drawn blood. Astonished at this circumstance, Ardeshir asked [Pg 355]if it was this that had kept her awake, and she replied in the affirmative. 'How, then,' asked he, 'did your father bring you up?' She answered, 'He spread me a bed of satin, and clad me in silk, and fed me with marrow and cream and the honey of virgin bees, and gave me pure wine to drink.'—Payne's *Arabian Nights*, vol. ix., note to p. 148. Cf. "the Tale of the Dragon," in Geldart, *Folk-Lore of Modern Greece*, p. 142.

The same idea is the theme of *Andersen's* "The Princess and the Pea."—Cf. Finnish verse about the lovely Katherine, p. 314.

Page 78. The castle turns round upon the approach of the dragon in the story of "Vasilisa," in *Naaké*, p. 51; see also *Ralston*, p. 66.

THE CHILDREN OF TWO RICH MEN. Kriza viii.

For another variant cf. the Magyar tale "The Poor Man and His Child's Godfather" in Merènyi's *Eredeti Népmesék*, vol. i. See also the Finnish story, "Lehmää wuohena myöjä," ("The Man who sold his Cow as a Goat") from Tavastland and Karelia, *S. ja T.* ii. p. 126, which tells of a man being fooled into the belief that his cow was a goat, but in the end he overreaches the sharpers.

Cf. Dasent's *Tales from the Norse:* "Gudbrand on the Hill Side," p. 172; "Not a Pin to choose between them," p. 198; and "Big Peter and Little Peter," p. 387.

Grimm, "Wise Folks," vol. ii. p. 73; "Hans in Luck," vol. i. p. 325.

Ralston, *Russian Folk-Tales*, "The Fool and the Birch Tree" (Afanassieff V. No. 52), p. 49. Also the latter part of the "Bad wife," *ib.* i. No. 9.

Gubernatis, vol. i. pp. 44, 200, and 388.

Dublin Magazine 1868, p. 707, "Bardiello."

Payne's *Arabian Nights*, vol. iv. p. 223, "The Simpleton and the Sharper."

Udvalgte Eventyr og Fortællinger ved C. Molbech. *Kjöbenhavn*, 1843, p. 317, "Lön som forskyldt, et jydsk eventyr."

Myllenhoff, *Sagen, Märchen und Lieder der Herzogthümer Schleswig Holstein und Lauenburg.* (Kiel, 1845.) "Die reichen Bauern."

[Pg 356]J. W. Wolff (Leipzig, 1845), *Deutsche Märchen und Sagen*, ii. p. 52, "Die betrogenen Schelme."

Kletke, *Märchensaal aller Völker*, i. p. 98, "Herr Scarpacifico."

Il Pentamerone, ii. 10, "Lo compare."

Grimm, vol. i. "Clever Elsie," p. 138; Stokes, *Indian Fairy Tales*; "Foolish Sachúli," pp. 27, 257; *Folk-Lore Record*, 1884, p. 40, Variant of "The Three Noodles." See also Halliwell's *Nursery Rhymes*, "Mr. Vinegar," p. 149, and the well-known verses about the pedlar called Stout, and "The Wise Men of Gotham," pp. 24, 56.

Amongst the numerous other simpleton stories we may note those where people harrow up their feelings about that which might happen to as yet unborn children.

The following are Magyar simpleton tales:—

The people in one village tried to carry a ladder through a forest *across* their shoulders and cut all the trees down so as to get through.

In another: A stork soiled the new gold nob on the spire and they shot it so awkwardly that it hung there and disfigured the place worse than ever.

In another: Some grass was growing upon an old church: so, instead of cutting it and throwing it down, they erected an elaborate scaffold and pulled a bull up by a rope tied round his neck. The poor brute, half strangled, put out his tongue, whereupon they said, "See, he wants it already."

In another: When the Turks were coming they put a foal in a little grotto, and when it grew they could not get it out.

In another: By mistake they made it out that they ate the *same* lentils twice, which is still a joke against them.

In Finland there are many such tales current, of which the following are specimens. There is a village called Hölmöla, the inhabitants of which are said to be very cautious, and who always considered well before doing anything, lest they might get into trouble by overmuch haste. For instance, when they are going to cut their rye, they always take seven persons, one bent the rye-stalk down; another held a piece of wood under it; the third cut [Pg 357]the straw off; the fourth carried it to the sheaf; the fifth bound the sheaf; the sixth piled the sheaves together; and the seventh ricked them. Matti chanced to see them one day, and was struck with their manner of working. When evening came there was but a quarter of the field cut; so he thought he would do them a good turn, and set to work to cut and bind the rest. When he had finished he laid his sickle on the last shock and went to sleep. Next morning, when the Hölmöla people came, they found all cut, and the sickle lying on the shock. They were all astounded, and came to the conclusion that work done in such hurry must have been done by witchcraft, and that the sickle was the wizard who had transformed himself into that shape, and concluded that he ought to be drowned in order to prevent him interfering with honest folks' work for the future. As it was not deemed wise to touch such a creature, they fished it down by means of a long pole with a loop at the end, and dragged it to the shore, although it was very troublesome, as it would stick into the stubble and ditches, and try to prevent them dragging it along. At last it was got into a boat, and rowed off into the middle of the lake. They then tied a large stone to the handle with a strong rope, so that it might not float, and then with joyous shout threw it into the water. Unfortunately the sickle caught the bulwark of the boat; and, being weighted with a heavy stone, the boat canted over, and the good folks barely escaped with their lives from the wicked wiles of the wizard.[26]

Once they built a hut, and did it so thoroughly that they forgot the windows. When it was done, it was very dark, and so they sat down to consider how to get the light in. At last they hit upon a plan: the light was to be brought in a sack! So they opened the bag wide in the sunlight, and then, when it was full, tied it carefully up, and brought it in; but alas! the darkness was not enlightened. They were very much cast down at this; and while they pondered over it Matti passed by, and, hearing of their trouble, offered to get them the needed light for one hundred marks; and they were delighted to get it for so little. Matti cut a hole in the wall, and lo! the hut was flooded with light. The people were so delighted that they [Pg 358]decided to take the whole wall down. Now they had light enough, but unfortunately, just then the hut fell down.

The writer of this has often heard in Holderness of a man who could not get into his trousers, and used to get up hours before his comrade, and get into his trousers by setting them up by a chair and jumping into them; till at last he was told to sit down, and put on first one leg and then the other. This was a great revelation to him. Another man took his wheelbarrow to wheel daylight in, and worked away till he was told to open his shutters, and it would *come* in. One day another brilliant saw some grass in a church steeple, and was just going to hoist his cow up to it, when a friend pointed out to him that it was easier for *him* to go up and bring it down. When at school at Newcastle-on-Tyne, some twenty years ago, we were very fond of the story of a Dutchman, who, with his comrades, went out walking one night; saw the moon's reflection in the water, and thought it was a Dutch cheese. He determined that the best way to get it was to go on to the bridge, and by taking hold of each other's feet to form a chain, and so reach the cheese. The Dutchman was top man, and held on to the bridge. Just when the bottom man was about to seize the cheese, the Dutchman hollowed out, "Hold on a minute, till I spit on my hands!" and so they all fell into the water, and destroyed the cheese, besides other calamities![27]

Amongst the Lapps, it is the Giants, and Stallo who are fooled, *e.g.*: "Patto-Poadnje hævner sig paa Stallo," "En Askelad narrer Stallo," and an amusing story of how a dressed-up log was palmed off as a Lapp girl ("Stallobruden"). *Friis*, pp. 78, 90 and 98.

See also "Den listige Lappen," Hofberg, *Svenska Sägner*, p. 195; and a Russian variant given in *Ralston*, p. 53.

Forgetting to put the spigot into the vessel, and so losing all the wine, occurs in "The Husband who had to mind the House," *Dasent*, p. 310, and in *Grimm*, vol. i.; cf. also note to "Frederick and Catherine," p. 238; and "Clever Hans," p. 381.

Page 82. In *S. ja T.* ii. pp. 113-126, under head "Kuolema Kummina" ("Death as Godfather"), two stories are given which resemble [Pg 359]this part of the Magyar tale. In "Taiwaan wuohen synty" ("Heaven's Goat's Origin") from Karelia, a poor man has a child, and goes to look for a godfather. He meets a stranger, who turns out to be God; but the poor man will not have him, as he makes one poor and another rich. Soon after he meets Death, and him he accepts, for with him there are no favourites. Death gives his godchild three gifts: a chair that whoever sits down on it cannot get up without leave; a bag that is never empty; and the power to know whether a person will recover, by noticing whether Death stands at the head or foot of the bed. The man lived to be over three hundred years old by tricking Death; and when he died he was not admitted into heaven because he called God a deceiver, and so he still goes wailing in mid-air: and this was the origin of the Snipe. In the other story, "Taiwaasen menijä," (Going to Heaven,) from Kivigari in Tavastland, Death gives the man an ointment, as a christening present, to heal all, providing the man sees him standing at the foot of the patient's bed. Death is grossly deceived, and when the man does die, he only gets into heaven by a fluke. A variant of the whole story is "Gambling Hansel," *Grimm*, No. 81. See also: *Grimm*, vol. i. "The Godfather," p. 168; "Godfather Death," p. 171, and note, p. 391; and "Brother Lustig," p. 312. Grimm, *Deutsche Mythologie*, ii. p. 951; *Dasent*, "The Master Smith," p. 120; C. Molbech, *Udvalgte Eventyr*, No. 70: "Döden og hans Gudsön," and "Brave Petrus en zign Zak," a Flemish Tale in *Volkskunde*. Tijdschrift voor Nederlandsche Folklore onder redactie van Prof. A. Gittée 3e Aflevering 1888, may be quoted as further instances.

Mistress Death appears in "Starving John, the Doctor," in *Patrañas*, p. 125; and in *Vernaleken*, "Hans with the Goitre," p. 238, it is a skeleton.

In a Wendish Story, St. Hedwige stands as godmother; see *Dublin Magazine*, 1861, p. 355.

In the Russian Story, "The Bad Wife," *Afanassieff*, i. No. 9, quoted in *Ralston*, p. 39, the devil flies out of Tartarus, to get out of the bad wife's way, and assists her husband to become a great doctor. See also a Lapp variant, from Utsjok, "Kjærringen og Fanden," in *Friis*, p. 138.

[Pg 360]

THE HUSSAR AND THE SERVANT GIRL. Kriza xix.

Cf. *Dasent*, "The Dancing Gang," p. 507; and the "Drop of Honey," in Payne's *Arabian Nights*, vol. v. p. 275, where, we are told, "a certain man used to hunt the wild beasts in the desert, and one day he came upon a grotto in the mountains, where he found a hollow full of bees' honey. So he took somewhat thereof in a water-skin he had with him, and, throwing it over his shoulder, carried it to the city, followed by a hunting dog which was dear to him. He stopped at the shop of an oilman, and offered him the honey for sale, and he bought it. Then he emptied it out of the skin, that he might see it, and in the act a drop fell to the ground; whereupon the flies flocked to it, and a bird swooped down upon the flies. Now, the oilman had a cat, which pounced upon the bird, and the huntsman's dog, seeing the cat, sprang upon it and killed it; whereupon the oilman ran at the dog and killed it; and the huntsman in turn leapt upon the oilman and killed him. Now the oilman was of one village and the huntsman of another; and when the people of the two places heard what had passed, they took up arms and rose on one another in anger, and there befel a sore battle; nor did the sword cease to play amongst them till there died of them much people; none knoweth their number save God the Most High." See also, "*The Book of Sindibad*," Folk-Lore Society, 1882, p. 133.

MY FATHER'S WEDDING. Kriza x.

Cf. Halliwell, *Nursery Rhymes:* "Sir Gammer Vans," p. 147.

Grimm, vol. ii., "The story of Schlauraffen land," p. 229; "No-beard and the Boy," p. 518; "The Turnip," p. 213, and notes, pp. 413, 442, 452.

Vernaleken, "The King does not believe Everything," p. 241.

Caballero, *Fairy Tales*, "A tale of Taradiddles," p. 80.

[Pg 361]Denton, *Serbian Folk-Lore*, "Lying for a Wager," p. 107.

Stokes, *Indian Fairy Tales*, Nos. 4, 8, and 17.

Ralston, *Russian Folk-Tales*, p. 295.

Mr. Quigstad has kindly sent the following Lapp variants collected at Lyngen. There was once a pot so large that when cooking was going on at one end, little boys were skating at the other. One of the men to whom the pot belonged set to work to make his comrade a pair of shoes, and used up seven ox-hides on the job. One of them got a bit of dust in his eye, and the other sought for it with an anchor, and found during his search a three-masted ship, which was so large that a little boy who went aloft was a white-haired old man when he got back again. There were seven parishes in that ship!

"Lügenmärchen" are common in Finland, and generally turn on a big fish, or a big turnip, and a big kettle to boil it in, giant potatoes, huge mushrooms, and so on. A schoolboy's story in Newcastle-on-Tyne relates how one man told his comrade of a remarkable dream he had had of an enormous turnip; whereat his comrade replied he had dreamt about an enormous kettle which was to boil the turnip in.

The other day a Boston friend told the writer a Lincolnshire story of a man who grew such splendid turnips that there were only three in a ten-acre field, and one grew so big it pushed the other two out. This man had a mate who made such a big kettle, that the man at one side could not hear the rivetting at the other! I am told by my friend Prof. Gittée that similar tales are current in Flanders.

Another north country yarn tells of a naked blind man going out to shoot, and seeing six crows, he shot them, and put them in his pocket.

Page 88. The river Olt rises in Transylvania, and flows into the Danube in Wallachia, in which country it is called the Aluta.

THE BAA-LAMBS. Kriza xiv.

Cf. "Saint Peter's Goddaughter," in *Portuguese Folk-Tales*. Folk-Lore Society, 1882, p. 54.

Dasent, *Tales from the Norse*, "The Seven Foals," p. 349.

[Pg 362]Naaké, *Slavonic Tales:* "The Three Brothers", p. 254.

Stokes, *Indian Fairy Tales*, "The King's Son," p. 234; and the Servian tale quoted on p. 294.

Page 93. Kriza notes that the "rotting, dead dog's head" occurs in the "Historiae Tripartitae ex Socrate, Sozomeno et Theodorico in unum collectae," by Cassiodorus; ii. 12. The first edition appeared in 1472.

FAIRY ELIZABETH. Kriza xv.

Cf. Vernaleken, *In the Land of Marvels*, "The Outcast Son," p. 151.

Page 98. The Judas she-devil's service lasted for three days in "The Three White Doves," *Vernaleken*, p. 269.

Amongst the many stories in which time passes rapidly, see Gilmour, *Among the Mongols*, "The Wizard," p. 344; Ralston, *Russian Folk-Tales*, p. 304; Baring-Gould, *Curious Myths*, "The Seven Sleepers," p. 93; and *Friis*, "Troldkjaerringen og Jes," from Swedish Lapmark, p. 38.

In the Lapp tale, *Friis*, No. 45, swan-maids come and steal the corn, and the two elder sons fail to catch the thieves, Gudnavirus (Ashiepattle) the youngest, succeeding in doing so.

Page 99. Concerning the bird enticing the boy, cf. the bird that steals the jewel in "Kemerezzam and Budour," in Payne's *Arabian Nights*, vol. iii. p. 157.

Cf. also Rink, *Tales of the Eskimo*, "The Sun and the Moon," p. 236; *S. ja T.*, i., "Lippo ja Tapio," from Ilomantsi, p. 6; and *Friis*, Nos. 44 and 45.

In some other Magyar tales a lame wolf or a lame eagle takes the woodpecker's place. Cf. Gaal, "Többsinsckirályfi" ("Prince Non-such"). In a Bohemian story it is a limping cock-pigeon, see *Vernaleken*, p. 359.

Page 101. Numerous incidents in folk-tales bear on the widespread superstition against looking (or going) back after setting out on a journey.

Cf. *Friis*, "Ulta-Pigen," where a lad is returning home with his [Pg 363]bride; the girl warns him not to look back but he does, and lo! there is a great herd of beasts his wife's parents have given him. The moment he turned all those outside of the gate vanished; in "Jætten og Veslegutten," the lad fools the giant, because he dare not look back; and in "Bondesønnen og Solens Søster," the hero stumbles and falls and so sees behind him and in a moment the king's town and palaces disappear.

See also Rink, *Tales of the Eskimo*, "The Revived who came to the underground people," p. 300; Hofberg, *Svenska Sägner*, "Soåsafrun"; Stokes, *Indian Fairy Tales*, "The Bél Princess," pp. 140, 283; and Gregor, *Folk-Lore of North-East Scotland*, Folk-Lore Society, 1881, p. 91.

A Lincolnshire labouring man, when I lived in the north of the county, told me he knew a wizard who wished to mend the road that led to his house across a field. He ordered one of his men to take a cartful of stones and a rake and to set off to mend the road, which was to be done as follows. The cart was to be taken to the far side of the field, and driven slowly along the road that needed mending, but the man was under no circumstances to look back. He did as he was ordered, but there was such a noise behind him that when he had got nearly over the field he looked round, and lo! there were thousands of devils at work, who disappeared the moment he looked round, and the road is not done yet.

In the same part of Lincolnshire, one day when a lady had gone out with a child to be baptized she turned back as she had forgotten something; when she entered the house one of the servants begged her to sit down before she went out again or something terrible would happen. The same superstition exists in Holderness, Finland, Hungary, Algeria, and Sweden.

Page 101. Amongst the numberless examples of swan-maidens, cf. the following:

Friis, "Pigen fra Havet," p. 27; "Bæivekongens eller Solkongens Datter," p. 152; and "Goveiter-Pige," p. 39, where the girls appear in gorgeous dresses.

S. ja T. i. p. 35, "Tuhkamo"; and ii. p. 53, "Ei-niin-mitä."

[Pg 364]Hofberg, *Svenska Sägner*. "Jungfrun i Svanhamn," p. 27.

A story is current in Småland of a clergyman's son who assisted his father as curate. One morning when the young man awoke he saw the sun-beams coming in through a knot-hole in the floor, and suddenly a woman of marvellous beauty came floating in on the light and stood before him. He sprang up and threw his cloak over her and took her to his parents. She became his wife and lived happily with him for many years. One day he chanced to say how strange her coming was, and in order to emphasize his words he took the knot out of the hole in the floor, and in a moment she was gone!

In a Lapp story, *Friis*, No. 7, the girl tells her husband to drive a nail into the threshold to prevent her going away. See also "Lappen i Skathamn." *Hofberg*, p. 174.[28]

Other examples of the swan-maiden kind are to be found in:—

Rink, *Tales of the Eskimo*, "The Man who mated himself with a Sea-fowl," p. 146.

Keightley's *Fairy Mythology*, "The Peri Wife," p. 20; also p. 163, where seals are said to put off their skins; and "The Mermaid Wife," p. 169.

Legends of the Wigwam, "Son of the Evening Star," p. 81.

Stokes, *Indian Fairy Tales*, "Phúlmati Ráni," p. 6.

Steere, *Swahili Tales*, "Hasseebu Kareem Ed Deed," p. 355.

Household Stories from the Land of Hofer, "The Dove Maiden," p. 368.

Vernaleken, *In the Land of Marvels*, "The Three White Doves," p. 263; "The Maiden on the Crystal Mountain," p. 274; "How Hans finds his Wife," p. 281; and "The Drummer," p. 288.

Grimm, vol. ii. "The Drummer," p. 333.

Ralston, *Russian Folk-Tales*, p. 120.

Croker, *Fairy Legends of the South of Ireland*, "The Lady of Gollerus," p. 177.

Sagas from the Far East, pp. 29, 91.

Payne's *Arabian Nights*, "The Story of Janshah," vol. v. p. 98;

[Pg 365]"Hassan of Bassora," and the "King's Daughter of the Jinn," vol. vii. p. 145.

Portuguese Folk-Tales, Folk-Lore Society 1882, "The Spell-bound Giant," p. 35.

Folk-Lore Record, 1879, p. 12; 1883, pp. 203, 250, 284, 320; and 1884, p. 11.

Wägner's *Epics and Romances*, p. 280, see "Valkyrs"; *Asgard and the Gods*, sub voce "Walkyries."

Baring Gould, *Curious Myths*, sub "Swan-maidens."

Page 103. Anent the wedding here mentioned, it may be interesting to note some ceremonies connected with Magyar weddings in olden times. Love-making was very simple: there was no long courtship before the betrothal, and one meeting of the couple was often deemed quite sufficient.[29] The young folks did not choose their future companions, that being the parents' prerogative; and very often the match was arranged when they were in their cradles. It was not considered desirable to make connections with foreign families, and in case a girl was given away to a foreigner, one of the conditions insisted upon was that the husband should learn the language of the country. Francis Csáky was thrown into prison by his father because he would not marry Miss Homonmay, who had been selected as his wife. Occasionally, however, some choice was allowed; thus, for instance, Nicholas Bethlen was allowed to choose his wife from among the daughters of Paul Béldy and Stephen Kun. It was considered an offence if a young man, not being a relative, paid a visit to a house where marriageable girls[30]were, as he was suspected of courting the young ladies on the sly; if the young man was one whom the parents approved, a day was fixed for him to come and "see" the girls. On the appointed day the young man started on his journey with great pomp, and generally arranged to arrive about supper time (7 to 8 p.m.); if the sight was satisfactory, the girl's hand was at once asked for.[31] During [Pg 366]supper the young couple sat opposite to each other, and after supper there was a dance. Some parents left it to their daughters to decide, while others endeavoured "to enlighten them." If the father was dead the widow sought the advice of her eldest son, or of the children's guardian. If the young man was refused[32] he left the place, sometimes carrying the young lady off by force, as John Mikes did Sarah Tarnóczy. The asking for the young lady's hand was performed by that member of the family who had the greatest authority; if the offer was accepted the bridegroom fixed a day for the betrothal. Then came the interchange of rings. The betrothal ring was not a plain hoop, but one enamelled and set with diamonds or rubies. From the day of the betrothal they were considered engaged, and henceforth called each other "my younger sister" (hugom), and "my elder brother" (bátyám),[33] and the young man was allowed to make his offerings of gold and silver. The betrothal—called in Magyar "the clasping of hands"—and interchange of rings was considered binding on both parties, and a breach of promise was considered the greatest insult. Sometimes a sort of preliminary wedding was celebrated, thus Nicholas Bethlen went through the marriage ceremony soon after the interchange of rings, but a whole year elapsed before, he took his bride to his house.[34]

Sometimes an agreement was drawn up; and the wedding-day having been fixed by the bridegroom, it was communicated to the bride's father, so as to allow him to make his preparations. The number of the wedding guests often amounted to several hundreds. At the wedding of Barbara Thurzó, in 1612, seventy Magyar nobles of the highest rank appeared personally, besides several from the Austrian dominions. The king of Poland sent his sons and several ambassadors, the [Pg 367]number of the guests' horses being 4324.[35] The wedding-feast was sometimes utilized for the discussion of politics. All the inhabitants of the village were invited, bullocks with gilt horns were roasted, and a goodly number of knives stuck into them for the use of the people. The bread was exposed in troughs, and the wine in vats. Amongst people of modest means the forms were the same, the supplies being smaller. The expenses of the wedding were borne by the serfs.

The bridegroom chose his best man from among his near relations, the groomsmen were young friends. A widower had neither best man nor groom's men. The bride had a matron[36] who gave her away, and who, together with the bridesmaids were chosen from near relatives. There was generally also "a host" chosen from the higher nobility, and he carried a gold stick in his hand; the deputy host carried a stick painted green; these two walked about and looked after the guests. A few days before the wedding the guests met at the bridegroom's house, and on the night previous to starting a weeping soirée was held, when the bridegroom took leave of his bachelorship.[37] On the night previous to the wedding the bridegroom and his guests journeyed to a village near the bride's residence, and slept there. So far the bridegroom had come on horseback; but now he took his seat in a carriage, and in front of him rode two young nobles clad in wild animals' skins,[38] who were called "fore-greeters" (elölköszöntök). These were followed by pipers, drummers, and buglers. In the bridegroom's carriage the best man sat by his side, his groomsmen in the opposite seat. The "matron of the bedchamber" (nyoszolyó asszony) followed in another carriage preceded by two young nobles dressed in skins and on horseback. The procession was closed by the servants, leading gaily caparisoned horses. The two "fore-greeters" [Pg 368]saluted the chief host of the bride, who returned the greeting, and sent a message saying that the master would be heartily welcome: this was conveyed to the assembled guests, who thereupon proceeded to the bride's residence. When they arrived at the outskirts of the village, the bride's chief host sent a gold ring and some saddled horses, and a horse-race was at once got up,[39] the prize being the gold ring. Then the bridegroom sent his presents to the bride; the guests, too, sent their presents; as did also the representatives of the united towns and counties.

If the wedding was kept in a fortified town the guests were saluted by the firing of guns. The best man greeted the family of the bride, to which the chief host replied: thereupon the best man asked for the bride[40] and the chief host replied, endeavouring to pass a joke on the bridegroom and his best man, to which the latter replied as best he could. Then the chief host delivered up the bride, and, with a long speech, invited the guests to the midday meal.[41] The meal was a sumptuous feast; musicians discoursing sweet music as it proceeded. The chief host assigned the proper places to the guests. The bride was not expected to eat, but to weep. The banquet over, dancing began. The first dance was danced by the best man and matron, who were followed by the bride and bridegroom; the former simply walking through her dances: several other dances followed. The bride appeared in three different dresses on the wedding-day;[42] the bridegroom in three [Pg 369]different dresses on the three days of the wedding. When the bride appeared they played the "bride's dance." During the parting ceremony the bride went down upon her knees before her parents, and was handed over to the bridegroom, who unsheathed his sword and cut off the wedding wreath.[43] This ceremony was called "taking possession of the girl." The fortress guns thundered out to let the world know when it took place. The young couple remained with the bride's parents till the third day, when she distributed her presents, and then set off to her new home.[44]

See also an account of the Palócz wedding customs in the Notes to the "Girl with the Golden Hair," *infra.*

[Pg 370]There is a host of wedding and love songs, especially in cases where the ardent lover had to go far to meet his beloved, as for instance, the Lapps had to do. Two are given in Nos. 366 and 406 of the *Spectator.* The following[45] I do not think has ever been translated before:

No, not under the wide spreading heavenIs there so sweet and rich a flowerAs my own, dear, sweet, beloved one, she has all my poor heart.

When I travel over the windy AlpsI remember my own belov'd one,And in a moment it's calm and warm, as after Midsummer.

The tune is very sweet and plaintiff, like so many of the folk-songs, the translation conveys no idea of the sweet and liquid music that even the words of the original are brimful of.[46]

"*Six-ox farmers.*"—To say that a farmer ploughs his land with six oxen yoked to his plough means that he is very wealthy.

Page 104. The giant in an Austrian story (*Vernaleken*, p. 95) draws circles in the sand and a fowl appears; and in the Lapp story ("Ulta-Pigen." *Friis*, No. 7) the lad marks out on the ground the plan of a house, &c., at night, and in the morning all is found complete.

"My lad, it is a *burial* feast." Halotti tors or burial-feasts are still very common among the Magyar rural population.

Page 105. The trouble that comes from those at home[47] occurs over and over in all manner of folk-tales, *e.g.*, in the Lapp story ["Fattiggutten, Fanden og Guldbyen"] the lad, after meeting a beautiful girl who becomes his bride, insists upon going home to tell of his good [Pg 371]luck, and when there wishes for his bride and her attendants to appear, to prove that his story is true. They come, but vanish almost at once, and then comes the numerous troubles before the lost bride can be found. *Friis*, p. 161. In another, the son of the swan-maiden shows his mother her dress, which she at once puts on and vanishes, "Pigen fra Havet," *id.* p. 27, with which Cf. *Dasent.* "Soria Moria Castle," p. 466.

Vernaleken. "The Drummer," p. 289.

Payne, *Arabian Nights*, "The Story of Janshah," vol. v. p. 109, and "Hassan of Bassoria," vol. vii. p. 175.

Page 105, "Johara." There is no town of *Johara* in Hungary, but there is in Russia a province of the name of *Jugaria* or *Juharia*—according to Lehrberg the Югра or Угра, of old Russian records—whence "the Hungarians (*sic!*) proceeded when they took possession of Pannonia [their modern home] and subdued many provinces of Europe under their leader Attila."[48] According to Lehrberg,[49] it comprised the greater parts of the governments of Perm and Tobolsk of our days. It was said in Herberstein's time—his journeys were made in 1517 and 1526—that "the Juhari ... use the same dialect as the Hungarians, but whether this be true, I cannot say from my own knowledge; for though I have made diligent search I have been unable to find any man of that country with whom my servant, who is skilled in the Hungarian language, might have an opportunity of conversing."[50] Since Ivan the Terrible, the province gives a title to the Emperors of Russia.[51]

Cf. Payne, *Arabian Nights*, vol. v. p. 121, wherein the maid flies to "the Castle of Jewels." The man only gets there by the aid of birds and beasts, and it is the*third* and most skilful magician alone who summons [Pg 372]a bird, which is the only one who knows the far-off place. In another story, vol. vii., p. 176, the maiden flies to the "islands of Wac."

Dasent, p. 212, it is "Whiteland," and an old pike knows where it is.

Vernaleken, p. 251, Moon and Sun do not know where the mysterious place is, but the wind does. See also "the Drummer," p. 289, where the bride flies to the "Crystal Mountain."

In the Lapp stories we find "Banka Castle" and "Bæive-kingdom," and in an Irish tale, "Grey Horn's Kingdom," as the mysterious land.

The three men (or women) to whom the forsaken husband goes occurs in the Lapp stories, "Bondesønnen," "Bæive Kongens Datter," and "Fattiggutten," Nos. 44, 45, and 46, *Friis.*

Finnish, *S. ja T.* "Tuhkamo," i. p. 35, and "Ei-niin-mitä," ii. p. 53.

Vernaleken, "The Judas She-Devil," p. 255. "The Three White Doves," p. 264. "The Maiden of the Crystal Mountain," p. 275.

Folk-Lore Record, 1883, p. 319.

Portuguese Stories, F. L. Soc., 1882, p. 108, "The Prince who had the head of a Horse."

Grimm, vol. ii. pp. 381, 399.

The Whistle and Whip as a mode of summoning in common, see "Fisher Joe," p. 16, *ante.*

Page 108. "The Lame Woodpecker" reminds us of the lame devil in "Stephen the Murderer," p. 10; in *Vernaleken*, there is "a limper," p. 265, and a "lame hare," p. 275, the reluctance of the birds to take the man to Johara, &c., occurs in the Finnish and Lapp stories referred to.

Page 109. "Youth-giving water." Cf. "The Fairies Well," in present collection, p. 295. In Hungary snow-water collected in March is said to possess the same virtue.

Cf. also *Finnish*, "Tuhkamo." *S. ja T.* i. p. 43, where Ashiepattle washes in a well and becomes marvellously beautiful.

[Pg 373]*Lapp*, "Bæivekongen.". *Friis*, p. 152. Where the lad dips his sore head into a kettle and becomes beautiful and golden haired. See also *Folk-Lore Record*, 1879. "Old Ballad Folk-Lore," p. 100. In "The Jewel in the Cock's Head," an Italian story, quoted in the *Dublin Magazine*, 1868, p. 706, the hero at once becomes young and handsome by the virtues of the jewel, and in a Finnish story, "The Enchanted Ship," the same end is attained by eating some berries. Cf. the effect of the Tàtos and baa-lambs breathing on anything, pp. 63 and 92 *ante*; also *Dasent*, p. 362; and such stories as "The Old Man made Young," *Grimm*, vol. ii., p. 215, and note, p. 444.

There are numerous springs and wells whose waters are said to possess marvellous powers, such as St. Winifred's in Flintshire, St. Keyne's in Cornwall, St. Bede's at Jarrow, &c. See Chambers' *Book of Days*, sub voce "Wells"; *Henderson's* "Wells"; Hardwick, *Traditions, Superstitions, and Folk-Lore*, p. 267; and Aubrey, *Remains of Gentilisme*, F.L.S., 1880, pp. 121.

THE THREE PRINCES. Erdélyi, i. 1.

Cf. *Grimm*, vol. i. "The Gold Children," and note; vol. ii. "The Two Brothers," p. 244, and notes, p. 418; in "Ivan Kupiskas Søn." *Friis*, p. 170, a bear, a wolf, and a dog help the hero.

See also *Dasent*, "The Blue Belt"; and Denton, *Serbian Folk-Lore*, "The Three Brothers."

Page 111. In explanation of the fact that the wolf, lion, and bear are sometimes called "dogs," and other times "servants," we may mention that is quite common in Hungary to address a dog as "my servant;" and the three brutes in the story are supposed to follow their masters like dogs. For animals and birds that help, cf.*Ralston*, "The Water King," p. 120. *Old Deccan Days*, "Punchkin," p. 14. *Vernaleken*, "The Three White Doves," p. 269, and "The Enchanted Sleep," p. 312.*Sagas from the Far East*, p. 137. *Friis*, "Jaetten Os Veslegutten." *Uncle Remus*, No. xxii. and notes to Prince Csihan.

[Pg 374]The sticking of knives into a tree to tell of the fortune or misfortune of the owner occurs also in "Knight Rose," see notes there, and p. 257.

A town draped in black cloth appears in *Grimm*, vol. i. note, p. 421. *Dasent*, "Shortshanks," p. 160. *Vernaleken*, "The Cobblers Two Sons," p. 197.

The dragon that devours a virgin every week reminds us of St. George, see Baring Gould, *Curious Myths*, "St. George," and *The Seven Champions of Christendom*. Cf. *Grimm*. *Stories from the Land of Hofer*, "The Three Black Dogs," p. 214. *Friis*, Bondesønnen and *Dasent*, p. 158.

Page 112. "The healing weed;" see note to "Knight Rose," p. 342.

The dragon in *No. 7, Pentamerone*, when one of its heads is cut off, rubs itself against a certain leaf and the head is at once fastened on again.

The treachery of the Red Knight which appears in this story has already been noticed in the notes to "The Hunting Princes." Cf. *Dasent*, "Big Bird Dan."

Page 113. Animals restore their master to life in *Grimm*, vol. i. p. 253. *Friis*, "Ivan," p. 170. *Ralston*, p. 231. *S. ja T.* i. "Här'än korwista syntyneet Koirat siw" (The Dogs who grew from the Ears of a Bull), p. 138; in another Finnish story, "The Golden Bird," the hero is restored to life by a wolf, after being slain by his treacherous brothers. In the Kalevala it is a bee that brings the honey which restores Lemminkäinen; Rune 15, 530.

The prince thinks he has been asleep, just as Lemminkäinen does in Kalevala, Song 15, 559. Cf. "Golden Hair," *Naaké*, p. 108; "Marya-Morevna," *Ralston*, p. 91.

Page 114. "Henczida to Bonczida," names of villages, the former in the county of Bihar, the latter in Kolozs.

Page 115. The witch throwing down a rod or hair; see also "Knight Rose," cf. *Portuguese Folk-Tales*, Folk-Lore Society, 1882, "The Tower of Ill-Luck," p. 49. Basile, *Pentamerone*, No. 7, where a fairy binds Cienzo by her hair. Denton, *Serbian Folk-Lore*, "The Three Brothers," p. 275.

[Pg 375]It is curious the part hair plays in popular lore.[52] According to the old idea that any part of a person, such as his hair, nail clippings, &c. was to all intents and purposes himself (see notes to "The Lazy Spinning Girl"[53]); so it appears here the witch's power would be conveyed by one of her hairs, just as the witch in the "World's Beautiful Woman" spits on the child's face with the hope of conveying her enchantment, p. 166. See *Henderson*, *sub voce*, "Hair." Black, *Folk Medicine in Wäs.*

Page 116. The unsheathed sword in bed occurs in the story of Siegfried and Brunhild. Cf. also *Dasent*, "The Big Bird Dan," p. 450; Payne's *Arabian Nights*, "The Story of Prince Seif el Mulouk," vol. vii. p. 94; *Pentamerone*, i. 9; and *Gubernatis*, vol. i. 330.

THE THREE DREAMS. Erdélyi, i. 2.

Cf. "The Secret-keeping Little Boy," p. 233, in this collection.

According to Ladislaus Arany,[54] an almost exact version of the tale is given in Schott's *Wallachische Märchen* (No. 9). Schott calls attention to the resemblance of this tale to the story of Joseph, in the Old Testament, who is released from prison and exalted for the successful solution of dreams. See also two stories from Radloff, *Proben der Volkslitteratur der Türkischen Stämme Süd-Siberiens*, quoted in *Gubernatis*, vol. i. pp. 139-142.

The "Operencziás Tenger," is the mythical sea of Hungarian folk-tales. With regard to the etymology of the word, it is said by some to come from the expression "ober der Enns," in the German name [Pg 376]of the Duchy of Upper Austria. The etymology is given for what it is worth. As to the cosmology of the story-tellers, all we can say is, that they appear to uphold the Zetetic school. The earth is flat, and surrounded by the Operenczian sea: beyond that is fairyland.

The Magyar peasants think much of dreams, as may be seen in their wonderful dream-book, "*A legrégibb és legnagyobb Egyiptomi Almoskönyv*," a work something in the same style as the dream-books that are still common in country places in England.

The significance of dreams is noticed in *Uarda*, cap. xv. Cf. *Denton*, "The Dream of the King's Son." *Horace*, c. *iii. xxvii.* 41; S. i. x. 33. *Homer* says that dreams of falsehood passed through an ivory gate in the lower world: true ones through a gate of horn.

See also Tylor, *Early History of Mankind*, pp. 5-10; and *Primitive Culture*, "Dreams."

There are many stories of dreams which foretold wealth and power, or were the means of the dreamer attaining them, *e.g.* "Gontram the good King of Burgundy," Claud Paradin, *Symbola*

Heroica. Also Chambers's *Book of Days*, vol. i. pp. 276, 394, 617; vol. ii. p. 188. The writer remembers hearing an almost precisely similar story to the last, when the ill-fated "Lifeguard" was lost on her way from Newcastle to London.

The Indians pay great attention to their dreams during the long fast at the beginning of manhood: see *Legends of the Wigwam*, p. 99. In some stories one of the chief characters pretends to dream that she may obtain certain information, such as "Luxhale's wives:" *Stories from the Land of Hofer*, p. 317.

It is a common superstition in Holderness that a morning dream is sure to come true, but if it is told to anyone before breakfast, it will not.

Page 118. "Immured alive": see a Magyar folk-song, "Clement the Mason," in the *Academy*, July 31, 1886. Cf. a paper read by Oscar Mailand before the Historical and Antiquarian Society of the County of Hunyad (April 29, 1885) on the legend of the building of the Monastery at Arges in Roumania. The story is nearly the same as [Pg 377]in the song of "Clement the Mason." Manuli, the master builder, has a dream, wherein he is recommended to immure the first woman that appears on the scene; the victim is Manuli's wife. During the discussion that followed, the president, Count Géza Kuun, mentioned that the same tale is told of the castle of Dévén in the county of Nógrád; the fortress of Dévény near Pozsony (Pressburg); and of another fortress in the Trans-danubian division, and that the legend is of Slavonic origin.

Grimm, ii. "Maid Maleen," p. 350.

Livius, viii. c. 15, "Virgo Vestalis damnati incesti, viva deforsa est."

The king vows to slaughter thirty Muslims at the gate of his palace, when complete, in "Ali Noureddin." Payne's *Arabian Nights*, vol. viii. p. 141.

Folk-Lore Journal, 1880, p. 282; January 1883, "A Bewildering Superstition."

Cf. also the incident in "Secret-keeping Little Boy", p. 238.

"*Dog-Headed Tartars*." Our story-tellers almost invariably use the epithet "dog-headed" when speaking of their old enemies, the Tartars. Medieval travellers, who wrote in Latin, speak of the Great Khan of Tartary as "Magnus Canis." Cf. *The Travels of Friar Odoric*, in *Cathay and the way Thither* (Hakluyt Soc. 1866). The learned editor remarks (p. 128, note): "I am not sure that a faithful version should not render 'Magnus Canis' as the 'Great Dog,' for in most copies the word is regularly declined 'Canis,' 'Cani,' 'Canem,' as if he were really a bow-wow. According to Ludolf, an old German translation of Mandeville does introduce the mighty prince as 'Der grosse Hund.'"

The irruption into Hungary of the Tartars under Batu Khan, in the thirteenth century, and their frightful slaughter and terrible devastations are sufficiently known, and need not further be enlarged upon here.

With regard to dog-headed people (cf. the Kynokephaloi of Ktesias), such people are often mentioned in ancient travels; thus, Odoric of Pordenone says: "[L'Isola che si chiama] Nichovera ... nella [Pg 378]quale tutti gli nomini [h]anno il capo a modo d'un cane." From an old Italian MS. text in the Bibl. Palatina at Florence, printed in*Cathay and the Way Thither*, p. 51.

The womankind of dog-headed people are always described as beautiful. Cf. the travels of Friar Jordanus, Odoric of Pordenone, Ibn Batuta. Cf. also the lovely wife of old Doghead in "Prince Mirkó" in this volume; and *Gubernatis*, vol. i. Preface, xix.

Page 120. "Born with a caul."

In Holderness and North Lincolnshire, a caul is said to prevent the owner from drowning. I have heard others say, that you can tell by its condition what the state of its owner's (the one who was born with it) health is, even if he (or she) is in a distant land. So long as it keeps as it is he is well, but if it "snerkles up" he is dead.[55] It is commonly called a "sillyhood" in the North.

Cf. *Henderson*, pp. 22, 23. *Aubrey, Remaines of Gentilisme*, p. 113.

Gregor, *Folk-Lore of North-East of Scotland*, p. 25.

Grimm, i. Hans in Luck. "I must have been born with a caul," p. 329.

Napier, *Folk-Lore*, p. 32.

Babies born with teeth are said by the Magyar peasants to be the children of witches; see Varga János, *A babonák Könyve*, Arad, 1877, p. 70.

Babies born with teeth are regarded as different to other children, in some parts of England, but the superstition is vague. A friend had a servant who was born with a grey lock, and the writer has often seen the girl; it was regarded as somewhat uncanny. Francisque Michel mentions in his *Histoire des Races Maudites*, that in the Valley of Argelès old women, when quarrelling with a cagot, shew their tongue "ou derrier l'oreille"; this is to remind the poor man of the wisp of hair on his ear, which is considered uncanny.

Page 120. The incident of the lad disguising himself so as to be exactly like his comrades occurs also at p. 241, in "The Secret-Keeping Little Boy." To be able to select the right person from several is [Pg 379]looked upon as a test of the magic power of the person tried as in this case.

Cf. *Naaké*. "Golden Hair," p. 107.

Vernaleken. "How Hans finds his Wife," p. 284.

Folk-Lore Record, 1883. Ananci Stories, p. 284; and the Polish story, "Prince Unexpected," *ib*. 1884, p. 13.

S. ja T. i. "Kulta-orit," p. 187.

Cf. *Folk-Lore Record*, 1880, "Mons Tro," p. 220.

Page 121. In the Lapp story, "Patto-Poadnje." *Friis*, p. 78, the Stallo's wife suspects there is something wrong with the soup, which is in reality made of her late husband, but the man fools her by saying he cut his finger while making it.

In the Finnish story, "Tynnyrissä kaswanut Poika," ("The Boy who grows in a Barrel"), *S. ja T*. i., p. 105, there are nine cakes made of a woman's milk. Cf. "How the widow saved her son's life," *Sagas from the Far East*, p. 207.

We may here note the constant difficulties that appear in the folk-tales, and thwart the love-making of the heroes and heroines. Commonly it is the king who does all he can to prevent the lovers being happy, or it is some one at home who causes infinite trouble. For examples of the tasks that the lover or husband has to accomplish, see the tales "Fisher Joe," "Handsome Paul," "Fairy Elizabeth," "The Three Brothers," "The Girl with the Golden Hair," &c., in this volume.

Cf. also *Friis*. "Ruobba. Jætten og Fanden," p. 67; "Bondesønnen. Kongesønnen og Solens Søster," p. 140; "Solkongens Datter," p. 152; "Gutten, som tjente hos Kongen," p. 167.

S. ja T. ii. "Leppäpölkky" ("Alder Block"), p. 2; "Maan, meren kulkija laiwa" ("The Ship that sails over Land and Sea"), p. 22; "Kaikkia, matkalla karwitaan" (All is useful in a Voyage), p. 29; and "Lakwan tekijät," (Ship Builders), p. 33.

Basile. *Pentamerone*. No. 23.

Schott. *Wallachische Märchen*, No. 24.

Ralston. "The Water King," p. 120.

Sagas from the Far East. "How Shanggasba buried his Father," p. 189.

[Pg 380]See also the troubles in getting to Johara in Notes to "Fairy Elizabeth," *ante*.

CSABOR ÚR. Erdélyi, i. 3.

According to some writers this story refers to King Matthias and his black troop. It is a Csángó tale.[56]

These traditional stories, as specimens of folk-history, are of great interest, showing how the kindness or tyranny of some lord or lady clings to the popular mind, and how all manner of stories attach themselves to great names.

Cf. "Herrn till Rosendal," in Hofberg, *Svenska Sägner*, p. 14; "Herrskapet på Ugerup," p. 17, where Arild dupes the Danish king by obtaining leave of absence until he reaps his harvest, he having sown fir-cones. (A variant of which the writer has heard amongst the peasants of the Eastern counties) and "Elestorps skog," p. 71, where the whole forest seems on the move as in *Macbeth*, act v. scene v. See [Pg 381]also "An ancient Arabian parallel," by Dr. Redhouse, in the *Academy*, July, 24, 1886. See also "Snapphane-grafven," *ib*. p. 75, a story of a heap of stones,[57] now known as the "freebooter's grave," that tells how a brave peasant slew the chief of the plundering band and so dispersed them.

"Grefvinnan på Höjentorp," *ib*. p. 97, which is a good example of how historic incident is moulded and blended in the popular lore, and it may be of interest to give it here. Shortly after Charles XI. had seized the greater part of his nobles' property, he went to see his aunt Maria Eufrosyna and was saluted with a sound box on the ear, and upon asking why she did it was told he got it for taking all her property from her. They entered the house where a herring tail and an oat cake was set before the king, and he was told as he had made his bed so must he lie on it. The king then asked his aunt if he might take care of her riches for her, but was saluted with such a box on the ear that he fled and left her to enjoy her estates in peace.

"Fru Barbro på Brokind," *ib*. p. 112, is an example of how the memory of a tyrant lives.

"Qvick i jord," *ib*. p. 122, tells of a terrible outbreak of plague, and how a Finn advised the people to bury a live cock, but as the plague raged as fiercely as ever a live goat was buried, and then a living boy.[58]

"Jonas Spets," p. 123, tells how the king found an old soldier sharpening (putting a point to) his sword and was warned to use it well on the morrow. After the battle the king ordered him to show his sword, and lo! it was dripping with blood. "Well done," said the king, "I will gild the point for you," and so he ennobled the soldier and changed his name to "Gyllenspets" (Golden-Point). This, according to the popular story, is the way the family of Gyllenspets in Vermland became nobles.

[Pg 382]The writer heard the following from old men in North Lincolnshire.

LIMBER.—There have been great wars and battles all over here and most of them are attributed to Cromwell. At Riby there was a fearful fight, the blood ran as deep as the horses' bellies, and to this day there is an opening in the hedge, where nothing will ever grow, known as Riby Gap, and there the blood flowed deepest.[59]

THORNTON ABBEY.—There was a great battle there and the soldiers knocked the church down and the town that used to be near it.

YARBOROUGH CAMP[60]—according to popular belief—was made by Cromwell's soldiers, who are said to have sat behind the entrenchment when firing at their enemies.

MELTON ROSS.—Perhaps the most curious is the tale told by an old groom about the gallows at Melton Ross:—

Some hundred years ago or so three or four boys were playing at hanging, and seeing who could hang the longest on a tree, when a three-legged hare (the devil, sir), came limping past; off ran the lads who were on the ground after him and forgot their comrade, who when they came back was dead. The gallows was put up in memory of that. The true story is that there was a rivalry between the Ross family and the Tyrwhits, and to such a pitch had it grown among their dependants that the two parties meeting on a hunting excursion got to blows and many were killed. James I. being in Lincolnshire shortly after, and hearing of it, ordered a gallows to be erected where the fight occurred, and enacted that in the future any persons slain in an encounter of this kind should be deemed murdered, and the perpetrators of the crime hanged. A gallows is always kept on the spot and when the old one falls to decay a new one is erected.[61]

Page 125. Permanent blood stains. Cf. those of Rizzio in Holyrood Palace; those in the Carmelite convent in Paris, said to have been made by murdered priests in the revolution; those at Cottele, on the banks of the Tamar, blood of the warder slain by the Lord of the Manor; those in Sta. Sophia, at Constantinople, &c.

[Pg 383]

THE DEVIL AND THE THREE SLOVAK LADS. Erdélyi, ii. 1.

Cf. *Grimm*, vol. ii. "The Three Apprentices," pp. 132, 418. *Stier*, No. 25.

A similar story used to be current among the schoolboys in Northumberland.

THE COUNT'S DAUGHTER. Erdélyi, ii. 2.

The writer of this remembers his grandmother telling him this story when he was a boy in Newcastle on Tyne.

Cf. *Grimm*, i. "The Robber Bridegroom," pp. 164, 389.

Chambers, *Book of Days*, vol. i. p. 291, "Mr. Fox."

Halliwell, *Nursery Rhymes*, p. 164, "The Story of Mr. Fox"; and Benedict, in "Much Ado About Nothing," act i. scene i.[62]

Cf. *Hofberg*, p. 14, "Herrn till Rosendal," where the horrors of the lord's house drives his betrothed away; and the "Iron Virgin," of Munich, who was said to clasp the doomed in her arms and pierce them with spikes. *Fraser's Magazine*, 1872, p. 354.

The story reminds us strongly of Blue Beard. Cf. *Notes and Queries*, 7th S. ii. p. 321.

THE SPEAKING GRAPES. Erdélyi, ii. 3.

Cf. Thorpe. *Yule-Tide Stories.* "Prince Hatt under the Earth," p. 15. Stokes' *Indian Fairy Tales*, "The Fan Prince," p. 195. *Grimm*, vol. ii. "The Singing, Soaring Lark," p. 5, and Variants given on pp. 378, 382. *Gubernatis*, vol. ii. Story from Piedmont, p. 381, [Pg 384]and a Tuscan tale, p. 382. In the latter, the father, who has promised his daughter a rose, forgets it, and his ship refuses to move on the homeward journey, and so he goes to a garden to get the rose, which is given to him by a hideous magician. This reminds us of the Finnish story, "Jykeä Lipas" (The Heavy Chest), *S. ja T.* ii. p. 146, where a man who was ploughing near a lake, went down to the strand to drink. When he had done drinking he tried to raise his head but could not, as a sea-troll had got hold of his beard,[63] and although the man repeated all manner of magic sentences he could not get away. The man at last had to promise his daughter, and so was set free: the story then turns on the forbidden chamber. In another, "Awaimetoim Wakka" (The Keyless Chest), *S. ja T.* i. p. 151, a man was lost and wanted to get home, when a being appeared and promised to take him if he would give him what he had at home, which turns out to be a beautiful child. Cf. "The King and the Devil," p. 189, in this collection. In Lapp stories the devil comes in. Cf. "Fattiggutten, Fanden og Guldbyen;" *Friis*, p. 161, where he promises plenty of fish to a poor man if he will promise what his wife "carries under her heart;" in another, "Gutten, Havfruen og Ridder Rød," *Friis*, p. 131,[64] a mermaid stops the king's ship and won't let it go till the king promises what his wife is bringing into the world. The latter part of the Finnish and Lapp stories is not like the Magyar, but rather reminds us of "Stephen the Murderer," and the latter part of "Shepherd Paul."

The "Dirty, filthy pig," that helps, is a variant of the huge frog that will not allow the girl to draw water from the well until she gives it her ring. Cf. "The wonderful frog," p. 224, and notes.

For the youngest daughter who wishes for such out-of-the-way, and in many cases utterly incomprehensible objects, Cf. Stokes' *Indian Tales*, "The Fan Prince," where the girl wants "Sabr," p. 195; and "The Rájá's Son," where the young man hears some parrots talk about the Princess Labám, whom he determines to find, p. 154; and the "Bél [Pg 385]Princess," p. 138. Mr. Ralston also notes *Afanassieff*, vol. i. No. 14, and vol. vii. No. 6.

Page 131. The king tries to deceive the pig, in the same way as he, the king, on p. 191 tries to deceive the devil.

Usually, there is a long series of troubles between the enchanted one appearing in some loathsome form and the revelation of the prince in all his beauty, as in the well-known story of "Beauty and the Beast."[65] Cf. "Prince Wolf," *Folk-Lore Record*, 1880, p. 227. "Prince Jalma," *ib.* 1885, p. 293. On the subject of "Husks," or glorious beings occurring under lowly forms, see in this collection the snake in "Knight Rose," "The Wonderful Frog," "Snake Skin," the youngest daughter in "The Three Princesses," and notes to "The Three Oranges," "Cinder Jack," and "The Widower and his Daughter."

Cf. also: The boy in the Lapp stories that wears a hat to hide his golden helmet. *Friis*, "Jætten og Veslegutten." *Stokes*, "The Monkey Prince," and "The Boy who had a Moon on his Forehead, and a Star on his Chin," pp. 126, 130, and note, p. 280. *Old Deccan Days*, "The wanderings of Vicram Maharajah," p. 119, "The Jackal, the Barber, and the Brahmin," p. 167, and "Muchie Lal," P. 221.[66] *Dasent:* Hacan Grizzlebeard. Also, "The twelve wild ducks" in the same collection, where the brothers appear under the form of ducks. Cf. the Finnish "Weljiänsä-etsijät ja Joutsenina lentäjät" (one who seeks brothers flying as swans): "Saaressa eläjät" (living on an island). "Tynnyrissä kaswanut poika" (a boy grown in a barrel); *S. ja T.* i. *Märchensaal aller Völker von Kletke*, No. 2. "Die Drei Königskinder." *Household Stories from the Land of Hofer*, "The grave Prince and the beneficent Cat." *Grimm* ii. "The Donkey." "The Goose-girl at the Well," and note, p. 441. *Sagas from the Far East*, pp. 28, 92, 222, 244, and 274.

[Pg 386]

THE THREE ORANGES. Erdélyi, ii. 4.

Page 133. In "Loving Lailí." *Stokes*, p. 81, the prince is commanded to open the fruit when he is alone, as Lailí will be inside quite naked. See also *ib.* pp. 251, 284, and *Grimm* ii. p. 496. *Pentamerone*, "The Three Citrons." *Portuguese Folk Tales*, p. 10, F. L. S. 1882; also *Dasent*, p. 437, "The Cock and Hen a-nutting."

Page 134. The changed bride occurs in the Finnish "Merestänousija Neito." (The Sea-Maid.) *S. ja T.* i. p. 77, and "Ihmeellinen Koiwu" (The wonderful Birch) *S. ja T.* i. p. 59. *Portuguese Folk-Tales*, "The Maid and the Negress," F. L. S. 1882. *Stokes, Indian Fairy Tales*, pp. xxiii. xxv. 3, 143, 284. *Dasent*, "The lassie and her Godmother," p. 219, and the "Bushy Bride," p. 376. *Grimm*, ii. "The Goose-girl;" "The White Bride and the Black one," and "The Maid Maleen," pp. 508, 525. *Friis*, Lappiske Eventyr, "Haccis-ædne," see "N. and Q." 7th Series, ii. p. 104. *Pentamerone*, "The Three Citrons." Geldart, *Folk-Lore of Modern Greece*, "The Knife of Slaughter," p. 63. *Folk-Lore Record*, 1884, p. 242, *ib.* 1885, p. 292. *Gubernatis*, vol. ii. p. 242. Thorpe, *Yule-Tide Stories*, pp. 47, 54, 62. Gerle,*Volksmärchen der Böhmen* No. 5. "Die Goldene Ente." Hyltén-Cavallius. *Svenska Folk Sagor*, No. 7, "Prinsessan som gick upp ur hafvet." Cf. also Steere,*Swahili Tales*, p. 398. Rink, *Eskimo Tales*, p. 310; and Denton, *Serbian Tales*, p. 191; also pp. 214 and 222, in this collection.

Page 135. The feigned illness occurs in numerous stories, *e.g.*: *Deccan Days*, "Punchkin," p. 5. *Dasent*, "Katie Woodencloak," p. 413. *Payne*, vol. i. "The first old man's story," p. 21. *Stokes*, "The Pomegranate King," p. 9. *Records of the Past*, vol. ii. "Tale of the Two Brothers," p. 149. *Friis*, "Ivan, Kupiskas Søn," p. 170.

Page 136. House tidying incident. Cf. *Grimm*, vol. i. p. 226. "Sweetheart Roland."

[Pg 387]

THE YOUNGEST PRINCE, AND THE YOUNGEST PRINCESS. Erdélyi, ii. 5.

Page 137. Good luck coming from being under a tree. Cf. p. 323 in this collection; and Rink, *Eskimo Tales*, "Kagsagsuk," p. 101. Stokes, *Indian Tales*, "The Fan Prince," p. 198, and "The Bed," p. 204. *Pentamerone*, "The Raven."

Page 138. Old one who helps. Vernaleken, *In the Land of Marvels*, "The Three Tasks," p. 226, and "Piping Hans," p. 221. *S. ja T.* "Maan, meren kulkija laiwa" (a ship which can sail on land and sea), vol. ii. p. 22, and "Ihmeellinen Sauwa" (the wonderful stick), *ib.* vol. i. p. 158. In Vicram Maharajah, *Old Deccan Days*, p. 101, the parents of Anar Ranee caused her garden to be hedged round with seven hedges made of bayonets, so that none could go in or out, and published a decree that none should marry her but he who could enter the garden and gather the three pomegranates in which she and her maids slept.

Page 139. The horse incident. Cf. Trojan horse, also *Gubernatis*, vol. i. p. 336. Geldart, *Folk-Lore of Modern Greece*, "The Golden Steed," p. 98.

Page 140. The marks of moon and stars. In *Payne*, vol. ii. p. 163, we read, that an old woman was taken "for a man of the flower of God's servants, and the most excellent of devotees, more by token of the *shining of her forehead* for the ointment with which she had anointed it." *S. ja T.* vol. i. p. 105, "Tynnyrissä kaswanut Poika" (a boy who grew in a barrel) p. 337, *ante.* Stokes *Indian Fairy Tales*, "a boy who had a moon on his forehead, and a star on his chin," p. 119. Denton,*Serbian Folk Lore*, "The Shepherd and the King's daughter," p. 173.

THE INVISIBLE SHEPHERD LAD. Erdélyi, ii. 6.

There is a similar tale in Erdélyi, iii. 5. See also *Grimm*, vol. ii. "The shoes that were danced to pieces," and notes, p. 430. *Roumanian Fairy Tales*, London, 1881, "The Slippers of the Twelve Princesses." |Pg 388|A sleeping draught is given to the prince in the story of the Enchanted Youth. *Payne*, vol. i. p. 59.

Page 142. A copper forest occurs in the Lapp story, "Jætten og Veslegutten." *Friis*, No. 18. Also in *Dasent*, "Katie Woodencloak," p. 414.

THE THREE PRINCESSES. Erdélyi, ii. 7.

Page 144. A girl finds her way back in a similar way in the Lapp stories. "Stallo og Lappe brødrene Sodno." *Friis*, p. 85, and "Stallo-vagge," *ib.* p. 106. Cf. also*Roumanian Fairy Tales*, "Handsome is as Handsome does," p. 81. *Pentamerone*, "Nennillo and Nennella." *Serbian Folk-Lore.* Denton, "The wicked stepmother." *Grimm*, vol. i. "Hänsel and Grethel," and note p. 355.

In the Swedish legend, "Tibble Castle, and Klinta Well." (Hofberg. *Svenska Sägner*, p. 146,) the princess coming to meet her lover is carried off by the Mountain King, and leaves her crown hanging on a fir tree, to show her lover what has happened.

Page 146. The acorn's rapid growth reminds one of Jack and the Bean Stalk.

For Magyar idea of giants and giantesses, see the Introduction.[67] The one-eyed monster occurs in the Lapp, "Ruobba, Jætten og Fanden," *Friis*, p. 67, and in the Finnish "Leppäpölkky." (*S. ja T.* ii. p. 2) nine daughters fall into Syöjätär's power, and are only allowed one eye amongst them. See also *Round the Yule Log.*

The Lapps tell of monsters which they call Bædnag-njudne[68] who had dog's noses, and one eye in the middle of their forehead.

Page 147. Cannibalism. Cf. the Lapp Stories, "Bædnag-njudne," "Stallo og Fiskerlappen," "En Datter af Stalloslægten |Pg 389|flygter fra sine Forældre og gifter sig med en Lapp," "To Lappepiger gifte sig med Stallo," &c. in *Friis.* Rink, *Eskimo Tales*, "The Brothers visit their Sister," p. 128. *Old Deccan Days*, "Brave Seventee Bai," p. 28. Payne, *Arabian Nights*, The History of Gherib and his brother Agib, vol. vi. p. 112.

Page 148. A monster is fooled in a similar way, in "The two Children and the Witch," p. 60. *Portuguese Folk-Tales*, F.L.S. 1882. See also *Grimm*, vol. i. Hansel and Grethel, p. 67. *Dasent*, "Buttercup," p. 146, and "Boots and the Troll," p. 253. Also other parallels noted in Ralston *Russian Tales*, p. 168.

The hair combing is a favorite incident in numerous Lapp stories.

The latter part of the story seems to be a compressed edition of the Cinderella incident.

CINDER JACK. Erdélyi, ii. 11.

The Magyar title of this tale is: "Hamupipöke," and as there are no genders in the Magyar language, the name may stand either for a male or a female.

Sports similar to those mentioned in the tale (but of course on a very much reduced scale, so as to suit ordinary mortals) formed part of the wedding festivities in Hungary in days gone by. Cf. Baron Radvánszky's work on *Magyar Family Life in the 15th and 16th Centuries.* 3 vols. (In Magyar).

For the whole story, Cf. the Finnish "Maan, meren kulkija laiwa" (*S. ja T.* ii. p. 22), a story from Ilomantsi, which tells of a king with an only daughter, whom he does not wish to marry, as he cannot bear the thought of parting from her, and so set as a task for any one who wished to marry her, the building of a ship that could sail over land and sea. Three brothers, who were merchants, lived in the land: the youngest was called Tuhkamo (Ashiepattle): these determined to try their luck; but the elder failed, because they rejected the offer of help from an old man;

Ashiepattle secured the old man's good [Pg 390]will, and so won the day. The latter part of the tale is something like that of Shepherd Paul in this collection.

A Karelian story, entitled "Tuhkamo" turns upon three brothers, whose father before he died bade them come and pray for him by his grave: only the youngest did so. He was rewarded, and by means of a wonderful horse, achieved marvellous feats of jumping, and so won the princess. Another story from North Finland: "Tuhkamo," relates how a dead father came to his three sons in their dreams, and ordered them to watch on the sea-shore; the youngest alone did so, and caught a swan maiden, whose father set him three tasks; viz. to fell all the trees near a bay; to set them up again; and to bring a golden chain from heaven. He managed all that by the help of his bride, but got into trouble over the last, as when he rode up to it, on his wondrous steed, and seized it, it was so heavy that he fell down to the earth, and was completely buried in the ground, except a little hair, which remained above ground; a duck made her nest on his head, and laid her eggs in it, and by means of a fox and other animals which came to eat the eggs Tuhkamo got out of his difficulty; he next fooled two men who were quarrelling over three precious gifts; he then went on to three houses asking for his bride; all the animals, &c. were summoned, and at last an eagle took him to his lost bride, who recognised him by a piece of the golden chain he put in the water the princess's servants drew.

In another Finnish tale, "The Golden Bird," the third son is the only one who can watch all night, and so finds out what it is that steals fruit from his father's favourite tree.

The Lapp story, "Ruobba,[69] Jætten og Fanden," *Friis*, p. 67, tells of *tools* of all sorts, axes and planes, &c. coming and asking the sons to give them some food; the eldest refuse, but the youngest gives them food, and so succeeds in finding out the robber.

Another tale, "Solkongens Datter," *Friis*, p. 152, relates how a man has a barn full of corn from which some one steals every night. [Pg 391]The man's two elder sons try to watch and fail; but Gudnavirũs (*i.e.* Ashiepattle) succeeds in finding the robbers—three swan-maidens—and securing one of them.

Cf. also Rink, *Eskimo Legends*, "Kagsagsuk," and "The Child Monster," where ill treated ones suddenly develope vast power. Dasent, *Tales from the Norse*, "The Princess on the glass hill." *Old Deccan Days*, "The Raksha's Palace," p. 205. Stokes' *Indian Fairy Tales*, "The boy who had a moon on his forehead," p. 126, &c. and p. 280. Mitford, *Tales of Old Japan*, "The story of the Old Man who made withered trees to blossom." Vernaleken, *In the Land of Marvels*, "Hondiddledo and his Fiddle," and "Mr. Chick," p. 228. *Roumanian Fairy Tales*, "The Hermit's Foundling." Geldart, *Folk-Lore of Modern Greece*, "The Scab Pate." Steere, *Swahili Tales*, "Sultan Majnún." Ralston, *Russian Folk Tales*, "The Norka," p. 73. Denton, *Serbian Folk-Lore*, "The Golden Apple Tree and the nine Peahens." "Who asks much gets little." *Grimm*, vol. i. "The Golden Bird," "The Three feathers." *Ibidem*, vol. ii. "Iron John," and notes, p. 434. *Gubernatis*, vol. i. pp. 25, 177, and 293, &c. where Russian variants are given. Thorpe, *Yule-Tide Stories* "The Millet Thief." *Polnische Volkssagen und Märchen*, Aus dem Polnischen des K. B. Woycicki von F. H. Levestam, "Der Glasberg." *Deutches Märchenbuch*, von L. Bechstein, "Hirsedieb." *Sagen Märchen und Gebräuche aus Sachsen und Thüringen*, Gesammelt von Emil Sommer, "Der Dumme Wirrschopf." *Svenska Folk Sagor*, Hyltén-Cavallius och G. Steffens, "Prinsessan uppå Glasberget."

THE THREE BROTHERS. Erdélyi, ii. 8.

The beginning of the tale reminds us of "The travels of Truth and Falsehood," p. 36 in this collection.

Healing Mud, p. 152. Cf. pp. 36, 53, 323, and 336, in this collection. Also, "Right is always right," a Wendish story, quoted in the *Dublin Magazine*, 1868, p. 356, and *Vernaleken*, "The Accursed Garden," p. 308.

[Pg 392]In Tuscany, the peasants believe that whoever washes his face in the dew before the sun rises on St. John's Day will have no illness all the year following. See*Gubernatis*, vol. i. p. 219. Cf. also Payne, *Arabian Nights*, vol. v. pp. 279, 281. A magic whistle appears in the Finnish story, *e.g.* "The ship that can sail on land and sea," *S. ja T.* ii. p. 22. See also in this collection, p. 192, and *Gubernatis*, vol. i. p. 289.

The envious brothers (or fellow-servants) appear in numerous stories, such as "Kulta-orit, Kulta-nuotta, wasta ja pilli (the golden stallion, golden drag net, broom and flute)," *S. ja T.* i. p. 187, and *Dasent*, "Boots and the Troll."

The tasks set are somewhat like those in "Fisher Joe."

In the Lapp story, "Gutten, som tjente hos Kongen" (*Friis*, p. 167), the hero is ordered to bring all the wild beasts of the forest into the King's courtyard. Animals help Hans in the "Maiden on the Crystal Mountain;" *Vernaleken*, p. 276. Cf. also notes to "Fisher Joe" and "Handsome Paul."

THE THREE VALUABLE THINGS. Erdélyi, ii. 9.

Cf. Naaké, *Slavonic Fairy Tales*, "The wise judgment." Caballero, *Spanish Fairy Tales*, "A girl who wanted three husbands." *Sagas from the far East*: "Five to one," p. 112; and "Who invented Woman," p. 298. Denton, *Serbian Folk-Lore*, "The three Suitors." Geldart, *Folk-Lore of Modern Greece*, "The Golden Casket," pp. 112 and 115, and *Arabian Nights*, "Prince Ahmed and the Fairy Banou."

THE LITTLE MAGIC PONY. Erdélyi, ii. 10.

A curious story of a magic horse is still told in Lincolnshire, which I heard the other day in Boston. This is *verbatim*. "Near Lincoln is a place called Biard's Leap; near there an old witch lived in a [Pg 393]cave, who enticed people in and eat them. One day a man offered to go and kill her. He had his choice of a dozen horses, so he took them all to a pond, where he threw a stone into the water, and then led the horses to have a drink, and the one which lifted its head first he chose. It was blind. He got on its back, and, taking his sword, set off. When he got to the cave's mouth, he shouted to the witch to come out.

"Wait till I've buckled my shoe,And suckled my cubs,"

cried the witch. She then rushed out, and jumping on to the horse stuck her claws into its rump, which made it jump over thirty feet (the so-called Biard's leap). The man struck behind him with his sword, which entered the old woman's left breast, and killed her."

The legend is given in a curious little tract, entitled "The existing remains of the Ancient Britons within a small district lying between Lincoln and Sleaford, by the Rev. G. Oliver, D.D. London, 1846." The man of the above version is replaced by a knight, who "cast a large stone into the lake, accompanied by a secret petition to the gods, that the chosen steed might raise his head from the water;" Biard rises, and they go to meet the witch, who has her left breast cut off by the first blow of the knight's sword; the second blow she evades by springing on to Biard's flank, where she fixes her talons, so that the horse took a series of prodigious leaps, three of which are at least sixty yards asunder, and are still marked by the impressions of his feet. The witch died from her wound, and was buried under a huge stone at the cross roads, and a stake driven through her body. *Gubernatis*, i. p. 338. Cf. Notes to Prince Mirkó.

Page 160. Obstructions placed in the way of the witch or giant who follows.

Cf. Finnish, "Awaimetoin Wakka" (the Keyless Chest), *S. ja T.* i. p. 151, and "Oriiksi muutettu poika" (the enchanted horse), *ib.* p. 142. Lapp. "Jaetten og Veslegutten." *Friis*, p. 49, and "Jaetten og Drengen hans," *ib.* p. 58. Rink, *Eskimo Tales*, "A tale about Two Girls," and "Giviok." Naaké, *Slavonic Tales*, "The wonderful hair," and "Ivan Kruchina." *Legends of the Wigwam*, [Pg 394]"Exploits of Grasshopper," p. 61. *Old Deccan Days*, "Truth's Triumph," p. 63. *Portuguese Folk Tales*, F. L. S. 1882, "The Maid and the Negress," and "St. Peter's Goddaughter." Ralston, *Russian Folk-Tales*, "Marya Morevna," p. 95: "the Baba Yaga," p. 141, and "the Witch and the Sun's Sister," p. 173. Dasent, *Norse Tales*, "The Mastermaid," p. 91; "Farmer Weathersky," p. 334, and "The Widow's Son," p. 363.*Grimm*, vol. i. "The Water Nix." Geldart, *Greek Tales*, "Starbright and Birdie," "The Golden Casket," p. 123, and "The Scab Pate," p. 164. *Vernaleken*, "The Two Sisters," p. 157. *Pentamerone*, "The Flea," and "Petrosinella." *Records of the Past*, vol. ii. "Tale of the Two Brothers," p. 142. *Gubernatis*, vol. i. pp. 166, 175. *Folk-Lore Journal*, 1883, "The Three Sisters and Itrìmobé," p. 235. A Malagasky tale. Ananci Stories, *ib.* p. 286. Irish Folk-Tales, *ib.* p. 323. *Ibid.* 1884. "Prince Unexpected," p. 15, a Polish tale, and "Isìlakòlona," *ib.* p. 31, a Malagasy tale.

THE BEGGAR'S PRESENTS. Erdélyi, ii. 12.

Cf. the wonderful gifts in: "Taiwaasen menijä" (one who goes to heaven) *S. ja T.* ii. p. 113, and "Ei-niin-mitä" (just nothing) *ib.* p. 53. "Bondesønnen, Kongesønnem og Solens Søster." *Friis*, p. 140. *Dasent*, "The Best Wish," p. 294, and "Katie Woodencloak," *ib.* p. 412. *Old Deccan Days*, "The Jackal, the Barber, and the Brahman." Stokes' *Indian Fairy Tales*, "The Story of Foolish Sachúlí." *Sagas from the Far East*, "The Avaricious Brother," p. 23. *Vernaleken, In the Land of Marvels*, "The Wishing Rag," "The Magic Pot." *Patránas*, "Matanzas." Caballero, *Spanish Folk-Tales*, "Uncle Curro and his Cudgel." *Pentamerone*, "The Months." *Grimm*, vol. i. "The Wishing Table, the Gold Ass, and the Cudgel in the Sack," and notes, p. 387. Also "The Knapsack, the Hat, &c." and notes, p. 409. Crofton Croker, *Irish Fairy Legends*, "The Legend of Bottle Hill." Payne, *Arabian Nights*, vol. vi. Jouder and his Brothers. *Folk-Lore Record*, 1878, "Some Italian Folk-Lore," p. 202. *Gubernatis*, vol. i. pp. 127, 154, 161; and Nordlander, *Sagor, Sägner och Viso* No. 4.

[Pg 395]

THE WORLD'S BEAUTIFUL WOMAN. Erdélyi, iii. 1.

Arany gives the following variants of this tale: *Mailath* 2, *Grimm*[70] 53, and *Schott*, Wallachische Märchen 5. See also in Russian poetry by Pushkin, in Bodenstedt's translation i. p. 100. In the German variants, twelve pigmies take the place of the twelve robbers in the Hungarian tale; and the queen thus addresses her mirror:

"Spieglein, spieglein an der WandWer ist die schönste im ganzen Land?"

And receives the reply—

"Frau Königin. Thr seid die Schönste hierAber Schneewitchen ist thausendmal schöner.Als Thr."

Cf. Pedroso *Portuguese Folk-Tales*, F.L.S. 1882. "The Vain Queen," and "The Maiden with the Rose on her Forehead."

Page 164. The love-stricken ones is a touch of the Oriental method of describing the power of love. See numberless examples in Payne's *Arabian Knights*.

Page 165. There is an Indian superstition noted in Temple's *Legends of the Punjáb*, p. 51, where we read, "he wore some coarse clothes over his own, so that her perspiration should not injure him," and in the footnote: "the woman's perspiration would take his 'virtue' out of him."

Page 165. Magic Mirror. Besides the variants at the beginning of the notes, we may compare the Magic Mirror in the Norse Saga, "King Gram" and the Hanoverian tale, in *Grimm*, vol. ii. p. 379.

For spitting as a mode of enchantment, see numerous examples in *Arabian Nights*.

Page 172. "The Pin, &c. which prevents the girl from moving." Cf. Stokes, *Indian Fairy Tales*, p. xiii., "The Pomegranate King," [Pg 396]p. 14, "The princess who loved her father like salt," p. 165; and notes on pp. 248, &c.

In the Finnish tale, "Här' än Korwista syntyneet Koirat siw" (Dogs which sprang from the ears of a bull), in *S. ja T.* 1, a girl scratches her brother's head with a devil's tusk, and so kills him; but his faithful dogs lick the wound, and so restore him to life.

In a Lapp story, "Bondesønnen" (*Friis*, No. 44) the son's sister awakes, when the hero pricks her hand, and sucks the drop of blood off.

Cf. Schott, *Wallachische Märchen*, p. 251. Pedroso, *Portuguese Tales*, F.L.S. 1882, "The Maid and the Negress." *Irish Folk Tales*, Folk-Lore Record. 1884, p. 197, "The Story of John and the Amulet." Halliwell, *Nursery Rhymes and Tales*, "The Red Bull of Norroway," p. 169. Thorpe, *Yule-Tide Stories*, p. 40, "The Princess that came out of the water." Payne, *Arabian Nights*, vol. i. p. 375. *Gubernatis*, vol. ii. p. 15, and a story from near Leghorn, p. 242, where it states that similar stories are to be found in Piedmont, in other parts of Tuscany, in Calabria, &c. and in the *Tuti-Name*. *Grimm*, vol. ii. p. 243, "The Glass Coffin."*Pentamerone*, "Sun, Moon, and Talia," and "The Three Citrons." Gonzenbach, *Sicilianiasches Märchen*, vol. i. p. 82.[71] *Old Deccan Days*, "Little Surya Bai," p. 83; "Chundun Rajah," p. 233; "Sodewa Bai," p. 240. In the two last, we also have examples of bodies remaining undecayed for months after death. Sodewa Bai looked as lovely a month after her death as on the night she died; cf. also the well-known "Sleeping Beauty."

The prince in the Greek story weeps and groans over a picture, just as this prince does over his dead princess. See *Geldart*, p. 95, "The Golden Steed."

Page 180. For a fuller note on witches see the Introduction.

[Pg 397]

THE GIRL WITHOUT HANDS. Erdélyi, iii. 2.

Cf. "Neitonen kuninkaan Sadussa" (The Maid in the King's Garden), and "Neitonen Hernemaassa"[72] (The Maid in the Pea-field). *S. ja T.* i. pp. 108-119.*Grimm*, vol. i. "The Girl without Arms," and note, p. 378. Molbech, *Udvalgte Eventyr og Fortaellinger*, "Pigen uden Haender."

THE KING AND THE DEVIL. Erdélyi, iii 3.

Cf. *Some Italian Folk-Lore*, "Lion Bruno," *Folk-Lore Record*, 1878, p. 209. *Portuguese Stories*, "The Story of a Turner," *Folk-Lore Record*, 1881, p. 152. *Irish Stories, Folk-Lore Journal*, 1884, p. 39. *Grimm*, vol. ii. "The King of the Golden Mountain," and "The Nix of the Mill Pond." Thorpe, *Yule-Tide Stories*, "The Gold Ring and the Frog," "The King's Son and Messeria," and "Goldmaria and Goldfeather." *Vernaleken, In the Land of Marvels*, "The Fisher's Son," and "The Stolen Princess."

S. ja T. i. "Awaimetoin Wakka," and *S. ja T.* ii. p. 146, "Jykeä Lipas" (the Heavy Chest). *Friis*, "Gutten, Havfruen og Ridder Rød," and "Fattiggutten, Fanden og Guldbyen." Ralston, *Russian Folk-Tales* p. 362-366, 124, 133.

Steere, *Swahili Tales*, "The Spirit who was cheated by the Sultan's Son." *Gubernatis*, ii. p. 382. One may also compare the Viennese Legends of the "Stock-im-Eisen," and of the "Baren-Häuter," for which *vide Pictures of Hungarian Life*, pp. 172 and 387. Cf. also the Swedish Legend,

"Friskytten," in Hofberg's *Svenska Folksägner*, and the well-known stories of Faust and Der Freischütz. See also p. 130 *ante*.

Page 191. The attempts to deceive the devil are found in numerous tales, e.g. *Friis*, "Stallobruden." *Grimm* ii., "The Iron Stone," p. 158. Lindholm, *Lappbönder*, "De bedragne jätten and; Quigstad og," Sandberg *Lappiske eventyr og folkesagn*, "Stallo og lappepigen."

[Pg 398]*Page 191*. "Owl's Feathers." Pillows of the same sort appear in "The Pelican," p. 255, and remind us of the superstitions connected with wild birds' feathers. In many parts of Lincolnshire, it is said, that it is impossible to die on a bed that contains them. I know of one old lady in Yorkshire, who when *in extremis* begged to be moved off her bed, as she was sure she could not die on it, as it had some bad feathers in it. In some places it is pigeon's feathers that the people particularly dislike. See also Henderson's *Folk-Lore of the Northern Counties*, p. 60.

Page 192. For different tasks, such as the millet cleaning, see also: *S. ja T.* i. "Ihmeellinen Koiwu" (The wonderful Birch). Stokes, *Indian Fairy Tales*, "The Rájá's Son," p. 163, and p. 180. Temple, *Legends of the Punjáb*, "Rājâ Rasâlû," p. 43. Thorpe, *Yule-Tide Stories*. "Svend's Exploits," p. 353. Geldart, *Folk-Lore of Modern Greece*, "The Snake, the Dog, and the Cat," p. 44. *Pentamerone*, "The Dove." *Folk-Lore Journal*, 1884, "Prince Unexpected," p. 13. *Gubernatis*, Vol. i. p. 38. Ralston, *Russian Folk Tales*, "The Water King," p. 126; also pp. 18, 153, 208 in this work.

The hairs that became serpents remind us of Medusa.

Page 193. The changes of the pursued, in order to avoid capture, occur in numerous tales, *e.g.* "Handsome Paul," and note 320 *ante*. Also *S. ja T.* i. "Oriiksi muutettu poika," and "Awaimetoin Wakka." *Friis*, "Jætten og Veslegutten," and "Jætten og Drengen hans." *Household Stories from the Land of Hofer*, "The Dove Maiden," p. 384. *Vernaleken, In the Land of Marvels*, "How Hans finds his Wife," p. 284, and "The Drummer," p. 292. *Folk-Lore Journal*, 1884, "Prince Unexpected," p. 15, and Malagasy Folk-Tales, "Isìlakòlona," p. 131. Campbell, *Popular Tales of the Western Highlands*, "The Battle of the Birds."

Page 194. The devil's limping and the woodpeckers and hares in other stories,[73] reminds us of an old Yorkshire saw, "Beware of those whom God has marked," and I know cases of people who regard any external deformity as the expression of internal malformation.

[Pg 399]*Page 195*. In the Lapp stories, the giants swallow so much water that they burst.

With the moral tacked on to this tale, cf. *Vernaleken*, "The Nine Birds."

THE THREE PRINCES, THE THREE DRAGONS, AND THE OLD WOMAN WITH THE IRON NOSE. Erdélyi, iii. 4.

Page 197. Tátos. Cf. notes, p. 345, also *Roumanian Fairy-Tales*, "The Hermit's Foundling" and "Vasilica the Brave." *Pentamerone*, "Corvetto" and Geldart,*Folk-Lore of Modern Greece*, "The Golden Steed," and "The Scab Pate."

The dragon vomiting out those it has eaten. Cf. The queen swallowed by the whale, in the story of the "Two Orphans," p. 223. Also Red Riding Hood. *Grimm*, i. "The Wolf and the Seven little Kids." Cf. old Greek legend of Kronos devouring his children.

Page 199. The bridge seems to suggest the bridge in the Koran. See also the bridge in *Pentamerone*, "The golden root."

This part of the story somewhat resembles that of "the Accursed Garden," in *Vernaleken*.

Page 201. The transformation of Ambrose and the Dragon. Cf. *Roumanian Fairy Tales*, "Vasilica the Brave," p. 73.

In the Lapp stories the hero calls for help to his gods. See *Friis*. "Stallo og Patto Poadnje," and "Stallo og Fiskerlappen."

Page 202. In the Finnish story, Alderblock turns himself into an ermine. See *S. ja T.* 2, "Leppäpölkky," a story which is very much like the Magyar in this part. Ralston, *Russian Folk-Tales*, "Ivan Popyalof," p. 69. Also *ib.* pp. 71 and 72. In the Finnish tale (*S. ja T.* i.) "Weljiänsä-etsijät Tyttö"—a little dog prevents the girl from bathing in water which would transform her. Cf. Pedroso, *Portuguese Folk-Tales*, "Pedro and the Prince," p. 26. *Gubernatis*, i. p. 191.

[Pg 400]*Page 203*. Ambrose sticks to the axle as the people did to the lamb, p. 14, *ante*. Cf. Story of Loki and the Eagle.

Page 204. The witch in the lower world reminds us of the Egyptian Legend of Ishtar, *Records of the Past*, vol. i. p. 144.

Page 205. The folk-tale-teller was ever fond of having a sly rap at the clergy. Cf. Lapp tale, where the priest wants to marry the goveiter girl himself, because she has a costly silver girdle; *Friis*, "Goveiter-Pige." Also Ralston, *Russian Folk Tales*, p. 27.

Page 205. Worming secrets out of witch, &c. by flattery. Cf. *S. ja T.* ii. "Antti Puuhaara," and *Friis*, "Stallo og Lappebrødrene Sodno."

Ib. Concealed Life. Cf. *Friis*, "Jætten, som havde skjult sit Liv i et Hønseaeg," and "Jætten og Veslegutten," where the giant has hid his life in the middle of a cow's heart. Rink, *Eskimo*

Tales, "The girl who fled to the Inlanders," p. 220. *Old Deccan Days*, "Punchkin," p. 13. Stokes, *Indian Tales*. "Brave Hírálálbásá," p. 58; "The Demon and the King's Son," p. 187, and note, p. 261. Dasent, *Tales from the Norse*, "The giant who had no heart in his body," p. 75.

Sagas from the Far East, "Child Intellect," p. 133. Steere, *Swahili Tales*, "Story of the Washerwoman's Donkey," p. 5. Ralston, *Russian Folk Tales*. "Koschei the Deathless," p. 103, and pp. 113—115. Mr. Ralston also gives *Asbjörnsen*, "New Series," No. 70, p. 39. Haltrich, *Deutsche Volksmärchen ausdem Sachsenlande in Siebenbürgen*, p. 188. Wenzig, *Westabauischer Märchenschatz*, No. 37, p. 190. *Hahn*, No. 26, i. 187, and ii. pp. 215, 294—5, *Vuk Karajich*, No. 8. Cf.*Records of the Past*, vol. ii. "Tale of the Two Brothers," p. 149. Geldart, *Greek Folk-Tales*, "The little Brother who saved his Sister from the Dragon," p. 56.*Pentamerone*, "The Dragon." Campbell, "Tales of the Western Highlands," vol. i. p. 81. *Grimm*, vol. ii. p. 564. Denton, *Serbian Folk-Lore*. "Bash-chalek," p. 172. Payne, *Arabian Nights*, vol. i. p. 118, and vol. vii. p. 91. Engel, *Musical Myths*, vol. i. p. 201. *Folk-Lore Journal*, 1884, "The Philosophy of Punchkin." Tylor, *Primitive Culture*, pp. 152, 153. *Gubernatis*, vol. i. pp. 131, 140, 269, and 412. Thorpe, *Yule-Tide [Pg 401]Stories*. "The Man without a Heart." Black, *Folk-Medecine*, p. 32. *Gesta Romanorum*, "The Knight and the Necromancer." Castren, *Ethnologische Vorlesungen über die Altaischen Völker*, p. 174. *Page 206*. A wonderful chest in the Finnish story, "Awaimetoin Wakka" (*S. ja T.* i.) opens as the golden apple in the Magyar tale, and out of it comes castle, servants, &c. See also Prince Mirkó, p. 74, *ante*.

THE WIDOWER AND HIS DAUGHTER. Erdélyi iii. 7.

There are some wild variants of this tale to be found amongst the Finnish Folk-Tales. See "Ihmeelinen Koiwu," the wonderful birch, "Kummallinen Tammi," the marvellous oak, and "Kolmet Sisärykset," the three sisters. *S. ja T.* i. pp. 59-77, also "Awannolla kehrääjät," the spinner beside the ice-hole, and "Sisärpuolet," the half-sisters. *S. ja T.* ii. pp. 161-172. Winther, *Danske Folkeeventyr*, "Den onde Skemoder," Asbjörnsen og Moe, *Norske Folkeeventyr*, "Manddattern og Kjärringdattern." *Deutsches Märchenbuch von L. Bechstein*, "Die Goldmaria und Pechmaria." Kuhn und Schwartz, *Norddeutsche Sagen*, "Das Mädchen im Paradis." Hyltén-Cavallius, *Svenska Folksagor*. "De twå Skrinen," Geldart, *Folk Lore of Modern Greece*. "Little Saddleslut" and the "Goat Girl," *Sagas from the Far East*, p. 180. Ralston's *Russian Folk Tales*, "The Dead Mother," and p. 260, where a Serbian variant is quoted, which apparently bears a strong resemblance to some of the Finnish. Denton's *Serbian Folk-Lore*, "Papalluga." Vernaleken, *In the Land of Marvels*, "The Blackbird," and p. 84. *Pentamerone*, "La Gatta Cenerentola."

Gubernatis, vol. i., pp. 31, 182, 195, 208, 241, 291, 293. Thorpe's *Yule-tide Stories*. "The Little Gold Shoe" and "The Girl clad in Mouseskin." *Grimm*, vol. 1, "Cinderella," "Allerleirauh," and notes, pp. 364, 416, 420. *Household Stories from the Land of Hofer*. "Klein-Else." *Folk-Lore Record* 1878. "Some Italian Folk-Lore," p. 188: *ib.* 1880. "The Icelandic story of Cinderella." *Portuguese Folk-Tales*, F. L. S. pp. 68 and 97: *Folk-Lore Record* 1884; Folk Tales of the Malagasy, p. 74, *ib.* Chilian Popular Tales, "Maria the [Pg 402]Cinder Maiden." *Tasks imposed*, p. 208; see *ante*, p. 398. The gold rose stuck into the gate-post (p. 211) occurs in one of the Finnish variants.

Page 214. The gipsy woman incident. Cf. *ante*, p. 386.

Page 215. The "feather picking" refers to gatherings of country girls held during the winter, to dress feathers collected during the year for bedding.

Ib. The golden duck incident is an exceedingly common one. Cf. *Old Deccan Days*, pp. 85 and 223. *Portuguese Folk-Tales*: F.L.S. p. 12. Stokes' *Indian Tales*, p. 284.

THE WISHES. Erdélyi iii. 11.

Cf. *Payne*, vol. v. "The man who saw the night of power." *Caballero's* Fairy Tales, "The three wishes." *Grimm*, "The poor man and the rich man," and notes; and a fragment in *Notes and Queries*. Finnish Folk-Lore, 6th S. viii., p. 201, also *Lewins* "A fly on the wheel," p. 81, where a Hindustani variant is given.

THE TWO ORPHANS. Erdélyi iii. 9.

In a Finnish Tale, "Weljiänsä-etsijät Tyttö," *S. ja T.* i. p. 119, the girl who seeks her brothers, the girl is warned by a faithful dog, from going near or touching water which a witch wishes her to do, and which entails misery on her; as also in another, "Leppapölky," where the witch tempts the heroes in like manner. Cf. Geldart's *Folk-Lore of Modern Greece*. "Starbright and Birdie," p. 33. *Grimm*, "Brother and Sister." *Gubernatis*, vol. i., pp. 175, 354, and 390.

P. 221. The cutting off of the lock of hair reminds us of the widespread superstitions connected with hair, or any other part of a person. Cf. *ante* pp. 332 and 374.*Archaeology*, "The Physicians of Myddfai," p. 113. I have also often heard the following in Yorkshire and Lincolnshire. That you must not give a lock of hair to anyone, or else you will quarrel with that person; that you must not keep the hair of a dead person unless it is "made up," or you will have ill-luck; and that all hair cuttings and nail parings ought to be saved and placed [Pg 403]in the coffin, so that the person may "enter heaven perfect!" A baby's hair and nails must not be cut until it is a year old, or else it will be a thief. Hair must not be cut when the moon is waning. It is also said that ague can be cured by hanging a lock of hair on a willow tree.[74]

Page 223. The witch wishes to get rid of the deer, in the same way that the gipsy does the golden duck, *ante* p. 215. Cf. Stokes's *Indian Fairy Tales:* "The Pomegranate King," p. 10; "Phúlmati Ráni," p. 4; "The Jackal and the Kite," p. 22; "The Bél-Princess," p. 144; and Notes, pp. 245-253. *Gubernatis*, vol. i., p. 412, and vol. ii., p. 31.

Page 223. In the Lapp Story, "Pigen fra Havet," *Friis*, No. 8,[75] a child is brought down to the sea-shore to bring mother back; and in the Finnish story, "Ihmeelinen Koiwu," The wonderful Birch, the child's cry brings mother back, just as the little deer's lament in this tale reaches the sister's ears at the bottom of the well.

In this Finnish tale the mother replies, and says to the reindeer, which are feeding near:

"Reindeer! Reindeer! feeding in the swamp,Come and take care of your child!Come and see the child you have borne!For the witch's daughter has neither food nor drink,And cannot quiet its cries."

See also *Finnish*, "Maid who rose out of the sea."

Grimm, "The lambkin and the little fish," and notes.

Pentamerone, "The two cakes." Theal, *Kaffir Folk-Lore*, "The story of Tangalimlibo," p. 61.

Page 223. Creatures inside others.

Cf. Theal, *Kaffir Folk-Lore*, "The story of the cannibal mother," [Pg 404]p. 142; "The story of the glutton," p. 175; "The great chief of the animals," p. 177; and the Finnish story, "Seppo Ilmarisen Kosinta" (Smith Ilmarinen's courtship), where the smith, after being swallowed by Untamoinen, cuts his way out.

Stokes's *Indian Fairy Tales*, "Loving Lailí," p. 76.

THE WONDERFUL FROG. Erdélyi, iii. 15.

My friend, Prof. Aug. Gittée, has kindly forwarded me a Flemish variant, "Van het Meisje dat met een Puits trouwde." "The tale of a girl who married a frog." See *Volskunde Tijdschrift voor Nederlandsche Folklore*, 1888, p. 48. Cf. *Grimm*. "The Frog King" and notes. Stokes, *Indian Folk Tales*, p. xvi. and "The Monkey Prince." *Gubernatis*. "The Frog." Max Müller, *Chips from a German Workshop*, vol. ii. p. 249. Cox. *Mythology of the Aryan Nations*. "Frog." Halliwell. *Nursery Rhymes and Tales*. "The maiden and the frog."[76] Dasent. *Tales from the Norse*. "Bushy Bride."

THE DEVIL AND THE RED CAP. Erdélyi, iii. 19.

Cf. Ralston, *Russian Folk-Tales*, "The Soldier and the Vampire," p. 314. Vernaleken. *In the Land of Marvels*. "How a Shepherd became rich."

[Pg 405]

JACK DREADNOUGHT. Erdélyi, iii. 16.

Cf. *Grimm*, "The Story of the youth who went to learn what fear was," and notes: *ib.* "The King's son who feared nothing," and notes. *Household Stories from the Land of Hofer*. "Fearless Johnny." *Afanassieff*, v. 46.

Page 232. The secret treasures guarded by ghosts, &c. is a world-wide tradition. Cf. Hofberg, *Svenska Folksägner*. "Skatten i Säbybäcken," Where a carriage full of gold and silver is said to be sunk mid-stream, over which a weird light flickers. Many attempts, we are told, have been made to rescue it, but each time some one has spoken, or else the bull-calves—which are not to have a single black hair on them, and were to be fed for three years on unskimmed milk—were not strong enough; and so the attempts have ever failed. See also, in the same work "Skattgräfvarna," where the searchers were frightened away by the Demon guardians of the hidden store. In Lincolnshire I have heard of a field where, tradition says, countless [Pg 406]barrels of beer, and a fender and fireirons of silver, are buried, and in my own parish I have collected three similar tales told of places here, and the other day a Negro from South Carolina told me another. Cf. Hardwick,*Traditions, Superstitions, and Folk-Lore* (chiefly Lancashire and the north of England), pp. 41, 46, 195, and 252. Cf. Baring Gould. *Curious Myths*. "The Divining Rod."[77]

THE SECRET-KEEPING LITTLE BOY AND HIS LITTLE SWORD. Erdélyi, iii. 8.

Cf. *Grimm*, vol. i., "Faithful John" and note. See *ante*, p. 350.

With regard to the sword growing in the garden, Cf. the Hunnish superstition mentioned by Priscus. "He (Attila) believes also that there will be before long some noteable increase of his power; and that the gods have signified this by revealing to him the sword of Mars, a sacred relic much venerated by the Huns, for many years hidden from their eyes, but quite lately re-discovered by the trail of the blood of an ox which had wounded its hoof against it, as it stuck upright in the long grass." *Italy and her defenders*, by T. Hodgkin, vol. ii. p. 92. No doubt Priscus makes use of the name of Mars to designate the Hunnish deity in the same way as Tacitus when he speaks of the Teutonic god of war. A naked sabre, fixed hilt downwards in the earth, was worshipped by the Alani. Cf. p. 33 of the above-mentioned work.

Payne, vol. vi. "Jouder and his brothers," pp. 129, 152, 164.

See also, Geldart, *Folk-Lore of Modern Greece*, "The Scab Pate." Payne, *Tales from the Arabic*, vol. i., "The story of the King who knew the quintessence of things."

"The Three Dreams," p. 117, in this collection, and notes, p. 375.

Page 236. The execution. The last ceremony with a condemned man when he is pinioned is to read once more his sentence to him. This is done by the sheriff, and concludes with "Hangman, do your duty!" After the execution is over, the military present are commanded to prayer; the helmet is taken off, the musket taken in the [Pg 407]left hand and grounded, and every soldier kneels on his left knee, and remains so for a few minutes till order is given "From prayer."

In olden times the sheriff, after he read the sentence, broke his judicial staff in twain, and threw the pieces at the culprit's feet: hence the Hungarian saying, "to break the staff near anyone," is equivalent to pronouncing sentence: *e.g.*, "I have done this, but don't break a staff over my action," *i.e.*, do not condemn my action.

Page 238. "Immuring alive." Cf. Roumanian legend "Manuli," and notes in this collection, p. 376.

Page 243. In the Finnish tale, "Alderblock," there is a sword, which cuts the enemy into fragments.

SHEPHERD PAUL. Erdélyi, iii. 17.

Cf. Finnish stories, "Lappäpölkky," *S. ja T.* 2; where Alderblock has five companions who assist him in his labours; also "Mikko Metsolainen" and "Mikko Miehelainen," *S. ja T.* i.; stories very much like the Magyar one. Also, "Maan, meren kulkija laiwa." In a Lapp story we find companions helping the hero. *Friis*. "Ruobba, Jaetten og Fanden."

Grimm. "How six men got on in the world," and notes; "The six servants," and notes; "Strong Hans," and notes.

Müllenhoff, *Märchen und Lieder der Hertzogenthümer Schleswig Holstein und Lauenberg*, "Rinroth." Molbech, *Udwalgte Eventyr*, "De fer Tienere." Cavallius och Stefens, *Svenska Folksagor*, "De begge Fosterbröderne," and "Halftrollet eller de Tre Swärden."

Bechstein. *Deutsches Märchenbuch*. "Der Hafenhüter."

Denton. *Serbian Folk-Lore*. "Sir Peppercorn."

Patrañas. "The ill-tempered Princess." "A tale of fourteen men," a Flemish tale; see *Magazin für die Literatur des Auslandes*, 1844. Caballero, *Spanish Tales*, "Lucifer's ear." Geldart, *Folk-Lore of Modern Greece*, "The Golden Casket" and "Little John, the widow's son." *Pentamerone*, "The Flea" and "The Booby."

Folk-Lore Record, 1881, p. 142. "The story of Mamma-na-Bura," a Portuguese tale: *ib.* 1883, p. 254, "Folk-Lore of Yucatan."

Page 246. The latter portion of the tale is to be met with in many [Pg 408]tales, *e.g.*, "Awannolla Kehräajät," where the girl goes through a hole in the ice, and finds a beautiful world there.

Dasent. *Tales from the Norse*. "The two step-sisters," p. 129; "Shortshanks," p. 166; and "The Big Bird Dan," p. 449.

Vernaleken. *In the Land of Marvels*. "The Taylor and the Hunter," "The Accursed Garden," and "The Three Princesses."

Denton. *Serbian Folk-Lore*. "The wonderful Kiosk."

Patrañas, "Simple Johnny and the spell-bound Princesses." *Grimm*, "The Elves," and notes. *Sagas from the Far East*, "How the Schimnu-Khan was slain." Ralston, *Russian Folk-Tales*, "The Norka," and variants there given on p. 80.

Geldart, *Folk-Lore of Modern Greece*, "The Prince and the Fairy." Steere, *Shahili Tales*, "Hasseebu Kareem ed Deen," p. 337.

Arabian Nights. "Ahmed and Pari-Banou," and numerous other examples of underground palaces, where distressed princesses lie awaiting deliverance.

Gubernatis, vol. i. pp. 25, 129, 193, 194; vol. 187, &c.

Rink. *Tales of Traditions of the Esquimaux*. "The woman who got connected with the Ingersuit or under-world people." There are numerous stories about the under-world and its people in Lapp stories, *e.g.*, *Friis*, "Cacce-haldek eller Havfolk," where a boy rows to the under-world. (*Notes and Queries*, 7th s. v. p. 381; cf. *ib.* 7th s. v. p. 501.) "Bæivekongens Datter," "Goveiter." There is also a tribe of underground people called Kadnihak, who are said to dress in red clothes, and have long flaxen hair reaching to their waists. Some people are said to have learned their songs, which are called "Kadniha-Vuolee." Cf. Baring Gould, *Curious Myths of the Middle Ages*, "St. Patrick's Purgatory." *Deutsche Märchen und Sagen*, Gesammelt und mit Anmerkungen herausgegeben von J. W. Wolff, "Der Kühne Sergeant." *Polnische Volksagen*, Aus dem Polnischen des K. W. Woycicki von F. Levestam, "Die drei Brüder."

See also, Friis, *Lappisk Mythologi*. "Under jordiske Guder."

Page 248. The Lapp tales say that the Stallos used to wear an iron shirt. See *Friis*, No. 26. Læstadius believes them to have been old Vikings.

[Pg 409]

THE PELICAN. Erdélyi, iii. 6.

Pelicans may occasionally be seen in the South of Hungary, but upon the whole the bird is unknown to the common people. The story-teller represents it as a little bird that sings most beautifully.

The hypercritical reader may be shocked at another natural historical blunder, viz., when the whale is described as "the king of fishes." But then we must remember that our own Sir Walter Scott speaks of the phoca as a fish in the last sentence of chapter xxxvii. of *The Antiquary*.

The Emperor Joseph II.'s edict expelling the Jesuits is still valid, we believe, but is not enforced. The Order has one or two houses in the country, and nobody disturbs them.

In a Finnish tale one half of a castle weeps while the other half laughs. Cf. also another Finnish story "The Golden Bird," where a king's son goes in search of a splendid bird which his father longs for. The hero is assisted by a wolf, which, amongst many other strange things, by rolling three times on the ground on its back, becomes a shop full of precious goods.[78] After many trials, chiefly due to the perfidy of his brothers, the hero, by the assistance of the wolf, wins the golden bird and a lovely princess. The golden bird will not sing till the youngest prince appears, just as in the present tale.

Page 251. "The old Beggar." This incident is common in folk-tales.

Page 252. "Dragon's milk," a favourite compound of mighty power in the magic formulæ of Finnish and Magyar folk-medicine.

Page 255. "Owls' feathers." *Vide* p. 398, *ante*, and *Notes and Queries*, 6th S. X. p. 401.

Page 256. "Traced triangle," *ante*, p. 370.

Page 257. "Pleiades." Stars and their lore is one of the most [Pg 410]interesting branches of Folk-Lore. Space forbids more than passing allusion to it here. In a note sent by Mr. Haliburton, he points out the important part this group of stars plays in the history of Primitive Man. There appears to be a mass of primitive traditions amongst savages, as to a primæval paradise with its Tree of Life and Knowledge being situated in the Pleiades. See also legends current amongst the Polynesians, Kiowas of the Prairies, the Abipones of the Pampas, Dyaks, &c. We may also compare the Cabeiric brethren in Phoenician tradition.

In the seventh star, say the Finns, is the sign of the slave; the ancient Finns having regulated their rising by the seven stars. A Finnish friend, Mr. K. Krohn, says he has obtained some forty old Finnish star names from an old woman, and hopes, by comparison of the same with the Arabic names, to obtain valuable results.

See also *Sagas from the East*, p. 53, and *Gubernatis*, vol. i., p. 228. Cox, *Mythology of the Aryan Nations*, "Pleiades."

Page 258. Just as the hero here goes to seek in an unknown land for what he needs, so does the hero in the Finnish tale, "Antti Puuhaara"; *S. ja T.* 2, go to Pohjola. (Darkness, *i.e.* the Northern Part). Cf. also Dasent's *Tales from the Norse* "Rich Peter the Pedlar," p. 236. Vernaleken, *In the Land of Marvels*, "For one Kreuzer a hundred." *Pentamerone*, "The Seven Doves," &c. and pp. 107 and 371 in this work.

Page 259. The threshold is a most interesting object in the lore and tales of the people. In Finland it is regarded as unlucky if a clergyman steps on the threshold when he comes to preach at a church. A Finnish friend told me of one of his relations going to preach at a church a few years ago, he being a candidate for the vacant living, and that the people most anxiously watched if he stepped on the threshold as he came in. Had he done so, I fear a sermon never so eloquent would have counted but little against so dire an omen.[79] In the Lapp tales the same idea appears, see *Friis*, [Pg 411]"Ulta-Pigen," the lad returning from a visit to his wife's parents (who are fairy folk) is ordered to step quickly over the threshold, and so saves his life. In the same story we read that a nail driven into the threshold will prevent a fairy wife from running away.

Ralston, *Russian Folk-Tales*, "The Fiend." Here Marusia gets entangled with the evil one, and death comes into her family; in terror she asks her granny what she is to do, and is told, "Go quickly to the priest and ask him this favour—that if you die your body shall not be taken out of the house through the doorway, but that the ground shall be dug away from under the threshold, and that you shall be dragged out through that opening." Rink, *Eskimo Tales*, "The Angakok from Kakortok," p. 391. Napier, *Folk-Lore from West Scotland*, p. 46, where, in the description of marriage ceremonies, we read "The threshold of the house was disenchanted by charms, and by anointing it with certain unctuous perfumes, but as it was considered unlucky for the new-made wife to tread upon the threshold on first entering her house, she was lifted over it and seated upon a piece of wood, a symbol of domestic industry."

Cf. 1 Samuel, v. 5, "Therefore neither the priests, nor any that come into Dagon's house, *tread on the threshold* of Dagon in Ashdod unto this day." Priests and dervishes in India still leap over the threshold of their temples, as they are considered too sacred to be trodden upon.[80]

Page 261. "The Organ Playing." Cf. a similar incident in the Finnish story of the Golden Bird.

Page 262. In the Finnish "Alder Block," the hero's father and mother have their age at once reduced by one-half, when the lovely Catherine embraces them. In the romance of Ogier le Danois sweet singing banishes all care and sorrow. "Et quand Morgue approcha [Pg 412]du dit chasteau, les Faes vindrent au devant dogier, chantant les plus melodieusement quon scauroit jamais ouir, si entra dedans la salle pour se deduire totallement," and so time is destroyed. "Tant de joyeulx passetemps lui faisoient les dames Faees, quil nest creature en ce monde quil le sceust imaginer se penser, car les ouir si doulcement chanter il lui sembloit proprement quil fut en Paradis, si passoit temps de jour en jour, de sepmaine en sepmaine, tellement que ung an ne lui duroit par ung mois."

THE GIRL WITH THE GOLDEN HAIR.

This story, with the four that follows, viz., "The Lover's Ghost," "Snake Skin," "The Fairies' Well," and "The Crow's Nest," are Palócz Folk-Tales, *vide Palócz Folk-Poetry*, by Julius Pap, Sarospatak, 1865.

The hatchet-stick (in Magyar "fokos") mentioned in the tale is an ordinary walking-stick with an axe-shaped brass or steel implement at the end. It is nothing else than the old Scandinavian "paalstaf," the "palstave" or "winged celt" of English antiquaries. It forms part of the national costume of the Magyars, and was carried by nearly everybody before 1867.

The ceremony of exchanging handkerchiefs alluded to in the tale requires some explanation, and we avail ourselves of this opportunity to give a few details of the marriage customs among the Palócz people as related by Pap.

On the first morning in May the lad erects a May-pole outside of the window of his lady-love, the higher the pole the more it pleases the girl, because the length is understood to be in direct proportion to the intensity of her lover's passion. On Whitsunday a pilgrimage to the Holy Well adjoining the monastery at the village of Verebély is arranged, and here the girl buys a nosegay made of artificial flowers for her lover, in return for the maypole, which nosegay is worn by the lad until next May-Day, or until the wedding. In the [Pg 413]meantime the lover visits the girl secretly once or twice at the house of her parents under the cover of night, and later on introduces himself to her parents. If he be well received he sends some friends to ask for the girl's hand, who state their request generally in very flowery language. If the lad's proposal be accepted, the ceremony of exchanging handkerchiefs takes place soon after, the lovers presenting handkerchiefs to one another in which they wrap apples or nuts. From this moment they are considered to be engaged.

The wedding is generally held after the vintage. On the day before the wedding a man, whom we shall call the master of ceremonies, perambulates the village and invites the guests to the festival. On the day itself the guests congregate at a place appointed by the M.C., and the whole company start in procession, headed by a band, to the house of the bride. They all stop outside the gate, and only the bridegroom's best man enters the house and invites the bride to start. The girl then, accompanied by her relations and bridesmaids, and a married woman, whom we shall call the Mistress of the Bedchamber, leaves the house and joins the procession, and they all proceed straight to the church. After church the young woman returns with the whole procession to her own house, and a light breakfast is served, at the end of which all the people adjourn to the bridegroom's house, leaving however the bride behind, until after lengthy coaxing, begging, and some elaborate ceremonies, she consents to go, and is led in triumph to her husband's house, where she is received by the father-in-law at the gate, who nearly overwhelms her with kind words, flattery, and congratulations, and holding her hand leads her into the house and introduces her to his wife, children, and relations. The rejoicing has now reached its climax, and the wedding banquet is at once commenced, to which each invited guest contributes a share according to his or her means.

During the banquet the bridegroom's best man waits at table, and ushers in the various courses reciting a verse for each *plat*, setting forth in most flowery language the various good points of the dish.

After supper the bridegroom's best man takes three lighted candles into his left hand and escorts the bride into her bedchamber, [Pg 414]where he removes the "párta,"[81]and confides her to the care of the Mistress of the Bedchamber. The best man lifts the párta high up in the air at the end of his palstave, and invites the company to bid for it, and then recites the so-called slumber-verses, which are attentively listened to by everyone present.

Next morning two married women from among the bride's friends arrive "to wake the bride," who awaits them sitting in a corner. The two females place the cap worn by married women only, on her head, and present the young couple with cakes and a mixture of spirit and honey.

In the meantime another procession has arrived from the bride's house with the wedding presents, and the people inquire of the Master of the Ceremonies whether he has not seen a "pretty little golden lamb that strayed from home and must have come here." The Master of the Ceremonies replies in the affirmative, but before producing the "lamb" requires a description of the stray one, and then produces some very old person bent with age and her face covered with wrinkles, and wants to know whether this is the lamb they seek for; of course they reply in the negative, and add that the missing one is young and pretty. The bride is then produced and shakes hands all round and receives presents from all present.

In some places the wedding lasts on and off a whole week, and sometimes ends with another ceremony of "searching for the lamb," similar to the one just described.

Such complicated wedding ceremonies are to be found all over Hungary, and in order to facilitate matters, the rules and verses for the occasion are printed and sold at all country fairs, the title-page generally representing the Master of the Ceremonies and the bridegroom's best man in their full festive attire.[82]

Cf. Finnish, "Kulta-orit, Kulta-nuotta, wasta ja pilli." "The golden Stallion, golden Drag-net, broom and flute." *S. ja T.* i. [Pg 415]and "Meresta nousija Neito," "The Sea Maid." Dasent, *Tales from the Norse*, "Bushy Bride," p. 374.

Payne, *Arabian Nights*, vii. pp. 70, 114, and ix. p. 23.

Payne, *Arabic Tales*, iii. p. 61.

Grimm, "The White Bride and the Black one."

In the Lapp Story "Bondesønnen, Kongesønnen og Solens Søster." *Friis*. It is the tail feather of a golden hen, that causes all the troubles. The beautiful girl, who is the Sun's sister, shone like a star, and whenever she entered a house it became as light as the brightest day, even if before it had been pitch dark. The whole tale is a most interesting one; the Sun's sister's sister, "Evening Red," being stolen by giants, who are turned into stone by looking at the Sun's sister, "Dawn." Cf. Princess Labám in "The Rájá's Son," Stokes's *Indian Fairy Tales*, p. 158. Also, pp. 43, 50, 54, 69, and 93.

Grimm, "The Devil with the three golden hairs," and notes. *Dublin Magazine*, 1868, Fireside Lore of Italy, "Corvetto." *Folk-Lore Record*, 1880. Danish Popular Tales, p. 217. "Mons Tro." Naaké, *Slavonic Fairy Tales*, "Golden Hair," from the Bohemian.[83] *Old Deccan Days*, "Brase Seventee Bai," p. 35; Panch-Phul Ranee, p. 141.

Haltrich, *Siebenbuergische Märchen*, pp. 61 and 171.

Mr. Ralston, in his notes in Stokes also gives the following examples of shining and glorious beings. *Indian Antiquary*, vol. iv. p. 54; *ib.* Jan. 1875, p. 10.

Schott, *Wallachische Märchen*, p. 125.

Mabinogion, vol. ii. p. 310; and Thorpe, *Northern Mythology*, vol. i. p. 47. Cf. Mailath, *Magyarische Sagen*, "Die Brüder," and "Die Gaben." Cavallius and Stephens, *Svenska Folksagor*, No. 7.

Records of the Past, vol. ii. "Tales of the two Brothers," a fragrant lock is found in the water, which is said to belong to the daughter of the Sun God.

Page 273. In the Lapp story of the Sun's Sister the King will not allow the lad to marry his bride until he has done certain tasks. So also in the Finnish stories of the Golden Bird and the Golden Stallion.

[Pg 416]*Page 273*. In the Finnish Tale "Totuus ja walte," the King's daughter is cured by being washed with dew. See also Notes to Fairy Elizabeth and the Fairies' Wellin this collection.

THE LOVER'S GHOST.

As pointed by Lad. Arany, the plot of this tale is, with the exception of the happy ending, essentially the same as in Bürger's beautiful poem, "Leonore," in which the bridegroom's ghost repeats three times the question—

"Graut Liebchen auch? Der Mond scheint hell!Hurrah! Die Todten reiten schnell!Graut Liebchen auch vor Todten?"

to which the girl each time replies—

"Ach! lass sie ruh'n, die Todten."

Arany mentions a Dutch and a Norwegian version of the same tale. Cf. *Grimm*, vol. iii. p. 75.

It cannot be supposed that the good Palócz folk have read Bürger, either in the original or in translation. They only read two kinds of literature, the prayer-book and politics. Pap relates an incident that is characteristic. He had to superintend some farm-work; and, in order to while away the time, was reading a book, which made an old Palócz remark that he would go straight to heaven if he read his prayer-book all day, as he did.

Cf. The old ballad quoted in Old Ballad Lore. *Folk-Lore Record*, 1879, pp. 111, 112.

Page 279. The charm given by the witch is one of the innumerable superstitions of a like class. Vide *Magyar Folk-Tales. Notes and Queries*, 6th s. ix. pp. 501 and 502.

Finska Fornminnesforëningens Tidskrift v. p. 106, "Folkströ och plägseder i Mellersta Österbotten," and *Notes and Queries*, 6th s. x. p. 404, and *ib.* 6th s. xi. p. 22.

[Pg 417]Cf. "The churchyard mould," in McGregor, *Folk-Lore of the North-East of Scotland*, p. 216.

Page 280. The ghostly horsemen recalls a strange story an old woman (nearly 80) told me some time ago, and which it is averred happened in Lincolnshire. One fine frosty night, as the Winterton carrier was going along the road, he met a pale man on horseback, who said, "It's a hard winter, and there's going to be a hard time: twenty years' disease amongst vegetables, twenty years' disease amongst cattle, and twenty years' disease amongst men, and this will happen as surely as you have a dead man in your cart." The carrier angrily declared that there was no dead man in his cart. "But there is," said the horseman. Then the carrier went and looked, and found that a man he had taken up to give a ride was dead. Turning round he found the horseman had disappeared. The potato disease, cattle disease, and cholera followed, said the old dame. This pale horseman is said to have ridden through the county, and I have heard of him at various places.

SNAKE SKIN.

In the Finnish Story, "Haastelewat Kuuset," the talking Pines, *S. ja T.* 2: a hunter is rewarded for helping a snake. See notes to "Woman's Curiosity," in this collection.

Pentamerone, "The Serpent."

Folk-Lore Record, 1883. "The good Serpent," a Chilian tale.

The king in this tale is angry at his daughter marrying such a husband, just as he is in the Finnish "Hüri Morsiamena," where the bride is a mouse.

Cf. *Grimm*, "The three Feathers;" "The poor Miller's Boy and the Cat;" and notes thereto.

Kahn und Schwartz, *Norddentsche Sagen*, "Das weisze Kätschen."

Asbjörnsen og Moe, *Norske Folke eventyr*, "Dukken i Græsset."

[Pg 418]Hyltén-Cavallius och Stephens, *Svenska Folksagor*, "Den förtrollade goodan," and "Den förtrollade fästemön."

Contes des fées par Mdme d'Aulnoy, "La chatte blanche."

Polnische Sagen und Märchen des K. Woycicki. "Die Kröte."

Cf. also an interesting article by Mr. Ralston, on "Beauty and the Beast." *Nineteenth Century*. December, 1878.

THE FAIRIES' WELL.

The chief points in this tale have already been noted in others. We may, however, note the following: The Devil in Stephen the Murderer, p. 7, in this collection, at once appears, when summoned, as in this tale.

Page 290. With regard to the *menu* of the devil, cf.

"Here lies the carcass of a curséd sinnerDoomed to be roasted for the devil's dinner."Poems of Robert Wilde. Strahan, 1870.

Page 296. There is a hunt for the father of a child in the Lapp. "Jætten, Katten og Gutten." *Friis*. Cf. Payne, *Arabian Nights*, vii. p. 227.

Page 297. Hot Bath, see p. 276, in this collection; and *Afanassieff*, v. 23.

THE CROW'S NEST.

The following version is still known to old nurses in Holderness, where I collected it. It is called "Orange and Lemon": "There were once a mother and a father who had two daughters, Orange and Lemon. The mother liked Lemon best, and the father Orange. The mother used to make Orange do all the dirty work, as soon as the father had turned his back. One day she sent her to fetch the milk, [Pg 419]and said, 'If you break the pitcher I'll kill you.' As Orange returned she fell down and broke the pitcher, and so when she came home she hid herself in the passage. When the mother came out she saw the broken pitcher and the girl, and took her into the house, when the girl cried 'Oh, mother! Oh, mother! Don't kill me!'

The mother said, 'Close the shutters in.'

'Oh, mother! Oh, mother! Don't kill me!'

'Light the candle.'

'Oh, mother! Oh, mother! Don't kill me!'

'Put the pan on.'

'Oh, mother! Oh, mother! Don't kill me!'

'Fetch the block we chop the wood on.'

'Oh, mother! Oh, mother! Don't kill me!'

'Bring the axe.'

'Oh, mother! Oh, mother! Don't kill me!'

'Put your head on the block.'

'Oh, mother! Oh, mother! Don't kill me!'

But the mother chopped off her head, and cooked it for dinner. When the father came home, he asked what there was for dinner.

'Sheep's head,' replied the mother.

'Where's Orange?'

'Not come from school yet.'

'I don't believe you,' said the father. Then he went upstairs and found fingers in a box; whereupon he was so overcome that he fainted. Orange's spirit flew away to a jeweller's shop and said—

'My mother chopped my head off,My father picked my bones,My little sister buried meBeneath the cold marble stones.'

They said, 'If you say that again we will give you a gold watch.' So she said it again, and they gave her a gold watch. Then she went off to a boot shop and said—

'My mother, &c., &c., &c.'

And they said, 'If you say it again we will give you a pair of [Pg 420]boots.' So she said it again, and they gave her a pair of boots. Then she went to the stonemason's and said—

'My mother, &c., &c., &c.'

And they said, 'If you say it again we will give you a piece of marble as big as your head.' So she said it again, and they gave her a piece of marble as big as her head.

She took the things, and flew home, and sat at the top of the chimney, and shouted down—

'Father! Father! come to me,And I will show thee what I've got for thee.'

So he came, and she gave him a gold watch.

Then she shouted down—

'Sister! Sister! come to me,And I will show thee what I've got for thee.'

So she came, and she gave her a pair of boots.

Then she shouted down—

'Mother! Mother! come to me,And I will show thee what I've got for thee.'

The mother, who thought the others had got such nice things, put her head right up the chimney, when the big block of marble came down and killed her.

Then Orange came down and lived with her father and Lemon happily ever after."

Cf. The story of the child that was murdered at Lincoln by a Jewess. See a fragment of it quoted in Halliwell, *Nursery Rhymes*, p. 276[84]. Shouting down the chimney occurs in several Lapp stories; also in the Finnish stories of the "Wonderful Birch" and "The Girl who seeks her Brothers," where songs somewhat like the above-mentioned occur. Also Cf. *Vernaleken*, "Moriandle and Sugarkandle," and Naake, *Slavonic Tales*, "Story of the little Simpleton." A story of a somewhat similar kind is current in Sweden. See Hofberg. [Pg 421]*Svsnska Folksägner*, "Mylingen"[85] and Hyltén-Cavallius *Värend och Virdarne*, ii. p. 1.

Also *Grimm*, vol. i. "The Juniper Tree" and notes, and *ib.* "The Brother and Sister" and notes; *ib.* vol. ii. "The Lambkin and the Little Fish," and notes.

WOMAN'S CURIOSITY. Merényi.[86]

Cf. *S. ja T.* ii. p. 73, "Haastelewat Kuuset" (the Talking Pines), which is very like the whole story.

Payne, i. p. 14. Dasent, *Tales from the Norse*, ii. p. 4. Denton, *Serbian Folk-Lore*, "The Snake's Gift." Naake, *Slavonic Tales*, "The Language of Animals" (from the Servian), and *Grimm*, vol. ii. p. 541. The power to understand the language of animals is often referred to in folk-tales, *e.g. Grimm*, vol. i. "The White Snake" and note, and *ib.* vol. ii. p. 541, *et seq.*

Gubernatis, vol. i. p. 152.

Tales of the Alhambra, "Legend of Prince Ahmed al Kamel."

Tylor, *Primitive Culture*, vol. i. pp. 190, 469.

The power of animals to speak still remains amongst the superstitions of the people. In Neudorf, near Schärsburg, there is a prevalent superstition that on new year's night—at midnight—the cattle speak, but in a language which man may not hear, if he does so he dies. See Boner, *Transylvania*, p. 372; and I have heard a similar story as to their speaking (or kneeling) on Christmas Eve in Lincolnshire. Curious remnants, too, are to be found in the doggrel rhymes of the people, *e.g.*, a few years ago I heard a woman in North Lincolnshire say,

"What do doves say?

[Pg 422]"Croo! pee! croo!

"Gillivirens and Jackdaws lay eight or ten eggs to my poor two."

It is very interesting to compare a Finnish fragment entitled "The Dove's Cooing" with the foregoing. A dove and a hen had each a nest, but the dove had ten eggs and the hen only two. Then the hen began to try and make the dove change with her. At last the dove consented, and gave the hen her ten eggs and took her two. Soon the dove saw she had lost, and began to repent her foolish bargain, and she still laments it, for as soon as you hear her voice you hear her sad song,

"Kyy, Kyy, Kymmenen munaa minä,waiwainen waihdoin tanan, kahteen munaan."

"I've foolishly bartered my ten eggsFor the hen's two!"[87]

[1]Cf. *Finska Kranier jämte några natur och literatur-studier inom andra områden af Finsk Antropologi* Skildrade af Prof. G. Retzius, Stockholm, 1878, p. 121. A most valuable and interesting work which ought to be known to all students of anthropology. See also Du Chaillu's *Land of the Midnight Sun*, vol. ii. p. 277.

[2]Hereafter quoted as *S. ja T.*

[3]This valuable collection will hereafter be quoted as *Friis.*

[4]Villon Society. London, 1884; and hereafter quoted as Payne's *Arabian Nights.*

[5]Such a window as they had in old times: a hole with sliding door or shutter. *Vide* Retzius, p. 110.

[6]The bath-house is a separate building with a stove in the corner covered with large stones which become red hot and then water is thrown upon them which fills the house with steam. Round the sides are shelves where the bathers (both sexes) recline, and whip themselves with branches of birch on which the leaves have been left to die. *Retzius*, p. 119. Cf. also *Land of the Midnight Sun*, vol. ii. p. 207.

[7]A John Twardowski is said to have been a doctor of medicine in the university of Cracow, who, like Dr. Faust, signed a contract in his own blood with the devil. He is said to have been wont to perform his incantations on the mountains of Krzemionki, or on the tumulus of Krakus, the mythic founder of Cracow. The demon was to do all the magician bade him and to have no power over him until he met him at Rome, where he took good care not to go. Whether this gentleman is supposed to have ultimately become the lame fiend I know not. See *Slavonic Folk-Lore*, by Rev. W. S. Lach-Szyrma, in *Folk-Lore Record*, vol. iv. p. 62.

[8]A division of South Sweden washed by the Skaggerack and Kattegat.

[9]Cf. "Haastelewat Kuuset" (The Talking Pines), *S. ja T.* ii. p. 73, where the man is about to reveal to his wife, who has been plaguing him to tell her, why he laughed when he heard some birds twittering, and, as this means death, he puts on all his clothes and lays himself out on a bench. Just then the hens are let loose, and as they run about the floor of the chamber where the man is the cock struts about and says, "Cock, cocko, cock, cocko! See, I have fifty wives and govern them all; the master has only one and can't manage her, therefore the fool is going to die." The man heard that, got up and kept his secret. Animals' language must not be revealed. Cf. Benfey, *Ein Märchen von der Thiersprachen* in *Orient und Occident.* Naake's *Slavonic Tales*, Servian story of the Language of Animals, 71-99; and "Woman's Curiosity," p. 301, in the present volume.

[10]*Old Deccan Days*, "Rama and Luxman," p. 66.—Thorpe's *Yule-Tide Stories*, "Svend's Exploits," p. 343.—*Grimm*, "Faithful John," vol. i. p. 33, and Notes, p. 348.—"Secret-Keeping Little Boy," p. 233, in this volume.

[11]Near the bath-house (*vide supra*, p. 308) is the kiln to dry corn, a most important building in the Finnish farmstead. It is built of wood like the bath-house. On one side of the doorway is a stove (built of stones, see *Land of the Midnight Sun*, vol. ii. p. 274, where there are illustrations of somewhat similar stoves or ovens), that gives out a great heat and *smoke*, which fills the inside of the building, especially the upper part. This "ria" or kiln is used to dry the corn in. All Finnish rye is dried in this way. *Retzius*, p. 120.

[12]Ruobba, scurfy skull, or Gudnavirus, *i.e.* Ashiepattle.

[13]Cf. *Dasent*: "Boots and His Brothers," p. 382, where Boots finds an axe hewing away at a fir tree, and a spade digging and delving by itself, and by their means he got the princess and half the kingdom.

[14]Wagner's *Asgard*, p. 208. Roman intruders are called "the Roman dragon, the bane of Asgard." Wagner's *Epics and Romances*, "the Nibelung," p. 3; "the Dragonstone," p. 243. Henderson's *Folk-Lore of the Northern Counties*, p. 283.

[15]Professor Ebers says: "Red was the colour of Seth and Typhon. The Evil One is named the Red, as, for instance, in the papyrus of Ebers red-haired men were *typhonic*." See "Uarda," note on p. 58. Red-haired people are still in some parts looked on as unlucky to meet when going to sea, or as "first foot." See also Black's *Folk-Medicine*, pp. 111-113. According to a Magyar jingle:

"A red dog; a red nag; a red man; none is good!"

[16]A finger song, common, with slight variations, in Sweden, Norway, and Denmark, and Swedish speaking people in Finland. Cf. Yorkshire—

Tom Thumbkins, Bill Wilkins,Long Daniel, Bessy Bobtail,And Little Dick.

See Halliwell's *Nursery Rhymes*, p. 206.

[17]It is interesting to note the finger-lore of the people, *e.g. Gubernatis*, vol. i. 166, says: "The little finger, although the smallest, is the most privileged of the five." It is the one that knows everything; in Piedmont, when the mothers wish to make the children believe that they are in communication with a mysterious spy, who sees everything that they do, they are accustomed to awe them by the words, "my little finger tells me everything." See also vol. ii. p. 151.

In Holderness, Yorkshire, it is a common superstition that if you pinch anyone's little finger when they are asleep, they will tell you their secrets; or, as some say, "if you can bear your little finger pinching you can keep a secret." If you see a white horse, spit over your little finger for luck. Schoolboys make their bargains irrevocable by spitting over their little fingers.[A] In Petalaks (a parish in East Bothnia, about twenty miles from Wasa) every one believes in a "bjero"[B] or "mjero," which is one respect resembles Sampo in Kalevala, insomuch as he brings good luck to his possessor. Sometimes he looks like a ball of yarn, but more often like a hare. The way he is manufactured is as follows:—A wafer spared from the Communion, some wool stolen from seven cow-houses on Maundy Thursday, and a drop of blood from the *little finger* of the left hand. During the performance the manufacturer must curse and swear without ceasing. The wool is to be spun on Easter morn when the sun dances; the thread to be wrapped round the wafer, and the whole put in the churn. Whilst churning, the spellmaker sings, "Milk and butter thou must bring to me; I shall burn in hell-fire for thee." After a time the "bjero" springs out, and asks, "What will you give me to eat?" "Raisins and almonds," is the reply. And all is complete. See *Suomen Muinaismusto-yhtiön Aikakauskirja*, ii.; *Helsingissa*, 1877, p. 133; *Vidskepelser insamlade bland allmogan i Petalaks*, 1874; *Skrock och vidskepliga bruk hos svenska allmogen i Vasabygden*. Af. Prof. Freudenthal,*Helsingfors*, 1883, p. 8; and Rink's *Tales and Traditions of the Eskimo*, p. 440.

[A]Cf. Tylor's Primitive Culture, vol. i. p. 103; vol. ii. p. 439-441.

[B]*Några åkerbruksplägseder bland svenskarne i Finland*, af. dr. J. Oscar Rancken, pp. 17, 24, 32.

[18]Tegnér: Prologen till Gerda.

[19]See variants given in *Henderson's Folk-Lore of the Northern Counties*, pp. 258, 262.

Cf. Riddle set to three soldiers by the devil, and found out by the help of his grandmother. *Grimm*, vol. ii. pp. 152, 425. Also, *Vernaleken*, p. 206.

[20]A similar plant occurs in "The Merchant," in the *Pentamerone*.

[21]Taylor's Edition. London. 1848.

[22]Of the word "devil" one cannot do better than quote Mr. Ralston's words: "The demon rabble of 'popular tales' are merely the lubber fiends of heathen mythology, being endowed with supernatural might, but scantily provided with mental power; all of terrific manual clutch, but of weak intellectual grasp." Cf. *Castrén, Finsk Mytologi*, p. 163.

[23]A similar tale still exists in Holderness under the name of "The Glass Stairs."

[24]*Morte d'Arthur*, book I, cap. iii. tells how "in the greatest church in London, there was seen in the churchyard a great stone foursquare, and in the midst thereof was like an anvil of steel a foot on high, and therein stuck a fair sword naked by the point, and letters there were written in gold about the sword that said thus: whoso pulleth out this sword of this stone and anvil is

rightwise king born of all England." Which sword was drawn out by Sir Arthur. Cf. book 2, cap. i. where a maiden comes girt with a sword, that no one could pull out but the poor knight Balin.

[25]This man-eating being was said to be something like a very big and mighty man, and was to be found in waste places. He was generally dressed in a white coat, with a silver belt round his waist, from which hung a silver-hafted knife, and a great many silver ornaments. He was exceedingly stupid, and the butt of Gudnavirucak. (Ashiepattle) They were probably nothing more than the old Vikings, and Stallo is thought to be derived from "Staalmanden," or men dressed in steel (Lapp, *staale* = steel).

[26]Cf. *Grimm*, "The Three Sons of Fortune," i. p. 291.

[27]I have heard similar stories amongst the peasants in Flanders.

[28]The magpie is an important bird in folk-belief, and Swedish peasants say you must not kill it lest it be a troll in disguise as in this story. If they build in a house it is a sign of luck; if in the fields and come to the house and laugh, woe be to the house.

[29]Cf. Amelia Ferrier, *A Winter in Morocco*, p. 172, *et seq.*

[30]It is curious that the Magyar word for a marriageable girl, "eladó leány," also means "a girl for sale."

[31]In old times in Finland, a "spokesman" used to go beforehand to the girl, in order to find out whether the young man was likely to be acceptable. Cf. Scheffer, *The History of Lapland.* London, 1751, p. 71; and Boner, *Transylvania*, p. 488.

[32]"Given the basket:" in Finland the same phrase is used. Cf. the English phrase, "to give the sack."

[33]Cf. Note to "Handsome Paul," p. 317, *ante.*

[34]In the Russian Church there are two distinct services, which are performed at the same time, the "betrothal" when rings are given and exchanged, and the "coronation." Lansdell, *Through Siberia*, vol. i. p. 168.

[35]Cf. Denton, *Serbian Folk-Lore*, p. 205.

[36]Cf. this with the Finnish "bride-dresser," who looked after the bride's toilette, even providing the necessary dresses if the girl did not possess them.

[37]See Scotch "feetwashing," *Folk-Lore of North-East Scotland*; Folk-Lore Society, p. 89. In Finland, before a wedding, the friends of the bridegroom-elect invite to a party, which is called the "bachelor's funeral," at which he is oftentimes carried on a sofa shoulder-high as a mock funeral.

[38]The royal Hungarian bodyguard wear leopard-skins clasped with silver buckles.

[39]I have heard of racing for ribbons, &c., at weddings in Yorkshire; and of young men racing home from the church to tell the good folk at home that the marriage was *un fait accompli.* Cf. Napier, *Folk-Lore*, p. 49, and *Henderson*, p. 37.

[40]A remain of the marriage by force. Vámbéry notes the existence of this amongst the Turkomans. The bride's door in Transylvania is often locked, and the bridegroom has to climb over; or sometimes he has to chase her, and catch her: *Boner*, p. 491. Cf. also *Tissot*, vol. i. p. 94;*Scheffer*, p. 75; Gilmour, *Among the Mongols*, p. 259; *Napier*, p. 50.

[41]For accounts of English wedding-feasts in the north, see Sykes' *Local Records*, Newcastle-on-Tyne, 1833, vol. i. pp. 194, 205, 209.

[42]The vizier's daughter is displayed in seven dresses in the story of "Noureddin Ali of Cairo, and his son Bedreddin Hassan": Payne's *Arabian Nights*, vol. i. pp. 192-194. And in old times the brides in Japan changed their dress three to five times during the ceremony: Mitford, *Tales of Old Japan*, p. 370.

[43]Cf. *Lappbönder, Skildringar Sägner och sagor från Södra Lappland.* af. P. A. Lindholm, p. 89.

Fra Finmarken. Friis, ("Laila" in S.P.C.K. translation), cap. xi.

Dancing the crown off the bride in Finland. See "A Finnish wedding in the olden times." *Notes and Queries*, 6th s. x. p. 489.

They cut the long hair off the Saxon brides in Transylvania; and in Spain, when the bride goes to her bedroom, the young unmarried men unloose her garter.

Just as in our land old shoes are thrown after the bride when she leaves home, and never matter how they fall, or how young relatives batter the backs of bride and bridegroom with aged slippers, you must not *look back*: so they say in Holderness, at least. The sumptuary laws of Hamburg of 1291, enacted that the bridegroom should present his bride with a pair of shoes. According to Grimm, when the bride put the shoe on her foot it was a sign of her subjection. (Boner, *Transylvania*, p. 491). See old Jewish custom, *Rath.* iv. 7.

See also *Napier*, p. 53, where he refers to the Grecian custom of removing the bride's coronet and putting her to bed.

Henderson, *Folk-Lore of Northern Counties*, pp. 36, 37, 42.

Aubrey, *Remains of Gentilisme*, Folk-Lore Society, p. 173.

Gregor, *Folk-Lore of North-East of Scotland*, pp. 96, 100.

[44]From a paper read before the Hungarian Historical Society, by Baron Béla Radvánszky, on Feb. 1st, 1883; Cf. *A magyar családi èlet a* xv. *es*xvi. *szàzadban*, by the same author.

Cf. Tissot, *Unknown Hungary*, vol. i. p. 227.

Boner, *Transylvania*, pp. 488-495.

Fagerlund, *Anteckningar om Korpo och Houtskärs Socknar*, Helsingfors, 1878, p. 42.

Lindholm, "Ett bondbröllop," p. 86; and "Ett lappbröllop," p. 91.

[45]Laulu Lapista.

[46]See also Swedish Songs in Du Chaillu, *Land of the Midnight Sun*, vol. ii. p. 424.

[47]Cf. another group of stories, where trouble comes from the advice of those at home, such as *Dasent*, "East o' the Sun, and West o' the Moon," p. 29; *Afanassieff*, vol. vii. No. 15, and "Cupid and Psyche," see also notes to "The Speaking Grapes, &c." in this collection.

[48]Cf. *Rerum Moscoviticarum Commentarii* by the Baron Sigismund von Herberstein. London, 1852. (Hakluyt Soc.) vol. ii. pp. 46 *et seq.*

[49]*Untersuchungen zur Erläuterung der ältesten Geschichte Russlands.* St. Petersburg. 1806.

[50]Loc. cit.

[51]Cf. Hunfalvy Pál, *Magyarország Ethnographiája*. Budapest. 1876. chap. 41.

[52]*Notes and Queries*, 7th S. ii. pp. 110, 111.

[53]Cf. also, *Folk-Lore Record.* 1879, p. 121; *Gesta Romanorum*, "The Knight and the Necromancer;" *Records of the Past*, vol. i. p. 136. "Tablet V."; Rink, *Tales and Traditions of the Eskimo*, p. 302; and Leland, *The Gipsies*, p. 159, where we are told gipsies object to having their photographs taken unless you give them a shoe-string.

[54]*Magyar Népmeséinkről* in the *Kisfaludy Társaság évlapjai.* New Series iv. p. 146.

[55]A Worcestershire woman told the writer that she had a nephew born with a caul, and when he was at the point of death it became quite moist.

[56]The Csángós are Magyar settlers in Moldavia; they are now assisted to return to Hungary by the Government. This story is told of the feud between two races. There are others which strike off the characteristics of neighbouring races, such as the story of the angels, current in Hungary, which is as follows:—

When Adam and Eve fell, God sent Gabriel, the Magyar angel, to turn them out of the garden of Eden. Adam and his wife received him most courteously, and most hospitably offered him food and drink. Gabriel had a kind heart, and took pity on them. He was too proud to accept any hospitality from them, as he did not consider it quite the right thing. So he returned to the Deity, and begged that somebody else should be sent to evict the poor couple, as he had not the heart to do it. Whereupon Raphael, the Roumanian angel, was sent, who was received and treated by Adam and Eve in like manner. He, however, was not above a good dinner, and having finished, he informed the couple of the purpose of his coming. The two thereupon began to cry, which so mollified Raphael that he returned to his Master, and begged Him to send some one else, as he could not very well turn them out after having enjoyed their hospitality. So Michael, the German angel, was sent, and was treated as the others. He sat down to a sumptuous meal, and when the last morsel of food had disappeared, and the last drop of liquor was drained, he rose from the table, and, addressing the host and hostess said, "Now then, out you go!" and the poor couple, though they cried most pitifully and begged hard to be allowed to remain, were cruelly turned out of the garden of Eden. See Arany's collection.

[57]The mound was opened in 1870, and found to contain bones.

[58]As late as 1875, a farmer near Mariestad buried a cow alive, upon disease breaking out in his herd. See also *Contemporary Review*, Feb. 1878, "Field and Forest Myths," p. 528, "Within the last few years, at least one Russian peasant has been known to sacrifice a poor relation in hopes of staying an epidemic."

[59]I heard this story again the other day in South Lincolnshire.

[60]Remains of a Roman camp near Brocklesby.

[61]Vide *A History of the County of Lincoln.* By the author of *The Histories of London, Yorkshire, Lambeth, &c. &c.* London and Lincoln: John Saunders gent., 1834.

[62]Boswell's *Variorum Edition of Shakespeare*, vii. pp. 162, 163.

[63]"Prince Unexpected." *Folk Lore Record*, 1884, p. 10.

[64]Cf. Lion Bruno. *Folk Lore Record*, 1878, p. 209.

[65]See Ralston's "Beauty and the Beast" in *The 19th Century*, December, 1878.

[66]In "The Raksha's Palace" in the same work, p. 203, the young princess found "the skeleton of a poor old beggar-woman, who had evidently died from want and poverty. The princess took the skin and washed it, and drew it over her own lovely face and neck, as one draws a glove on one's hand."

[67]The giant who demands human flesh of his wife, and the giantess who has only one eye in the middle of her forehead, are proofs of the foreign origin of this tale.

[68]See p. 340 *ante.*

[69]Ruobba, or Gudnavirũs, *i. e.* scurfy skull, is the Lapp for Ashiepattle. See "Jætten og Veslegutten," *Friis.*

[70]See note, vol. i. p. 407.

[71]*The Death of Dermid*, by Ferguson, may also be compared. Where the hero is slain by the envenomed bristle piercing his foot. For this part of the poem, vide *Dublin Magazine*, 1868, p. 594.

[72]See p. 335, *ante.*

[73]The witch's daughter in the "Two Orphans" is lame of one foot. See p. 221.

[74]There is a curious tale of a relation of my own who was popularly said to be able to cure people of ague by going to a thorn and shaking while she said: "Shake, good tree, shake for So-and-so," and then the disease fled. I have heard that the good old dame was herself always very ill after this operation. The hanging of a lock of hair on a tree, I presume, was understood to be the same as taking the afflicted person to the tree.

[75]See also another Lapp tale, "Haccis Ædne." *Notes and Queries*, 7th s. ii. Aug. 7, 1886.

[76]I have often had this tale told to me by my nurse when a child, and heard the following version a short time ago in Holderness, and was informed it had been told thus for ages: "There was a stepmother who was very unkind to her stepdaughter and very kind to her own daughter; and used to send her stepdaughter to do all the dirty work. One day she sent her to the pump for some water when a little frog came up through the sink and asked her not to pour dirty water down, as his drawing-room was there. So she did not, and as a reward he said pearls and diamonds should drop from her mouth when she spoke. When she returned home it happened as he said; and the step-mother, learning how it had come about, sent her own daughter to the pump. When she got there the little frog spoke to her and asked her not to throw dirty water down, and she replied "Oh! you nasty, dirty little thing, I won't do as you ask me." Then the frog said "Whenever you speak frogs, and toads, and snakes shall drop from your mouth." She went home and it happened as the frog had said. At night when they were sitting at the table a little voice was heard singing outside—

"Come bring me my supper,[A]My own sweet, sweet one."

When the step-daughter went to the door there was the little frog. She brought him in in spite of her step-mother; took him on her knee and fed him with bits from her plate. After a while he sang

"Come, let us go to bed,My own sweet, sweet one."

So, unknown to her step-mother, she laid him at the foot of her bed, as she said he was a poor, harmless thing. Then she fell asleep and forgot all about him. Next morning there stood a beautiful prince, who said he had been enchanted by a wicked fairy and was to be a frog till a girl would let him sleep with her. They were married, and lived happily in his beautiful castle ever after." This is one of the few folk-stories I have been able to collect from the lips of a living story-teller in England.

[A]There is a traditional air to which these lines are always sung.

[77]See also notes in the Introduction.

[78]There is a similar incident in *Grimm*, "The Sea Hare," where a fox changes himself by dipping in a spring.

[79]In Finland they say that if two persons shake hands across the threshold they will quarrel. In East Bothnia, when the cows are taken out of their winter quarters for the first time, an iron bar is laid before the threshold, over which all the cows must pass, for if they do not, there will be nothing but trouble with them all the following summer. Cf. *Suomen Muinaismuisto Yhdistyksen Aikakauskirja*, v. p. 99.

[80]On entering a house, especially a royal house, it is improper to use the *left* foot on first stepping into it; one must "put one's best (or right) foot foremost." Malagasy Folk-Lore, p. 37. *Folk-Lore Record* 1879.

[81]The "párta" is a head-dress worn by unmarried women only, in the shape of a "diadem" of the ancients in silk, satin, or velvet, and generally embroidered

[82]Cf. p. 365 *ante.*

[83]Cf. Gerll, Volksmärchen der Böhmen, "Die Goldene Ente."

[84]See also *Folk-Lore Record*, 1879, "Old Ballad Folk-Lore," pp. 110, 111.

[85]Myling, myring, or myrding generally means the ghost of a murdered person.

[86]Arany says he dare not accept the collection from which this story is taken for scientific purposes, as Merényi has drawn very liberally on his own imagination.

[87]*S. ja T.* iii. "Pienempiä Eläin-jutun katkelmia," p. 37. The whole of the Finnish beast stories are most interesting, and the resemblance in many cases to the negro variants in *Uncle Remus* very striking.

[Pg 423]